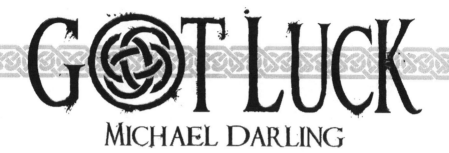

GOT LUCK

MICHAEL DARLING

Got Luck

FHP

Future House Publishing

ISBN-10: 1-944452-99-0 (paperbound)
ISBN-13: 978-1-944452-99-5 (paperbound)

Cover illustration by Jonathan Diaz
Developmental editing by Mandi Diaz
Substantive editing by Helena Steinacker
Copy editing by Jenna Parmley
Interior design by Emma Hoggan

Acknowledgements

First of all, I owe a debt of gratitude to Mom and Dad, who bought books for all my birthdays, transcribed stories I made up before I could write them myself, and enabled frequent access to the library as an act of self-preservation. I'm also glad they didn't hide the Edgar Allen Poe.

Thanks also to Mrs. True, my third-grade teacher, who instilled in me the idea that writing a novel was possible as long as I kept putting the right words together.

Thanks to my Beta Darlings who read through the early roughness of Got Luck and helped polish the facets of the story until they sparkled: Sharee Hughes, Carrie Held, Davor Ninic, Kyle Shields, Jared Barneck, and my wonderful Shaunabella. I couldn't have done any of this without you!

Thanks to Callie Stoker who gave the manuscript its first professional edit and got Got into shape as a character. Your instincts and edits are always invaluable!

Many thanks to "Doey" of Ireland who helped with the pronunciation guide. Foreign words and phrases give the Behindbeyond it's otherworldliness but it's difficult to invent a language that sounds consistent and real. Since I was borrowing from Gaelic mythology, I borrowed Gaelic as well. Of course, you are welcome to pronounce the language of the Fae however you like, but if you prefer authenticity, there's a guide further on.

Finally, thanks to the staff of Future House! It's been a great adventure working with Adam, Ami, Helena, Jeff, Jonathan, Mandi, Ryan, and the crew. Your expertise and thoughtfulness has come in equal measures and I'm very grateful.

Pronunciation Guide

Characters

Béil – bale
Brón – brohn
Caimiléir – cam-ih-LAIR
Deamhan – day-VAWN
Fáidh Bean – FAY-ah ban
Fiach Dubh – FEE-ock dohv
Greim – GREE-um
Láir – lair
Laoch – LAY-ock
Madrasceartán – MAW-drah-skar-TAWN
Prionsa – PRIN-sa
Stail – stall

Places and Things

Ail Bán Dearg – ale bawn JAR-ig
An Taobh Thiar Agus Níos Faide – on TAY-iv here OG-us niece FAY-dah
Corrchnámhach – kor-kuh-NAW-vock
Liagán – leah-GAWN
Tairseach-Cosantóir – TAR-sock ko-san-TOR

Phrases and Commands

Briste briosc broiscaí – BRISH-tah BREE-osk BRIS-key
Ithe – IH-uh
Leigheas – lice
Maraigh tú féin – MAR-ig too fayn
Oscailte – OS-kull-cha
Sciath – SHKEE-uh
Tine – CHIN-na
Tar anseo – tar ON-shuh

CHAPTER 1

A Woman and a Bullet

The woman outside the door was Stained. She stood outside, reading my name on the door and walking back and forth. If she realized I could see her through the glass, she didn't seem to care. The Stain shrouded her like a torn mantle of dark, writhing ribbons, and nobody could see them except me. I'd seen Stain like hers before, but I couldn't remember where.

I sat on the edge of my desk and watched her check the door again. Maybe she was trying to figure out how to pronounce my name, which was painted in silver lettering on the door. Goethe Luck. People always had trouble with the last name. Kidding.

Finally, she opened the door and leaned in. Somewhere outside, someone was playing Gloria Estefan. She looked at me and then backed out. The door closed itself. She read the door again. I wanted to go ask, "May I help you?" but hesitated. I could use the work, but I didn't want to scare her off.

She opened the door again and stepped inside. I watched her check my second floor office, placing the closet, back room, and bathroom. She was pretty in a debutante kind of way: confident and likely spoiled. Her looping ash-blonde hair was underwire length, and she wore too much makeup for my taste. I guessed she was trying to look older than she was. A light strawberry scent drifted in with her, delighting my nose. The Mama would call her a harlot, but she looked like most twenty year-old girls walking around on your average summer day in Miami. Her clothes were expensive but looked like they came from unrelated shops, as if she had strolled through Bal Harbour and purchased one item from each store with no consideration for color or texture.

"Welcome to the Pizza Shack," I said. "Table for one?"

"Someone killed my husband. The police can't help me." She said it flatly, like she'd been practicing until she'd wrung all the emotion out of it.

No wonder she hadn't caught my joke. She'd walked in with a script.

"I'm sorry to hear that. Won't you have a seat?" I turned the single chair in front of my desk partway around. Like her clothes, the chair didn't match anything else, so at least the office coordinated with the client. The chair was one of those plastic office creatures that had been ergonomically designed to death. She sat and looked at me with dry eyes.

"Did you say this was the Pizza Shack?" she asked.

Ah, there we go. Just took a minute. "It used to be. We still find pepperoni under the rugs." I sat back on the edge of my desk and clasped my hands. "Tell me about your husband."

She took a deep breath, sat down, and launched into her speech. Her voice was husky yet soulful. "They found Barry in his hotel room. He was wearing the shirt and tie I gave him for his birthday. And the pants. And the shoes. He'd been stabbed once in the heart. They said that's what killed him. He died quickly. But he was also cut open. His belly. They cut open his belly after he was already dead." She moved her hand in front of her own abdomen with her fingers splayed apart like she was feeling his pain. "His insides were still there and all. But they can't tell me why he was cut open like that."

"I'm sorry for your loss. Sounds like you've told that story a few times."

"About a million. Don't worry. I've already cried it out."

"You're fine," I smiled warmly. "When did this happen?"

"Six months ago."

"How long had you been married?"

"Less than a year. Our first anniversary would have been two weeks after he was killed."

"Again, I'm very sorry for your loss."

She shifted in her seat.

"I don't even know your name," I said.

"Are you going to take notes?" she replied. "If you're going to help me, you should take notes."

"All right."

I stood up and walked around to the other side of the desk. So far, the girl was sincere. Her tone told me that she was accustomed to having people do what she asked, but she wasn't a brat about it. She paid attention to detail and expected other people to do the same. Her husband had been gone for several months but, for some reason, she wasn't happy with the answers she'd been given. Maybe there was something in her subconscious that didn't agree with what she'd been told. Maybe she just wanted a second opinion.

My chair was one of those great wooden office monarchs made of oak with dark green real-leather upholstery that weighed about two hundred pounds. It reclined so you could lean back and put your feet up on the desk—also oak—and take a nap. I sat in it and opened the desk drawer. No pepperoni. Just a few notepads and pens that I'd gotten from the nearby office supply. Been here six months and this was the first time I'd used them.

"Milly," she said. "Milly MacPherson Mallondyke."

While I tried, unsuccessfully, to prevent my left eyebrow from rising, I made notes including all the information she had given me so far. I asked, "So, your husband was Barry Mallondyke?"

Milly nodded. "The fourth."

The fourth? I guess men with a name that sounds like it was made up for the sole purpose of sounding pretentious have no problems attracting mates.

"I want to know more about you," Milly said. "I want to know who I'm hiring."

"I haven't agreed to work for you yet," I replied. Her request was a smart one though. Not expected. Milly might turn out to be even deeper than she appeared. I answered, "I'm twenty-seven years old. When I was eight, I died from a fever. I don't remember what happened, but the doctors told me I was clinically dead for almost three hours. Apparently, they cooled my body in ice and revived me. From that moment, I found a desire to live every day as if it were my last. I also found out that when I touch somebody I can see their future."

"Is that true?" The wry wrinkle in the corner of her mouth told me she didn't believe all of it, but she was willing to play along.

"Most of it. It's true that I have a better appreciation for life than most people because it's also true that I died when I was eight. The part where I can see a person's future by touching them is from a Stephen King novel. The Dead Zone. Ever read it?"

"No. But if you could see the future like that, you could touch me and then we'd know if you find out who killed my husband. Right?"

Point for her.

I suddenly remembered where I had seen a twisting mantle of black ribbons like hers. The Stain she wore had also been on a child. A little boy whose parents had both been shot in the head, but no bullets, no bullet casings, no gun, and no residue were found. The case was never solved. If the Stains matched, could the same perpetrator be involved? I'd probably never know, but I made a mental note.

"You're right. I can't see into the future, but I'd be glad to help you with your problem. Just so you know, I'm ex-military and ex-police. I have a private investigator's license, which gives me access to records that are not available to the general public."

"That will help." She pressed her lips together in a half smile.

I went on. "I can also interview people who don't want to talk to me and make a general nuisance of myself with local law enforcement. I also have a gun permit, so I can shoot anybody who tries to kill me before I find out what I want to know. I have a library card too, so if you need a good book to read while you wait for me to figure things out, just say the word."

"I have my own library card, thank you." Her smile ratcheted up a bit. She was warming to me. Not always the easiest thing.

I nodded. "Milly, there's a very good chance that I won't find anything new about your husband's murder. Most of the time, the police do a good job of finding whatever there is to find.

There may be nothing new, and it will cost you the same amount of money to find out. If you're willing to take that chance, I'll give it my best shot."

The widow Mallondyke looked at me for all of three seconds and then stood up. She'd come to my office to meet me face-to-face, and she seemed to like making her own decisions. She pulled out a cashier's check from her mismatched purse and handed it to me. It had her business card clipped to it and was made out in my name with a lot of zeroes.

"If you run out of money, let me know." She turned and walked to the door that had my name on it. She looked over her shoulder and said, "My father is friends with your former chief. He's the one who recommended you. He said if anyone could find out who killed my husband, it was you."

Milly MacPherson Mallondyke opened the door and walked out. The swirling black ribbons of her Stain trailed after her like a sentient shroud.

About five minutes later, while I was pacing behind my desk and pondering the unpredictability of financial fortune—and the unpredictable nature of a certain police chief who, I knew, hated my guts and everything they stood for—my front window exploded.

Whatever chunks of my brain that would be dropped into a jar someday and labeled "instinct" quite capably liquefied my knees and sent me to the floor. Be small! Be still! Be alive!

The sound of shattered glass scattering in shards across the floor seemed unnaturally loud but didn't last long. I waited for about ten seconds and then peered out from the side of my desk. The window next to the door had been a floor-to-ceiling piece of glass about six feet wide. Now it was effectively distributed across the tile floor all the way from the front of the office to the back. Glass had been thrown to either side of the desk and across the top.

There were a few drops of blood on the floor. Since I was the only person in the office, I expertly deduced that the blood must be mine. I privately investigated my hands and face and found a few small cuts on my cheek and forehead. Thankfully, my hair was okay.

I thought about getting my gun, but my gun was hanging in my holster, which was hanging in the closet about fifteen feet away. Another ten seconds went by as I looked around behind the desk. There was a new hole in the wall, about eight feet up, just below the ceiling.

"Son of a poodle," I said.

At great personal risk, I finally stood up. I stepped out through the door onto the open balcony that ran around the outside of the building. I saw no one fleeing the scene. No manic scrambling. No ninjas in the daylight. I didn't see Milly and there were no cars moving in the parking lot. I had to assume my client was gone. There were a couple of bystanders going to their cars, but they were looking up at me instead of looking around. If the shooter had used a suppressor, the breaking window had made a bigger noise and that's what had drawn their attention.

The ancient shop-owner from downstairs, who ran the Korean cafe on the ground floor, hobbled out into the lot and turned to look up at the damage. He shielded his eyes from the sun and shouted, "You okay?!"

"I'm good, Qui-Gon!" I replied. His name was Quy Nguyen and he was about eight hundred years old, but he only looked five hundred fifty. Five hundred sixty max. I called him Qui-Gon because I'm such a kidder, and George Lucas isn't really using the name anymore.

"You want lunch?" That Qui-Gon. Always making a sale.

"Yeah, all right."

Qui-Gon nodded and hobbled back into his shop to fix me some bulgogi and kimchi.

Adrenaline pooled now in my stomach, making it ache, and my muscles everywhere felt jittery and unsettled. I went back to my desk and picked up the phone. The Mama had always called the police "them popo-pigs" even after I'd become one. But I was going to need them popo-pigs to file an incident report. I called and informed them of the attempted homicide and coincidental murder of my window and gave my name and location.

In the next room I had some exercise equipment. Since I couldn't go anywhere until the cops arrived, I went in and started working off the adrenaline. It was surreal spinning on the stationary bike while looking at the hole in the wall. The hole with the bullet that had almost killed me just a few minutes ago. The thought made me pedal faster. I hoped Qui-Gon would get here with lunch ahead of the police.

Although I was not yet aware of it, in twenty-four hours my life would change forever.

CHAPTER 2

Attack of the Invisible Liondog

Qui-Gon brought a couple bags of food. I paid him and started unpacking about a pound of lean, steaming, marinated beef and four kinds of spicy kimchi, along with a small mountain of steamed white rice.

I had made quick work of most of it by the time local PD rolled up with flashing lights but no sirens. I found myself heaving a sigh and shaking my head in disappointment. Sirens are cool. I'd used the siren every chance I got when I'd been on the force. On the other hand, nobody was dead or wounded and that was a good thing. The two uniforms had already given the place the once over when Sergeant Kapok from homicide popped in.

Kapok was a frumpy, grumpy Puerto Rican I'd run into from time to time when I'd been a uniform myself. I didn't have a great name for him because he was no fun and didn't deserve one. If he ever became Commander though, I was all ready to go with Commander Commandant "The Commandman" Kapok. If Shakespeare could use alliteration for comic effect, so could I. It's all about the timing.

Kapok observed the scene like he was lost.

"You hoping to see a body, Sergeant?" I asked.

Kapok nodded, "Yours." He shrugged and indicated the floor with a sweep of his hand. "No luck. Ha ha."

I think he was serious. "You're all heart."

"I heard the word 'gunfire' and your address on the radio. Thought I'd come check it out for myself. Hope springs eternal." He shrugged again. "So whatta we got here?"

I'd already had a lengthy conversation with the uniforms and I was annoyed at Kapok, but I might need a favor from him someday so I went along. Cooperation comes easier with feathers unruffled. I pointed at the hole in the wall. Then I pointed at a bullet bagged for evidence on my desk.

"One of the boys there dug it out. My guess is a 7.62 mm from an SR-25. Military sniper rifle with a suppressor. But the shooter is an amateur."

Kapok kept looking up at the hole in the wall. "How do you figure?"

"Professional wouldn't try to shoot through a plate glass window. He'd wait for a clearer shot. And he pulled it high. Had to come from ground level, but even if he'd been aiming at my head it shouldn't have gone two feet over even with an upward angle. Nervous shooter."

"Got it all figured out," Kapok said.

"Just a guess," I replied.

"So who did it?" This time, Kapok seemed almost interested in the answer.

"No idea."

"Who'd you tick off most recently?"

I scratched my chin. "I could go a couple of ways on that one. The self-deprecating 'so many, I'll make a list,' or the patently untrue 'everybody loves me, who'd want to kill me?' What do you recommend, Sergeant?"

"Make a list. Get me a copy. My paper shredder is lonely."

"Hey, Sarge," I ignored his comments, "You work the Barry Mallondyke case?"

"Not my case. Old news anyway. Why?"

"His widow wants me to take a look."

"I see. You want to waste her money, it's up to you Luck. Come down to the station. I'll see if the Chief will let you look at the book."

"Appreciate it, Sergeant." I didn't mention the fact that the Chief had already recommended me for the job to Milly's dad. Of course he'd let me look at the book.

Kapok looked around, nodded to the uniforms and left. I saw him snatch a piece of kimchi on his way out. He almost made it to the stairs before I heard a whole lot of coughing and swearing. Kapok coughing on cucumber kimchi. Take that Bill, you ol' spear shaker.

Tomorrow, I'd get a look at the murder book. All the important details of the homicide would be in that book, from photos to witness statements to police reports. Everything that could be put on a sheet of paper and three-hole punched.

Other than the desk and chair and my exercise equipment, there wasn't much else in my office. I had a drawer partially full of case files, my gun and holster and a jacket, and a few other office supplies that fit into a couple of boxes. I packed everything downstairs and put it in the trunk of my car. The uniforms told me they'd continue to patrol the area in case the shooter came back. I called the landlord's office and let them know the window had been shot out. They said somebody would be over to replace it.

I got into my car and drove. I owned a 1965 Mustang that I'd spent the last two years fixing. She had a great paint job, but it was all I could do to keep her running. Parts were hard to find, and Craigslist and eBay had become my favorite haunts. I figured by the time I replaced the last part that was worn out, I'd just have to start back around at the beginning again. She was definitely a problem child, but the car was my baby and I loved her.

She had a kick-butt sound system. The original radio had been trashed when I'd bought her from the wrecker so I'd replaced it, which let me blast music while driving around with the top down. I punched up the volume and Geddy Lee wailed about racing his uncle's red barchetta.

I had a choice of getting on the I-95, but I wasn't in a hurry so I got on Biscayne Boulevard and headed south toward Coral Gables.

While I drove, I phoned my partner, Nat. Nat was born with the burdensome name of Tiziano Neckersteinach. He emerged from the womb as a U.S. citizen, but only just. His parents emigrated from Germany the week before his birth. He and I served together in the Marines. When we came back, I joined the police force in Miami and he ran with some mercenaries in North Africa for about the same amount of time. Nobody ever dared call him Tiziano except his parents, and almost nobody could pronounce his last name properly, so everyone called him Nat.

Nat ran a local gym and health spa called the Iron Foundry. He gave classes on yoga and Pilates and provided personal training services. This meant he regularly had his hands on some of the best-toned female bodies in Miami. I didn't ask, and he would consider it dishonorable to share. Nat had no Stain, but I suspect if he had, it would be all kinds of pure. When you get to know Nat, you understand. Nat was also my best friend.

The phone rang and one of the aforementioned bodies answered the phone. "Iron Foundry Health Club," she said. "May I help you?"

"Mr. Neck-uh-stone-sack please," I replied.

"Um. You mean Nat?"

"Yeah. This is Counselor Smallwater's law office. May I speak with Nat?"

"Well, he's in a class right now. Can I take a message?"

"Hmm. I suppose it's all right. You can just tell him that his annulment is official now. He and his sister are no longer married."

"Oh. Oh-uh. Ok."

"Crazy to go all the way to Vegas and the girl you meet is the sister you haven't seen for years. Right?"

"Uh. Right."

"Anyway, have him call this number as soon as possible."

"Yes. I'll have him—uh, he—he'll call you back."

"Thanks."

Some fine Florida scenery rolled by. I cruised down Biscayne until it turned into SE 2nd and turned again into Brickell. The CD changed. ZZ Top. "Just Got Paid." The cell phone rang.

"Yo," I said.

"What the hell, Luck?" It was Nat.

"Hey! Pretty good news about you and your sister, right?" I said.

"Got, I keep telling you not to mess with my people. They

don't know you're kidding."

"I cannot be contained," I replied. "But I can be shot at."

There was a long moment of silence. Then, "What happened?"

I told Nat about the window and the hole in the wall at the office.

When I was finished, he asked, "You all right?"

"Sure."

"'Kay." Nat. Not just a man of few words. A man of few syllables.

"Also got a new client."

"Good."

"You heard about the Barry Mallondyke murder a few months ago?"

"On the news."

"His widow wants to know who killed him."

Nat didn't say anything. Waiting.

I forged ahead. "I'm going to go down to the station and take a look at the murder book tomorrow. Maybe have Erin take a look at the ballistics report."

"Sounds like a plan," Nat hung up. Guess he needed to go tone more bodies.

Brickell ran southwest and passed near a bunch of parks. Simpson Park—D'oh!—was a block off and was a quiet spot surrounded by a dense screen of trees and low stone walls and fences. Down a little further was Alice Wainwright Park. I don't know who Alice Wainwright was, but she apparently didn't like trees. Her park had a few palms but was mostly grass running down to the beach. Had a beautiful view though. There, Brickell turned into the South Dixie Highway, which was a block east of the Vizcaya Museum & Gardens. The gardens there included Italian-style landscapes to explore and a sprawling mansion built in 1914. Also, the world's largest collection of Vizcayas. That's what I was told.

Miami-Dade County boasted two hundred sixty parks. I appreciated the patches of green interspersed with the concrete and glass. Each green space was a welcome hunk of refreshment. Passing every single one was like passing a friend. I wanted to wave.

I got off the highway and drove into my neighborhood: a well-heeled section of Coral Gables where the houses were large and had a street in front and a river behind.

Everybody calls the place where they live "my house," but the house where I lived wasn't really mine. It was a big, airy French Colonial, but I didn't own it. I didn't pay rent for it. I didn't lease it.

I can't remember anything about my life before my death and resuscitation. I was told that I had no parents or relatives, and I was sent to live with The Mama in a foster home. She's a story all her own. I graduated high school at age seventeen, and I was told when I reached the age of twenty-one I would be able to move into a house that was waiting for me in Miami. I have never known who owns the house or why I am allowed to reside in it. Once a year, an attorney comes over to check things out and I sign some papers. Then he leaves and that's it.

So, the house is where I live. The house comes with two other built-in perks: Maximilian and Sandretta. Max is a culinary genius in addition to being groundskeeper and handyman. When I need help fixing my car, Max is my mechanic. If I had a boat, like all the neighbors, I bet Max would know how to take care of that as well. Sandretta cleans and washes and basically covers all the housekeeping duties. She's also my relentless piano teacher and that's another story as well.

The house is nice but you can't eat it, so all other expenses have to be covered by me, and that's why I work.

I pulled through the archway into the carport next to the house and took the stuff from the trunk of the car. It would all be going back to the office in a day or two, so I put it in the entryway for the time being. I called out but the house was empty. Not unusual. Max and Sandretta often ran errands before I got home. I headed toward the kitchen for a snack.

Something felt wrong.

I walked into the great room en route to the kitchen, and the air around me suddenly felt different. I held my breath. There was other breathing I could feel that wasn't my own. It was larger and deeper. Lungs with enormous capacity were working the air around me. I felt something watching me. The small hairs on the back of my neck were at attention and caught movement. I felt the displacement of air and heard something scratching the tile floor.

I couldn't see anything out of the ordinary, which really got me scared. I told myself to calm down as goose bumps erupted all over me.

The great room had couches on one end, arranged facing the wall and the fireplace I almost never used and the television screen that I used a lot. They were all in their places with bright shiny faces so no clues there. Over by the door near the middle of the room was a full-size grand piano that I played every day. On the nearest wall was a long set of shelves with a sound system and tons of books that I often bought from the sale table at the library, including graphic novels; copies of National Geographic; old hardback editions of detective novels; and books on literature (including Shakespeare), philosophy and history, and nature. There were also about two thousand music CDs. Those were all where they belonged. There was a table behind the couches that had fresh tropical flowers on it, courtesy of Sandretta.

The flowers were swaying.

Something was moving. My brain chunks screamed at me.

I turned to scan the room behind me. I felt the press of air before I felt anything else. Instinctively, I dodged to the side and started to roll between the table and the piano. Something caught my foot hard and threw me off my roll. My leg slammed into the table and I heard a crack. Instead of gracefully rolling toward the window, I fell sideways and hit the floor on my side. The air came out of me with a "whoof" and pain shot up my ribs. Tile was not a great material for cushioning a fall.

I heard a snarl. Deep and big. Really big. I still couldn't see anything, anywhere in the room. What the . . . ?

I got to my feet. The crack must have been the leg of the table instead of my leg. Still hurt.

I moved around the piano, trying to put something large and

solid between me and my invisible adversary. I tried to catch my wind while my heart pounded out of my chest.

Another snarl. The sound was moving toward me. Something landed on the piano with a thud. Gouges appeared in parallel tracks on the lid as if a giant cat had put a paw there to use my Steinway for a scratching post.

If that was supposed to be intimidating, it worked. I skirted around the side of the piano, hoping another avenue of escape would present itself.

I felt the thing coming around and instinctively dashed the other way. Those claws skittered on the tile, and whatever-it-was slammed into the bookcase. Dozens of CDs and copies of National Geographic went flying. There was a flickering in the air and I saw an outline. Bits of colored light, like lens flares in a J. J. Abrams movie, shattered and cascaded around the edges of an enormous beast. It was roughly the shape of a lion, but blockier and twice as big. It turned toward me as it gathered its uneven legs, and I looked into a face that was more like a big dog. Rottweiler maybe. It snarled again.

"I can see you now, Toto!" I yelled. "You're not in Kansas anymore!"

I had a sudden flashback. For a moment, I was a ten-year-old kid again in the bayou by The Mama's house. I'd snuck out of bed in time to witness a knight-in-armor riding a giant lizard through the cypress trees.

This was not a good time for nostalgia.

I kept circling the piano going the other way, and the beast leapt at me again. My dodge-and-roll was successful this time. Cue the Olympic theme.

The beast skittered some more, off-balance. It was learning how not to slide on the tile though and hardly slowed.

The lights filled the outline now, and the thing was becoming less ephemeral by the moment.

Where was my gun? Oh yeah. In my shoulder harness, which was now in a box. In the entryway.

While I calculated the length of time I'd need to run down the hall, open the box, find my gun, unlock the gun, load the gun, and defend myself, the beast moved closer.

It was going to take me.

We were both breathing heavily now. The pain in my side was starting to overshadow the pain in my leg.

"Play dead!" I yelled. Toto kept coming. It was worth a try.

It continued coming at me, walking now—with me in reverse, keeping its iridescent outline in view.

I bumped into something solid behind me. I'd misjudged the exit to the hallway and now I was backed up against the wall. The beast gathered its legs under itself again, preparing to pounce. It was almost completely solid now. Sparkles flickered in bright trails around the edges still, like it was Stained all over. I could see its eyes now. Green. Intelligent. Ageless as the stars.

The doors of the house were solid oak. If I could get through one, slam it shut, it might keep the thing off me long enough for me to get to my car and get out of here. Then I'd make one extremely terse and pointed call to animal control.

The lion-dog-hyena was ready to take another shot.

"Squirrel!" I yelled. I pointed as I shouted, feinted right and ran left, heading for the nearest door.

It wasn't fooled.

I ran, but the beast caught my legs with a swipe of its paw. I slammed into the wall and then fell on the tiles a second time. My side erupted in fire. I felt the weight of a good-sized planet on my back. Toto used a paw to flip me over so I was facing up. It pinned my shoulder to the floor. There was no way I could move.

It didn't eat me. It did breathe on me. I expected a fetid, rotting stench to wash over my face. Instead, I smelled wildflowers, dewy grass, and sunshine.

One last pleasant surprise before I died.

With one paw holding me down, Toto used the other paw to draw on my face. More specifically, it used the tip of a claw to etch the skin of my forehead. I heard screaming and realized it was me. The lines felt molten but instantly cooled. When Toto was done, it backed away. It looked at my forehead almost approvingly. Then it met my eyes and snorted once and disappeared.

Blink.

A few leftover sparks drifted up toward the ceiling and faded away.

At lunch, eating kimchi, I would have bet good money that getting shot at would be the strangest and most frightening thing that would happen to me today.

I sat on the floor and unashamedly moaned in a way that wasn't masculine at all. From fear and pain but also relief that it was over and I was alive. My leg hurt and my side hurt worse, so sitting got uncomfortable pretty quick.

Gravity played devil's advocate, but I finally won the debate over getting to my feet. I padded down the hall. No need to hesitate or be afraid. There was nothing in this world that could scare me anymore.

My reflection stared back at me from the bathroom mirror, and I thought that guy looked as shocked as I felt. How about that? Since I was already staring, I examined my brow. There were faint lines in my skin, thin as threads, in a gently-glowing baby blue. I had seen a pattern like that somewhere before, but I couldn't place it or imagine what it might mean. It was like a Stain but contained in a small circle instead of a ribbon.

The lines were fading. Over the course of about ten minutes they became fainter and fainter until they melted away altogether. Other than Stain, I hadn't seen anything this messed up for at least ten years. Maybe my teenaged misbehaviors at The Mama's were coming back to haunt me.

I sat on the side of the tub and fingered my bruised leg and ribs. I said some bad words.

The tub was right there, all handy-like. I filled it up with hot water, and while the faucet ran I got some Ibuprofen out of the medicine cabinet and swallowed four of them. When the tub was full, I stripped and eased into the hot water. More bad words ensued.

I soaked for a good thirty minutes, until the water had cooled and I had let some drain out and refilled it. I wondered if I should report this latest attack to the police. What would I say? A giant liondog got in the house and used my head for a neon art project? Oh, and don't forget, Officer Friendly, it was invisible. Make sure you write that down.

The pain wasn't getting better but it wasn't getting worse. I wrapped myself in a towel and gimped to the bedroom. I put on some sweats and gimped to the kitchen, but I wasn't hungry for anything even though I knew my body would need fuel for repairs. I poked around in the fridge. A sandwich would be easy to make, so I assembled a ham and cheese with some brown mustard and ate it standing over the piano. It hurt to swallow.

Big long gouges still adorned the wooden top. I could see quite a few shattered CDs on the floor. I'd have to replace some Peter Gabriel and Frankie Goes to Hollywood. Chopin was all broke up too.

The tile looked cold and hard, especially in the places where I had fallen. I needed more rugs.

I thought I'd lie down for a few minutes, just until Max and Sandretta got back. I curled up on my bed and fell asleep.

When I woke up it was dark. Four in the morning by the clock. I thought I could hear music, but it was only a lingering melody from a dream I couldn't otherwise remember. I got up to walk off the tightness in my leg and side. I walked down the hallway and cursed at the pain as I stretched.

The French windows were open in the great room. If I had opened them, I had forgotten. Probably hadn't been me. There was a nice waning moon over the river, and its reflection flickered at me from the water. The reflection changed and for a moment there was a face. Female. Human but with an exotic glimmer of something other, and it was all just a trick of flowing water and light and me with a fuzzy head. That's what I decided.

I took more Ibuprofen and went back to sleep.

CHAPTER 3

Office Visits

Erin O'Connell was the sexiest medical examiner in the world. Her career trajectory had been notably meteoric because she had an uncanny ability for analyzing information, and she was also famously beautiful. When you watch a television drama and see an impossibly attractive woman working as a lab technician or forensic pathologist and you say to yourself, "There's no way a woman that gorgeous would be stuck in a regular job because she'd be earning a million dollars as a supermodel," well, Erin is that woman. In a regular job. And that gorgeous.

She wasn't freakishly tall, but she always wore high heels to work so she stood about 5' 11" and that made her taller than almost everyone in the office. The heels never seemed to bother her in the slightest even when she spent the whole day on her feet. Her deep oak-shaded hair was cut past the shoulder and arranged to set off the heart shape of her face. Her mouth was small but her lips full. A heart within a heart. Her eyes were the color of warm toffee, but I'd seen them change to emerald green when she was angry or upset, which has been known to happen with me around. She always wore a lab coat at work which somehow did absolutely nothing to hide her curvy figure. except where it better served to lead the imagination to speculation.

I might be in love with her a little.

I'd met Erin at a crime scene. I was on the force and we were canvassing the street where a serial killer had left another victim. Erin was comforting the wife. At one point, when she was alone, I said "Hi." She instantly replied, "Nope. Don't do drugs," which made me smile. I later found out she helped the wife get into counseling, and she volunteered once a week at a women's shelter.

She was much more than a pretty package.

Oh. She was also Stained.

I strolled into the lab. Okay, limped.

"Of all the gin joints, in all the towns, in all the world, I walk into yours," I said.

"Luck, when are you going to stop mangling Casablanca?" she asked. She didn't look up from the lump of something pink and squishy that she had in a metal bowl. She was poking it with a scalpel.

"When you come with me to Paris," I replied. "Then I'll be able to say 'We'll always have Paris.'"

"Can't happen," she said. "That'd only work if I got on a plane after and you never saw me again."

"That does seem to be a flaw in the plan."

Erin set the metal bowl and scalpel down on a table. She looked up then and I caught the full impact of those smoldering toffee eyes.

"Got something for me?"

Boy did I ever have something for her. Plus, she'd given me a tempting straight line. I took the high road. "Two things. A bullet and a story," I replied.

"Okay. Bullet first," she said.

"It's in evidence." I did have my copy of the incident report, which I held out to her. That simple motion was enough to make me wince. I hoped she hadn't noticed.

"Then you can tell me about those ribs."

She'd noticed.

She took the report and started reading. She hummed a little while she read and I just waited, not wanting to rush her.

Erin's Stain was actually quite beautiful. Instead of the oppressive, ugly black ribbons that Milly carried, Erin's Stain was a forest green band that encircled her torso, right over her heart. It had a pattern that looked like stylized leaves and vines, although that was just my interpretation. Not a Stain really. On her, more of an embellishment.

She finished reading. "So when ballistics are done, I can check it against the database for you, okay? See if I can find a match."

"That would be great. I don't think the police will pursue it themselves." I smiled.

"And now the story," she replied.

I told her about the meeting with Milly MacPherson Mallondyke. Erin's left eyebrow went up at the name. I could respect that. And I told her how, after Milly left, the bullet had presumptuously shattered the front window of my office and ended up in my wall.

She listened carefully. When I was done, she said, "You don't think your new client shot at you?"

"Why would she? She just hired me to do a job."

Erin moved her lips around in distracting ways while she thought. "Maybe she just wanted to identify you. You said she checked the door repeatedly before she came in. So she was really intent on making sure she had the right place. Then she talks to you and gets a good look. She hires you to make you comfortable. Justification for checking you out. Then she leaves, sets up with the rifle. Kills you. The check she gave you never gets cashed. It serves as her alibi."

I nodded while she spoke. I nodded a lot. "This is why I like talking to you. The feeling that you're dangerously close to putting me out of a job," I said. "But my feeling is she's sincere."

Erin shrugged. "So cash the check. If it clears, she's probably legit. If it bounces, keep looking over your shoulder."

"You are wise," I replied. I made to give her a bow, Jackie Chan style, and groaned.

"I'm guessing the bullet had nothing to do with your limp and your ribs," Erin said.

She'd noticed the limp too. I thought she'd been completely focused on the pink and squishy thing in the bowl.

"Sit over here," she said, indicating a stool.

I sat. She brought another stool and sat across from me. She pointed at my leg and gave me a "gimme" gesture. I entrusted my left lower extremity to her tender care.

"How did you injure your leg?"

"Bumped into a table," I said. I left out the part where I was being chased by a giant, invisible liondog.

She gently rolled up my pants leg a little and slid a warm hand up along my shin. She carefully manipulated my leg and foot. Her probing fingers were firm and—yowch! That hurt. "Not a fracture," she said. "Open your shirt."

I unbuttoned my shirt. Her hands ran along my side and then along each rib, starting at the bottom and working her way up. It both tickled and hurt at the same time, which was just wrong. I held myself together with some effort. I wanted to giggle and swear simultaneously.

"Take a deep breath," Erin said.

I inhaled and stopped halfway and groaned again.

"Uh-uh," she said. "Deep breath."

I had to clench my teeth together, but I managed to fill my lungs with air and expand my chest.

"How did you hurt your side?" she asked.

I let the air out of my lungs, relieved. "While I was distracted by the table, the chair snuck up on me."

Erin looked at me with her head tilted to the side and gave me a dubious expression like she was watching I.Q. points falling out of my ears.

I laughed, which hurt, and said, "I'm just stupid clumsy. It was embarrassing. Like I was trying to dance with the furniture but the furniture was drunk."

"Ok," she replied. "There's nothing broken but stay off the leg as much as you can and take ten deep breaths every hour. It'll keep you from getting an infection in your chest."

"That's it?"

"Can't put a splint on a rib," she replied. "Just barbecue sauce."

I laughed again. It hurt again. She smiled. "Ten breaths. Go."

"I already did one. Plus, you made me laugh several times which counts for another one."

Erin rolled her toffee eyes at me and waved me off. I took ten deep breaths and every one set my side on fire.

"Can you look at one more thing?" I asked.

Erin kept her expression neutral but I could tell she was thinking. I pointed at my forehead so she wouldn't get the wrong idea. "The skin across here hurts. Weird, right?"

The circlet of her Stain touched me when she drew close. I swear I felt a tingle. Unless it was just my imagination. She frowned a little and squinted and ran a finger across my brow. She smelled like soap and jojoba and cinnamon and butter and sugar. Sexy and clean. Possibly edible.

"What happened to your forehead?"

"Shaving accident?"

"Uh-huh. No abrasions. No bruising. Not even a pimple," she said. "Maybe you just slept on it funny."

"Maybe," I said. The symbol on my head had faded completely. Or my imagination was trying to kill me. And kill my piano.

I looked into Erin's eyes and she backed away.

"I'll see what I can find out about that bullet for you," she said, getting back to business.

"Sounds good," I replied. Señor Nonchalant. I buttoned my shirt back up and readjusted my pants leg. "Thanks for your help."

"Mmm-hmm," Erin said. Already back to the pink and squishy.

I made my way over to the downtown police station, which was only one rock song away as the crow drives. Practically everything in Chief Cuevas's office was brass. Brass bookends on the shelves, brass paperweights on the desk, brass pen-and-pencil set. If the Chief had thought of a more subtle way of making it clear he was the top brass in the building, he'd long ago shot it down with a brass bullet.

Cuevas motioned me into the brass fortress the second he saw me.

"Luck, get in here," he said. Ah, just like old times. Dumbrass.

"You're reviewing the Mallondyke case for Milly," he stated.

"Good to see you too, Chief," I replied.

The Chief ignored me. He stood up and unlocked a filing cabinet and pulled out a binder. As far as I could tell, there wasn't anything else in the drawer. He shoved the binder at me. I took it and tucked it under my arm.

"Before you take another step, you're going to keep your trap shut and hear me out," he said. "I continue to maintain you're a colossal screw-up. You don't like following rules and you have a pathological dislike for authority. In this case, I decided that kind of behavior may be just what Milly needs. I had a long talk with her father and he wanted someone who wouldn't mind coloring outside the lines. I thought of you. We play golf at Palmetto every week. I want you to meet us there next Sunday at ten in the morning and tell us what you find. We'll let you know what Milly should be told. Anything you find out between now and then, you keep to yourself until you clear it with me. I know how you operate and I don't want to hear any baloney about how Milly is your client. I can see that coming a mile away. You drop that kind of thinking into the toilet right now and flush it. Her daddy's money is paying for this and he's willing to go along with bringing you onboard because his daughter is hurting."

He handed me a pen and pointed a thick finger at the piece of paper that was sitting on the edge of his desk. I bent down to read it. Standard sign-out sheet for the murder book. City of Miami PD loves its documentation. A brass monkey—one of Cuevas's paperweights—was looking up at me to make sure I was behaving myself. I stuck my tongue out at it.

Cuevas said, "No photocopies of the book. No taking anything out of it. The book doesn't leave the building. You return everything back to me." I signed and Cuevas kept the paper. He fixed a particularly dangerous expression on his face and half-squinted at me. "You go ahead and find out what you can. I'm relying on you not to mess it up. Are we clear? Do you have any questions? Good. Now get out."

Of course I was clear—and that's precisely why I had questions. In typical Chief "Tequila Cuervo" fashion, he was dictating his terms and leaving no room for argument. If the Chief believed

I was going to fall in line just because he was yelling at me, he was conveniently ignoring precedent. He could think whatever he wanted. Since I needed to read through the book, I didn't say anything except, "Thank you, Chief."

I stood in place and let Cuevas glare at me for a second while he tried to decide if I was being smart. I entertained the possibility of the Chief owning a large, invisible liondog. Then I left.

CHAPTER 4

Symbols

I found a quiet spot outside the break room where there were some unoccupied tables and chairs. Most of the policemen ate at their desks or in their cars while on duty, so there were rarely any crowds. I had some snacks, the murder book, and the rest of the day to see what I could find out. Perfect.

At the front of the book was a summary of the case notes. These were used to give an overview of the investigation, primarily so the District Attorney could determine what kind of case the state would present if it went to trial. Since there hadn't been an arrest, the summary was brief.

The rest of the book went more or less in reverse chronological order. The first material entered was at the back. As the case progressed, papers were added at the front so the most recent additions were behind the summary. I flipped to the back in an effort to see the case as it unfolded.

The responding officers' report was the first entry. The body was found by the hotel maid, who used her master key to access the room for housekeeping at 11:14 in the morning. The door had a "Do Not Disturb" sign on the handle, so she had skipped the room until it was the only one remaining to be cleaned on that floor. She knocked and announced herself because people sometimes forget to take the sign off the door when they leave. When there was no response, she went in and found the body. She contacted the hotel manager with a frantic call and the manager called the police. When they arrived, the responding officers secured the scene and did some initial interviews until the detectives arrived along with the medical examiner.

There wasn't a lot to be gleaned there, except the killer had probably left the "Do Not Disturb" sign to delay discovery.

The medical examiner's report was a little more useful. Another examiner from Erin's office had been on the scene. Erin hadn't done the examination herself. I flipped forward and saw that the same examiner had done the autopsy as well: Sean Graver. I guess he was a new examiner. I'd never met him before.

The initial report stated that Barry Mallondyke had died sometime between midnight and 4:00 in the morning. There were no defensive wounds visible. The cause of death had likely been the stab wound to the heart due to the location of the blood that had pooled under the body. The examiner would not confirm until the autopsy had been completed. The wound was approximately an inch and a half long. The lower edge of the wound was sharp and the cut was clean. The upper edge of the wound was torn and ragged. The examiner determined the victim had simply lain there and bled out. No sign of thrashing on the bed or fighting against the assailant. The blood had bubbled up and run down the sides of the victim's chest and soaked the bed, but had not been disturbed.

The secondary wound, in the abdomen, was longer. About seven inches. Almost no blood had come from this wound, indicating that the heart had ceased beating when several cuts had been made. While the wound to the heart had been violent, the wound in the stomach had been careful and methodical. Multiple cuts had been made to get through the various layers of skin, fat, and muscle. The examiner could not see any trauma to the organs visible in the abdominal cavity, including the stomach, liver, or intestines. Again, however, the examiner would confirm later. There were no other signs or scars indicating surgeries or previous wounds.

I liked Sean's work. His report was thorough and well-written, and he didn't throw in a lot of extraneous detail.

The report went on to describe the condition of the victim's extremities and other observations made before the body was moved. I didn't see anything else that would be useful. There were some photos, and I looked at the ones showing Barry's face, his expression oddly serene. He looked like he was sleeping. Maybe dreaming about a nice dinner or walking on the beach with the young and beautiful Mrs. Mallondyke. The rest of the photos, showing the up-close details of the murder and mutilation, I could do without.

Next, I skimmed through the witness statements and detective's reports to see if any other information would jump out at me. Nothing did.

I got to the autopsy report. C'mon Sean, my man. Gimme something I can use.

There was a boatload of scientific description which went over my head. The gist of it all appeared to confirm the examiner's original findings. Barry was murdered by a single knife wound into the heart. After bleeding out, his heart no longer functioning, his abdomen had been carefully cut open for reasons unknown. And Barry hadn't seemed to mind. He'd smiled pleasantly while a knife of some kind had been plunged into his chest and his life bled away.

I flipped through the pages, finding more photos. Suddenly, I had to stop.

I was so shocked by what I saw, I pushed the murder book away from me like it had caught fire. For a few long seconds I froze in place.

My mind didn't want to process what I had seen. A nice, juicy clue had just walked up to the door of my brain and knocked, and my subconscious took a quick li'l peek through the spyhole and didn't want to answer that particular door right now. Thanks anyway. Never mind what was standing out there. Not interested. No solicitations. Don't bother the conscious part of the brain. Let it sleep.

I forced myself to look again. The image burned its way into my mind and memory.

A medical examiner starts with the outside and works inward. Eventually, a body is stripped and photographed to create a record of anything and everything that might be important. Got a nice little tattoo of Tweety Bird somewhere secret? Put there so only you and your closest companions will see it? Better add the medical examiner to the short list and be aware that if you die under questionable circumstances, everybody concerned with the investigation of your death will get the privilege of saying, “Hey there, Tweety! Did that bad ol’ Puddy Tat getcha?”

Barry Mallondyke had a tattoo all right. But it was no Tweety Bird. I would have preferred a Tweety Bird.

Between Barry Mallondyke’s supple shoulders, just below the nape of the neck, was a black circle with a design inside it. Like a Stain. Initially, my mind jumped to a terrifying conclusion: the tattoo had led to his death and I was next. The more closely I looked, however, the more I told myself to calm down. There was a design—but a much different design than the one I had seen on my forehead.

I grabbed a pen and sketched the design on a paper napkin. Chief hadn’t said anything about taking sketches.

I stuffed the napkin into my pocket and referred to the description of the tattoo in the examiner’s report.

As I read, I felt a little better. Mallondyke’s tattoo was temporary like one of those you get wet and press against your skin or gets painted on. After the examiner had completed his report, he had washed the body so it could be re-dressed and turned over to the mortuary. The design came most of the way off although traces of the ink remained faintly visible.

The design was also in a different place on him, of course. I had no idea what that might mean, but the more differences I could find, the better I would feel. The design was also very different from what I could remember about mine. The design on my forehead was an interlocking set of elements that filled the circle it was in. Mallondyke’s design was contained in a circle as well but was more like a triangle shape with odd curlicues at the corners and lots of white space.

Those might’ve been gang signs except they were too complex and delicate. Gang signs were meant to be intimidating, not pretty. These intricate symbols had to be something else.

I bought a fruit juice and cinnamon bun from the cafeteria—

Aha! That's why Erin smelled that way! Cinnamon bun!—and tried to settle down with the food. I took ten deep, agonizing breaths, per doctor's orders. I forged ahead and hoped there wouldn't be any more surprises.

Two hours later, I felt I'd gotten everything I was going to get out of the murder book. All I really found out is that Barry Mallondyke had no enemies. He had been, by all accounts, a loving husband, responsible citizen, and friendly guy. He'd been vice-president for his family's export business, Mallondyke South African Mercantile, since he graduated from college at the age of twenty-two. The company was almost seventy-five years old and owned, among other things, a diamond mine outside Johannesburg, South Africa. He had not been involved in any legal suits or bar fights, and he had no debts except for a mortgage and a couple of credit cards. His vehicles were leased by the company. He didn't gamble. He drank socially when the occasion called for it but preferred a beer on the weekends. He had a million-dollar life insurance policy, but he made more than that in a year so he was worth more alive than dead.

I stood up and stretched—carefully—still hurt—and took the murder book back to the Chief's office. He was on the phone when I knocked, so I left the book on his desk.

A pair of workmen had almost finished installing the new window at my office. The landlord was on top of his game for once. Of course, this was an image thing. Having a broken window that could be seen all the way to the street was bad for a location's reputation. Quick action was real estate self-preservation. The property had to look well-maintained to keep its value. If I had a problem with the plumbing though, it would be months before anything got done.

I had decided to go by the office to see what was going on, and I was pleased to find everything was almost done. I could go to the house and bring my stuff back.

Then I found the strangest thing. Sitting in the dead center of my office desk was a bullet casing for 7.62 mm rifle load.

I asked the window installers if they had found the casing and put it there. The older of the two men shook his head and said it was there when they started the job this morning. Suspicion crept up the back of my neck. It was just too weird. It had to be the casing from the bullet that had found its way through my window and into my wall, didn't it? I wanted to circle the desk and see if there was anything else I could see there. But I didn't want to look like a goofball in front of the workmen. I knew I should call the police and have them pick it up. Chain of evidence and all that. Impatience won. I still had the napkin in my pocket with the symbol on it so I used it to pick up the casing and deposited it in my shirt pocket.

Qui-Gon caught me on the way out to my car.

"Hey! You want lunch?" he asked.

"Not now, thank you," I replied. "I'll be back later."

"Okay. You see the little boy?"

That stopped me. "What little boy?"

"Little boy wearing funny shirt. He came past this morning before I open up. He walk upstairs to your office. He never come down."

Pretty much anybody going to my office had to walk past Qui-Gon's restaurant. And he had eyes like a hawk so he saw everything. Always looking for the next hungry customer.

"How old was he?" I asked.

"Dunno. Maybe eight. Maybe ten years-old."

"What did he look like?"

"Dunno. Just little boy. Funny shirt. He went upstairs. Later, guys bring window. Little boy still never come down."

"Did he look lost? Was he with anybody?"

"No. Not lost. Walked straight up like he know where to go. All by himself."

I tried to think.

I think I'll move to a different location. Somewhere normal. I can't imagine where that might be.

"The shirt. You said it was funny. Like a cartoon shirt? With a funny drawing on it?"

"No. Funny like old. Like nobody wear anymore. Like . . . Robin Hood!" Qui-Gon smiled at me. His little dark eyes sparkled from his wrinkled face like chips of obsidian set in a prune. He was proud to have come up with an explanation he thought I would understand.

"Okay," I said. "I'll check it out. Thanks."

I was going to look like a goofball after all.

The workmen ignored me and I ignored them as I made a tour of my office, discretely bending to look under things and sneaking peeks behind shelves and cabinets. They finally packed up their tools and left, and I explored the closets in peace.

No little kid here. I sat at my desk to think.

The small windows on the back of the office were usually cracked open for air. I didn't think a kid could climb through one and safely drop the fifteen feet or so to the ground, but I was losing my grip on what was possible and what wasn't. I told myself that the kid had likely gone down the same way he had come up and Qui-Gon simply hadn't seen him go. I wanted to find the kid if at all possible since he was the most likely candidate for leaving the bullet casing on my desk and that meant he might have seen the shooter.

I had no idea how my life had become so weird. It was about to get weirder. I was an hour away from ten-thousand dawns.

I went out to my car and sat for a few minutes, thinking. I thought so hard that my forehead started to itch.

I realized what I needed right now was a feather.

It was a short drive to the Alice Wainwright Park with its convenient access to the beach. After a stroll along the sand, I found a herring gull feather caught in some grass, which was perfect. I took it home.

In the back of my mind, I wondered what had happened to

Max and Sandretta. They weren't here when I'd come home from the office, and I hadn't seen them this morning either. What I really need though is a stone from the back yard. I quickly found one. A round, smooth, fist-sized hunk of sandstone, which was perfect. I took it into the house.

I pushed the piano away from the middle of the room and it crunched over some of my CDs. I should have picked those up. Really though, a candle is what I need most. I had candles in the bedroom. They had never been lit, which was a little sad, but they were perfect. I brought one out to the great room along with a box of matches and put them on the floor.

I should take that bullet casing over to Erin, so she could look it over. Maybe after I get a glass of water. I really needed a glass of water.

I stood at the sink, filling a tumbler from the faucet, when I looked up and saw the ghost of my reflection in the window. It was light outside so my reflection was faint. There was no mistaking the design on my forehead though, glowing brightly blue. I could see it now, in complete detail. I don't know why I wasn't able to recall it before. It was elegant. Simple. Perfect.

Salt. That's what I really needed. I had a container of salt, which was perfect. In fact, I had three. When had I bought those? Probably planning a margarita party that never came to fruition. Ha! Fruition. I'm all about the fruition. Need a knife to cut fruit. Get a knife from the drawer.

I looked at everything I had on the floor. Feather, stone, candle, matches, water, salt, knife. That was everything. Perfect.

I think I'm coming down with a fever. My forehead felt incredibly hot.

I got to work. I stood in the middle of my great room floor and started pouring salt in a line around myself. I drew a circle and then started filling it in. The pattern was vivid in my mind and I sketched it from memory. Interlocking lines with ancient power waiting. I used all three containers of salt. When I was finished, I stood back and looked at my creation.

Perfect.

It was crazy how satisfied I felt to get this done. To complete the design the way it needed to be. It was so right.

I situated the other items at the compass points. Feather for Air in the North. Stone for Earth in the South. Water for Water to the West. Candle for Fire to the East. I lit the candle. Almost finished. I held the knife with the point against my thumb. I pressed. Blood welled up on the pad of my thumb. I walked around the circle and let seven drops of blood fall onto the salt to give it fuel. With each drop, the sky grew darker, and somewhere a breeze became a storm. I knelt in front of the circle and touched the knife to the salt.

I knew exactly what to say.

"*Oscailte.*"

A thunderbolt of energy shot from my forehead and down my arm and traveled around both sides of the circle. The energy met itself on the other side with a clap that shook the house. The sound rolled across the floor in a wave and a pale, translucent column of blue light shot up from the floor to the ceiling.

Some small part of me said to another small part of me, "That was nifty."

The circle and the design it held solidified while the spaces between the lines faded away. A rush of wind came up from the floor, and I took a deep breath of fragrant air from a faraway place. There were trees and grass and flowers below. The design became a silver gate with a hinge directly in front of me. The gate dropped away. A meadow lay below me, extending downward at an angle perpendicular to the floor. The silver gate lay on the grass at ninety degrees from where it had started.

I stood in front of the open space and let myself fall.

CHAPTER 5

Realm of the Alder King

I landed on the grass after pivoting through the hole. Gravity had altered its angle with me, and I found myself walking along a faint path. An honest-to-goodness shaft of moonlight lit the way like a spotlight on a hazy evening. I turned and looked behind me. The silver gate lay on the grass and the hole attached to it remained right where it had been conjured. I could see the ceiling of the great room through the hole.

What . . . ?

The Mama would have called this a "cluster monkey," and I could picture her saying it with her ham-sized fists on her ample hips, shaking her head in dismay, making her pink hair curlers smack against the side of her head. I'd created a few cluster monkeys in my time with her, and it seemed I'd created one again, although I was at a sudden loss to know how I had done so.

I followed the path away from the gate. It felt like the right thing to do. My forehead didn't itch anymore.

There was motion in the woods behind me, and a single, audible step on the ground. Without turning my head, I tried to see if there was someone moving through the trees in my peripheral vision. Nothing that I could see.

The path was clear. Wildflowers dotted the edges and spread off into the distance in tiny splashes of red and purple and blue and yellow. The air was cool and light and my lungs took it eagerly in.

I heard a little girl's laughter in the distance. Another voice hushed her. Someone was expected. Maybe me.

The air behind me became suddenly denser and I turned in reflex. Toto had come back. My heart leapt in my chest and started playing marimba with my ribs. What could it want with me this time? It looked at me with those intelligent eyes, impassive, impossible to read.

I took a few steps, walking backwards. Please don't follow.

Toto followed.

I stopped because my knees decided a refresher course in walking would be in order right about now. Toto sat back on its haunches. Patient. Just a twitch of a pointed ear.

The liondog was possibly not interested in chasing me down. I tried to put it out of my thoughts. For maybe three milliseconds. I urged myself sideways, keeping an eye on the liondog and an eye on the path.

There was a stand of willow trees ahead, towering shoulder-to-shoulder. Their slender branches and leaves created a curtain of sorts. Behind them, shy lights danced. I reluctantly let Toto herd me in that direction.

I went through the willow curtain and emerged into a moonlit glade.

Dozens of creatures surrounded an open area in the center. Together, they created a ring of fantastic colors and shapes and sounds.

Most of the beings there were human in appearance. Some had eyes that were overlarge or ears that tapered toward the back of their heads. Some had wings that were almost clear but caught the silver of the moon and a hundred other tiny, twinkling lights that were floating through the air.

Others weren't human at all. There was the whispering creature that was built like a centaur but with a feline body and a regal, hawk-like face. And the family of bears with serpent-scaled spines that scrambled up a tree, twitching their long hairless tails for balance. Voices, from guttural to flute-like, spoke and sang in hushed tones.

They were also Stained. All the colors of the worlds, real and imagined.

All those things The Mama talked about—maybe she wasn't crazy after all. Or maybe I'm the crazy one.

I felt Toto come up behind me and bump into my left shoulder, making sure I'd remember who was there. My breath caught in my throat as a hundred pairs of eyes looked my way.

I turned my head and scanned from one side of the circle around to the other.

In a voice that rang out louder than I intended, I said, "Who ordered the kung pao chicken?"

A few of the faces stared back in shock. Most gave no reaction at all. I realized it was entirely possible that none of them understood what I had said. I didn't know if we spoke the same language. They certainly didn't look like the kids I'd grown up with.

A woman—no tail, no wings—detached herself from a group of confidantes and came languidly toward me. One of her friends had scaly skin and another looked like she was made of papery, white tree bark.

The woman who approached was as human-looking as any here. Her face was long with delicate features, almost like a living Modigliani. She had eyes that were tilted and shaped like almonds and a mouth that was a little too wide. Still spectacularly beautiful. She would have blended in with the girls at Nat's gym, except for her outfit and her Stain. Instead of workout clothes, she wore a tight, shimmering gown. It was silver with a blue pattern of stripes like a zebra. Or a tiger. The skirt was split up the side to an alarming height, revealing long, sensual legs. She walked on her toes as if she wore heels but her feet were bare. The dress left her shoulders exposed. It was a feat of engineering that the dress stayed in place at all as she walked.

She stopped in front of me, standing entirely too close. Desire came off her skin, infectious. I cleared my throat.

Her gaze ran down my body all the way to the ground and back up again.

When she spoke, she paused and breathed between the words as if there was nothing more savory than her own thoughts. "Thou art. So deliciously. Broken."

Her long, delicate finger wove a sinuous path toward me.

Her fingertip brushed my chest, ever so slightly.

I wanted to die.

I felt my chest split open. Acid poured down the splayed interiors of my skin and the edges caught on fire and rolled back, layer after layer until the bones were exposed. It lasted only a moment, but it was long enough for me to realize that life was the last thing I wanted to cling to. Then the pain went away just as quickly as it had started. I found myself kneeling on the ground, my trembling hands pressed against my chest. I looked down. I was unharmed but my breath had left me completely.

"Thou shalt. Respect. Thy masters. And kneel," she said.

I coughed. My breath returned in great, heaving gulps. I continued to stare at the ground in front of me. Those stripes she wore. Definitely not zebra. I wrested control of my body back from the memory of pain.

When I was finally able to look up at her, standing over me with a sneer on her face, I said, "No fortune. Cookie. For you."

She giggled. "So very. Broken," she said. She bent over and touched me with her finger again. Pleasure ran through me in great shuddering waves like a top-ten list of life's best experiences rolled into one.

"We can. Also. Reward," she said.

A long double note from a horn sounded in the air. The woman turned her head and sighed. Playtime over. She straightened to her full height and tip-toed away.

The horn sounded again, closer this time, and the sound was accompanied by a thundering riff of deep drums.

On the third sounding, the willows parted on the opposite side of the glade. A procession entered, led by a dozen massive warriors in silver armor. The armor was intricately detailed, showing deer running through forests and bears rampant on stony hills. The warriors moved with inhuman fluidity. Their helmets were slotted and I could see no details of their faces, except for their glowing emerald eyes.

Behind the warriors rode a man on a pure white stallion. His head was bare, save for a simple silver circlet. Instead of armor, he wore a plain tunic and a waistcoat along with breeches and boots. The man stood in the saddle and raised his hand. Everyone with two legs knelt and bowed. Those with four legs put their bellies to the ground.

The man dismounted. Clover sprang up everywhere he walked.

A pair of attendants brought out a simple oak table and chair. They were taller than their master by at least a foot, but they moved bent over, keeping their heads lower than his. Servants brought a plate of bread and cheese along with a chalice and placed them before their master as he sat.

He looked at me. Raw power emanated from him like a wall, and he had a Stain like earth-toned armor. He was the shortest person in view, of the humans at least, but he was the most splendid specimen of any species I had ever seen. I felt an incredible sense of loyalty and admiration sweep over me. In that moment, I would have followed him to the brink of Armageddon and fought every demon on the way before I would have allowed a single hair of his head to be harmed.

It was all I could do to keep myself from running to kneel at his feet. It helped not knowing what was expected of me. What if he didn't want me to approach? Who was I to even look upon him? I was an insect looking upon a god. I stayed where I was. But I prayed for some direction from him so that I could fulfill his wishes.

Honeysuckle had emerged from the ground and was climbing the legs of the master's chair, blooming as it went. All of nature worshipped this man.

A functionary with a cat-like face stood in front of me. He gave me a bow but I hardly noticed.

"With the Alder King as witness, and before the assembled court of the Fae, we are gathered. Thou art known among mortals as Goethe Luck," he said.

It seemed I should be paying closer attention. This might be about me. The master's power . . . the Alder King's power . . .

The functionary went on, "Thy days have been numbered and thou dost approach ten-thousand dawns. The time has come to test the vessel of thy true self."

I felt silver encircle my wrists. The bindings were fashioned to resemble flowering vines with little moons and stars along the borders. I had a feeling the manacles weren't a birthday present. At first, I almost laughed. The silver was so delicate I could easily break it. As soon as I had the thought, however, the thought left me. In the back of my mind, I understood that without the desire to break free, the flimsy manacles might as well be inch-thick, cold-forged iron. Then that understanding also fell inaccessibly deep from useful thought.

The cat man placed a long silver dagger between my hands. The handle was wrapped in soft leather and the sharp end was pointed at my chest.

"Thou wilt be victorious or thou wilt end thyself." It couldn't tell if it was a prediction or a command.

I turned and looked at the expectant faces surrounding me. One or two of them held unconcealed bloodlust in their eyes, but most appeared to be indifferent at best. Potential self-evisceration apparently wasn't fresh enough to entertain this crowd. Toto sat directly behind me. Probably, the liondog would finish any uncompleted death-dealing. Comforting.

The last eyes I met were the Alder King's. He nodded to me and raised his chalice.

Darkness. Nothing more.

I was suddenly free of my bonds, but limited since I couldn't see anything around me. I felt something underfoot, holding me up, so I had to be somewhere. I bent down and felt around, but there was nothing for my hands to touch. It might be a mistake to try walking. I might fall off of whatever molecules are holding me up. I saw light over my shoulder.

There was something behind me.

It turned as I did. It was human in shape and masculine, exactly my height. But it was featureless, barely three dimensions, and composed of the same pale blue energy I had learned to associate with magic. I moved my arm and the figure did the same. I raised my foot and the figure did the same. I moved my foot ahead of the other one and gradually transferred my weight. The figure did the same. I didn't fall. Neither did he.

Cautiously, we approached each other. Like a reflection in a mirror, it copied everything I did, except it had its own left and right sides.

When only a few feet remained between us, I stopped.

I heard my heart pounding in my ears. How many times in a day would I feel fear? What kind of test was this? Was this an enemy? The functionary had said I would be victorious or die. I stretched out my right arm and it did the same with its right arm. Our palms faced each other. The most bizarre high five in history. At least in my history.

I feared there would be a jolt of pain when contact was made. There was a vibration to it but the energy was cool and soothing. It clung to my skin like water.

Holy mostaccioli. That felt amazing.

I took a step back. Fascinating. But I had no idea what it meant or what I was supposed to do.

We stood looking at each other for a minute.

I almost felt betrayed when it attacked. Blink of an eye and the thing had its hands around my throat. Cool and soothing—but getting tighter. Choking the life out of me. I grabbed its wrists and pulled. It didn't yield. I tried turning and throwing it. I tried kicking it. I had no mass to use against it. Nothing solid to make contact with. I started to see lights dancing at the edges of my vision.

They had given me a silver knife, but it had vanished along with the silver manacles.

Wait. A knife. I still had the knife that I had used to cut my thumb and open the circular gate in my house. It was in my back pocket.

I pulled it out and slashed through the thing's wrists. The energy divided and my own wrists erupted in sudden pain. I could still use my hands but it hurt. I backed away from the energy. The parts that had been the figure's hands were floating in the air. They were losing their shape and energy seeped out of them and floated away. They grew incrementally smaller, like squashy blue balloons with slow leaks.

I could whittle it down, I decided. Cut it into small chunks and let the energy drift away.

"Don't!" A voice, quiet but urgent, echoing inside my head. "Don't hurt it!"

Forget that! I was going to take a step forward and let this thing walk itself into my knife.

"You need it!" The voice was muffled and warped, like listening to a conversation through a wall using a glass like in old movies. But the glass was full of water.

"What for?" I thought.

The voice did not respond. I waited. I didn't hear anything. Screw it. I took a step and the figure did the same. The blue light guy bumped into the blobs I had carved off and absorbed them again. Shoot! I raised the knife.

"Stop! I'm risking everything!" The voice was female at least. I could tell that much.

"What?"

"What I'm doing is dangerous!" She sounded desperate.

"Who are you? How are you talking to me?"

"I can't tell you."

"Well, that's too bad. For all I know . . ."

"There isn't time . . ."

". . . you're making it worse."

". . . it's almost dawn."

I sighed. I didn't know what to do. If time was running out, maybe it didn't matter what I did. But this felt so real. And I was tired of being afraid.

The blue man had not moved at all during my exchange with the voice. Perhaps, since I had thwarted its attack, it was just going to wait me out. What possible purpose could there be for this scenario?

"It will need blood now," said the voice.

"That's handy," I thought. "Since I'm the only source. Shall I just kill myself? Save you the trouble?"

The voice sounded irritated. "It's important for you to survive. More than you know."

I wanted to believe that. I'm sure the voice wanted me to believe it too.

I raised my hand with the knife.

The figure raised its corresponding hand but it wasn't a hand anymore. Its shape had changed and now it had a knife of its own.

Great. If I cut or stabbed the thing now, it would do the same to me. Mirroring me. Except I can't reabsorb my body parts if they get cut off. It would kill me before I could kill it.

"Think about what the chancellor said." The voice bordering on panic. "You have to figure it out."

"What's it to you if I don't?"

No response. I needed to do something. Anything.

Then, "Don't say my name."

"I don't even know . . ."

"Of all the gin joints, in all the towns, in all the world, you walk into mine."

She just told me not to, but I almost said her name right out loud, Erin. I was stunned. I could trust this voice. "What do I do?"

"Give it blood. Figure it out. Hurry. It's almost dawn."

I tried to focus. If I attacked it, it would attack me. Make me bleed. Then what?

I had a better idea. If I cut myself, it would cut itself too. But it wouldn't hurt itself. It would be like water attacking water.

I turned the knife. I cut my thumb again. The being made the same motions, cutting its own thumb to no effect. That's good, I think. I put the knife back in my pocket as a crimson line ran down along my thumb to my palm. I tried the high five again. When the blue guy's hand touched the blood, there was a flare of light. The being absorbed the blood for a full minute. The dazzling flare of light stopped, but the aura surrounding the blue guy was vital and bright.

The chancellor had said something about this test. What had it been? I'd been so distracted by the Alder King's power. What were the words? A test of my true self. That wasn't it. There had been more. Vessel. The vessel of my true self.

Vessels held things—other things—inside them. A glass was a vessel for holding liquid. Could it be something simple? Just holding . . . I stepped into the blue light and embraced the energy. It clung to me, embracing me as well. My skin began to tingle. There was no pain but it filled me to the point of satiation. I felt refreshed and at the same time barely able to contain the power that surged through me. I started to shake. It was too much. I closed my eyes, clenched them shut. My hands became fists and the bones and tendons groaned as my entire body went rigid. I threw back my head and roared.

I opened my eyes when I felt grass on my face. I was no longer in the empty space. I heard a voice say, "Call for a healer." Then I blacked out.

CHAPTER 6

Gifts

"Well done, Fáidh Bean. He awakens."

I'd been hearing voices for a little while, but those were the first sounds that had formed themselves into something recognizable.

"I'm fading?" I mumbled.

I felt a warm hand on my forehead. "No. I'm Fáidh. That's my name in this realm. It sounds like 'Fae' but you have to add an 'ah' sound on the end."

Okey. And also dokey.

Recent events came swimming up to my consciousness. The glade. The creatures. The strange people. The empty space. The blue guy.

"Did I fall on the knife?" I asked.

"No. You dropped it before you came back."

I let that process for a minute. "Why do I need a healer then?"

"You landed on your face."

That would explain the pounding in my temples. I ventured to open my eyes.

There's that moment in the Wizard of Oz where Dorothy steps out of her house and the world is no longer dull and monochromatic but filled with color. I was old enough to remember VHS tapes; for years, they were the only way to watch a movie at home. The Mama played that tape over and over because she said she had seen Judy Garland in concert once. Then came digital technology and high definition. When I later saw the movie again on disc, the contrast was even more striking. When I opened my eyes, the world had changed like that.

I was lying on my back and no longer bound. Dawn had broken and the early light filtered through the glade. The colors were different and I could see more of them. Everything was more detailed than I had ever noticed before. I looked at my own hand, front and back. I wasn't looking at skin. I was looking at a collection of textured flesh with whorls and ridges and different gradations of small hairs and pores and wrinkles and tiny flakes of skin that were coming loose. Underneath were networks of veins, protrusions of bone, and overlays of muscle. Although incredibly more delicate and soft, the pattern of my skin wasn't all that different in its basic structural pattern than that of an alligator.

And I had a Stain. White and as gossamer as a baby's ghost, but it was there. A single ribbon woven from a million tiny symbols encircling my chest.

My head hurt.

I transferred my gaze to a particularly well-constructed face.

"Hello," I said. I had to blink and look again.

The woman smiling at me really was Erin, even though she said her name was Fáidh. Maybe she was a superhero. Her eyes were perfectly emerald green. "Are you all right?" she asked.

"I think so," I lied. I tried to think of something to say that wouldn't betray my shock at seeing her here. I couldn't think of a thing.

"You broke your nose when you came back and fell on the ground," she said. From her expression, I think she was trying not to laugh. "I fixed it for you. While you were out, I also took care of your ribs and your leg. I can heal you faster here than in the mortal world."

I tried moving and found that all my aches and pains, except for the one in my head, were gone. "That's really nice," I said. Awkward seconds passed.

A shadow fell upon us. "Can he stand?" It was the chancellor.

"I think he can," I said. I got to my feet. It took a moment for me to catch my breath. The vista before me was dazzling. The willow trees were sparkling gray-green and I could see the veins in the leaves from where I stood. The wildflowers were pin-sharp points of bright color that were almost painful to look at.

The menagerie had grown. The four-legs were running

through the trees, enjoying the fresh morning air. The two-legs had assembled around small tables or on the grass. Breakfast had been served, and there were beverages to sip and cakes to eat.

The chancellor led me back toward the Alder King's table. Erin had disappeared.

When I looked upon the Alder King now, I could still feel his power drawing me in, but the effect was muted. I didn't feel the same sense of blind loyalty that I had felt before. Something—maybe it was me—had changed.

The Alder King stood up from his seat and gazed upon me with a serious expression. "Thou hast not disappointed," he said. "I am pleased to see thee in one piece." He smiled for a moment. "It is my duty now to show thee the additional benefits that come with thy new station."

It seemed appropriate to say something. "Thank you," I said.

A hush dropped on the glade, and it was so quiet you could have heard a feather hit a pillow. The menagerie was listening. A dangerous gleam came instantly into the Alder King's eye. He took a moment to compose his words carefully.

"It is ill-advised to utter any expression that would put thee in debt," he said. "Take care that you do not create the need for a payment that could be most cruelly claimed. It very literally could mean your life."

This was confusing, but I could see that the Alder King was extremely intent on teaching this lesson to me. "What should I say?"

"It is safest to acknowledge a gift with a nod. No words are needed," the King replied. "And be wary of those who expect words from thee."

I gave him a nod to let him know I understood.

We walked through the glade toward a stand of poplars. They rose straight and pointed like leafy arrows aimed at the heart of the sky.

"There may come a time when I will ask of thee a great task. Thou wilt perform it under my aegis, but thou wilt be expected to use all the might and power thou hast—and all the gifts given to thee, now or in the future—without hesitation. Dost thou understand?"

I nodded. I couldn't imagine what sort of task the Alder King would require of me. I was certainly less capable than pretty much any of the people or creatures in the realm around me.

The King seemed pleased. "Now, one or two more bits of business."

We proceeded past the poplars to a circle of elm trees. There were three creatures there. A cat, a raven, and what looked like a frog. The frog was enormous, at least two feet tall. It also had sharp claws, and when it yawned I saw a dozen sharp teeth in its cavernous mouth.

The cat was completely disinterested in everything going on around it. Typical cat. Then a dragonfly cruised past, and the cat opened its mouth to spit a thin stream of fire through the air. The dragonfly dropped to the ground and the cat pounced on it instantly. I wasn't much of a cat person, but I could think of a Chihuahua or two I'd like to introduce to that cat.

The raven was methodically still, perched on top of a rock. It watched the other creatures, assessing everything around it.

"What a beautiful bird," I said.

"Excellent," said the King. "I was hoping one of these would appeal to thee."

What?

The King went on. "This realm can be dangerous and one can easily become lost in its ways. When thou needest a guide, thou mayest call upon this magnificent creature to lead thee. What wilt thou name it?"

"Midnight Dreary," I replied. I didn't know if anyone from this realm was familiar with Poe, but the first lines of "The Raven" popped into my head as soon as the question was asked.

"As thou wishest," said the King.

He addressed the bird, "Fiach Dubh! By thy Eternal name I call thee. From this time forward thou art bound to this man. Be his guide in all the Ways and come to him when he calls thee Midnight Dreary."

Be my guide? Come when I call? Was this a twilight zone pet shop?

The bird croaked, harsh and loud, and flew to my shoulder. It sat there, surprisingly lightweight. It adjusted the glossy black feathers of its wings by shrugging its shoulders. I felt pretty awesome.

We left the circle of elms. The sun was climbing now and had just cleared the horizon. We crested a hill and before us was a vast forest. Rolling hills covered with trees extended as far as I could see. In the distance atop the hills there were conifers but the trees nearest were fruit trees and ornamentals. A cluster of stone towers huddled nearby, which I guessed belonged to the Alder King.

The next group of trees were cherry trees. It was a long time yet before spring, but these trees were blossoming. The ground was covered with petals like a layer of pale pink snow and the air was incredibly fragrant. Several women loitered among the trees.

The Alder King approached them with some relish, rubbing his hands together and strutting just a bit. Since he was short, he had a good view of some of their best features. "Gather round!" he said. "Present yourselves to the man of the hour."

The women stood in a loose line of ten or twelve with the King off to the side. I suddenly felt like I'd been wrangled into judging an impromptu bikini contest. Except that none of the women wore bikinis and at least one of them wasn't wearing much of anything at all.

The first woman in the line had an orange ribbon of Stain complementing a pair of red boots and was otherwise completely enveloped in her long blonde hair. It's possible she had clothing on under the hair but I didn't feel comfortable enough to look more closely to find out. I nodded to her and looked away.

The women were different in height and shape and Stain, but all were incredibly lovely. They seemed pleased by my appraisal and I nodded at each one in turn. It was still awkward. I was supposed to make some kind of determination, but I didn't know what that was.

At the other end of the line, opposite the girl possibly covered by only her hair—whom I was studiously trying to avoid staring at again—was a dark-haired beauty with a golden Stain in a black gown that had no sleeves. The skirt went down to the ground and was tailored perfectly in a sheath that went all the way up to her neck. She had hazel eyes and flowing hair that cascaded down her back almost to her ankles. I'm pretty sure the raven was staring at her too.

A giggle came from somewhere behind me. The woman with the blue tiger stripes had reappeared. Oh, goody. She took a place next to the vixen in black. She looked down the line and got a sour look on her face. A few of the women took a step back, conceding territory.

"Majesty, we are missing the healer." It was the dark-haired vixen in the black gown who had spoken. The blue tiger girl snapped her head around and I swear she actually hissed.

Erin stood next to the King. She hadn't been there a moment ago, I was sure. "Not missing, Majesty." She strolled to the end of the line. I noticed her dress for the first time. It was several shades of green in a leaf pattern, cut just below the knee. It clung to her body and moved attractively with every flexing muscle.

"Thou mayest choose an helpmeet," said the King to me.

An helpmeet? What the great googly-moogly was that?

Erin appeared to be composed, but there was an undercurrent of stress. Where had she been while I was getting the grand tour from the King? I didn't know what a helpmeet was, but she was always helpful. Right? I looked at her and she was giving me a little head motion. I looked at the other girls and back at Erin.

"Thou mayest wish to choose quickly," the Alder King said to me. "If thou delayest, they may compete for thine attention and blood could be spilt."

This all seemed greatly amusing to the King. And the girl in the blue tiger stripes, who extended a hand toward me as some kind of invitation. The Princess of Pain and Pleasure. Whatever she intended, it wasn't going to happen.

"Her," I said, pointing at Erin. "I choose her." I didn't know anything about these other women. Why would I want help from them?

"Well chosen," said the King. He clapped me on the shoulder. He propelled me toward Erin who remained standing stiffly in her place.

Blue Tiger giggled again as I passed. "If thou wishest. Thou mayest. Make me. Thy courtesan," she whispered. She was laughing but her eyes were hard and icy.

What? Courtesan?

The Alder King took Erin's hand and placed it over mine. I wanted to ask what was happening, but before I could say a word Erin put her finger to her lips. She was afraid of something. Her green eyes were dark.

The King went on. He had not noticed our brief exchange.

"Be ye one," said the King. "Ye have my blessing, and I wish ye long life and unending happiness."

Realization settled over me like a burning blanket.

What had I just done?

CHAPTER 7

Dangerous Females

"We're married?" I shouted.

"Don't yell!"

"I'm not yelling. I'm shouting. Because I'm confused."

Erin and I had found a quiet place to talk. The raven had flown off my shoulder. Maybe it sensed the turmoil brewing inside me and wanted no part of it. I looked around because I didn't want to look at Erin. There were lilacs growing over an arbor and little finches singing all around us and the whole beautiful thing was ticking me off.

"I didn't know what was going on out there, Erin. Why didn't you tell me?"

"Call me Fáidh in this realm," she insisted.

"Sorry. In my head you're Erin."

"Don't say you're sorry either! An apology is a hundred times worse than saying 'thank you.' Words like that have special power. One apology and you are indebted with a powerful burden that could leave you enslaved for a hundred years. Never apologize.""

"Fine! Whatever. Fáidh."

She took the points with a nod and said, "I didn't know myself. Not until it was too late. You don't interrupt the Alder King unless you want a long and painful death."

"Well, I figured that out at least."

"When you first arrived I was so surprised to see you."

"I was surprised to see you too," I said. "Stunned. I guess you come here a lot."

"This is my birthplace," she replied. "Right now, in the mortal world, it's my lunch hour. There was an announcement of a Quickening from the Alder King and all the Fae were invited. I decided to take a break from the lab to see what was going on."

I sighed. So much weirdness. My head was killing me. "Heckuva party," I smiled ruefully. "I don't even know how I got here. That story about tripping over the furniture was a lie. Some huge lion-and-dog-hyena-thing just appeared inside my house and attacked me. How does that make any sense to a normal person? I guess you'll believe me."

"The creature is Madrasceartán," she replied.

"Mad-who?"

That made Erin smile a little, which was a huge victory, I thought. For a moment we were back in the Medical Examiner's office and Erin was just Erin. The moment didn't last.

"Madrasceartán. The king's beast. She serves as the king's messenger and, when needed, assassin."

"I can believe it. Wait a second, that enormous, vicious thing is female?"

"She is."

"Wow. Okay. Why is it that the most dangerous things in the world are female?" The little smile grew.

"That is a fact you would do well to remember."

Hmm.

I continued, "She drew some kind of symbol on my head with her claw. It was circular with some design in the middle. But after a while I couldn't see it anymore and you couldn't see it either."

"Not without magic," Erin nodded. This was a common thing, apparently. "She put the instructions in your mind with that sigil and also gave you some of her power so that you could open the gate. It also made you think that it would be a really good idea to complete your task. You could have stopped at any time if you really wanted to. Did you have the feeling that you were doing something important? Something right?"

I remembered. "Yeah. Even though I didn't even know what I was doing or why."

"That was her sigil working on your mind. If you hadn't finished the job, you would have felt disappointed about it for the rest of your life. Although they probably would have taken more direct action. But if the Fae don't have to, they won't. The more they can get people to do things willingly, the better. She also gave you some power because you didn't have any of your own. Not before the Quickening."

"What's a Quickening?"

Erin sat down on the grass, spreading her gown away from her long legs. I stayed on my feet, pacing.

"A Quickening is when you receive your powers," Erin replied. "You and I are both Halflings. Part Human, part Fae. We have powers and they are different for everybody. I've always had mine. Yours have been dormant. The Quickening is a ceremony that awakens the powers inside you. It traditionally takes place on the morning of your ten-thousandth dawn."

I thought about the ordeal. "Is it supposed to be dangerous?" I asked.

Erin shook her head. "No. It's symbolic. The binding and the knife represent your soul as a mere mortal, trapped without power and vulnerable. When you accept your power, you become free from your mundane prison. But the ceremony shouldn't hurt you."

"My power tried to strangle me."

"That's what was happening?"

I nodded.

"Someone was interfering. When I saw it was taking too long and you were lying so still on the ground I got worried. As a healer, the King gave me permission to check on you so I put my hand on your forehead. I didn't get permission to speak to your mind and it's lucky I didn't get caught."

"People can do that?"

"Eternals—the Fae—and some Halflings can. Anyway, a formal Quickening happens infrequently, maybe once in a decade, and the King does not often attend. Even when he does, he doesn't make gifts afterward. Today he was a congenial host. This is not historically common. The Alder King is ruthless and arrogant. He's been known to kill for sport and if you offend him, he will not forget. Ever."

"He's standing right behind you," I said. Lying.

Erin's eyes flashed green. "Don't be an imbecile. What I'm trying to tell you is that the Alder King has taken a special interest in you and that has me worried. What I found out, while you were talking with the Alder King, is that you might be his son."

Something clicked into place with that. "I think he probably pays for my house," I said. "And my caretaker and housemaid."

Erin's thoughts came tumbling out now. "If it's true, he would also be interested in you having children. That 'impromptu' wedding was probably planned."

"Look, I didn't know there was going to be a wedding. He said choose a helpmeet. I thought he meant a helper."

"Helpmeet means wife. It's archaic but—didn't you ever read the Bible?"

"Well, yeah. The Mama . . ." I snapped my fingers. "That's where I heard it before."

Erin shook her head. "Above all, you have to remember that the Fae love their deceptions. They have raised gamesmanship to an art form. They love to play tricks on humans almost as much as they love to play tricks on each other. The one thing the Eternals cannot do is lie. And they always know when someone else is lying."

"Okay," I said.

"So they strategize. They brought you here and it's all new to you. The King wanted you to get your powers. The thing that concerns me is that you were attacked while you were in the ceremony. Later, we'll have to figure out why. After you were Quickened, the King gave gifts to you. At the end he said you may choose someone and made it sound like just another favor. You weren't forced into it. They made you think you were just getting another servant."

"We didn't say 'I do,'" I said. I felt the need to point that out.

"Doesn't matter," Erin replied. "The mortal realm has made some great strides in equality and choice. But the Faerie world hasn't changed for centuries. If the Alder King says we're married, we are. I have less right to object than you do."

We didn't kiss either.

I looked at the ground. My head was killing me. "I'm sorry . . ."

"NO! No you are not!" Ow! Now who was shouting?

"Yes, ma'am," I said. I almost said I was sorry again because I wanted to make her laugh, but it seemed important to her that I was taking this seriously.

Long moments of silence followed then in which I pondered the situation and tried not to look at Erin. After a while, she broke the silence.

"Any one of those girls would have been happy to be your mate. A chance to bear the grandson of the Alder King? Quite an honor."

"An honor? It's a mess," I said.

"So you're unhappy?"

"Picture the Hindenburg falling onto the Titanic, carrying the Black Plague."

"I see." It took me a half-second too long to notice Erin's voice growing cool. "Well, I guess the day is just filled with disappointment," she said.

Mayday.

"No," I replied. "I just assumed we were both feeling . . ."

"What, Luck? Feeling what?"

This was going badly and I didn't know where the conversation had gotten off the tracks.

Erin's eyes were emeralds. Emeralds on fire. She folded her arms tightly under her breasts and crossed her legs, closing herself off. "So if I hadn't shown up, who would you have picked? Which of those girls would you have chosen?"

"The girl who was probably naked under all the hair!" I snapped.

"You're either an idiot or that's a real crummy defense mechanism you have there," she replied. "Please tell me you always make jokes when you screw up."

"I always make jokes when I screw up. Better?" My head was about to explode.

The lilacs stirred and Blue Tiger slinked in through the arbor.

"How is. Everyone?" she asked.

"Peachy," I said.

Erin remained quiet, her arms and legs and probably her toes crossed by now.

"Oh," Blue Tiger made a pouty face. "Not a happy. Honeymoon?"

"There is no honeymoon," I said.

"This is not a honeymoon," Erin said.

We both spoke at the same time and the word "honeymoon" came out simultaneously. In other circumstances, it would have made me laugh.

"Oh, yes. Ye are so. Incompatible."

"Please leave, Béil." Erin's voice was glacial.

Blue Tiger remained unfazed. "I just came so. He could thank. Me," she said. She looked at me and gave a little curtsy. "Art thou. Not going. To thank me?"

I played dumb. "For what?"

"For teaching. Thee. Respect."

"Ah. If only I could," I said. "Unfortunately, I am prohibited from expressing thanks for anything. King's orders."

Béil licked her lips. "Thou art learning," she said. "Very good." She reached a finger toward my chest. I stood up and moved away. She giggled at me and I felt a shiver like ice water down my back. My head was trying to beat me over the head with itself. Béil probably liked drowning puppies in her spare time and I wasn't eager to see what her touch would do now that I had been Quickened.

"Back off!" I was very pleased to see a sudden look of shock and fear on her face.

Erin, unfortunately, had a similar expression.

I looked down and saw the knife in my hand. I don't remember pulling it out of my pocket. Why was my head pounding? Why did my hand hurt?

"Thou darest?" Béil hissed. "Fool!"

Erin was shying away from me too, looking at me like I had

a handful of rattlesnakes. I looked again. The knife seemed to be glowing with an aura of dark purple. Looking at it made me feel nauseated.

"Goethe," Erin said. "That knife is steel. It has iron in it. Throw it away. Please!"

I didn't throw the knife away. I took a step toward Béil instead and jabbed at her with it. She said no words I could understand but she gasped and snarled at me. I backed her through the arbor. "Leave us alone," I said.

She threw a baleful—Ha ha! Baleful!—grimace in my direction and tip-toed away with as much of her dignity as she could retain.

"Put it away," Erin begged.

Feeling suddenly sheepish for no good reason, I slipped the knife back into my pocket. My headache flared. I tried to think of something competent to say.

"I wish to make amends," I said. They were the only words I could come up with besides, I'm sorry.

Erin looked at me, but I couldn't read her. "Go home," she said.

I knew I'd wounded her but I couldn't think of anything else to say that would be of any real use. "All right," I said.

I abandoned her to the lilacs and the finches in the arbor. I called, "Midnight Dreary!" and the raven came from some nearby shadow and settled on my shoulder. She rapped on the top of my skull a few times with her beak. It didn't hurt but I got the message. "Yeah, I know," I said. "I'm a knucklehead. Please show me the way back to my home."

The raven took off, circled above my head once, and flapped in the direction of the morning sun.

I emerged from the silver gate, righting myself around that ninety-degree angle. The column of pale blue light winked out and all the objects on the floor were now nothing more than a mess waiting to be swept up. It felt like I had been gone for hours, but the light outside had not changed, as far as I could tell. It was the same day. While I hadn't noticed the exact time when I left, my best guess was that I had been gone for a few minutes and no more.

I pulled the knife out of my pocket again and dropped in on the nearest table. Instantly, my head stopped hurting.

Well crap. I was affected by iron now too. How many things were made of iron? Like my beautiful car, for starters?

"Welcome back to the mortal realm, sir."

I jumped. A little.

"Sandretta!" I said. "I'm . . . uh . . . that's quite the mess. On the floor." Is it okay to say I'm sorry here?

"Not a problem, sir. I'll be happy to clean it. Max and I have been waiting for this day for many years. You are one of us now."

Sandretta and Max and I had always had a comfortable working relationship although, clearly, I had never gotten to know much about them. They were both Stained with ribbons in different shades of blue, though, and I'd always thought of them as special. The fault for not knowing them better was entirely mine. I was unpredictably home, except to sleep, and I confess I took them both for granted.

Now that we were all in the same club de Fae, I wasn't sure how our relationship would change. They probably had powers that could toast me to a cinder, and for all I knew they were centuries old. They could be, in every respect, my superiors. The Mama had always taught me that respect for one's elders and superiors was paramount. Of course, I was the lowest creature on Earth, which is another thing I was taught by The Mama. So everybody was my superior.

With new eyes, literally, I took stock of Sandretta. She was always immaculately dressed in functional clothing that didn't seem dowdy but still let her do what she needed to do through the day. She had wrinkles at the corners of her hazel eyes that were laugh lines, not crow's feet, and smiling came easily to her. Her hair was always pulled back in a smooth chignon that would be at home at a cocktail party.

"I appreciate you, Sandretta." I didn't know what else to say, but at least it made her smile and she gave me a nod.

I looked at my home. The home my apparent father provided with all the fine construction and the fine people to care for it. My father had given me everything I needed.

Except a father.

I noticed the folded up napkin on the counter. I had forgotten about the bullet casing and the design I had drawn earlier.

"Hey, Sandretta," I said. "Can I show you something?"

"Certainly, sir." She folded her hands together and waited.

I scrounged around in the drawers and found a plastic baggie. I let the bullet casing slide out of the napkin and into the baggie and then I sealed the baggie shut. Evidence preserved. With the napkin folded, I approached Sandretta. As soon as I opened it, her hands went out in front of her like she wanted to push it away.

"Oh no." She turned her head, looking to the side. "Take that to Max, outside in the garden."

Her reaction prompted me to look at the design again. The symbol was just some standard ink on crummy paper and there hadn't been anything of note about it when I had drawn it. Now there was a dark aura around the symbol. I watched as it twisted and writhed on the paper like a living thing trying to escape. Tortured and seeking freedom, the symbol was like a Stain that wanted to fulfill its own purpose and it was surrounded by an undeniable wrongness.

I went outside. The garden had tons of vegetables, a slew of herb plants, and exactly three citrus trees: orange, lemon, and lime. Max used the produce to make some amazing dinners, and I think he liked being out in the yard. The garden kept him from getting bored. I found him putting some mulch from a wheelbarrow around the fruit trees. He was dressed in lightweight overalls, with a white t-shirt that showed his tanned arms, and a safari hat. He looked up as I approached and took his hat off, giving me a little nod. The action was habit for him and I had never found it annoying until today.

"Max, can I have you look at something?" I started. "You may be able to tell what it is."

"Certainly, sir," he replied.

I showed him the design.

Max didn't ask me where I'd seen the symbol or how it had gotten on the paper. He just shook his head and in his deep voice said, "I recognize this. Very dark magic. Dark magic used to control the will of another. This makes a person a puppet. Anyone under this symbol will do anything the caster asks. Even kill or jump off a building or walk into a lake and drown. Anything. They will not be able to resist."

That sparked another question. "Will they even lie still while someone stabs them in the heart and cuts them open?"

Max nodded curtly, "Yes. They will feel the pain but they will lie complacent and unmoving if the caster asks them to remain so. Inside, they will want to scream and run away. Outside, they will remain still."

I couldn't imagine the nightmare Barry Mallondyke must have endured before he'd bled out. Death must have been a welcome release.

"You are not thinking of using this?" Max asked. "Adding magic will awaken it."

"No, Max. It was found on someone. They were murdered."

"Using this is punishable by execution," Max said. "Better for them if you catch them here and not in the Behindbeyond."

"Okay."

"Please. Destroy this paper as soon as you can. It can only bring evil."

He made perfect sense. "I will, Max."

CHAPTER 8

Milly in the Sky with Diamonds

I stood in the middle of the bank lobby, appreciating the fact that there were no giant liondogs, no fluttering faeries, and no blue guys. Just the magic of commerce at work. I inhaled and took a deep, delicious breath of capitalism.

Driving over hadn't been too bad. Sitting in my car, I could feel the hum of iron surrounding me, but the padded seats and all the non-iron components insulated me from any ill effects. I was able to crank up the music—Tom Waits, "Long Way Home"—and enjoy the ride.

In the bank, I remembered I should make a call.

Nat answered the phone himself.

"Iron Foundry," he said.

"Hey. Me."

"What's going on, Luck?"

"The office. They replaced the window already."

"That's good."

"I'm cashing the check from Milly Mallondyke right now."

"That's good."

"If it bounces, I'll be worried she's the one who shot at me."

"Not good."

"Can you think of any reason a kid would go up to the office and leave a bullet casing on my desk and then sneak out?"

I let Nat try to think of any reason.

After a while, he said, "Nope."

I couldn't think of anything else to say. Under other circumstances, I'd be telling my best friend that I'd just gotten married. Under the circumstances I had to live with, I couldn't. I was sure he'd be happy for me. He might not even be mad that he wasn't invited. All I said was, "Okay. Good man talk."

I hung up.

The check didn't bounce.

So, back in the real world, safe and sound. I hoped the lovely Erin was back too. Also known as the enchanting Fáidh. Also known as the newly-minted Mrs. Luck.

I needed someone to look at the bullet casing. I should give it over to the police. There could be fingerprints leading to the shooter and, if I found the weapon, it could be matched to the firing pin. I'd rather saunter back over to the medical examiner's office and see if someone toffee-eyed and leggy could check it out for me. I should send some flowers first. Even then, I'd feel stupid walking into her office and asking for a favor after all that had happened today. I'll probably just take a chicken approach and submit it to the police.

In the last twenty-four hours, I had been shot at, attacked by an enormous magic beastie from Nightmareland, and been brainwashed into going to a Faerie realm where I was almost strangled to death by my own nascent magical power. Then I broke my nose, got healed, and accidentally got married. What a party. The next twenty-four hours should be epic.

Plenty of daylight left.

Barry Mallondyke's office was on the eighth floor of a nice building with lots of windows in Miami Beach. The address came from Milly's business card. The receptionist's desk was set facing the elevator, and behind her was a broad, brilliant view of the Atlantic Ocean. There were no chairs to sit on in the receiving area, but there was artwork on the walls showing a lot of diamonds and other gemstones cut and set and looking priceless. The receptionist wore an eggshell linen blouse, buttoned up to the neck, and square hipster glasses that were too small for her face.

"Good afternoon, may I help you?"

She looked invitingly into my eyes and actually sounded like she wanted to help.

"May I speak with Ms. Mallondyke please?"

"Sure. Is she expecting you?"

"I don't think so. She gave me her card and told me I could get in touch with her if I needed to."

"Okay. May I have your name please?"

I thought about using one of my patented comic aliases. Skip Tracer was one of my favorites. But the darn receptionist was being so nice.

"Goethe Luck," I replied. "Most people just call me Got. Or Mr. Luck."

The receptionist gave me a half-smile and looked over her glasses at me. "Got Luck? Why not Good Luck? It's closer to 'Goethe' isn't it?"

"The woman who raised me told me every day that I was anything but good," I replied.

"That still doesn't sound like a real name," she said.

Just can't win.

"Wanna see my driver's license?"

The girl shook her head. "I'm sure Ms. Mallondyke will vouch for you." She tapped on her computer screen and spoke into the nearly invisible headset she wore.

"Ms. Mallondyke? A Mr. Luck to see you."

After a moment, the receptionist looked back up at me. "She'll be here in a moment. Would you like a juice? Wine? Some coffee or tea?"

"Sure a juice would be great. Pineapple if you have some."

She rolled six whole inches on her chair and opened a mini-fridge under her desk to find a can of pineapple juice and a chilled glass. Nice. She poured, then served it on a napkin with great efficiency, and covered what might have been an awkward wait. Especially since some overpaid business analyst had probably told them that chairs in a reception area were passé and open space was feng shui and thus, no place to sit. Not that I minded. This place had style and I didn't mind standing in it.

"Mr. Luck," said a voice. Doesn't sound like Ms. Mallondyke. I turned to see a slender guy wearing a summer jacket over a t-shirt and khakis standing in the hall. In his hand, he had a cane with a silver handle shaped like the head of a snake. "This way."

His face was fine-boned with small features, his hair was very blond, slicked back tightly over his skull, and he had a miniature soul patch under his lower lip. The soul patch, in contrast to his hair, was bright red. His look was intended to be chic to impress people who might look down on him as Milly's administrative assistant. He had that sour expression indicating that, whoever I was, I shouldn't be wasting his boss's valuable time.

I followed the guy, who walked slowly, using the cane for support as he limped. I stayed a few steps behind, sipped my beverage and resisted the urge to walk ahead of him.

As we proceeded up the hall, the offices got bigger, along with the titles. The first doors were for managers, then directors, and then vice-presidents. People looked up from their work as we passed, and I got the feeling they hadn't gotten a lot of visitors lately. Milly's office didn't have a title on the door, but it was next to the president's office, which was empty.

Milly sat in a chair by the window. She was wearing a white silk blouse that was long and a black skirt that wasn't. Her hair was held up with a dozen mismatched hair clips and there didn't seem to be any organization to the arrangement of her tresses. Somehow, she pulled off the look. I was also struck again by the virulent and ugly Stain that wound around her like serpents bearing a plague.

As a kid, I didn't have anyone to talk to about Stain, except The Mama, but wondered a lot about why some people had Stain and some had none. Why some Stain was beautiful and some was ugly. After a while, I just got used to seeing it and didn't wonder so much. Now, looking at such a sweet girl as Milly marked by such a nasty Stain, I was starting to wonder again.

The room didn't have a formal desk but there were a couple of low tables and an extra chair. A few papers were on one of the tables, but Milly was busy assembling them into a folder. She looked up and smiled thinly as I came in.

"Have you found something already?" she said. I was surprised again by her husky voice.

"I have," I replied. "I also wanted to see where Barry worked and see how you are getting along."

"How thoughtful. Please, have a seat."

"If it's all right, I'd like to take a look at Barry's office."

"Sure, but everything's out of there. All that's left is the furniture."

"Okay. It still might give me a feeling for how he spent his time."

Milly thought about it for a moment. "How about you tell me what you've found first and we'll go in after?"

"That's great," I said. "By the way, this juice is delicious."

"I'm glad you like it," she replied.

I finished it off and I was about to hand the glass to Milly's assistant but changed my mind. The poor guy looked like he was about to fall over already. The added weight of a glass might topple him. I put the glass on the floor and rubbed my hands together to remove the condensation. I reached into my pocket and brought out the folded napkin. I kept my eyes on the guy in the jacket and said, "It's probably best if we keep this between ourselves," I told Milly.

"Oh. Anything you have to show me you can show Amad."

"How about I show you first, we'll talk about it, and if you want to tell Amad—or anyone else—you can disclose it later. Just to be safe."

Milly shrugged. "All right. Amad, if you wouldn't mind, I'll need to be alone with Mr. Luck."

"Of course, Ms. Mallondyke. As you wish."

"And would you take that glass with you, please? Let's keep the carpet nice."

"Oh, that's all right," I said, swooping down to snatch the

glass. "I think I'll get a refill on my way out."

Amad stood with his hand half-outstretched, his head bobbing up and down, his programming stuck between the command of his boss and the wishes of a guest.

"Really," I continued. "I'd rather keep it."

Amad gazed back and forth between me and Milly for another few seconds. His in-between expression was comical, but laughing would be unkind. Finally, he gave a little bow and limped out.

"Amad is so sweet. I don't what I would do without him," Milly said.

Pointing at the files in front of her, I asked, "Still settling things?"

Milly nodded. "You've no idea. There are so many things to sort out. Barry hated using computers. He was always afraid of information getting lost or stolen. So he wrote notes in longhand, and I'm the only person, it seems, who can read them."

"Sounds like a challenge."

"He'd fly to Johannesburg for meetings and on those long flights, he'd compose whole notebooks of letters and meeting notes and things to remember. To be honest, I haven't been able to find anything all that important for weeks. Barry's father has been running things just fine from South Africa, but I think he keeps me on because he feels bad for me."

"And what does Amad do?"

"Well, I can read the notes but I don't always know what's important. He tells me what to keep and what to file away and what to forward to somebody else."

"I see. Did you ever go to Johannesburg with Barry?"

"Sure. Sometimes. The first time was when we were engaged. He took me to the corporate offices and his parent's house and even the mining facility. Barry showed me how the diamonds are mined and cut and graded. Unlike other companies, we do everything ourselves. It's how we became the only company in the diamond trade able to remain completely independent from the practical monopolies in South Africa and Belgium and the Netherlands."

"I'd imagine the security there is pretty tight."

"Unbelievably. Theft and smuggling are a problem, and Barry was constantly worried about it. Of course, there are security cameras everywhere. There are only two exits and both have a security checkpoint. Only one person at a time can pass through. As often as medically allowed, x-raying the workers will sometimes catch a thief. They have used radioactive paint on diamonds so that anyone taking stones out of the mine will be caught with a Geiger counter. Mostly though, Barry managed a group of spies and informants to keep the theft down. The reward for reporting a theft is higher than the value of a few diamonds. If you keep the workers paranoid and unable to conspire with each other, they tend to behave."

I was impressed with the depth of her knowledge. "What about the diamond cutters? What happens after the diamonds are brought in from the mines?"

"There are only a few diamond cutters. It takes eight years to get certified, and by the time they have reached that position in the company, they are very loyal."

"You were only married a few months," I said. "You must be a quick study."

"Oh, Barry shared everything with me. He didn't have anyone else he could trust so he would go on for hours. I liked to listen to him talk and I remember things."

Milly was growing wistful and I had no intention of making her sad. But I had one more question. "Did Barry have access to diamonds without restrictions or supervision?"

"Yeah, sure. He had samples brought in all the time for review so he could make sure the quality remained consistent and the grading was accurate. The workers gossiped about Barry, saying he had a stockpile of diamonds large enough to swim in. They weren't entirely wrong. He had a very large collection of diamonds in reserve. But he had no reason to steal from his own company. He took extraordinary pride in the bottom line. He wanted to make sure all our employees would have a good job and a good wage, and that meant carefully controlling the value by controlling the sales."

I nodded. "Well, I have something to show you. It probably doesn't mean anything, but there wasn't a lot of detail in the police report, so I thought you might know more about it."

"Okay," Milly replied. She sat up straight in her chair. Of course, the sigil was pretty darn significant, but if it didn't mean anything to Milly, it would help rule her out as a suspect. I unfolded the napkin and watched for her reaction. It still looked alive and nauseating to me.

"Oh," she said. "They found that on the back of Barry's neck, right?"

"That's right."

"I have no idea what that was. It was painted on, and Barry had never done anything like that before. I guessed that maybe he was thinking about getting a permanent tattoo or something." Milly wiggled on the chair and shrugged. "I think tattoos are sexy, you know? Maybe he got the design inked on first and he was going to ask me if I liked it before making it permanent?"

I believed her story. She hadn't reacted suspiciously to the image on the napkin and the thought of her husband getting a tattoo for her would make sense to a young girl like Milly.

I folded up the napkin and tucked it away. "That's most likely what it was then," I said. There was no way to explain to Milly that the sigil was part of a magic spell designed to make her husband passive while he was murdered. "Well, I have a few other leads I'm pursuing," I said. "Do you mind if I take a look inside Barry's office?"

"No problem." She stood up and led me next door.

Barry's office was designed to entertain as much as to conduct business. The walls were soothing tones of blue and white. It had a large desk, as expected, but it also had a seating area with comfortable couches, and a sideboard that would have held all sorts of liquor. A cabinet on the wall was closed but would hold a screen and other electronics since a video projector on the ceiling was pointed at it. A neighboring counter would be used for preparing and serving food. The table between the couches was spacious enough to hold a lot of paperwork. There was a private bathroom attached and it was nicely appointed as well. I could imagine Barry easily having several clients in meetings all day and deftly mingling meals and business without a hitch.

"This is a beautiful office," I said.

I turned to find the door closed and Milly slumped against it. Her eyes were wide as she looked at Barry's desk. With effort, she forced her eyes shut and covered her mouth. Tears rolled over her cheeks as a quiet sob struggled to come up. I resisted the urge to put my arms around her. It wasn't easy.

The first time I'd almost gotten fired from the police force came about because I never gave tickets to women who cried. If they were hardcore criminals, that was different. But a soccer mom who knew she'd gone a few miles an hour over the speed limit and was already blubbering by the time I approached her window? I'd just give her a warning every time.

"I thought I'd be okay," Milly mumbled. She started sliding down the wall.

That's all it took.

I caught her in my arms before she hit the floor and tried to make a comforting cocoon she could cry in.

"I thought I'd be okay," she repeated. "I thought if I didn't come in here, didn't look at this room for long enough, I'd be okay."

I cleared my throat. Gave her a pat on the shoulder. "Grief has its own needs. The passing of time is only part of it." I sounded like I knew what I was talking about.

That's when she tried to kiss me.

CHAPTER 9

Warning at Yoga

According to popular culture, private detectives are third in line for romantic entanglements. They fall behind the pizza delivery guy and the pool boy for misadventures in the company of lonely women. I hadn't been doing this job for very long and it seemed unlikely to me that there would be anything to it in reality. However, clichés arise, I guess, based on facts and here I was, alone with a vulnerable woman who was also my client.

She stepped in—wet eyes closed and lips at the ready—but I caught her by the shoulders. She leaned back to look up at me. Her arms stayed around my neck.

"I haven't been held by a man since my husband died." She took a deep breath and sighed, the sound uneven. "Do you think six months is a long time? It feels like a long time."

A century passed before I was able to regain some measure of composure. And rework one of Newton's laws: a jaw once dropped tends to remain dropped. I finally found my voice and my short-circuited brain said, "I'm sorry. I just found out that I'm married."

Milly tilted her head ten degrees sideways, which was also cute as a puppy. The tears on her face changed course, adjusting to the new down.

"You say the funniest things, Mr. Luck. I can't tell if you mean them or if you are just weird."

"Ah. Well, in this case, I do mean them. I was recently married. We're completely in love and I would feel terrible if I were to betray her trust. As my wife. Whom I am in love with."

Milly blinked at me twice and said, "Oh." Emotion started to swim again in her eyes. Her loneliness was palpable and I felt a pang of guilt. Still, I reached around my neck, took her wrists, and gently pulled her arms around to the front. It had to be the most awkward extrication of my person from another ever. The only thing that would make this situation more awkward would be if the door opened.

The door opened. Amad, who evidently made a career of looking judgmental and suspicious, looked at me with judgment. And suspicion.

I still held Milly's wrists in my hands and they waved in the air, useless. I nodded sagely and turned back to her and said, "So, Mrs. Mallondyke, as I was saying, I don't think those spots on your hands are at all cancerous. But if they're bothering you, I'd suggest you contact your health care provider for a referral since I didn't actually graduate from medical school."

I shouldered my way through the space between the door and the perplexed Amad.

"Missed it by one semester," I said.

Although the spouse is always the first suspect in a murder, I was pretty confident Milly Mallondyke was not involved in her husband's death. He'd given her love and comfort and nothing to provoke her. His life was remarkable for being mostly unremarkable. His wife was young and beautiful and a little kooky, but rich guys often landed the beautiful girls on wealth. The special thing about her was that she was smart and he had earned her devotion, which said a lot for their relationship. I hoped she'd find another man to love her, and soon.

The sigil was the key. I had to find out who would use magic on Barry and why they would need diamonds. The motive would seem to be greed, but why would someone cut Barry open after his death? What I needed was a way to determine who used magic and who did not. There had to be a spell for that.

Overall, I felt that I was accepting the new paradigm of my life rather well. The Mama had been incredibly superstitious. My experiences in her care had always included a mix of religion and magic to explain the world around me. There was no sense arguing against the existence of magic in the world. I had seen things with my own eyes. I had experienced things that could only be explained with magic for as long as I had reckoning. I saw Stain on people and nobody else could. I'd learned to be adaptable, and my way of thinking was to accept whatever came my way. Better than sitting in a corner, gibbering.

I drove to the Iron Foundry.

It wasn't lost on me that my best friend owned a club called the Iron Foundry and I had just acquired an aversion to iron. I might have to find an alternative to weight training. Any iron weights and other components of the machines could be toxic. I took some laps in the pool to loosen up, swimming half a mile. Then I toweled off and went looking for something else to do.

I found Nat leading a yoga class and thought, "Why not?"

There were mats rolled up on a nearby shelf so I grabbed one and set up in the back of the room. There didn't seem to be any men besides Nat in the class. Maybe if I was quiet, nobody would notice. Twenty minutes later, doing what was called the "Child's Pose" I decided I didn't need to move again. For the rest of the day. Maybe the week. I was neither as flexible nor as strong as I thought.

"Tired? Already?"

I couldn't see the girl's face because her arms were stretched out above her head but she was wearing a tank top and capris with a blue tiger stripe. And a crimson Stain.

Ho. Lee. Crap.

Nat called for a new pose. "Bridge position."

I moved up until I was kneeling but the girl continued rotating backward until her feet were flat on the floor and she was facing the ceiling with her back arched and her shoulders on the mat. Some bridge.

"Looking at you. Will take. Me out of. Alignment," she said, turning her face towards me. "But it's. Worth it. Call me. Evie. In this world. Or not. You choose."

This morning, her speech pattern had seemed sinister. Now, in this world, the staggered syntax of her speech brought my stupid compassion to the surface.

"Hi, Evie," I said.

"I think. We got. Off. On the wrong. Foot. This morning," she replied. She spoke in a hushed voice that didn't carry past the two of us.

I didn't say anything. She came here to find me for a reason. She'd either tell me or she wouldn't.

"I Come. With a. Warning. You're going. To need help. There are. Things about. To happen. Terror and. Destruction from. Other realms. You are. Not prepared."

"And you're the person to help me?"

"You are. A child. Lost in. The woods. And the woods are. Very large. And wild."

It was probably a bad idea to offend this creature—any more than I had already—since she has likely had full use of her powers for a millennium and didn't mind using them. "I appreciate your warning, Evie. I have Erin—Fáidh—to help me," I said.

Evie laughed. "She will. Help you into. An early grave. She cannot. Help you. Fight what she. Doesn't know."

"Why not just tell me what I need?"

"Ah," she smiled. "I cannot. Give it. All away. The Alder King. Has not. Had a son in. Hundreds of years."

I remembered Fáidh's warning about how much these people took delight in tricking humans so I said nothing.

"I cannot let. You. Just win. However. If I am. Seen as part. Of your victory. I will. Secure. My position. In the. Courts forever. You have no. Idea what. That means."

She looked up at the ceiling again before she continued, "I will. Let you. Stumble about. For now. Pray you. Find use of me. Before it is. Too late."

Evie stood and rolled up her mat and walked out. I noticed that her exit this time was much less frantic than the last time.

So, things are about to happen. Worse things than what had happened already, if she was to be believed. I sat on the mat, closed my eyes, and listened to the women around me. There was a kind of steady poetry to their breathing. In through the nose, out through the mouth. Constantly in rhythm. Inhaling oxygen to feed the muscles. Exhaling carbon dioxide to eliminate the waste. Outside the walls, the city had its own rhythm. A pulsing of cars on the road and the evening breeze shushing through the palms. Beyond the city, the Earth spun on her axis, locked in her dance with the sun as she swung through space in a predictable orbit. But, under the surface, in the Behindbeyond, there was something more. I could almost feel it there, pressing against our world. Probing for weaknesses.

In stillness, I felt some peace.

I stayed where I was and kept my eyes closed. The new power rested inside me, quiet but present, like a subterranean lake. I listened to the women applaud the end of their class, roll up their mats, and pick up their water bottles. I listened as the life in the room diminished and dwindled. Then there was just me and one other person in the room.

"Got. What's going on?"

"Don't know what you mean, Nat." I said, opening my eyes.

"You're acting strange."

"Same as always."

"Not the same. You're doing yoga." He stared me down.

"Trying to."

Nat had a light sheen of sweat from instructing and his shirt clung tightly to his muscular frame. He'd trimmed his hair since I'd seen him a few days ago. I wanted to tell him what was going on but I couldn't.

"I confess," I said. "I'm dealing with a lot of stuff. I've been going through some changes. Could be early onset menopause."

Nat smacked me in the head.

"Tell me if there's something you need," Nat said. It wasn't a question.

I gave him a shrug that he didn't see.

CHAPTER 10

Lunch Date with Death

I felt terrible.

And I'd overslept. This was after Max had prepared an especially fine Orange Chicken last night, using our own garden oranges, which I'd washed down with some wine. Then I'd washed the wine down with some wine. Somehow my goblet was magic because I only had the one glass to drink but the whole bottle had been inside it. It was almost enough drink that I didn't think about Erin. Almost. Additionally, the events of the day had worn me out. Probably more than anything was the trip to the Fae realm. But the workout last night and the drink had taken their toll as well. And by my body's reckoning, I'd lived through a 32-hour day. Thanks, Faerieland. Let's do the time warp again.

I stumbled to the kitchen and found Sandretta making a late breakfast. She efficiently dispensed lightly-buttered toast, grape juice, and coffee, which was exactly what I needed. Instead of thanking her I said, "That looks great."

She nodded and said, "I was about to wake you." She placed a glass vase in front of me with a peach-tinted rose and a card with my name on it.

"What's this?" I asked.

"It arrived about thirty minutes ago," Sandretta replied.

"For me? Who is it from?"

"Read the card, silly sir."

I did.

The card said, "Meet me for lunch. Robaccio Restaurant. 11:30." It was signed "Erin."

Huh.

The rose was a nice touch but I couldn't decide if it was a

good thing or a bad thing. I hadn't bought roses since high school prom, when I'd been forced, and I couldn't remember if a peach rose meant "Let's get together" or "Sorry for your loss."

I checked the clock.

Nuggets.

I had an hour to get cleaned up and make it downtown.

I showered and shaved and put on some slacks and a button-down shirt. I jumped in the car and headed out. It took a minute to find a CD, but I finally settled on Queen. Usually, I picked "I'm in Love with My Car," but today I felt more like "Somebody to Love."

The Robaccio Restaurant was one of those places that sounded like a nice Italian trattoria—and it was. The funny thing about the place was the name: a blend of two Italian words. The word "robaccia" meant "trash" in Italian and "bacio" was "kiss." Putting the two words together was like naming a British pub the Rubbish Smooch, which someone in London really needs to do. It was a popular spot with new couples because it was fancy enough to make an impression on a date but not expensive enough to create an expectation of romance. Best of all, the food was really good. I couldn't vouch for their kisses.

I parked around the corner and walked past a screen of palms and myrtles. Erin was already outside the entrance. She was standing with her hip stuck out sideways and her arms crossed like she was impatient although I was early. She had a little clutch purse in one hand. In the other, she had a rose to match the one I'd gotten this morning.

She saw me. She didn't wave or anything but she looked at me with a funny expression.

"Hey," she said.

"How are you?" I asked.

"Fine. How about we talk?"

"How about we eat?"

"Okay. Talk first, then eat, if you still want to."

We sat on a bench between the door and the corner of the building where people could wait for a table when the restaurant was busy. There was nobody else in the parking lot, except for a few empty vehicles, so we could be alone for a few minutes.

"So, what did you want to talk about?" she said.

"Uh. Whatever you want."

"You invited me here," she continued. "I assumed it wasn't just for lunch."

This wasn't right.

The truck coming at us was pushing fifty when I caught it in my peripheral vision. The driver stomped on the gas and the engine roared, splitting the air. Five thousand pounds of metal barreled towards us. All I could see was about a mile of steel grill between a couple of headlights. Instinctively, I pulled Erin into my arms and dove sideways. She screamed. I turned my shoulders as we fell. She was on top of me when we hit the ground. Continuing the motion, we rolled on the sidewalk. There was a sickening crunch as the truck demolished the bench and slammed into a trio of date palms. My foot erupted in fire. I heard the pop of airbags through the truck's open windows. It was over as quickly as it had begun.

Erin said, "Oh, wow."

We were both panting like dogs. I tried standing up, hoping the driver of the truck was alive so I could kill him. The bones in my foot ground together and I grunted.

Erin said, "Oh, wow."

I eased back down to the sidewalk. I wasn't going to be walking on my foot for a while. Gritting my teeth, I looked at Erin. "Are you all right?"

"Oh, wow," she said.

"Hey! Erin!" I looked at her until our eyes met and she focused on me. "Are you all right?"

She didn't say "Oh, wow" again. She shook her head and then she nodded. She looked okay, just shaken. "You just . . ." she began. She looked down at my foot and must have seen the blood that I felt soaking into my sock and shoe. "Your . . ."

I shifted on the sidewalk. My foot didn't hurt yet, but I could feel it throbbing. It felt like a bag of rocks on the end of my leg.

Heavy. Wrong.

The noise and kinetic violence had attracted a small crowd.

I saw someone on their phone, punching three digits. 9-1-1.

Erin started moving like a person who just woke up and realized they were late for work. She scrambled on her knees to get her purse, which had fallen a couple of feet away.

"Lay back," she said. There was an urgency in her voice that was new to me.

"What?"

"Lay back!" she hissed. She started pulling off my shoes and socks.

"What are you doing?"

"Putting you back together before the police get here."

That sounded like a great idea. Over Erin's shoulder I saw somebody from the crowd coming our way. A woman.

"Get back!" I said. She hesitated. "Keep everyone back. Check on the guy in the truck." That would give the woman something else to do for a minute.

I leaned back on my elbows. "Why take off my shoes and socks?" I asked.

Erin's reply was almost too quiet to hear. "Your body pretty much knows how to heal itself. But I need to give it a little guidance and speed up the process. I'll reference the good side to help the other side be correct."

"Well, there goes my career as a dancer," I said.

Erin was busy with the task at hand but she heard me. After a minute, she said, "Dancer? What do you mean?"

"I think you just said you were giving me two left feet."

Erin shook her head and I could tell she was trying not to smile. Or cry. "You are so dumb," she said. "Hold still."

She opened her purse and pulled out what looked like a medallion about the size of a silver dollar. She put the coin on my broken foot and held it there while her right hand grasped my other foot. There was a pulse of pale blue light from her hands, and the bag of rocks started rearranging itself. In looking at the process, I felt I ought to be screaming at the top of my lungs as the bones shifted under my skin. But I felt oddly at peace. There was no pain. The experience was fascinating to feel but nauseating to watch.

I tried to keep my breakfast down while my bones and muscles and tendons and vessels resumed their traditional places and knit themselves together. A smear of blood was left and that was the only sign on my body remaining from the ordeal. "Oh, wow," I said.

"Unhn," Erin put a hand to her head. She had a number of abrasions on her wrist and forearm and a bump was emerging on her forehead.

"You're hurt," I said. I didn't know if she was feeling the effects of nearly getting killed or from the healing. Or both.

"I need something to drink. Sugary," she replied.

By now, the restaurant staff had been informed of the problem. A waitress and a guy in a vest with a red carnation boutonniere and a nametag were over by the door, looking concerned.

"She's in shock," I hollered. "Get her an iced tea or a coke."

The waitress dashed into the restaurant and came out with large glasses of both. She stepped around the truck carefully, glancing into the cab through the window with a fleeting expression of panic. Erin drank the tea first. A siren wailed, heading our way.

"Better?" I asked.

Erin nodded. She bent toward me, her head giving my shoulder a bump. "You saved my life," she said. "You saved us both."

I put my arm around her, giving her shoulder a squeeze. "I had to. You're twenty kinds of amazing," I said.

I got to my feet. I really wanted to get a look at our would-be killer before the cops arrived. I left Erin sipping her cola on the sidewalk and ventured toward the truck. The rose Erin had brought was destroyed. Its peach-colored petals were blowing all over the parking lot in sad little tatters. I dug out my private detective's license from my pocket and held it up as an all-purpose get-out-of-my-way talisman. People moved aside and let me peer into the truck. The airbag had blood on it. The driver's head was tilted sideways against the headrest. The impact had split his lip, and his face had been roughed up, turning it red. His eyes were closed. He had a thin horseshoe of hair and he was wearing a shirt and tie. He looked like a businessman who'd left the office for a little munch-and-murder. He was also Stained. The pattern was ugly and familiar. It was the same as Milly's.

I didn't recognize the guy. "Hey, buddy," I said.

He opened his eyes halfway and looked at me. He got his head up off the headrest and mumbled through the blood that was sticking his lips together.

"Kill you. Mon-stah," was all he said.

"He's asking for you." Just our good fortune that Lieutenant Kapok was in charge of the case. He'd spent the last three hours telling me there was no chance I'd be able to talk to the guy who had tried to run over Erin and me and make us permanent residents of the Robaccio Restaurant parking lot. Instead, I'd spent the time explaining that I didn't know who this guy was, I'd never met him before, and I didn't know why he was trying to kill us. I'd also spent the time trying not to picture how we could have been, smashed and broken and bleeding, pinned between a truck bumper and a stand of date palms. My stomach was in knots.

"Well, Luck, this guy knows your name and what you do. He admits to taking a shot at you with a rifle a couple days ago. Mostly, he's clammed up and won't talk, but that's the sanest thing he's said. Otherwise, he's nuttier than a fruitcake on Christmas day in Squirreltown."

"Why do you say that?"

Kapok shrugged. "Go talk to him. You'll find out. I'm going for a smoke."

I went into the interview room and took a seat. There was a file folder on the table containing the first reports. Our erstwhile hit-and-runner had been cleaned up and there was a white bandage on his upper lip that made him look like he had a narrow mustache. Sort of an inverse Hitler. The Stain around him shimmered balefully and I felt like it was watching me. The sensation was unpleasant and the feeling was hard to shake off. His hands were cuffed and locked to the underside of the table and the table itself was bolted to the floor. His eyes were bloodshot and held nothing but venom and murder.

From the file, I got his name: Charles Mayer.

"Hey, Charles," I began.

"I'm gonna kill you for what you did," he replied.

I nodded. "I'm sure you will. Just not today. So, since we have a minute and you wanted to talk to me, let's talk."

"Monster," he said. It came out again as "Mon-stah." Through his bandaged lip I could hear that Charles had a bit of an accent, and I placed him as coming from Boston.

"You're right. I'm a monster. As far as I know, my parents weren't even the same species. You seem to know a lot about me. So what about you, Charles? What do you do?"

"Try to kill you," he replied.

"Well, I appreciate your single-mindedness. You must do something for a living though. To finance your attempts to kill me."

"Yeah. I work."

"And where is that?"

"Dying is too good for you."

"All right. Let's do this. Let's pretend, for just a minute, that I have no idea what you're talking about."

"Mon-stah! You know what you done!"

"Of course I do. And I deserve to die. I realize that. But I said pretend, remember? I just want to hear you tell it in your own words. From the beginning."

Charles took his eyes off me for the first time since I'd come into the room. He looked from side to side like he was trying to access a part of his brain that he hadn't used for a while. Man, this guy was focused.

He looked up at me again, remembering something. "The pictures. They got my pictures." He couldn't point with his hands cuffed under the table so he jutted his chin in the direction of the file folder. "They got them out of my truck."

"Pictures?" I asked. I shuffled through the folder and came up with several pieces of glossy photo paper. They were blank. I laid them out on the table.

Tears starting rolling down Charles' face and the floodgates opened. "My baby," he said. "Look at her. With you! She was such a good girl. You turned her into somebody we couldn't even recognize no more! Mon-stah! You ruined her! Look at that one! You and her. What is that? Why'd you do it? And that one. You filthy . . . damn you! You got no right! She was so sweet. So pure. I wish I'd never seen her like that. How can I ever forget what you done to her?"

All I could see was white paper, but I had no doubt he saw everything he described. His pain was genuine. He hadn't told me any details. Maybe he couldn't say out loud. And I couldn't be sure that the things I was imagining were worse than what he apparently could see. I listened to his heaving sobs and I felt ashamed of what he thought about me even though I had never met his daughter. Never done the things he thought I had done.

"Where is she now?" I asked. My voice came out thick and heavy.

"Dead!" Charles replied. The tears were flowing freely and a trail of shiny snot had started under his nose as well, running over the bandage. "Her mother and I put her in the ground last spring. I spent months tracking you down so I could kill you."

He looked at my face with utter disbelief. Watched what was rolling down my cheeks. His expression changed from sorrow back to anger again. "Why're you crying?" he demanded. "You don't get to cry for her! You are not allowed to cry for her! You did this!"

I carefully stacked the sheets of blank paper and put everything back in the folder and then closed it up again. Then I wiped the dampness off my face with my hand and stood.

"I don't blame you for wanting to kill me, sir," I said. "And I don't know if you believe me when I say I want to get you some help. But I'm going to try."

"Don't you leave! Mon-stah! Get back here!"

I left the room with Mr. Mayer cursing and vowing to kill me.

Kapok was standing in the hall, hunched over like always. "You got more out of him in ten minutes than we did in three hours," Kapok said. "Maybe we won't let him kill you after all."

"Appreciate that," I replied.

"He's nuts, right?"

"Like a fruitcake in Squirreltown," I said. "Got something for you though."

"Go ahead." Kapok frowned, already not liking what I was going to say.

"Check him for tattoos. He might have one on the back of his neck. If it's temporary, wash it off. Let me know what happens."

"Now you're nutty," Kapok replied.

"Never can tell."

CHAPTER 11

Some Enchanted Evening

While I'd been at the police station, Erin had taken refuge in her lab. She appeared to be lost in thought. Lost deep.

"Hey. How are you?" I asked.

She roused herself and gave me half a smile. "Okay."

"You had some scrapes and bumps. Do you need anything for those?"

"I heal quickly. It's hard to use magic on yourself but I don't need it. I'm fine."

Upon inspection, the bump on her head was almost gone and the scrapes on her arm had all but vanished.

"How about you?" she asked. "Any other complaints?"

I had a few, where I'd landed on the sidewalk. "Only that we didn't get to have lunch."

"Mmm," she replied.

"Would you show me how to use magic?"

She took a deep breath. "I guess that is my duty now, isn't it," she said. "As your undesired helpmeet."

"I didn't mean it that way. I didn't . . ." I hated sounding defensive. "You don't have to do anything. Just tell me who else to talk to and I'll . . ."

"No, no," she stopped me. She put her hand on my arm for a moment. "I didn't mean anything against you. It's this whole . . ."

"Deception thing?"

"Yeah."

"I understand. Look. How about you come over to my house, okay? Max will make a great dinner for us and we can talk like we thought we would at lunch. There won't be any truck-driving assassins. You can teach me to make a nickel float in the air or something."

Erin smiled and it was two halves this time. "Okay. Dinner's on you. Lesson's on me."

"Sounds good."

She got serious again. "What happened with the guy in the truck?"

"You'll find that very interesting. I'll tell you after dinner. I have something else to show you and I think they may be related." I wiggled my eyebrows. "The plot will thicken."

Erin rolled her eyes just enough to make it cute. "So dumb."

I was waiting at home, nervous like a teenage kid pacing around before a date with the prom queen. Which this wasn't. Not a date. Just two professionals, talking business over dinner, who were married. Why be nervous? The phone rang. Kapok.

"How did you know?" No graciousness at all. Not a drop from this guy.

"Hello, lieutenant." I said.

"How did you know about the tattoo?"

"Just a hunch, Kapok."

"Hunch. Baloney," he replied.

"I prefer malarkey over baloney. Except on a sandwich. Then it's the other way around."

Kapok ignored me. "What's going on? What do you know about this mess? Who is this guy?"

"Never met him before today. But I'll make a deal with you. I have some leads I want to follow. If they pan out, I'll give you a heads up and the arrest will be all yours."

"Why not tell me now?"

"Wouldn't want to waste the time and resources of the City of Miami Police Department on baloney."

Even over the phone I could hear Kapok licking his lips while he took a minute to think it over.

"This could be the beginning of a beautiful friendship," I said.

"Screw your friendship. I expect you to tell me everything you know when you know it."

Kapok would have to get in line behind Chief Cuevas and Milly Mallondyke's father.

"It's a deal, detective. So what happened with Mr. Charles Mayer?"

Kapok coughed it all up like a cat with a hairball.

"This is really beautiful," Erin said. She was walking around the house checking the layout and the decorations. She'd kicked off her shoes the second she'd come through the door and I realized I had never seen her without heels. She was still tall and gorgeous. She'd changed into a deep maroon summer dress before coming over. I wore jeans and a pullover.

I'd told her it was the Alder King's house by mortgage, but I had done the interior design, and the furniture and artwork were mine. I was pleased she thought the place was beautiful.

I followed her into the great room. The piano remained unrepaired.

"Ooo," she said. She ran her fingers into the gouges on the piano. "Madrasceartán?"

"Yep. Madeira-is-certain. Whatever you said."

Erin laughed and it was musical. "You'll need to learn how to pronounce words precisely if you expect to cast a spell," she said.

"Then I will have to work on that."

She lifted the fallboard and ran her fingers down the keys, but not hard enough to make a note. I could still hear the whispering sound of her skin caressing the keyboard.

"Do you play?" she asked.

"But of course," I replied.

I sat down on the bench and pretended to crack my knuckles. "Name a song. Any song at all."

She thought for a moment and said, "'Claire de Lune.'"

I placed my hands on the keyboard. I closed my eyes and

tilted my head back and struck a key, sounding a single note. "There you go. Gimme another one. I can play the first note of anything. As long I get to choose the key it's in."

Erin laughed again. "So you're a poser."

"I am. I really am."

Then I played. The selection included a lot of runs up and down the keyboard and the music flowed with a lyrical style that was satisfying to play. After the first couple of minutes Erin sat down on the bench. By the time I finished the piece, she had her head on my shoulder. The world was a bright and shining place.

"What was that?" she asked.

"Beethoven. Piano Sonata Number 21. Third Movement. I picked it because when I'm not a poser I'm a shameless show off."

She was quiet for a minute. Then, "How long have we known each other, Got?"

"Four years. At least that's when I remember meeting you. It was when I was on the force. Popsicle Killer case."

"Oh. I guess I didn't notice you then. I just remember when you got in hot water with the Chief. About six months before you quit. Or were told to quit."

"Not my finest hour," I said.

"Everyone at the station knows you were railroaded out. And now you're a mysterious private investigator. Like Sam Spade."

"Ah. Now we're back to me being a poser," I said. She smiled. "Hey, I have a question for you."

She lifted her head off my shoulder and I instantly wished she would put in back. "All right," she replied.

"Since we're allergic to steel, what do you use for tools in the lab?"

"Sterling silver," she answered. "It's just the iron in the steel that affects the Fae. Iron weapons can make wounds that won't heal in our folk. So my instruments are sterling silver. It costs a lot more but there's no iron. Just silver and copper. A dwarf makes them for me."

"A dwarf? As in a short guy or an actual . . ."

"Dwarf. Yeah. A race of people whose stature is naturally under five feet tall, just like in the movies. Impeccable craftsmanship. Great beards."

Sandretta appeared at the entry for the dining room. She stepped softly, not wanting to break the moment, and she waited until both Erin and I noticed her before she gave us a nod and said, "Dinner is ready."

"Okay. Dinner and then magic," I said.

I followed Erin and made sure she was seated comfortably. The place settings were silver—always had been—and it occurred to me now that there was a reason for that. Max had gone Italian since we hadn't been able to have an Italian meal earlier in the day. Pasta primavera followed by a saltimbocca, which was a veal dish with sage and prosciutto di parma. Tender and flavorful enough to put any Robaccio chef to shame. This was served with a Barbaresco wine, perfectly matched. There was no wine with dessert, which was probably smart, but there was sparkling San Pellegrino along with some fruit and cheese and sweet little cannoli Max had made.

During dinner we had managed to avoid the subject of work until the cannoli.

"So what happened with the guy in the truck?" Erin finally asked.

"He was enchanted," I said. "He was convinced that I was somehow involved in the death of his daughter. He said he'd been trying to kill me out of vengeance. He confessed to shooting at me through the window of my office. The police found a sniper rifle in the back of his truck."

"What had him so convinced?" Erin asked.

"He had some photos with him. They looked blank to me. To him, however, they looked like photos of me and his daughter." I didn't tell her what Mayer had accused me of doing. "He also had a tattoo on the back of his neck. I think it was magic. They washed it off and now he's a completely different person."

"They don't think it was magic, do they?"

"I've already got the detective in charge thinking that there's some kind of drug responsible."

"Okay. Maybe we can work with that," Erin said. "People are rather blind to magic. They'll be more likely to accept that story."

"I thought they might. They're holding Mayer overnight. I'm going to see him again in the morning."

"Did he really have a daughter?" Erin asked.

"I checked into it. He had a daughter all right. She died about a year ago of a drug overdose. Sad story."

"The best deceptions are based on fact," Erin said. "Someone knew about this poor man and used the tragic events of his actual past to turn him against you."

"That's my guess."

"Too bad we don't know who did this to him. That's the person we need to find. That's the person responsible for almost killing us."

"Ah. But I do have a connection." Luck the Triumphant. That's me.

I led Erin from the table to the couch. Sandretta brought out coffee while I retrieved the napkin and the bullet casing in the baggie. I showed her the casing first. "We probably don't even need this anymore, now that we have Mayer in custody. But this should match the bullet I brought in."

I held up the folded napkin. "This is a little more interesting. I don't find it agreeable to look at and I'm guessing you won't either." I unfolded the cloth.

As before, the drawing was alive. Erin's reaction was quick. "Where did you find that?"

"It was on the back of Barry Mallondyke's neck. I copied this from the medical examiner's report."

Erin looked more closely. "I must have missed seeing this when the report was filed."

"It was faded. The tattoo was temporary and was gone when the body was washed. I copied it because it was the only thing that jumped out at me. The Alder King's liondog placed a sigil on my forehead and here was this on Mallondyke. Max told me it would allow the caster to control him."

"It would." Erin went back to the table and grabbed a knife.

She brought it back and cut through the circle of the drawing. The symbol almost gave a sigh and the lines coalesced. It was just a drawing now.

"If you'd put a little power into it, that would have been a working spell," she said. "You were playing with fire, Got."

"I didn't know," I said. Lame.

"Lucky for you, you've got me," she replied. "Which way to the kitchen?" I led her there. The kitchen was already immaculately clean after the dinner Max had made. Everything was put away and there was no sign that a culinary artist had been at work.

We found some matches and burned the napkin in the sink. We watched the flame consume the paper, then we washed the ashes down the sink and the design was no more.

Erin put a soft hand on my arm and said, "I think it's time for that magic lesson."

CHAPTER 12

Magic Lesson

"My first partner, the guy who trained me on the force, had a saying. He said that coincidence is what happens before you have enough information."

"So Mallondyke and Mayer are part of the same plan?" Erin asked.

"I need more information, but I don't believe in coincidence. A few days ago, I'd never seen anyone with tattoos like these and now I've seen two of them connected to tragedy and murder. There's something going on."

I related my encounter in the yoga class at the Iron Foundry with Evie, a.k.a. Béil, a.k.a. the Blue Tiger.

"She said something is coming. Something is happening in the other realms that we aren't prepared to fight. She said terror and destruction were coming and we would need her help. She wants recognition, which she was completely open about. She also has a hard time talking. I felt bad for her."

"Don't. She's a predator in every sense of the word."

"I see," I said.

"Plus she's crazy," Erin added.

"That's also true." That green tinge had come up in Erin's eyes. I wondered if Erin was feeling a little jealous, which was fine with me. "So you can heal. Can I do that?"

"Too soon to tell," she replied. "We'll have to see what you're good at. There are different talents for different people. They can be loosely classified as one of the four elements: Earth, Air, Fire, and Water. I'm primarily Water, which gives me an affinity for healing. Water is like the blood of the world, constantly moving and nourishing and cleansing everything. There are resources formed into oceans and lakes and rivers and, of course, rain. My power feels a lot like that, especially in the Behindbeyond."

"You are definitely amazing," I said. "I'm glad you have that ability."

"I'm also good at Psychometry, which allows me to see the history of objects. Who has touched something and where it came from. Comes in very handy for solving cases."

"Wait, you can tell where an object has been?"

"It's not like I see the history of something just looking at it or picking it up. It takes a spell and a substantial amount of magical power. But yes, when I want I can see where an object has been. And who has handled it. How do you think I made medical examiner so young?"

"You cheated."

She laughed at that. And it sounded just a little bit evil.

We were back in the great room. She pointed at my collection of magazines on the shelves. "You have National Geographic, Nature, Science—quite the collection."

I shrugged. "I've always been interested in the physical world." I pointed at a row of photos. Me on Mt. McKinley. Me snorkeling in Hawaii. Some of the photos had me smiling with pretty girls. I hoped Erin wouldn't mind. "Getting out into nature is relaxing."

"Then you might be attuned to Earth, which would be amazing. There hasn't been a real Earth Mage for centuries. Except for the Alder King."

Erin's eyes were full-on green now. She was excited about this.

"What's so special about being an Earth Mage?"

"Earth Mages have an affinity for almost everything. They can be immersed in all the elements. They could be adept at Water, Air, or Fire magic. Or all of them. And they have abilities usually unique to them alone."

"Like what?" Seeing Stains?

Erin shook her head. "Not yet. We're going to try a few things first. And you have to be very careful."

"Why is that?"

"The Earth is full of her own power. Earth Mages hear the call of Earth and feel the power that is just beneath us all the time. Earth Mages recharge their powers very quickly, especially when in contact with open ground. But you can never be tempted to use that power directly. Ever."

"No?"

"Everyone who's tried to use the power of the earth as a source died instantly and messily. The power is too great to be borne by flesh and they basically exploded, killing themselves and anyone and anything nearby."

"So I could use it once." I smiled.

"That's not funny." Erin looked appalled.

"Okay. No direct use of earth power. Got it."

"It would also be good to talk to Keeper, I think. Maybe we can do that tomorrow."

"Who's Keeper?" I asked.

"Oh, you'll like him. But you're going to have to let a girl keep her secrets for now."

Hmm. That was pretty much the same thing Evie had said. Women.

"We have work to do," Erin continued. "And the first thing to consider are the words you'll need to use. Some spells require long phrases to accomplish. Like a summoning. But a lot of spells use a single word."

I'd picked a good helpmeet. You can always tell when a teacher likes the subject matter. Erin tucked her hair behind her ear, probably to cut down on the wind resistance, because she spoke a mile a minute.

"The words themselves have no power. It's like a trigger on a gun. If you found a trigger lying on the ground, it's just a piece of metal. If you attach a trigger to a gun, though, and load the gun with bullets, then you have a lethal weapon."

"Gotcha."

"Similar to a gun, magic needs three things: a power source, a focus, and a trigger. A lot of people can use magic without a separate focus—but they're using their own bodies for a focus and that can be detrimental. It can kill you. It's much better to use another object for a focus. Then if the magic destroys it, you can always make another one. It's how magic wands came to be so widely known. Nowadays, we'd look ridiculous carrying wands around, so we use other things as a focus."

"I think I could pull off carrying a wand around. I make everything look good."

Erin shook her head with a smirk. She went to her purse and brought out her medallion, the one she'd used to heal me. She laid it in my hand. "Now sneeze," she said.

"Urm. What?"

She laughed. "You have to draw out your power so you can use it. It's kind of like making yourself sneeze by just thinking about it. It's the energy inside you, but you have to open your mind and mentally produce a natural physical action. It probably won't be that hard for you. Your power wants to be used."

She turned her back and slipped her dress off the curve of her shoulder. Zowie. Nice shoulder. Across the top of her shoulder blade were the remains of an ugly bruise. That must have been really bad if it hadn't healed by now.

"Put the medallion on the bruise," she said. I wanted to do what she asked but I hesitated. "Are you shy, my husband?"

That threw me off. "Well. Uh. I don't want to make a mistake. Or hurt you."

"You won't," she said. "I'll guide you the whole way."

This conversation was getting awkward fast.

I put the medallion on top of the bruise as gently as I could.

"Good," Erin said. "Now open up and let some power flow into the silver. Imagine a thread of blue flowing from the center of your body and out through your hand. You'll feel it physically when it happens."

I tried to imagine it happening the way she said. It didn't work.

I closed my eyes and gave it all my concentration for a full minute but there was nothing. I tried again. And again. The wait was getting embarrassing.

Just as I relaxed, I felt a pleasant tingle flash from the middle of my chest and dart down my arm and through my hand. It threatened to grow into a flood. The power had found an outlet and it urgently wanted release. It felt like the silver was pulling the energy out of me and I had to make an effort to slow it down. Erin had said only a thread was needed. In time with the beating of my heart, I let thread after thread pulse from my center. I opened my eyes and found a cool, blue glow forming beneath my hand.

"Achoo," I said.

"Very good," Erin smiled. "Now you have to say the magic word."

"Please?"

"No, but you're going to laugh. The word to heal is '*leigheas*.'"

I did laugh. It sounded like "lice." Usually not a word associated with healing. Dutifully, however, I said it. "*Leigheas*."

There was a feedback thrum of sensation that filled me at the same time my power left me. My body was lost for a moment within a sense of wholeness and warmth.

"Mmm," I heard Erin say.

"Whoo," I said.

Erin's bruise was gone.

I pulled the medallion away, and she touched her shoulder with her fingertips. "Nicely done," she said. "You could do very well as a healer."

"I had a good teacher," I replied. "I felt, I don't know . . . fulfilled somehow."

"That's good. You're supposed to feel that way."

She pulled her dress back up to cover her shoulder. Deep sigh.

"So this is how you use magic directly."

"Power, focus, trigger," I said.

"Good. You get an 'A' for the class. We can talk later about making a focus that will best suit your purposes. For now, we should talk about enchantment. I have something for you." From her purse she produced a silver dollar.

"Looks like a silver dollar," I said.

Erin's smile and flashing eyes tipped me off. She was quite proud of something. She pressed the face of the coin and it pivoted to reveal a secret compartment. Inside rested a silver sigil. "For an enchantment to work, the focus represents the purpose it serves. That's why I could tell what the tattoo you copied was used for. Because of the design. But also how it felt."

"So what's this one for?"

"You've gotten pretty beat up the last couple of days. So more than anything, you need a shield. That's a protection from physical attack. There are protections against magical attacks as well. Those are called wards. Considering your recent history though, a shield is what you need."

"Wow. That's very thoughtful. Never got a shield from a woman before."

Erin's hair had fallen off her ear with her animated teaching. She curled it back again.

"It's not much different from the last spell. You just put the spell on the focus instead of through it. Magic has its own set of rules. Some of it resembles physics. Other stuff makes no real-world sense at all until you understand magic better. For an enchantment, the power remains ready until it is used. It never dissipates. There is no entropy so it never grows weaker, unless the object is damaged or destroyed before you use it."

She handed the silver dollar to me. The sigil inside it was a stylized four-leaf clover. "For Luck," she said.

I laughed, "That's very nice. Thank you."

"Shame on you for thanking me—but you will next time you're attacked. Remember, for a shield, the focus represents you, but you have to have it with you. You can also create a shield for another person or even a place. The simplest way to enchant it is to hold it in your hand and look at it."

She tipped the sigil out of its compartment, and I held it in my hand. It was thin but still heavier than it looked.

"Now put power into it like you did before."

This time the power flowed instantly. The blue glow surrounded the silver, bathing it in light.

"You can put as much power into as it will accept." Erin put her hands underneath mine as if she were measuring my progress.

After a minute or so I felt the flow hit a dead end. "Good," she said. "Now, the word for shield is '*sciath*.'"

"*Sciath*," I said. The blue light snapped into the sigil in an instant, and I felt the air around the sigil being displaced like a popping balloon. Strangely, the sigil was lighter now than it had been before.

Erin put the sigil inside the silver dollar and snapped it closed. "Here you are," she said. "Just keep it in your pocket and it will protect you until its energy is used up."

"How will I know if it works?"

"You won't die next time someone fires a bullet in your direction," she said. "If you want to test it, get a gun. I have no problem shooting you." There were those flashing green eyes again.

"That won't be necessary," I replied. "Appreciate the offer."

"Good. So, I'm going to go home. In about five minutes you're going to be asleep. Your power will demand recharging. Thanks for the nice dinner."

"You're going home?"

Erin found her heels and her purse, and I followed her to the front door, practically begging, "But, but, but . . ."

She turned when she reached the door.

Some part of my brain switched on and I found myself saying, "I don't know why I'm telling you this."

"What?" she said.

"My client, Milly Mallondyke, tried to kiss me. Nothing happened. I told her I was married."

Erin's face was unreadable. She looked back and forth from one eye to the other, looking for something. I let her look.

She took a breath. Then another. "I'm trying hard to find a reason not to like you," she said. "You are making it difficult, Mr. Luck."

That was good, I think.

She opened the door and moved under the portico toward her car. Halfway there, she turned and raised her forefinger to ask one last question. "If I hadn't been there, would you really have chosen that girl?"

I replied without hesitation. "No. I didn't know what a helpmeet was, but it sounded like it would entail spending time with someone. I'd have picked the girl that was the most like you."

She paused for a heartbeat, then spun around so quickly her hair flowed like liquid around her head. She took two steps and spun back, and her hair settled over one shoulder. "Good answer. Okay. Bye."

CHAPTER 13

Connection

Erin was right. Exhaustion settled over me within a minute of her leaving, and I barely made it into bed before falling unconscious. No dreams. No half-awake rolling over in the middle of the night. Boom. Sleep. Morning. Just that fast.

I felt great.

It was too early to go down to the station and I needed a run. I found myself doing laps around a place called Merrie Christmas Park. I'd been told the park was named after a little girl who had passed away and her parents had dedicated the spot to her memory. That reminded me of Mr. Mayer's daughter for a moment, and I distracted myself by drinking in the scenery. There wasn't a single evergreen tree in sight, but there were lots of banyan trees for shade and walkways to jog down. I had my silver dollar in my pocket. I was almost hoping someone would take a shot at me. I was curious to see what would happen. No snipers though. Not even a drive-by. Probably for the best.

After a couple more miles, my heart rate had been duly accelerated and my muscles were loose. I made my way back home and showered and changed into some comfortable slacks and an ecru shirt.

In the kitchen, Max had prepared bacon and eggs and hash browns—just on the right side of crispy—and fresh-squeezed orange juice. Exactly what I was craving.

I ate modestly and jumped in the car.

The soundtrack for the day started out with some Rolling Stones. I drove to the sounds of Mick Jagger and friends delivering some emotional rescue. Perfect.

Charles Mayer had not slept well. He might not have slept at all. He sat in the same clothes in the same chair in the same interview room, looking like a teddy bear that had fallen out of a car on the I-95 and then got run over for an hour or two. His eyes were so dark he looked like he'd been in a bar fight, and his hair on the left side was doing a fine impression of a cockatoo's crest. I was curious to see if he was still carrying a Stain or if it had disappeared along with the temporary tattoo. The black ribbons still curled around him with a hateful darkness. Interesting. His hands weren't cuffed today and I was glad to see him nursing a cup of coffee.

"Mr. Mayer, do you remember me?"

"Oh. I am so sorry, sir. So unbelievably sorry." He blurted it out, the words tumbling over each other in a rush.

He remembered all right.

"I got no idea what happened to me."

"It's okay, Mr. Mayer. You weren't yourself."

"I was not," he agreed.

"The only explanation I can come up with is that you were drugged," I said. Of course, that wasn't the explanation, but it was the only thing I could think of that could be accepted by poor Mr. Mayer—and local law enforcement. "Did the police here tell you anything?"

Charles nodded more energetically than I thought possible for a man in his state.

"They said there was some kind of tattoo on the back of my neck. When they washed it off, I felt better."

"There is a certain class of drugs that can enter the nervous system through the skin," I said. "Some of them are helpful, like when you put a patch on your arm to help you stop smoking."

"Okay, okay. That makes sense."

"Other drugs can be harmful. Yesterday, you were acting like you were on PCP, although it could have been something else. If it's a new drug, it may not be easy to detect. The question is, how and when did you get that tattoo?"

Charles shook his head. "I don't go into those places. I've

never been in a tattoo parlor." He said it "pah-lah" and I found his Bostonian accent charming today.

"It could have been somewhere else. Gymnasium? Swimming pool? Spa?"

Charles snapped his fingers. "That coulda been it," he said. "I got a free massage at this company I was consulting for. We got some coupons for free massages from our client."

"Did the masseuse come to your location or was it at a massage parlor?" I was desperately hoping he'd say "pah-lah" again.

"We all went down to this place in Hollywood."

Darn it. No "pah-lah."

"I had the flyer with the stuff from my truck," he said. He was excited he was helping. I was excited he was helping. I felt a rise of adrenalin begin to push into my system.

We opened the file folder that had again been left on the table. I watched as Charles flipped past the "photographs" without a blink or a twitch. He found the piece of paper he was looking for. The Starlight Spa in Hollywood. I tried to maintain a calm demeanor.

"That's very good, Mr. Mayer," I said. "May I take this?"

"Yeah, sure. Why would I want to keep it?"

"Thank you. And do you mind my asking who your client is? The one that gave you the coupons?"

"Yeah, sure. Mallondyke South African Mercantile."

And that, ladies and gentlemen, is what we call a solid freakin' lead.

I was pumped enough that I almost forgot my other question.

"Do you know where you got the rifle that was found in your truck, Mr. Mayer? Or who gave you the ammunition?"

He shook his head. "No idea. I know I had the rifle and I used it, but I don't have any idea where that rifle came from or how I got it. Again, I'm so sorry."

"It's all right now."

I believed him for reasons of my own.

"Thank you, Mr. Mayer. This is all very helpful," I said.

"Yeah, yeah. You bet."

"And may I say I was very sorry to hear about your daughter. My condolences to you and your family."

"Yeah. She done it to herself. We couldn'ta helped her any more than we did. And I know you didn't have anything to do with her dying."

I nodded gently. "Well, I'm going to follow up on this information you've provided and maybe we can find out what happened to you."

"That'd be great. Thanks."

I found Kapok in the hallway.

"I gotta couple gangbangers to interview next—you wanna talk to 'em for me?" he asked.

"Do they want to kill me?" I replied.

"Not yet. Maybe they will after they meet you."

"Well, apparently, wanting to kill me is a prerequisite to a good interview."

"You're probably right," Kapok said. "I'm going to get a warrant for that massage parlor. See if we can get their records."

"First, put Mr. Mayer into protective custody," I replied. "Him and his wife. The people who did this to him might come after him. Then get your warrant."

Kapok chewed on that for a minute.

"Remember, the arrest is all yours," I said.

"Don't get cocky," Kapok replied.

I peeked into the medical examiner's lab. Erin was in there, wearing an electric blue dress with matching pumps under her lab coat. She looked really good. And really busy. There was another examiner in the lab, working at a table near the door. I deduced he was Sean Graver based on the detailed and focused way he was approaching his work and taking meticulous notes. And from the nametag he was wearing on his lapel. This detective stuff. Woo hoo.

"Hey, you must be Sean," I said.

He didn't look up from the microscope slides he was preparing.

It appeared he was examining some dirt with sparkling minerals of some kind in it. “Mm-hmm,” he said.

“I wanted to tell you that I read the report you wrote for a murder I’m working on. It was really well written.”

“Mm-hmm.”

Wow.

“So. Uh. Good to meet you.”

I could have asked him if his family always dealt with dead people. Uncle Graver the Mortician. Cousin Graver the Gravedigger. Sean Graver the Examiner of Dead People. But he was dead people. Where’s the fun in talking with that?

Erin was more responsive. She actually smiled when I approached.

“Hey,” she said.

“Hey, hey.”

“Always gotta one-up me, eh, Got?”

“Best I can do is catch up.”

That earned me another smile.

“I brought the casing for you to check,” I said. “Hope you don’t mind.”

“Nope. I’ll be glad to see what I can find.”

I handed her the baggie with the bullet casing in it. “I got a lead from Mr. Mayer this morning, and I have to say, he is in a much better mood.”

“That’s good. On both counts,” she replied.

“I’m going to run up to Hollywood and see what I can find out. Is that anywhere near the place you were going to show me?”

“Not even close,” she said.

“Can I call you later?”

“You’ll be in trouble if you don’t.”

I liked the sound of that.

I made another stop at the Iron Foundry.

Nat was in his office working on his accounts for the month.

He loves doing that. Almost as much as rubbing cinnamon sticks on his eyeballs. He didn't have much choice though. He'd had to fire the college kid he'd hired to keep the books a couple of months ago. The kid had been a whiz at making the numbers crunch. He was also a whiz at harassing the patrons. After the cops had hauled him off to jail, Nat found his system completely blocked by passwords and firewalls and who knows what. Then he'd had to hire another college whiz to get him back into his own system and he'd vowed to do the job himself from then on.

"Can I drag you away?" I said.

"Please," he replied.

"We're going to go check out some massage people."

Nat looked at me. And waited.

"What?" I said.

"No joking around?" he said.

"No."

"Okay." Nat stood up and got his gun, which he tucked into the back of his jeans. Inwardly, I smiled.

Technically, I should be going by myself. Nat didn't have a private detective's license like I did. He was just a civilian with a very useful set of skills. Skills that had saved my backside more than once.

I told him the situation, more or less. I explained that Charles Mayer had been under the influence of something unsavory and had tried to run me over yesterday. There was a tattoo painted on the back of his neck, which was identical to the tattoo found on Barry Mallondyke. We were going to go find out if Mayer had gotten the tattoo at the massage parlor and if Mallondyke had ever been to the same place.

I fed Nat the theory I'd concocted: they'd get people all relaxed on the massage table and then put the tattoos on while they were face down and chilling out. Probably told them it was some kind of new treatment to ease tension and improve circulation or something. I didn't know if the tattoo had the drugs in some kind of solution that would penetrate the skin or if it was something else. I just knew there were similarities, and it needed to be checked out. And, in a fit of practicality, I needed backup.

As I offered my explanation, I started to feel bad. I don't lie to my friends. While I wasn't lying completely, I was leaving out some information, which made me feel like a complete jerk. The main reason to go there was valid. I was just hoping that we could find out what we needed when we got there and leave without a fuss. If it was a quick in and out, I'd told Nat what he needed to know and kept it simple. That was for the best, right?

I climbed into my Mustang and Nat got into his personal Escalade. He owned three. Two of them were black and had Iron Foundry advertising all over them. The one he drove today was white and unmarked. I copied the address of the massage parlor and gave it to Nat through the window. Nat followed me to I-95 and we headed north.

CHAPTER 14

Spa Giant

The Starlight Spa was in the middle of the block, surrounded by exotic-looking restaurants, a martial arts dojo, an ice cream pah-lah, a pet store, and several hotels. The outside had Japanese screens behind the windows and bamboo trees painted on the glass. Underneath the name of the shop were some Kanji characters that probably said "Starlight Spa" in Japanese.

Nat parked on a side street across from the spa and I parked around the corner.

I waited while Nat took a walk around the block.

"Back entrance," he said. "No windows. Steel door looks solid."

"Okay. I'm going in. Appeal to their sense of public duty. You follow in five in case they have no sense."

"Got it," Nat replied.

"Or in case they try to massage me to death."

"Good way to go." I saw a miniature Nat smile flicker into existence for a heartbeat.

I opened the front door and stepped into an Asian paradise going to seed. There was an elevated koi pond in the corner with a pair of orange-and-white fish barely swimming. The pump was moving water like a terminal emphysema patient moving air. There was a Buddha on the reception desk along with a Japanese lucky cat, and on the other side was a statue of Ganesh, the Hindu elephant god, sitting next to a Chinese dragon. Behind the counter was an oil painting of Mount Fuji but the frame was decorated with Korean characters. The decor was either an attempt to accommodate every flavor of Eastern culture imaginable or the interior design had been turned over to a small tribe of clueless white people who lived in a flea market and were substantially blind.

Across the countertop and underneath in a display case were about a hundred different oils, salts, candles, lotions and other small containers with big price tags.

A bubble gum girl sat behind the counter. Her gum and her hair were the same shade of cotton candy pink.

"Hey there," I said. "May I talk to your manager?"

I pasted a pleasant smile on my face.

Bubble gum girl gave me a seen-it-and-heard-it-all-before look. Then her eyes latched on to the gun in its shoulder holster and she froze.

"Manager?" I reminded her.

She stood up and scuttled through a beaded curtain. The curtain gradually settled, and I watched the scattered pattern of different colored beads reassemble themselves into a representation of a pagoda.

Female voices hissed intently at each other behind the beads and the girl returned, preceded by an older woman with a well-coiffed mane of black hair. She had a billboard of green eye shadow on each lid and thin lips run over in a bright red. She used her thin lips to say, "Hello. Welcome to the Starlight Spa. Do you have an appointment, please?"

I showed her my license and said, "I don't have an appointment, darn it. But I just need to speak to the manager."

"He's not in," Geisha Granny said. She didn't even look at my license. "Sorry. You make an appointment and come back later."

"That's okay," I said. "I'm working on a murder investigation, and I know what I'm looking for. How about I just go back to the office and find it?"

I moved toward the beaded curtain. Geisha Granny jumped in front of me. Pretty spry.

"No murder," she said. "We too busy. You make an appointment and come back later."

I stepped in and took her hand in mine and slipped my arm around her waist. "I'll bet you were quite the little dancer in your day," I said. We swayed together and I turned her around. She didn't exactly follow my lead, but she weighed maybe ninety pounds so there wasn't much resistance. "What was your favorite? The Lindy? No. No. You strike me as a tango kind of girl."

I'd made a full circle and then another half when I let her go. Now I was next to the beaded curtain and she was nearer to the reception counter. I walked through the curtain.

There was a central hallway with a number of rooms along its length. I startled a woman getting a mani-pedi from a girl who looked up at me with surprised almond-shaped eyes as I passed. "Ladies," I said.

I checked each room going down the hall. There was a space for hairstyling, but most of the rooms had massage tables, except for the one on the end, which had a hot tub and sauna jammed together in the same room. Across from the sauna was the manager's office, the door standing open.

"We call the police," Geisha Granny said from behind.

"They'll be here in about an hour anyway," I replied over my shoulder. "They're talking to a judge right now to get a warrant. I just need to see your files before they come down and confiscate all your computers."

I don't know where the baseball bat came from, but Granny had a pretty decent swing. There was a sharp "Crack!" as an honest-to-Betsy Louisville Slugger collided with the back of my head. It wasn't a home run kind of swing as Granny didn't really have the strength. But she had good bat speed and I was willing to give her a ground-rule double out of courtesy.

I'd hardly felt the hit. There was a little nudge and it felt like someone was bumping into the entire back half of my body all at once. That was it. The shield was working. It spread the impact over a wide area so the overall effect was minimal. Almost non-existent.

Cool.

I was probably less surprised than Geisha Granny, if that's possible after being sucker-whacked. I managed to turn around and keep a straight face. More-or-less. Geisha Granny's eyebrows shot up and almost disappeared underneath her hair. I snatched the bat out of her hands and she unleashed a string of Mandarin at me. She was either swearing or trying to exorcise a demon. Maybe both. Her gestures told me volumes about what she thought of me and, most likely, the legitimacy of my birth.

I went into the empty office. The computer was up and running and ripe for the picking. I tapped on the keyboard and the system prompted me for a password. Fortunately, I had a master key. As Luck would have it.

Before Nat had fired that college kid, the one who was the poster boy for harassment, I'd hired him to do a job for me. His work now resided on a thumb drive that I, with malice and forethought, plugged into the Starlight Spa's computer.

A prompt came up on the screen: "Continue?"

I clicked "Yes." Then I kicked back and watched the fireworks on the screen as the software chewed up the computer's password request and spit out the bones. Then it began copying files. It plowed through the directories like the Miami Dolphins' offensive line in Super Bowl VIII, which was impressive.

The task was well underway when an eclipse happened.

The light in the room dimmed by half and I looked up to see a moon-sized man standing in the doorway. More like filling the doorway.

He was wearing an enormous Hello Kitty shirt, large enough for an entire three-generation Japanese family to picnic under.

In the face, he was Polynesian. Odds were even money he was Tongan. In the body, he was a mountain ape. Heavy on the mountain. I guessed he was about six-four and three-hundred fifty pounds. He was Stained too and the pattern was familiar enough that it made me gulp.

I sat back in the chair feeling a first rush of panic. This was Not Good.

"Are you the manager?" I said. "Boy, I'm glad to meet you. I was just going to leave a message for you on this computer but it's not letting me in. Guess I don't need to leave a note now. What's your name?"

The Tongan stood there, blocking my only avenue of escape. He gave me the "come on, let's go" sign with a hand the size of a pot roast. I got up off the chair.

"Okay. I know. I make an appointment and come back later."

I saw the punch coming. The guy was too big to move fast but he had momentum on his side. He was probably used to knocking guys out with one of his eight-pound fists and then chucking them out. Once the fist started moving, it was hard to stop. I leaned away from it and squinted, anticipating the blow instinctively. The meat of his knuckles mashed up against my shield. I simultaneously felt the impact across the whole left side of my body and heard the pop of several bones in his hand breaking.

He grunted and that was the whole of his reaction. I'd fought big men before. Not this big, but the Marines were a breeding ground for Neanderthals with something to prove. While they had size and strength, it usually came at the cost of stamina and speed. Not this guy.

I tried to edge around the Tongan's side, but there was no way to get through the door as long as he was standing upright. He still had one good hand, which he used to grab me by the arm and toss me across the room like Jaws tossing James Bond. I caught myself on the edge of the desk and went at him, punching him on his weak side. It was problematic at best to reach his head with any force. He was just so darn tall and wide. My fist barely snapped his head back. I took a shot at his midsection, but it didn't connect with any solidity. It was like fighting the marshmallow man from Ghostbusters with fists instead of proton packs.

He let me take a few more ineffectual swings at him. I knew he was just letting me find out how much he could take opposed to how much I could dish out. That equation was definitely in his favor. I got too close to his good hand and I found myself flying into the nearby wall. I was either landing harder or my shield was wearing down.

I tried to figure what his endgame might be. He clearly didn't want to move from that doorway. When I feinted and dodged he wasn't tempted to come after me. He swung at me if I got too close but otherwise he was rooted to the spot between the jambs. I could pull my gun on him but we both knew I wasn't going to shoot him.

Finally, he stumbled forward into the room.

Nat had bulled his way in from the hall and had enough mass to displace the Tongan a couple feet, at least when the big guy wasn't expecting it.

The Tongan turned to face the new threat.

Outside the Marines, everything I needed to know to fight giants I'd learned from watching movies. I jumped on the Tongan's back and locked up his head with one arm around his neck and used the other to add leverage. Following suit, the Tongan backed up hard and we slammed into the other wall.

Oof. I felt that one.

"Got him?" Nat asked.

"This is going to take a while," I replied. "He's still getting air."

I could hear the Tongan's inhalations growing breathier, but his neck was so thick I was having a hard time choking him out.

"Heavy bag," I said.

Nat picked up on my cue. The heavy bag is the big hanging sack of sawdust that boxers use to build their stamina and practice body work. It took a lot of energy to punch the heavy bag again and again. It raised your heart rate pretty quickly when you worked it. I was hoping the same would be true for the heavy bag getting worked.

Nat was an expert. It would have been a pleasure to watch him go at it if I weren't hanging on for dear life. Nat danced in and landed a few blows and hopped back out, changing positions and staying away from the Tongan's wide swings. I couldn't cut off his air completely, but we could make his body work harder so he'd need more oxygen. Plus he was bearing my weight, which stressed his system even more. His breathing grew more labored as Nat kept up the strike-and-retreat. The Tongan wasn't getting enough air to keep up. It took a couple of minutes but the big man finally sank to his knees. I held on to make sure he wasn't faking it. After another long minute he grew woozy. His brain was starved and at last he slumped to the floor.

I rolled off and checked his pulse and it was strong. I was glad.

"I know your head will be . . . wait." I looked at Nat. "What is the line? Your head will ache when you wake but dream of big girls? What's that line from the Princess Bride?"

Nat was no help.

I looked down at the sleeping giant. I wasn't eloquent, but I meant it when I said, "Sorry about the headache. Have happy dreams of fat chicks."

I grabbed my thumb drive and we moved into the hallway.

"Get what you need?" Nat asked.

"Think so. What took you so long to get in here?"

Nat didn't answer directly. When we reached the reception area he pointed at the corner with his chin. On the floor were three Asian guys, all of them unconscious but still breathing.

Then I understood the Tongan's plan. He was just keeping me busy until these guys could get here. Didn't turn out to be a good plan though—my cavalry beat his cavalry when Nat came in and cleaned up.

"Oh," I said. "Okay. So you got these three guys while I was taking care of the Tongan. Pound for pound, that makes us even."

Nat showed no reaction at all.

Geisha Granny and the Bubble Gum Girl had pressed themselves against the wall. Granny cut loose with another string of Mandarin as we walked out the door. I didn't understand anything she said, but I was pretty sure it wasn't "Thanks for coming."

CHAPTER 15

Psycho Stuff

"Got some results from your bullet and casing," Erin said.

She was alone in the lab now. Sean "Mt. Graverest" Graver having been called out to examine a crime scene at the beach.

Erin gave me the casing first, back in its baggie. It had been dusted for "friction ridges" and was covered in pink swirls. "Ah, you've given it a woman's touch," I said.

"All about the contrast," she replied. "If you don't mind my saying so, your handling was pretty sloppy."

This was the police professional in her coming out. I didn't take offense. "Why do you say that?"

"The only fingerprints I could identify on there are yours."

"What?" I looked at the prints though the plastic. My new eyesight made it easy for me to see the whorls and lines of pink on the brass. I compared my thumb with one of the prints. There was a little scar that I'd had since before I could remember. That, along with the pattern of ridges, confirmed she was right.

"I found this at my office. Right before the King's liondog had me going home to open the silver gate. Actually, the Korean guy downstairs said a little kid had gone into my office. If anyone's prints should be on here, they should be his. I remember picking up the casing with a napkin—the same napkin we burned last night. I don't remember ever touching it with my bare hands."

Erin patted my shoulder. "Those prints are yours. 99.9% certain."

"No, I'm sure you're right. How about the bullet?"

"I read a copy of the report. No prints, but the bullet and casing are the same round and they were used in the sniper rifle collected from Mr. Mayer. Mr. Mayer has already admitted to the attempted shooting. We can corroborate with physical evidence now, if we need to."

"It's up to the district attorney," I said. "I'm not pressing charges. Especially since I know he was being manipulated."

"Do you know where he got the rifle and ammunition?" Erin asked.

"He doesn't remember."

Erin smiled. It was electric.

"Mr. Mayer may not remember, but the bullet does."

I recalled Erin talking about this before. "This is that psychotic thing you were talking about," I said.

"Psychometry," she corrected me. "I can see the history of an object. Who has touched it, where it has been. I just got a hold of the bullet, so I haven't taken a magical look yet. Would you like to see?"

"Absolutely."

"Then come along, underling," she said.

"Underling? Is that what you call the mate of a helpmeet?"

"No. That would be 'helpless,'" she said.

"Ouch." Man, she made me smile.

I followed her into the back of the lab where there were several small rooms. There were offices for each of the medical examiners, some storage spaces, and some rooms for processing evidence.

Erin entered the last room and I followed, the helpless underling.

There were stacks of supplies for analyzing different things, including boxes and bottles labeled things like "cyanoacrylate" and "glacial acetic acid" alongside a small refrigerator with a glass door holding more bottles. All Erin was looking for was a silver bowl. It was at the bottom of a stack of plastic bowls. She took it down off the shelf.

"Better lock the door," she said.

I closed the door and locked it. "Could be scandalous," I said.

She didn't respond to that. I wondered if I shouldn't have said it or if she was just preparing to focus on the job at hand.

The bullet went into the bowl along with enough water to fill it halfway.

"I can get a clearer impression if I'm touching the object directly. But this way . . . well, you'll see," she said.

Erin put her fingers on the silver rim. I deduced that the rim of the bowl was the circle she would use in creating the spell. She spoke softly and the words were melodious and strange. That pale blue glow emanated from her fingertips and she drew a neon line around the rim of the bowl. The circle snapped shut with the sound of a bell. She continued half-chanting, half-singing. As she moved her fingers around the rim of the bowl, images surfaced on the top of the water. The first image was Erin. It looked like her face had been projected onto the water's surface.

"Cool," I said.

The next image was me. She continued moving her hands. I realized that when she moved her hands counter-clockwise, the images shown receded backward in time. She spun the images backwards, going faster. Sometimes she stopped and moved clockwise, going forward in time, to catch a glimpse of something or someone that she had passed.

Most of the images were of Charles Mayer. Some of the images included his surroundings, like the interior of his truck. Sometimes there were stretches of darkness with no discernible details. Sometimes there were sounds, ragged voices. Ranting. Crying. The voices were loud in the closed room.

With a deft touch, Erin spun the images until she found the day Charles Mayer shot at me. It wasn't like watching a movie, the images sometimes moved, stuttering, repeating or jumping. Or not doing anything at all. But one image was clear, sharply detailed, and as heart-wrenching as it was frightening. The image of Charles Mayer, rifle at his shoulder, finger on the trigger, and pure hatred shining in his eyes.

I forgot to breathe for a minute until Erin started spinning the images again. Through the scenes, we met Mrs. Mayer as well. A middle-aged housewife, confused, trying to calm an unreasoning and angry husband. Back further. Mr. Mayer, looking at blank photos, weeping. I was glad she didn't dwell there. Finally, there were new people. Possibly in the massage parlor, but the details were blurry and non-descript. Then a face, warped by the speed of the image.

"Wait! Go back," I said.

Erin dutifully moved her fingers in the opposite direction around the bowl. She had never stopped her song.

"I know that guy!" I said.

Erin stopped moving and the blue light of her fingers illuminated the surface of the water with a wavering light. The face was distant, but I recognized it. He had a sour expression on his face and a triangular patch of beard beneath his lip. Bright red.

"His name is Amad and he works for Milly Mallondyke," I said.

Erin stopped singing and pulled her hands away from the bowl. The image faded and there was an ethereal sound in the air, like the ringing of a bell in reverse. Also cool.

Erin swallowed thickly. Her breathing was heavy like she'd run a mile or two. "I know him as well. In the Faerie Realm, he is known as Caimiléir," she said. "Among other things, he is a necromancer and an enemy of the Throne. He was sentenced to banishment but pled for mercy as the King's nephew. The Alder King forced him to renounce his path and set him upon a new path of tasks to demonstrate his fealty. As far as I know, he has yet to complete his trial of penance."

I thought for a long minute. Amad—Caimiléir—was my cousin, possibly. He had seemed rather weak and almost comical in person. And he hadn't had a Stain. As I'd discovered, mortals sometimes had a Stain but the Fae always did. I stowed the thought for later.

"Well, we can connect him to Charles Mayer and the bullet he shot at me. We know he works for Milly Mallondyke. If we assume the people responsible for the tattoos did them both, we still don't have a solid link with between him and the murder of Barry Mallondyke. But it's a start."

"Got. Stay away from him," Erin said. There was sudden quaver in her voice and an urgency in her eyes. "He's an Eternal. One of the few comfortable in both this realm and the Behindbeyond. He has followers and comes here all the time. Béil is bad, but she doesn't allow herself to be summoned here unless she really needs to and she can't tolerate being here for long."

"Wait. Summoned?"

"Yes. Halflings like you and me can come and go between realms whenever we want. Eternals have to stay in the Behindbeyond and can't come to the mortal realm unless they're summoned by somebody who's already here."

So, somebody brought Béil here. And somebody brought Amad. Good to know.

"Caimiléir wants power. He doesn't care if it's in the Behindbeyond or here, and he doesn't care who gets in his way. If I had to guess who tried to attack you during your Quickening, it would be him. As a way of hurting the King."

The concern in Erin's eyes was sweet, but I also saw she was deadly serious.

"I'll stay away from him, if I can," I said. But if Amad did kill Barry Mallondyke, I might not be able to avoid a throw-down. I had an obligation to my client.

I changed the subject.

"Can you look at the casing too?" I asked. "Because a little boy was apparently involved in delivering it to me."

"All right," Erin replied.

"Don't exhaust yourself."

"I won't."

She put the casing into the water and sang the spell. The images danced while we watched and after a minute or two, Erin found him. Qui-Gon had been remarkably accurate. The image floating at the surface showed a boy, about ten years-old, with sandy hair and a shirt that looked exactly like something out of Robin Hood. He must be the boy who'd delivered the casing. I wished he could jump out and tell me who he was. He looked familiar somehow and I felt it should be easy to place him. But I couldn't.

"Do you recognize him?" I asked Erin.

She ended the spell again and shook her head. She was breathing heavily again. I was going to owe her another meal to recharge her physical batteries. "No. Do you?"

"I feel like I ought to."

"Well, in any case, we have even more reason to see Keeper now," Erin said. "To find out more about you and to find out what Caimiléir is up to."

We unlocked the door and I followed Erin into the main area of the lab. Sean Graver had returned. If he noticed us coming out of the back room together, not at all sneaky, he didn't show it. He didn't even look up from the report he was writing.

"I'm going out for lunch," Erin said.

Sean looked up. "Sounds great! Have a good one!"

I gave Graver a quick stink-eye on the way out, but he'd already gone back to his report.

Out in the hall, I told Erin, "I had a one-sided conversation with that guy where he didn't say a word. But you say you're going for lunch and he goes all chatterbox for you."

Erin winked at me. "It's good to be the boss."

"Guess so. Are you tired from the spell?"

"Some spells are easier than others," Erin said. "Healing takes a lot of energy because there's a huge physical effect. Psychometry is about thoughts. It's all mental, so it didn't take as much out of me. Actually, it's nice that we're going to the Behindbeyond. We recharge our power there from the energy around us. We don't need to sleep to gain our powers back quickly."

"What if I cast a spell there?" I asked.

"Easy as pie."

"Let's go."

We decided to take my car. Erin settled into the passenger seat like she belonged there.

"Nice," she said. I told her to check the glove box and choose something to play. She flipped through the selections and slid a disc into the CD player. Van Halen. I smiled.

"No, I will not discuss David Lee Roth versus Sammy Hagar," she said. "I like them both."

I just pulled out of the parking lot. Still smiling.

"So who is this Keeper? Is that his name? Or what he does?"

"Yes." She was laughing now.

"Okay. And where is this place? Where Keeper is?" I asked.

"It exists in many locations," she replied. Enigmatic on purpose.

"Ok. Where is the one we're going to?"

"Closest door is Key Largo."

"That's about an hour and a half from here," I said.

"Yes. If you think like a mortal," Erin said. She was taking great delight in my lack of experience. "Otherwise the nearest portal is only ten minutes away."

She gave directions and we soon arrived at a pretty bungalow surrounded by tall fences drenched in bougainvillea.

"Whose place?" I asked.

"Mine," Erin replied. "Come in."

The interior of Erin's house was decorated in white with aqua accents. Instead of a beach theme, however, she had memorabilia from old movies all over the place. Posters and props hung from the walls or sat on shelves, and an ancient arc light projector stood in an alcove. It was like being in a 1940's boardwalk movie house.

"Awesome," I said.

"Glad you like it," Erin replied.

She had a familiar poster with Humphrey Bogart and Ingrid Bergman hanging next to the window. I stood next to it and admired it. "Hey, was it me who mentioned Casablanca first?"

"It was you," Erin replied. "One of the things that made you interesting. Or made me wonder if you were looking in my windows at night."

I shrugged. "Either way."

Erin laughed. "Give me a minute. I'm going to change."

She disappeared and re-emerged literally sixty seconds later. When she said a minute, she meant a minute. The last dress she'd worn in the Behindbeyond had been a green gown with a leaf pattern. This dress was like a waterfall. A pattern of ripples in a gorgeous shade of blue cascaded from shoulder to hem and she had heels to match. Her hair flared out away from her face to create a wild mane of flowing locks. She had redone her makeup, giving her eyes a smoky allure that made the whole package breathtaking.

"Whew," I said. "Wow."

"Glad you like it. Again."

I looked down at my clothes. They were nice, for South Florida, but I looked like a street beggar compared to her. She was out of my league as the human Erin. But compared to this gorgeous creature from a hidden realm, I wasn't even in the same universe. "What do I wear?"

"You're fine," Erin said. "The Behindbeyond, or *An Taobh Thiar Agus Níos Faide* when you're there, is hopelessly chauvinistic. You can wear whatever you want and nobody will think less of you. But me, as the wife of the Alder King's son, I have a different standard." She held her hands up and turned slowly in a circle.

On impulse, I stepped in and wrapped my arm around her waist. "You're the royalty."

Erin put her hands on my chest. She didn't pull away—but she was ready to push.

"Got. I've had a couple of days now to think about things. I wasn't sure how to react when all this happened. In a lot of ways, it was kind of exciting on its own. But I'm not sure this will really work. As a marriage, I mean. Of course, I'll be your helpmeet in the Behindbeyond. I won't cause dishonor to you. I'm just . . . I'm not sure if . . . I need some time. Is that all right?"

I looked into those warm toffee eyes. I wanted to be with her. She was in my arms and it was very, very nice. Part of me—a small part—wanted to enforce my claim to her body. But I couldn't be that guy. I sighed inside. Men don't get their feelings hurt. But if a bruised heart felt anything like I felt right now, it would suck.

I'd never let her know. I'd keep it light. I cleared my throat and said, "There's an old Japanese saying: 'The man owns the house but the woman owns the bed.'"

Erin laughed, deep and throaty. Good. She didn't know what I was feeling.

She needed time and I would need to give it to her. I let her go.

"Is that a real Japanese saying?" she asked.

"No," I had to admit. "But it's good, right? Nice combination of sensitivity and pathos."

"It's good," she said. "Let's go."

She led me to a storage room with a wood floor. In the center of the floor was a silver inlay that looked to be permanent. An empty circle. Against the wall was a set of shelves with a collection of silver patterns that looked like they fit into the circle.

"This is like the portal I made," I said. "To get to the Behindbeyond."

"Exactly. Instead of making a portal every time from scratch, I use these. Different patterns are for different destinations."

She took a pattern off the shelf and dropped it into the center of the circle. It was very similar to the design that came out of me. Same kind of design but instead of a real feather, rock, cup of water, and candle, there were symbols at the compass points.

"Would you care to do the honors?" she said.

All righty.

I knelt down and touched the circle. I took a moment to make sure I remembered the word that Madrasceartán had etched into my mind. Then I took a breath and fed a thread of power into the silver. I said, "*Oscailte.*" The whole pattern flashed to life and a column of blue light shot up to the ceiling. The gate pivoted down into the floor.

"That was easy. When I made mine, I had to put blood into it."

"Silver doesn't need blood, it's a natural essence of the Earth herself," Erin said.

"I like that."

Erin took my hand. I tried to keep it light. Like we were friends. She said, "Don't forget to call me Fáidh in the Eternal realm. It's a matter of honor."

"Okay," I replied. "Fáidh it is."

"Shall we?"

I squeezed her hand, and together we fell in.

CHAPTER 16

Keeper

Our ninety-degree turn put us onto a wooded path. Immense oak trees towered over everything, their trunks were at least thirty feet in diameter and they soared to least five-hundred feet tall. A few stray leaves sailed down through the air, each one the size of a kite.

"This isn't Key Largo," I said.

"I didn't say it was. I said Key Largo was the closest door. Come on. I'll show you."

We followed the path around the trees. There was an inn on the other side. Maybe more of a lodge. Or a mansion converted for public use. It had a thatched roof and mullioned windows and couldn't have been more filled with charm. A sign hanging from a post by the road said "*Corrchnámhach.*"

Erin saw me reading the sign and said, "Newcomers refer to this place as 'The Angle.' That's the meaning of the word you're trying so studiously to read."

"Gotcha."

We pushed open the heavy door to find the place stocked with patrons. The room was constructed at odd angles. It had pillars in what appeared to be random locations. There were tables with odd assortments of individuals eating and drinking and talking. There were no musicians visible, but I heard an unobtrusive and simple melody playing. At the center was a bar with seven counters facing each of the seven sections where the patrons could sit. I just stood a pace or two from the door and tried to take it all in.

Erin pointed to a nearby door. It had a palm tree carved into it. "That door exits into a janitor's closet in Key Largo," she said. "The door is always open, if you know where to look. It doesn't take any will or word. This place is a sanctuary, open to all."

"That's fantastic," I said. "How many doors are there?"

"There are seven direct doors. Other doors exist that lead to the seven doors. Have you heard of ley lines?"

"Uhhh."

"Guess not. You can think of them as lines of supernatural power that connect areas of the world that are significant to the Fae. Places of historical or mystical importance. There are lots of minor lines but only a few major lines. Where those lines cross is called a nexus. Sometimes you'll get more than two major lines intersecting. Those places are the most important. There's only once place where seven ley lines intersect."

"Let me guess. Right here at The Angle."

"Correct. And they generate the power needed to travel from one place to another using the ways between the doors. You're a quick learner, underling."

"Careful. That kind of nickname could stick to a guy."

"You'll just have to deal with it then."

"Very well, helpmeet. So where do all these lines come from?"

"Okay. So the Earth has her own magic, but she can be affected by magic as well. The ley lines are bands of magical power, almost like magnetic fields, that circle around and through her."

Holy whoa. Ley lines are the Stains around the Earth.

I didn't have time to geek out about my revelation. I needed to listen.

Erin continued. "And ley lines are not straight. They curve and bend from any number of influences and they're also affected by belief. A lot of the changes over the centuries have dealt with what people believed, where they lived, and what they did. For example, a ley line was once located in Greece. As power shifted westward with the Roman Empire, the mythology and belief shifted with it. That ley line moved from Greece to Italy." She pointed at a door with, no kidding, a pizza carved into it. "That door will take you to an alcove underneath the Coliseum in Rome."

"Why not the Vatican?"

"That's a different set of beliefs," Erin said. "Beliefs aren't necessarily incompatible with each other and systems can even overlap, geographically as well as philosophically. But they are expressed in different ways."

"I see."

"By the way, the source where Key Largo is located now was once located in Bermuda," Erin said.

"Bermuda Triangle?" I asked.

"Exactly. Science has removed a lot of the myths surrounding the Bermuda Triangle. The source shifted towards Florida as the beliefs are stronger in Florida now."

Erin indicated a large group of retirees wearing golf shirts and polyester pants. They were drinking beers and Bloody Marys.

"So the source is in Florida now because there are more old people?"

"You could say that."

"Who are they?"

"Vampires."

"You must be joking," I said, moderately aghast.

Erin grinned. "Think about it," she said. "Vampires are among the oldest beings on Earth. Even they age, albeit slowly. Eventually, they need to find a place where they can blend in with the local populace. And, due to the latitude in southern Florida, there's a more consistent cycle of day and night there than almost anywhere else. They need nighttime to travel and feed and the nights in Florida don't vary much during the year."

"Okay." I stared at her. "If you hear what sounds like bubble-wrap popping inside my head, that's just my brain exploding. So I'll just deal with all this at a later date." I took another peek. "They look like attorneys. Shall we get a table? Then you can tell me what other creatures of the night are stalking the Behindbeyond."

"Like werewolves? Basilisks? Various forms of other undead?" She had to be teasing.

"Those exist too?"

"Didn't you say your brain was exploding? Let's just say there are fewer fictitious creatures in existence than you might think. Come on. Let's see if Keeper can speak with us."

We moved toward the bar. As we went deeper into the building, I saw that the ceiling was very high. Or . . . "Hey, are those stars?" I asked. "In the middle of the afternoon?"

"This is a special place, remember? It's the most powerful nexus that we know, and the ley lines aren't all parallel to the Earth," she pointed up. "Some are perpendicular. Besides, some customers don't walk."

As if on cue, a pair of Pegasi flew down from the midnight sky and landed in an area with straw on the floor and stalls like a barn. Their hooves hit the floor and I felt the impact when they landed. They shook their manes and tucked in their wings, and I had to say, "How cool is that? I'll answer with 'extremely cool.'"

"Fáidh Bean! How are ya lass? You're looking as lovely as ever. And what is this with ya? Ye're supposed to take the trash out, not bring it in."

Erin laughed warmly. "Keeper! Let me introduce you."

The man addressing us was about five feet tall. He was layered in brilliant white hair with his features fitted in between, almost as an afterthought. The white hair was shockingly bright and finely-trimmed on his face but untamed everywhere else. A thick tuft sprouted from the collar of his shirt. Then there was a beard across his chin, a smiling mouth, a bristly spray of a mustache, a round nose and mischievous dark eyes, eccentrically bushy brows, a broad forehead, and a final tuft of white to cap it all off. As if that weren't enough, his Stain was a silver work of art with multiple ribbons of exquisite design interlinked. I looked down at my poor little band of a Stain and felt inadequate. His Stain was . . . magnificent.

"Keeper, this is Goethe Luck," Erin said.

"Pleasure to meet you," I said.

Keeper extended his hand, which took mine like a vise. More thick white hair covered his forearms.

"Oh, aye. I know who ya are, lad. I know who ya are. But I'm not sure you do."

Kind of an odd thing to say.

"Sit yerselves down. We have a lot to talk about. I'm sure ye have some questions. Ye may have more by and by." His speech had a certain brogue that caught the ear. But it was hard to listen closely as he still had my hand. It felt like it was encased in granite and he kept a hold of it as he escorted us to a big wooden table in a nearby corner. I was wondering if I was going to get my hand back and what condition it might be in once I did. Finally, after Erin and I were seated, he let me go. I put my hand beneath the table and squeezed it with the other one to make sure the blood hadn't been banished entirely.

"I've been waitin' for this day," he said. He was looking at me with an appraising eye, and I felt he was seeing deep into the spaces where I kept my inner soul. "Make yerselves at home. And call yer friend, the raven. This concerns her as well."

Keeper walked off in the direction of the kitchen. It seemed he knew a lot about me. "Midnight Dreary!" I called. Less than a minute later, she flapped down through the stars overhead and landed on the carved back of a chair.

"Just in time, Fiach Dubh." Keeper had appeared at my elbow but I never heard him coming. He placed flagons of ale on the table. He also brought salt-and-vinegar potato chips and some cheese.

"Here are some starters, for starters," he said. He had a bowl with grubs and berries in it, which he placed in front of the raven. In this setting, no dish was a surprise. Midnight Dreary waited quite politely until Erin had tasted a chip and sipped some ale. Then she began consuming her meal with delicate precision.

The chips were perfectly seasoned, and the ale and cheese complemented each other so well I could have made a whole meal of everything and been content.

Keeper disappeared and reappeared after a minute, catching me by surprise again by approaching from the other direction. He had a large book.

"Sorry to come between ye." He rearranged the table so he could place the book where we could both see it. He turned the thick pages. They were well-preserved and smelled faintly of dust and parchment.

"Naturally, there are many history books concerning the Alder King," he said. "Yer father was most insistent I show this to ya."

Why not tell me himself?

Keeper mumbled, "I'm looking for . . . here we are. Johann Wolfgang von Goethe."

Of course, I'd heard of Goethe. Ever since I could remember, I'd wondered why my name was the least pronounceable—and least cool—of the selections available. The Mama said the name came with me, but she never would tell me anything else. Goethe was awkward but Wolfgang was awesome. I could have told people I'd been named after Mozart or after a gourmet chef with the name Wolfgang. Even Johann was preferable to Goethe. There were Strauss and Bach, at least.

Keeper stopped on a page with a poem written by my namesake, in 1782, and titled Der Erlkönig.

"A poem about the Alder King," I said.

"Aye, lad. You know it?"

"Oh, I've had an ongoing education about all things Goethe."

"Well the original was in German," Keeper said. He slid a piece of paper out from under the book and laid it across the pages. "I took the liberty of having it translated."

Erin and I leaned in together and read.

Who goes riding fast in dark and wind?
The father 'tis with his only kin.
He holds him tightly in his strong arm,
To hold him safely, to keep him warm.

"My dearest son, why hidest thy face?"
"My father, I see the Alder King's grace!
The Alder King flies with crown and tail—"
"My son, it is just the mist so pale."

"Come now dear child, come away with me.
The loveliest games I'll play with thee.
Colorful flowers grow in my world,
Mother will dress thee in robes of gold."

"My father, my father, canst thou hear
The King's promise whispered in my ear?"
"Be calm, stay calm, my most precious child;
The wind in the leaves is sounding wild."

"Wilt thou, handsome boy, fly with me on?
My daughters will treat thee as our son.
My daughters will dance with thee at night,
And sing you to sleep 'til morning's light."

"My father, my father, see ahead
The Alder King's daughters stand in dread?"
"My son, my son, all poor father sees
Is moonlight gray on the willow trees."

"I love thee, thy form is strong and fair,
By force then now I shall take thee there."
"My father, my father, feel his hold!
The Alder King hurts me in the cold!"

In horror, the father speeds along,
His shuddering child held in his arm
Through hardship at home they end the ride.
In his arms, the dearest child has died.

"I've read this before," I said. "It's the feel-good poem of the 18th century." Actually, The Mama showed this poem to me. It was in a book that, like my name, came with me.

"It's so haunting and sad," Erin said.

"It's a steaming load of twaddle," Keeper spat. "'Tis tragic, aye. But the mortals got the details completely wrong. Goethe only wrote what he knew, of course. Can't blame him for that. He was visiting a friend when a man rode by on horseback, carrying a feverish boy. The man was all but a stranger. He'd moved into a farmstead nearby with his wife and this child. They claimed the child belonged to some distant relative, and they'd been asked to take the boy to the countryside. There were issues with his health and he apparently had visions of the Alder King and his daughters. The boy did die that terrible night."

I glanced at Erin, who was wrapped up completely in Keeper's story. She was smart, for certain, and accomplished, but she let herself be a woman. Even better, she let herself be a human being. She was touched by the tale and I found the funny and soft sides of her incredibly appealing.

"Problem was," Keeper continued, his audience now firmly in his granite grasp, "'Twasn't their child. The man and his wife had stolen the child and run off with him, hoping to hide the boy from his true father. The Alder King wasn't trying to take the child, ye see. He was trying to take him back."

"So who is the child?" I asked.

Keeper smiled. "Considering, I think ye have enough to put the two and two of it together," he said. "'Specially since the boy didn't stay dead."

Erin who was much more accustomed to living in the fantastic, was quicker to draw a conclusion.

"Got, it's you!"

CHAPTER 17

Jeweled Gate

On some level, I knew Erin was right. But denial is always the first reaction to crazy.

"That's crazy," I said.

"There are some, like me, who may know more about ya than ya know yerself," Keeper said. "That's what I'm a-tellin' ya. Ya did die when only a child, didn't ya?"

"Yes. But if what you're saying is true, that means I died in 1782."

"Exactly. As the mortals reckon it."

"This is cocoa puffs," I said. "Cuckoo for."

Midnight Dreary, whom I'd momentarily forgotten, chimed in, "Caw-caw!" she said.

"My point precisely." I gave her a nod. Her grubs and berries were all gone so I offered her a piece of cheese. She took it delicately at the tip of her shiny beak and tossed it back into her throat. "Good girl," I said.

"I see ye're having a hard time believing, lad. Ya say yer name is Luck?"

"That's right."

"How about 'Laoch?'"

The way he pronounced it was, "Lay-ock" but I wasn't going to quibble. "Close to the same."

Keeper turned more pages. "There's more in here about ya, when ya have time. But this is what the King is wanting me to show ya next."

It was a simple entry, with the name of a hospital in Louisiana and my modern date of birth and a name, "Goethe Laoch."

Some memories of my early life came floating up to the surface from a cornered abyss of my mind. "My foster mother told me I had a different version of my name when she took me in. I remember she said she just called me 'Luck' because it was simpler and I already had one name she couldn't pronounce."

"Aye, but 'Laoch' is yer name as given ye by the Alder King. It means 'Hero,' lad. Ye're all but walking around with a label on yer forehead."

Every day had a new shock, it seemed.

"I'm not surprised to find out that there are things in the world, unseen and magical, that I didn't know were real," I said. "I've always known there was more to our existence than everything we can see and feel. It's the idea that I have some part of that world that's more difficult for me to accept. I've always been just . . . me. And there's all the strange stuff my foster mother taught us."

"What do ya know about yer foster mother?"

"She's The Mama. An enormous Cajun woman who cared for me and about five or six other boys at a time. She preferred to be called La Mere, but she'd accept The Mama. Once, I called her 'Mother' and she smacked me across the face with the back of her hand and kicked me out of the house until it was dark. She wouldn't have anything to do with me until morning. I had to eat dinner outside in the cold. She told me I only had one Mother, and she was dead, and she didn't want to be compared to a dead woman."

Erin said, "Not exactly a good caregiver."

"She had an interesting way of tracking how mad she was at you. If you did something wrong, she'd hit you and leave a bruise on your arm or face. She never bothered to remember what exactly you did wrong but she knew if you had a bruise on you, it was something she was supposed to be mad about. When your bruises healed, she wasn't mad at you anymore."

"That's horrible!" Erin said.

"It had its own kind of logic. Except I'd sneak into her make-up and cover my bruises with foundation so I could have dinner in the house instead of in the yard. We had a real jerk of a kid come in for a while. He was a year older than me and stole my food. So I hit him and gave him a black eye. The Mama didn't let him eat with us for more than a week, until his eye wasn't swollen anymore. Kid didn't mess with me again."

Erin didn't say anything, but I couldn't misinterpret her disapproving expression. "Hey, it was dog-eat-dog. The Mama had a lot of weird ideas. Superstitions and rituals. She went to the Protestant church five miles away every Sunday, but she also had a whole lot of beliefs you won't find in the Bible. She talked to the spirits in the trees and in the river. Sometimes too, in the dark, I'd see lights floating around the swamp outside. We often had visitors in the middle of the night. I'd sneak out of bed and try to see who it was. One of the visitors had a triangular face, and I thought her overcoat looked really funny. Then I realized she had wings like a dragonfly on her back. I grew up with weirdness. It made me believe. I figure that's why I can see the Stain."

"The what?" Keeper put his hand on my arm like a boulder on a stick.

"I can see patterns on certain people, like ribbons with designs on them. I've seen them for as long as I can remember." I looked around the room. "Every living thing in here has a Stain. I don't know what else to call it. I just made it up when I was a kid."

"I have a Stain?" Erin's brow was furrowed as if I'd just told her she had cancer.

"It's beautiful. Like a forest of ferns and grapevines reflected in a rippling stream." I smiled at her, reassuring. "Keeper's Stain is like finely-crafted silver bands of chainmail with little symbols worked into the metal. Don't ask me what mine looks like," I glanced at my chest and my wispy Stain and bluffed. "There aren't words."

"And you've always seen it?" Erin asked.

"Yeah. As far as I know, I'm the only one. I only told The Mama I could see Stain because she believed a lot of stuff. She called it a gift from the Fae and told me to keep it to myself. I haven't told anyone else until now."

"That's amazing!" There was a glint of something new in Erin's eyes. "What does it mean?"

"I think it means there's magic in the person. Or they've been touched by magic. I've seen the same Stain on a couple of different people now, and I think they've been enchanted by the same person."

Keeper cleared his throat before I could continue and finally lifted his hand off my arm. "The Mama was right to tell ya to keep it to yerself," he said. "'Twill be to yer advantage. The Mama's in service to the Fae. Has been for decades. She cares for all the illegitimate children and orphans that are shunned to the mortal realm. All those lads ya grew up with, they had at least one Fae parent who either wouldna claim 'em or had died. She kept your mind open to the idea of magic in the world. She did that for all the lads in case they came in touch with Faerie again. She wasn't Fae herself, but she accepted the Good Folk and their children without question. Contact with the Fae might have made her eccentric, but there's nothin' wrong with her believin.'"

Huh.

"That explains a lot," I said. "So, according to this, I was born sometime in the eighteenth century. And I was kidnapped by mortals?"

"With help, of course," Keeper said. "Someone took ya from our realm and handed ya over to them."

"Who would do that?"

"Someone opposed to the Alder King. Someone angry enough, or insane enough, to take the only male child he'd had in more than five hundered years and whisk him off to the humans."

I wasn't sure how I felt about a father who would let his own son die so that other people couldn't keep him.

As if reading my thoughts, Keeper continued, "Ya had to die, lad, to throw the enemy off their purpose. The King couldn't kill the mortals. That's against his own laws and how would he know if he got them all? But if the mortals and the Fae all think ya dead and gone, well, they don't keep looking for ya, do they?"

"I guess my father knew he could bring me back to life," I said, chagrined.

"Aye lad. Your father took your spirit and captured it with a most powerful magic. Your body was buried that night and then taken from the ground by the King as well, with no one the wiser. Then ya were made whole again and kept out of the world for two hundred years and then some. Until the King felt the danger was passed. He sent ya off into the mortal realm again where ya could grow unmolested until yer ten-thousand dawns. Now ya can take care of yerself and ya have yer powers."

There was a lot of weight to the information I was being given. A lot of responsibility. "So why doesn't everyone call me 'highness?' I notice they call me 'sir' instead."

"Aye, well. Yer father will have to declare ya his son official-like before that. He hasna done it yet, though we all know who ya are."

"Hmm," I thought for a long moment. "Still, great lengths have been taken on my behalf. A whole lot of trouble for one little Halfling."

"Well, the Fae have trouble conceiving offspring. There's many a reason for that. Part of it has to do with how few of us there are any more. There are very few full Eternals who are also fertile. And almost all of them are spoken for."

I could think of one fertile female who was an Eternal and unattached. But who would want her? It was probably my right to choose my own mate anyway, but I was suddenly grateful I hadn't been forced to marry Béil. Besides, she probably had all the partners she could trap at her disposal.

Keeper went on. "Another part of it is how few there be who believe in us. We were gods once. But the mortals and their science have killed us off and made our power dwindle as sure as any war might've done. Anyhow, we took to mating with mortals long ago as well as with each other. A Halfling is better than no child at all, and the fertility of the mortal stock gives us Eternals a better chance. The two of you, should ye conceive, could bring an ordinary mortal into the world. Most likely ye'll have Halflings same as yerselves. But there's a chance—a glorious and much-desired chance—that ye'll have a full Eternal child. If that happens, it will mean a great deal to us all. A great deal."

He looked back and forth between us with a soulful gaze that was both tender and intimidating.

"Uh, we're still working out the details of our relationship," I said.

"Ye best be," Keeper replied. "Long as ye know what's expected. What's being hoped for by so many."

I looked at Erin and tried to read her expression. She looked pensive but that was all I could sense.

The words "Thank you, Keeper," nearly crossed my lips before I remembered where I was and who I was talking to. Instead I said, "This is a great help."

"There's a good lad. Now we'll have a proper dinner. Ye stay right here." Keeper turned his attention to Midnight Dreary. "Fiach Dubh, quit thieving yer master's chips, ya sneaky creature. Fly off and tell the Alder King that I've had my talk with his boy and his bride now, and the hospitality of *Corrchnámhach* is theirs for as long as it's wanted."

Midnight Dreary launched herself skyward and flew up into the stars. She circled once and found a heading she liked. I watched her until she was out of view. "She can talk?" I asked. On my plate was a single potato chip. She hadn't eaten all of them, which I found quite polite.

"She'll remember everything said and done here, lad. The Alder King will know what he needs to know. Now sit ye here and I'll be right back."

Keeper took the book and other papers with him. I'd reached my capacity for surprises in a day. Perhaps he sensed that or perhaps he was just very careful with the things he was assigned to keep.

"Well, well," said a familiar voice. Another surprise after all.

"How are the. Lovebirds?"

"We're fine, Béil," Erin replied.

The cut of Béil's dress was as provocative as ever, but today it was all snakeskin leather with a short jacket and boots to match.

"Fine? Without cuddling? Or shy. Hand holding? Not even.

A blush. In the cheek?" She looked at me with a smirk. "It's been days. Since the. Wedding."

"You don't see me complaining," I said.

She laughed and the sound was oily and mean. "I don't see. You doing. Anything. Maybe I should. Cast a spell. On the two. Of you. Put you. In a. Romantic mood."

"Sadly, you can't use magic in here," Erin chided. "As you well know, this whole place is neutral ground and warded by Keeper and the Alder King himself."

"Sadly true. So, Got. Have you found. Any reason. For my help yet?"

"Not yet," I said. It was with some effort I kept my tone even. I placed my hands on top of the table and grasped them tightly. I wanted to slap her.

"Well. I can. Wait," she cooed. She leaned over and it was all I could do to sit still. Her breath burned into my ear. "For anything. You need."

I finally turned and gave her my best rolling-eyes-for-whatever expression.

She went back to torturing Erin. "Have you told. Him your. Secret yet? Is that why. You're afraid to. Take him to. Your bed?"

Erin didn't speak but she hunched her shoulders and shied away. Whatever she meant, Béil was making Erin very uncomfortable.

"Consider this," I said. "I can't call you for help if you don't go away."

That didn't make Béil angry exactly, but the laugh that erupted from her was rough.

"All right. Dear ones. I've had my. Fun for. Now."

She spun and strode away, her hips set to swinging more than was strictly necessary.

I said, "Snakeskin clothes. Isn't it wrong to wear your own species?"

Erin thought about that for a second. I knew she got it when she smiled—but the smile was decidedly weak.

"Look," I said. "Whatever secret she was referring to probably doesn't matter and if it does, you'll tell me when you're ready.

Until then, don't worry about it. I'm very understanding. Usually, I'm the one making true confessions."

Erin nodded. She slid her chair closer and slipped her arm through mine. She was nervous and in need of comfort at the same time.

She changed the subject. "I knew Keeper would have some answers. Are you glad we talked to him?"

"I am. I had no idea I was so old. I better get some life insurance before I keel over and leave you a destitute widow."

Erin laughed a little then and the tension in her shoulders melted a bit.

"When Keeper gets back, I have another question for him."

"It can wait, lad." Curse his supernatural ninja skills! Keeper had materialized out of nowhere again. He put two bowls of stew on the table, a full roasted chicken, a loaf of dark bread, and two mugs of something dark. He said, "Eat."

We did as he commanded.

The stew was made with root vegetables and wild game, Erin informed me. The chicken was infused with rosemary and the drink went perfectly with the black bread. It was all incredibly delicious. When I had finished, I was just the right amount of full. Satisfied but not uncomfortable. This place is amazing. Too bad it isn't on a map where I can find it again, in case I'm not able to go to Erin's portal first. Or drive to some janitor's closet in Key Largo.

I was just considering the possibility of dessert when Keeper appeared again. "Now, lad, let's have yer questions."

I got to it. "You know I'm a private detective? That's my work in the mortal realm."

"'Tis what I've been told."

"I've run across some circumstances that I've never seen before. And I'm wondering, is there any reason you might kill a man by stabbing him through the heart and then cutting open his abdomen but leaving all the organs intact?"

"Ya would if you're a right bloody bastard."

Well, yeah. "But no magical reason?"

"Well, there's a type of divination using entrails, but you need to take them out of the body. We put that kind of crude magic behind us long ago."

"Right. Okay. This may be an odd question."

"This is no place to be timid, lad."

"Very well. Is there any magic that requires diamonds?"

Keeper thought for a moment. "Ye can enchant diamonds for any of a hundred purposes. Same as most things."

"Would there be any advantage to using diamonds specifically?"

"Well, like other gems, they're pretty to wear. As foci, they're rather small, but they can transmit a lot of power because of their perceived value."

"Wait, how's that again?"

Keeper pulled up a chair from a neighboring table and sat on it backwards. He crossed his arms on the top of the backrest.

"Ya see, lad, almost everything we do, whether we be mortal or Eternal, is based on belief. When ya get up in the morning and go to work, ya do so because ya believe it will reward ya with pay, am I right?"

"Sure."

"Another kind of belief made gods out of us Eternals. As I told ya before, we have lost much of our power and influence in these realms when belief in us dwindled down."

"I remember."

"Another kind of belief relates to the value of things."

"Like diamonds?"

"Exactly, lad. There's really nothin' very special about a diamond. Every diamond were once just a melted slab of liquid carbon. Somewhere, deep in the womb of Mother Earth, it cooled and became a crystallized rock. Then it were found and cut and polished. It's extremely hard, of course. Only another diamond can cut a diamond. But they're rather common and unremarkable otherwise. Their price is high because the supply is tightly controlled. But the smartest thing the mortals did with them was tie them to a woman's heart. All that stuff about diamonds bein' a girl's best friend and expectin' a diamond as a weddin' ring—that only became common in the last century. Before that, a diamond were just a gemstone without color. Now, they have meanin' for people. Now they have value because people believe they have value. Now they can draw a lot of power from the universe. Now a diamond is powerful enough to conjure with."

Keeper was surprisingly knowledgeable about the mortal realm. I had to wonder how much time he spent away from *Corrchnámhach*.

I had another question. "What if you had a whole pile of diamonds? Could someone create something specific if they put them together?"

"Well, there was an ancient construct, just a rumor really, called a Jeweled Gate. But it was . . . *briste briosc broiscaí*!" Keeper looked suddenly stricken and he jumped up from his chair so fast, he knocked it over. He leveled a thick forefinger in my direction and said, "Ya have to tell me more about what ya got goin' on in that head. Soon as I get back."

He dashed off and he moved surprisingly well for a short, ancient guy. He could have been a running back for King Arthur.

I watched him go and then turned to Erin. "What did he say?" I asked.

She laughed. "It's as close to swearing as you're likely to hear from Keeper. The literal translation is 'broken brittle biscuits.'"

I laughed too. "For a man in the restaurant business, that would be worth cursing over."

Keeper returned. He had a book in his hands with a cover that was dark brownish-red. There were cobwebs in his hair, and it looked like he had tried to wipe off the layers of dust from the book with his bare hands, getting most of it on his shirt and pants.

"Why is the cover of the book that color?" I asked.

"Not all leather used for bookbindin' comes from cows, lad. Now tell me what led ya to ask about usin' diamonds for magic?"

I told him how I'd been hired to find the person who killed Barry Mallondyke. How I'd been shot at by Charles Mayer. How they both had controlling tattoos painted on their necks that meant there was a larger mystery going on. How I'd met a guy named Amad who was Caimiléir here, working for Milly Mallondyke who was also involved somehow with Charles Mayer. And how the Mallondykes had been in the diamond business for generations.

"Maybe there's a correlation, maybe there isn't," I confessed. "But I have a hunch and asking irrational questions might help find a connection. The life of Barry Mallondyke centered around diamonds and his new wife. And, considering the tattoos and the possible involvement of this Caimiléir, it's a possible next step. I'm trying to find out if the correlation is there."

"And ye know Caimiléir is involved?" Keeper asked.

"Fáidh found out," I replied.

Erin nodded. "In some way, he's connected to this."

Keeper stiffened and his face became solemnly grave.

"We canna speak any more of this here. Ye'll be comin' with me now," he said.

We rose immediately and followed Keeper away from the public room and the music and the light.

CHAPTER 18

Deamhan Realm

We followed Keeper down a flight of sturdy wooden stairs. It smelled like new potatoes and straw bales and fresh, fertile dirt. We passed a room with a dozen kinds of mushrooms growing. There were also rooms full of kegs labeled "Whiskey" and barrels of pickles. Along the other side was a wine cellar that must have been four square city blocks. Hardly a speck of dust anywhere.

At the end of a very lengthy hallway was a room with a heavy door, held together with metal straps. The door was twenty feet high and a foot thick and it looked like it could withstand a good-sized army wielding a battering ram. I guessed there was a reason for the reinforcement of the door and that made me a little nervous. The door made my head start to pound, and I confess I practically jumped over the threshold. I felt better as soon as put some distance between myself and the door.

"Iron bound?" I asked.

"Oh aye, lad. And warded to the teeth as well," Keeper confirmed.

On the inside, I could see that the door could be barred with a massive oak timber like a castle gate. There was a table in the middle of the room and a chest. Keeper put the book on the table then lifted up the bar and put it in place. The bar looked like it weighed a good five-hundred pounds, but Keeper handled it without a grunt.

I looked around the room and realized it had no corners. It was round. On the floor was a wide silver circle that sat just beneath the wall and followed the circumference of the room. For all I knew, there was a million dollars worth of silver inlaid there. Good luck digging it out and getting it past ninja Keeper.

Keeper knelt on the floor for a moment and murmured with his hand on the silver. An invisible wall closed us off. All the sound that had been filtering in through the walls and door suddenly stopped. The music and conversation and the sounds of hooves on the floor overhead, which had only been background noise, were suddenly conspicuous by their absence. By contrast all the sounds in the room were magnified. I could hear Keeper's hands rubbing together and the rustling of the fabric in Erin's dress as she moved around the room.

"So lad, what do ya suspect?"

"I honestly don't know if Caimiléir is up to something unsavory," I said.

"With that one, experience shows 'tis best to assume he's guilty until proven innocent. Because he's rarely innocent."

"Béil also told me that there's something terrible on the way, so she knows—or claims to know—something about it."

"Well, it will be a chore getting anything out of her," Keeper said, dismayed.

I protested, "But she has to tell the truth, right?"

Erin chimed in, "Getting her to tell the truth isn't a problem. Getting her to talk is the hard part. If she doesn't want to say something, we can't make her."

"She has told me more than once now that there's something evil on the way, and she's told me I'll need her help."

"Ah. That's her game," Keeper said. "She's a political beast, make no mistake."

"She's made a point of letting me know it. She's told me she wants to make sure she's there to get her share of the glory. Whenever whatever it is goes down."

Keeper clapped his hands to the side of his face and rubbed his gray whiskers. The minutes of silence passed strangely in our cocooned room while he thought. We could hear each other breathing and when the tang of the air made me sniff, it sounded too loud.

"Well, I can conclude one of two things," Keeper finally said. "Either she's foreseen the events about to take place by magic or she has some kind of stratagem that will put you in place when the time is right. You may not be able to avoid what's coming, lad, even if you try."

"I don't plan on avoiding anything," I said. "I'm stubborn that way."

"Well, make sure ye're prepared. Fáidh's a good woman and she'll help ya."

"She has already," I said.

Erin smiled at that. "Well, we're not done yet."

I pulled my silver dollar out of my pocket and opened the face. I held up the medallion so Keeper could see it.

Keeper took the medallion between his thick fingers and held it up to the light. "That's a fine piece of work," Keeper said. "'Tis a shield focus, isn't it?"

"It's already saved me from having my head bashed in." I said it with some pride. "Ouch!"

Erin had punched me in the shoulder. Hard. Her little fists had bony knuckles. "You didn't tell me about that," she said. She sounded peeved.

I shrugged. "Didn't have a chance yet. It just happened. Well, not long ago, depending on how time is passing in the mortal realm." I rubbed the spot where she had punched me. Keeper gave the medallion back. He was trying to hide a smile underneath his whiskers. I said, "I should recharge this. May I do it here?"

"No better place," he replied. "This room is one of the only spots in *Corrchnámhach* where magic is permitted."

The power came easily here and when I said "*Sciath*," the medallion hit full in about two seconds. "Wow," I said.

"Ya won't be tired from it either. Not here," Keeper said. He went to the chest nearby and opened it. He produced two silver chains with small silver pendants and gave one to me and one to Erin. The pendants were in the shapes of lions.

"These will bring ye back here to this very spot from anywhere in creation. They're amulets, which means ye don't have to use any will or word. Wear them whenever ye may be near danger. If ye need to escape, ye just break the pendant off the chain and ye'll be brought back to the safety of *Corrchnámhach*."

"They're beautiful," I said.

"So beautiful," Erin said at the same time.

Keeper chuckled. "Ye're a pair all right."

We put the chains on. Mine felt so light I hardly noticed it was there. It was hard to believe it was anything other than a frail accessory.

Keeper nodded, satisfied. "Now I've a few more things ye'll need to know and then I'll get ye on yer way."

He went back to the trunk and brought out a silver oval in a frame. The frame was intricately crafted and the silver at the center was polished so perfectly, it was like a mirror. Keeper held the mirror over the middle of the table and murmured a long phrase I didn't understand. A ring of blue light flashed around the perimeter of the mirror. When he let go, the mirror remained suspended over the table.

I had to admire that. "Fantastic," I said.

"'Tis more than a parlor trick," Keeper said. "There are dangers in what I'm about to show ye. The creatures we're about to visit would love nothing more than to come through and consume us, body and soul. To do that, they need something physical to hold onto. Even a small thing. With the mirror floating in the air, they'll have nothing to grasp. Be careful to keep yerselves apart from it. Any physical contact and ye could die. Or worse."

I found myself taking a step back. And another. The Mama didn't raise any morons.

Keeper started his spell. Like Erin had done with her Psychometry, he sang the spell. Keeper had a mellow baritone that you could feel in your chest as well as hear. The blue light began to condense on the silver surface of the mirror like fog on a window. The blue color of Fae power filled the disc. Droplets started to fall onto the table. Keeper sang on.

All at once, the blue light flared up and then vanished altogether. We beheld a blasted landscape through the mirror. It was like looking down from an airplane window. The viewport moved past a rust-colored field of slag where the sand had been turned to glass. Nothing moved except us.

Our view turned as we traveled across a barren flat. Keeper's song took on a questioning tone and I felt he was looking for something or someplace. We saw massive pillars of rock that climbed up into a blood-red sky. Smoke and ash drifted overhead in heavy, choking clouds that blocked any possible view of stars or moons. Fissures in the ground spewed fire, and while there was a sulfurous glow that lit the landscape in a sickly yellow hue, much of the light came from the abundant flames that erupted in spurts and gouts across the plain.

Keeper kept singing as he raised his hand to indicate a structure that was not created by nature. It was a stair-stepped triangular gate in the distance. As our viewport drew closer, I could see it was a pyramid shape. Three of the sides were constructed like a letter "A" with a triangular window cut out of the wall while the fourth side was almost completely open. It was about the size of a twenty-story building.

There was energy inside the apex of the structure but instead of blue, it was the orange-red color of magma. Shafts of power routinely jumped from the top of the pyramid to the ground. Finally, inscribed in stone, was a circle that covered the floor of the structure. Dozens of runes or other symbols I didn't recognize danced in shiny black shapes. Their appearance was similar to the shifting ink that had been on the napkin where I had drawn the tattoo design from Barry Mallondyke's neck.

What was this place?

Erin yelped and we both jumped back when a scaly claw burst out of the mirror into the room. It was a cheap ambush, like the cat that jumps out of a dark closet in a horror movie. My heart started pounding hard nonetheless, and I bit back a curse.

The claw had seven talons, sharpened like daggers. It felt the air around the mirror tentatively, sweeping as far as it could reach, seeking for something it could touch. It had a Stain, of sorts, but instead of floating over the skin, the pattern was under the skin. Like a living tattoo. I shuddered. Keeper, with ice-cold veins and nary a flinch, kept singing.

The claw withdrew and a face came to fill the empty space. A row of eyes beneath a spiky brow looked out at us and then a snout tested the air. A gravelly voice that rumbled like thunder made sounds I couldn't begin to interpret. The face pulled back until its entire visage was visible to us. The creature's glamour struck me with force. It reminded me of the Alder King's glamour, except instead of filling me with loyalty, it enveloped me in despair.

Surrender to me, was its message. There is no hope.

Keeper made a wave of his hand, a dismissive gesture, and stopped singing.

The viewport snapped shut and the power drained away. Keeper took hold of the silver mirror and laid it down on the table as its power faded. Erin and I looked at each other, then back at Keeper who turned to face us with a grim expression.

"Okay," I said. "I have some clean underwear back in my car, so I'm just going to go change and then you can tell us what that was all about."

Keeper gave half a smile and put his hands together. He cracked his knuckles, which sounded like walnuts breaking, and took a deep breath that he let out through his nose in a long, cleansing stream.

"The being you saw was a deamhan," he said. "We call that place *Tairseach-Cosantóir* or the Guardian Gate. The gate prevents the deamhans from entering our realm. This, in turn, prevents the deamhans from entering the mortal realm."

He held his hand out in front of him, opened flat with his palm facing down. "This is a crude representation, but you can think of the mortal realm as a plane of existence like this." Keeper then put his other hand underneath the first, at a ninety-degree angle. "Ya know that when ya enter the Faerie realm, it is a plane of existence that is perpendicular to the mortal. The two planes intersect and that's why ya can go back and forth between them."

Keeper moved the first hand to a position underneath, keeping it oriented the same direction. "This is the Deamhan realm. It is perpendicular to the Faerie realm. Again, the two realms intersect. But the Deamhan and mortal realms are parallel to one another.

They can't intersect."

"So you can go back and forth between the Faerie realm and the Deamhan realm. But why would you want to? Who would want to go to that hellish place?"

"No one, lad," Keeper replied. "But once in a great while, a new deamhan is created. The new deamhan is banished to that lower realm. The Guardian Gate is the only way in, and 'tis usually a one-way trip. The deamhan is put through the gate into the lower realm where it remains for eternity."

"Holy crap. Where do these new deamhans come from?"

Keeper put a heavy hand on my shoulder. "They're us, lad. Mortals and Eternals and Halflings alike. Them that have turned aside from all that is good. Deamhans make themselves from the cloth of Humankind and Fae. It's our job in this realm to find them and condemn them and make sure they never again return. That's our work, ya see? One purpose of our realm. And there are those who would take our work and make a ruin of it. On their way to becoming deamhans themselves, usually, or misled into falsehood by wicked people."

Keeper held his hands out again, flat, with his palms facing together but separated. "The mortal realm above and the Deamhan realm below never cross ways. Always near but never touching." He turned one hand ninety degrees. "Only by the Faerie realm is there a passage. That's why the Faerie realm has the task of keepin' the world safe."

He picked up the book he had brought and laid it on the table. As he thumbed through the pages, he continued, "Ya heard of summoning, I suppose?"

"Yes. Eternals have to be summoned to the mortal realm, but Halflings, like Fáidh and I, can go between realms whenever we like."

"Good. In a similar vein, 'tis possible for a deamhan to be summoned, but only to the Faerie realm because here is where the planes are joined. When a summoning is made, it creates a way between the Faerie realm and the Deamhan realm. The caster must also know the deamhan's name and he also has to make a sacrifice to do it. It's possible for the deamhan to later reach the mortal realm from the Eternal, but they lose much of their power in the doing of it."

Keeper stopped on a page. He jabbed a stout finger at a diagram there and then put his arms around both Erin and I. "I tell ye all this so ye can understand the importance of what this all might mean. This is the Jeweled Gate. The making of such a gate is likely impossible. Even less likely that it'll work. However, there could be lives lost even in the attempt. So trying to stop it, if this is indeed what's happening, would be well worth the effort."

Keeper nodded at the page. "That's a crude sketch at best. Done that way for a reason. There's no need to be giving anyone instructions for making one. But at least ye'll know it if ye see it."

The line drawing depicted a circle, of course, with an intricate pattern around its circumference and several lines crossing through at different angles. I recognized the design. It was a pentagram. There were indications of other components but the overall symbol was unmistakable.

"How long would it take to build one?"

"Oh, lad. Would likely take a dedicated mage many months. Years even. 'Tis a highly-complex design and there are several layers to it. Each layer has to be completed in order before the next layer can be added upon it."

Erin was smart enough to ask the important question: "What does a Jeweled Gate do?"

Keeper sighed. "The most horrifying thing possible, I reckon. It opens a passage directly between the Deamhan realm and the mortal. Worse than a summoning and passing by the Faerie realm, it would set loose deamhans in all their strength upon Humankind."

CHAPTER 19

Corporation

I'd never experienced a deamhan's power before, but I knew I never wanted to feel that way again.

"If Caimiléir is building a Jeweled Gate, we have to stop him," I said. "The thought of deamhans entering unhindered into the world—our world—has me on edge like you wouldn't believe."

"Me too," Erin said softly.

We had departed *Corrchnámhach* with an admonition from Keeper to watch out for each other. Sounded good to me.

Outside, we walked shoulder-to-shoulder through the titanic oak forest. We had a lot to think about so we walked in silence. My ego was still feeling bruised because Erin wasn't sure about us as a couple. I hoped that the quiet wasn't uncomfortable or awkward for her. I didn't mind it. I needed to think.

The portal we had used to come here was still standing at the edge of the path.

"How long do these portals stay open?" I asked.

"Isn't your brain exploding?" Erin replied. "Are you sure you can handle more new information?"

"You're right. I'll have to throw out some old information to make room for more new information. What was your name again?"

"Ha ha."

"So, how do the gates work? What if someone went back and closed the gate? Would we be stranded? Or what if someone was stalking you and followed you here and then killed you and went back through. They'd never find your body."

"And people say I'm morbid."

"Legitimate questions."

"All right. There are different gates or portals. Ours employs a spell that is safer than most. Magically, portals have only one side. They originally face toward you and when you go through, they turn inside-out and face the other way."

"And turn ninety degrees," I said. "Quite the gymnastics."

"Right. But don't think of it in terms of geometry or physics. Magic is magic." I nodded and Erin went on. "Right now, at my house, there is no portal because it's facing here. And a portal imprints on you at the moment you use it. Basically, only we can see it because we came through together. We could take other people back through the gate with us though."

"Over the river? Maybe through the woods?"

"Shut up!" Erin rolled her eyes but smiled too. "And the portal remains tethered to you as long as you are in the same realm. If you leave the realm, the portal closes itself. A gate, on the other hand, is a door that stands open both ways until it runs out of power or is closed by breaking its pattern. Got it?"

"Got it. I'm still getting used to the idea that I'm an eighteenth-century prince. The more I can learn, the more real it becomes for me."

"I understand. I'm sure I'd feel the same way. We both address problems by gathering all the information we can, don't we? Then we decide what to do."

"Probably led to our choice of careers."

We went back through the portal together, arriving in the storage room. Erin picked up the insert and the light faded. Then she put the pattern back on the shelf.

"How long were we gone?" I asked.

"A few minutes," Erin said. She pointed to a clock on the wall.

"Cool. So when do I get an awesome name for the other realm? You're Erin here and Fáidh there. I'm just Got. Or Luck."

"If you like, you could go by 'Prionsa.' That means 'Prince,'" Erin offered.

I wrinkled up my nose. "For a second I thought you were going to say 'Princess.' Don't think I'm ready for a tiara."

Erin changed her clothes again and I drove her back to the

station in my car. We listened to Bon Jovi, "Livin' on a Prayer."

She hopped out but before she shut the door, I asked her if she had any workout clothes.

"Yeah, I keep a bag here at work," she replied.

"Will you help me with some more magic lessons tonight?"

"Absolutely, helpless."

I didn't even blink. "Great, helpmeet. My business partner runs a gym called the Iron Foundry." I gave her the address. "Meet me there and we'll see what kind of progress we can make. Six o'clock."

Erin smiled, "I'll be there. Prionsa."

Still not growing on me.

Back in my office again, at last.

Everything was set up as it had been before, including my laptop. The only problem was an uncomfortable urge to look out the new window to make sure nobody was walking around with a gun. I was going to have to get some curtains.

I tried to stay focused on my work. I connected the thumb drive to the laptop and copied all the files I'd stolen from the Starlight Spa. Going through them was a laborious process, but what else can you do?

Finding Charles Mayer was easy. I knew the day he'd gone to the spa thanks to our last conversation. He'd gotten the massage with the coupon, but he'd also paid for a wrinkle-reducing facial treatment. Male vanity, alive and well at $136.00 an hour.

Finding Barry Mallondyke proved more difficult. It should have been within a day or so of his death. The tattoo was temporary, after all. I had to assume it would only be effective while it was fresh, like Mayer's. The spa was busy enough, for a seedy dump. I had to wonder if some of the entries were code for less-than-savory services. And the list of clients included an abundance of "guest visitors" paying cash. Ultimately, Barry could have been any of the anonymous clients over the few days prior to his death.

Because the spa appeared to be suitably busy, it looked like they were keeping track of their income. The goods and services might be questionable but it appeared, at first blush, that there wasn't a lot of money going under the table.

I moved on to other files. I found I had records for their payroll. None of the names were ones I recognized. There were receipts for equipment like massage tables and laser treatment machines which didn't interest me. Then I found a spreadsheet for the regular monthly expenses and things got interesting. There were the expected monthly utilities: electric, gas, garbage, water. And a lease payment to a property management company. I searched online and found a website and social media accounts. Most interesting was the notation on their website that they were a subsidiary. Another quick search and I found the parent company. The CEO was none other than one Lonnie MacPherson.

Sweet. I bet myself a shiny nickel that the Lonnie MacPherson would turn out to be the father of Milly MacPherson Mallondyke.

Another day, another lead.

Two more minutes online and I got to keep my nickel.

I found a photograph, about three years-old, with Lonnie MacPherson, his wife, and their only daughter. The tag on the photo said "Milly Graduates from Brown University" and showed a slightly younger version of my client.

Boo plus yah.

Milly's dad held the lease for the Starlight Spa.

Amad was at the spa when Charles Mayer had been given a magical tattoo.

The tattoo on Mayer was similar to the tattoo on Mallondyke.

Ergo: cahoots. Milly's dad was connected to Amad the Merciless.

I doubled up and bet myself a shiny dime that at least one of the two either killed Barry Mallondyke or knew who had.

The analytical part of me tried to remember if Milly's dad had an alibi for the night of the murder, and I couldn't remember if the subject had even come up. I'd have to check it out, but the magical part of me insisted it didn't really matter. If you had a buddy that could open a portal for you to the Behindbeyond, you could be halfway around the world and it wouldn't matter. You could establish an alibi, travel anywhere in a matter of moments to commit a crime, and travel back before anyone missed you.

The thought was chilling. The conventional wisdom in law enforcement was that there's no such thing as a perfect murder. I was starting to peel back the lid on just how wrong that idea could be.

The biggest question was still why.

Unless I found another reason, the mutilation of the body was done out of spite. I wasn't a father, and history was replete with dads who wanted to murder their sons-in-law, but I looked at the picture of Lonnie with his arm around his daughter and just couldn't give it any weight. Milly had been so happy in her marriage, and Barry had been a good provider. What was there to hate?

I leaned back and rubbed my eyes with the heels of my hands, making little stars wash across the view inside my eyelids. There had to be more to this.

I searched for all the holdings linked to Lonnie MacPherson's business and subsidiaries. He had a dozen small business locations that he was leasing out, a few larger office buildings—but none in Miami Beach—and even a couple of apartment buildings. Diversified real estate. Those were the commercial properties. I searched for industrial properties and, holy mostaccioli, he had about twenty. Most were south, starting at Wynwood and going as far down as Leisure City. A spread of more than twenty-five miles.

Well, I had my work cut out for me tomorrow.

A split second later, I realized tomorrow was Sunday. I had an appointment to meet Chief Cuevas and Milly's father at the Palmetto Golf Course in the morning to talk about my progress. I had precious few things I could talk about.

How much should I disclose? MacPherson might know that Nat and I had forced our way into the Starlight Spa. He'd be worried about what I'd found out. I'd have to skirt around that incident. Until I had more information—like actual evidence—I couldn't tell a potential suspect too much. Until I had proof, I wouldn't want to let him know he was even on my radar.

I started to wonder if MacPherson was into diamonds. It could all come down to how MacPherson was using his ample resources to help Amad acquire diamonds because they were building a Jeweled Gate. There was a lot of supposition in that. Dangerous waters.

Still, I got excited and searched some more into MacPherson's background. I quickly found that he didn't own any jewelry stores that I could find. None of the commercial buildings he owned had jewelry stores as tenants either. I wasn't sure how one invested in diamonds. It wasn't traded like gold or silver or stocks or bonds.

Crap.

I needed a walk. I went downstairs and bought a late lunch and a soda from Qui-Gon. He had a group of thirty Koreans jammed into the cafe; otherwise, he would have chatted non-stop about everything under the sun. I went back up to my office and brooded over pork.

Where would I go for a source of diamonds? I asked. Why, I would go to Barry Mallondyke, that's where, I answered. He would have been a good source. So why kill the diamond goose?

Other places to get diamonds would be jewelry stores themselves. And pawn shops.

I logged in to the police database and ran a search for articles on diamond robberies.

There were reports on diamonds that had inexplicably gone missing from shops. Reports on people detained or accused of stealing diamonds but released due to lack of evidence. Once, a suspect had been arrested with about fifty diamonds on him, but the case never went to the district attorney because the stones vanished before they were filed into evidence. Internal Affairs had gotten involved on that one. I also found reports of diamonds being packaged for shipping but never making it to their destination. Diamonds missing from safe deposit boxes.

Diamonds stolen during house burglaries. Overall, it looked like there were a hundred ways diamonds had been stolen or gone missing. There didn't appear to be a real pattern though. No particular type of story predominated.

Then I found another article that caught my attention. A recent report stating that jewel thefts—diamonds in particular—had actually declined over the past two years.

Poodle monkeys.

I was out of lunch and out of soda and out of ideas.

I went for a drive.

It took only minutes to find the nearest industrial property owned by MacPherson, in the Wynwood neighborhood. I found the property at the back of a dead-end street. It looked like it wasn't earning MacPherson a lot of revenue. At one time it had housed a distributor for imported goods of some kind. There was a chain link fence around the property, but the gate wasn't even locked. The windows were boarded, but a couple of the boards had fallen off. The building was long but shallow, and it didn't take a detective to see that the building hadn't been used for anything in a while except as shelter for rats and the occasional vagrant.

MacPherson's next property was about four miles away. It turned out to be filled with workers prepping flower bundles for distribution. I parked up the block and scouted the place through binoculars, but didn't see anyone I recognized. There was absolutely no security and loads of chaos. Nobody in their right mind would keep anything more valuable than a ten-dollar watch in that place.

It was almost time to meet Erin at the Iron Foundry, so the day was looking up again. I checked the list of properties and there was another one a few blocks away. Worth a shot.

The third place was tucked behind a solid vinyl fence. It had a gate that had to be opened by a keypad, and it looked like the buildings were compartmentalized into small units for storage. Each unit had a different number on its door and most of them had locks. Finding out what might be stored here would be daunting—but I made a mental note to keep this spot on the list for further investigation.

In the meantime, I had a date with my wife and my best friend.

CHAPTER 20

Of Wards and Fire

Erin screamed as two strong arms caught her from behind, grabbing her and lifting her off the ground. She struggled and kicked and threw her head back against her assailant's face, aiming for his nose. She kicked between his legs while he had her in the air. The attacker started to put her back on the ground and she brought her heel down on his knee, scraped her foot down his shin and stomped on his instep.

"That's good," I said. "Make a lot of noise and go for the vulnerable points."

Nat gave her a half-smile and a nod. Eloquent as any attacker could be. He came over and whispered, "I like her. She's tough."

High praise from the man. There was so much I wanted to tell Nat. How this woman was my wife in a faraway land that was really just around the corner. How she and I were second cousins to an ancient race with magical powers. How something scary was on its way and we had to stop it, and he might end up in the middle without a clue about any of it. I just nodded. He clapped me on the shoulder and left the workout room.

I said, "Remember you can also go after the eyes and throat. Especially if you're face-to-face. Those bony knuckles of yours can deal some damage."

Erin flipped her hair out of her face. Her eyes were bright and there was a light sheen of sweat on her face. She had never had self-defense training and Nat had been willing to help.

"You also have the element of surprise on your side. A bad guy won't expect you to fight because you're . . ."

"Weak?" she interjected.

"Beautiful," I said immediately. That earned me half a smile.

Only half? I forged ahead, "When it comes to the real thing, don't pull any kicks or punches. Give them all you got. You might only get one shot."

"Tell me why we're doing this again?" Erin asked.

"Remember what we learned from Return of the Jedi?"

"No. What?"

"We learned you can be the most powerful sorcerer in the galaxy, but if someone grabs you and throws you down an energy shaft, you die like everybody else."

Erin rolled her eyes at me.

"So, you teach me to use magic and I teach you to fight. It seems to me that if someone needs a few seconds to prepare a spell, then you have a few seconds to take them out with a punch or a kick. They can't zap you if they're unconscious. Okay?"

"Zap me?"

"What? Isn't there a zap spell? I was hoping you could teach me a zap spell." I did my best to sound incredibly disappointed.

Erin crossed her arms and screwed her mouth up in a sour-pickle expression. I knew when to surrender.

"I think we've had enough," I said. "That was a good session. You did great. And I can tell you don't like to sweat." I threw her a towel and she patted her face. She was tired but she still looked perfect. How did she do that?

"Women don't sweat," she informed me. "They glow. Or glisten. At worst, perspire." She sounded more than just tired.

"Was this a bad idea?" I asked.

"Nope," she replied. "I like anything that will help me kick your butt if you get out of line. And anyway, you called me beautiful." There was that smile. The wicked one I liked so much. She threw the towel back at my face and headed out of the workout room. "Give me twenty minutes and we'll go," she said.

I watched her leave the room and wished the next twenty minutes were already over.

I had a theory. "So are you going to teach me about wards?"

We were home again and Max was making dinner. Erin had gotten cleaned up at the gym and emerged looking amazing. She had followed me in her own vehicle, which I found out was a Porsche convertible. When I turned down my sound system in my car, I could hear Belinda Carlisle cranked up in hers.

Now the two of us were on the back lawn. The sun was down and if the vampires were out, they were hopefully very far away.

"Wards are useful," she replied. "They are placed on locations or objects more than people. You can put a ward on a person, but that can interfere with their shields, and they will have a hard time casting other spells. Wards keep spells or even entities from getting in. Or getting out. You can cast magic inside one or near one if it's designed to let you. You can't walk through one if it's designed to prevent you. Wards are more powerful if they're specific. You can cast a general protection ward but it will be pretty weak. On the other hand, if you cast a ward to keep a specific person out, it will be almost impossible to break."

"Good to know," I replied. "So could Caimiléir put a ward on himself to hide his identity, for example?"

"Absolutely. If the Alder King sent Madrasceartán to this realm to find him, she'd have a hard time sensing him if he's warded to appear human."

"As a side effect, he wouldn't show any Stain. His Stain is invisible to me because his power is hidden. But I can see the Stain on people he has touched. I meant to tell Keeper about that. I'm sure Caimiléir's magic marked Mr. Mayer, and before that Milly and her husband."

Erin thought about it. "That answers a lot of questions."

"Caimiléir tried to kill me through Mayer." Saying it out loud made it all too real.

"Now I'm sure he attacked you during the Quickening."

It was impressive and frightening that he could do that. He must have been nearby, but he hadn't even had his hand on my forehead.

Erin went on like she'd remembered something she wanted

to tell me earlier. "Your entire property here is warded like crazy. Did you know?"

I looked around. I didn't see anything.

"Are you sure?"

"I can feel it when I get close. Max and Sandretta are responsible for keeping this place safe, and they're doing a great job. Thankfully, they didn't set any wards against me."

"What happens if you encounter a ward that's against you?"

"Usually, you can't move through it or cast through it. It can be painful to touch. Even lethal. You might not be able to see through it. Or hear sounds. Or you may only be able to see and hear what the caster wants. Really sophisticated wards will let some people cast through it and others not. Those can take hours to set up."

The king's liondog didn't have any problems getting in my house. "Sounds complicated."

"It can be. For now, you just need to learn some spells that are offensive."

"Oh, I'm offensive enough already. Ask anybody."

Erin's laugh sounded deep in her throat, and I noticed how nice her teeth were in the evening light. Yeah. That's what every guy looks for. A woman with nice evening teeth.

"So what do you suggest?" I asked.

"Well, one of the four elements we haven't tested is Fire. We can see if you have an aptitude for that," she replied.

"Are you sure? I might burn the place down."

"I doubt it. We'll stay outside just in case."

"What do I do?"

Erin took my hand and held it in both of hers with my palm up. Her touch alone was magical.

"First, just let a drop of power into your palm. Let it bloom and then cut it off. Try making the smallest speck of power you can and don't feed it."

I concentrated but having her hands on mine was distracting. Finally, a blue glow emerged and pooled in the middle of my palm. Once I saw it shining, I stopped the flow.

"Too much," Erin said. "Take it back." The power seeped back into my hand, reabsorbed by my interior reservoir.

"Try again. This time anticipate it and cut it off right at the point it appears."

I tried. The next pool of blue was smaller.

"Still too much," she urged. "Try again."

I gradually developed a feel for controlling the power until I could make a miniscule droplet pop up into my hand consistently.

"Good! Very good!" Erin was getting excited. "Now I have absolutely zero ability for this, so I can't show you what it's supposed to look like, but I have seen mages put on a fire symphony. They created the most amazing displays of controlled flame you can imagine. Everything from bouncing little fireballs to a whole flaming whirlwind. Almost anything is possible."

"Okay," I said. "Let's give it a shot."

Erin still held my hand. "As you release just a speck of power, say the word, '*Tine*,'" she said.

She was looking at my hand so eagerly now. I was just hoping it would work.

I popped up a droplet of power and said, "*Tine*."

The erupting ball of flame just about took my head off. Erin's reflexes were faster, but we both fell back instinctively and landed on the grass as the fireball went straight up into the air like a flare, only ten times bigger.

Erin was sitting on her butt with both hands covering her mouth. She was trying to keep the giggles from overwhelming her and she was losing. I was trying to recover from the shock and wondering if I had any eyebrows left. I looked at my hands. Not a mark on them. Not even a sensation of heat. Erin gave in to the laughter and fell back on the grass, looking up at the sky and pointing.

"It's not that funny," I said.

"That was a little one," she replied. "The look on your face! Your eyes were like grapefruits! I'm gonna die!"

Yes, she was going to die. I was going to kill her. But the more she laughed, the funnier it got, and I started to chuckle.

"I take it it's not supposed to be that powerful?"

She rolled back and forth on the grass. "No!"

Overhead, about fifty feet up, the fireball was still going.

"Whoa! We have to make it stop!" I said. "Someone's going to call the cops!"

"9-1-1!" Erin yelled.

She was making me laugh too, but the ball of fire overhead worried me.

"Hey! If the cops show up we'll be answering questions all night. How do we make it stop?"

Erin sat up and wiped the tears from her eyes. Or tried to. She was still laughing, barely under control.

"Foom!" she said and lost it again.

I could take a joke but . . . "Seriously," I said. I was sort of laughing and sort of ticked.

Erin got to her feet and came over to me and held out her hand. I was reluctant to accept but she looked at me with toffee-colored puppy eyes. Darn puppy eyes. I gave her my hand and she dragged me down near the river. She squatted near the edge and pointed at a space about twelve inches in front of her. "See it?" she said. "C'mon. You're supposed to have enhanced sight."

I bent over and tried to see. "I just don't know what I'm looking for," I said.

Erin let go of my hand. She closed her eyes and I could feel her drawing power from inside her. As she spread her hands, I saw a trickle of water falling from her fingertips. She puckered up her pretty lips and blew some air at the water. The droplets floated out, slower than they should have under normal circumstances. Suddenly, they hit a barrier and shot out in a million different directions. They traced a lattice of fine lines, like a web spun by a million spiders determined to illustrate the word baroque. On crack. There was a basic form to it, but it was amplified and augmented by curlicues and fans and little zig-zags. The lines sparkled, iridescent.

"Oh that," I said.

"That's the ward around the perimeter of your land,"

Erin said.

"Pretty," I said, looking into her eyes. "And that ward thing isn't bad looking either."

"Flirt," she said.

"So the ward around the land is doing something besides catching water drops?"

"I talked to Max, to ask him about the wards. He said the wards will keep magic inside, which is why the fireball you made stopped rising. It's safe to practice outside that way. He also said the wards are always set so that anybody looking this way will just see a house and yard. Nothing special. They can't see us or anything suspicious at all. It's all hidden. You could be doing anything out here and nobody would be the wiser."

"So that's why the neighbor lady refuses to be impressed by my barbecuing skills," I said. "I was starting to get a complex."

We walked back to the patch of ground where we'd been and lay back on the grass together. Erin scooted over and put her head on my shoulder, which confused me. This is what a woman does when she's not sure about a relationship? I pushed the thought away and watched the ball of flame roll and flash.

"I'll get you back for this you know," I said.

"You will?"

"Probably. When you least expect it."

"Okay."

"How long do you think that fireball will last?"

"Like any flame, it will end once it runs out of fuel and oxygen. There are lots of counterspells. I could douse it if you really want me to, water does that, but I'm kind of interested to see how long it will burn. It'll be good to get a feel for the potency of your power."

"Potency," I repeated. "Oh, yeah."

"Like everything else in life, some people have greater capacity for power or better quality. Potency. Or adaptability for using power for different things. We're just finding out what qualities you have."

The fireball continued to spread flickering orange light across the yard.

"Isn't this supposed to be harder to do?" I asked.

"It's new to your conscious mind, but magic has been a part of you since birth. Some children can cast spells before they can walk. Your body has always had potential for doing this stuff. You just didn't have the power or knowledge to use it before."

"So. Fire. Pretty hot."

"Ha ha. Fire is the element most useful for offensive spell casting. You can be deadly with other kinds of spells, but fire is pretty much a universal weapon. I wouldn't want to battle you—especially after you've gained some experience."

Finally, there was a little pop! The fireball snuffed itself out.

"Try again?" Erin said.

"Don't think my eyebrows could handle it."

She giggled. "I should tell you, if you use an object to focus the spell, it can help you direct its effects and enhance them. Silver would be especially good. Like a silver pen or a letter opener. And if you feed the flame with power while you chant the word, you can really make an impressive attack. Some longer phrases will give the fire added life. It's like singing a song. You can make your voice loud or soft, but you can also make the notes high or low. You can shape the sound to be constricted or open or rough or smooth. It's like that. And the fire will react and behave differently as you bend it to your will. Some mages spend centuries perfecting their craft. That goes for all spellcasting. On the other hand, sometimes a huge flaming explosion is all you need to get the job done."

I made no reply. I could see the stars coming out above us, everything in order, and I was content to just listen to her talk.

"Can I make an observation?" Erin's voice was hesitant. "It's not a criticism. I just notice you kind of fly by the seat of your pants. What we're doing is necessary practice. But we'll get to the point where we'll have to make a plan. We can't get ready for anything and everything. We'll have to get ready for something specific. You'll tell me when you find things out, right? I feel completely inadequate for the task as it is. So I need you to help me help you."

She rolled on her side and propped her head on her hand so she could look at me. I looked back. I looked at her eyes and then down at her lips and then back to her eyes. I think she was as surprised as I was that we were this close. Then the moment passed.

"Sure," I said.

CHAPTER 21

Evidence

Max tried to feed us a late dinner, but Erin said she wasn't hungry and she needed to get up to do autopsies starting at five in the morning. I told her she worked too hard, and she touched my cheek before she left.

I didn't want Max to feel bad, so I ate a plate of salmon and homemade scones. The meal wasn't heavy—just right—and thoroughly delicious. I told Max and Sandretta that because we were in the mortal realm, I was making the choice to thank them and let them know I appreciated the things they did for me and especially for keeping the house safe.

If I hadn't been thinking about my meeting in the morning at the golf course, I would have slept better. The conversation that hadn't happened yet persisted and repeated in my dreams. Cuevas and MacPherson circled around me so I could never address them together. Each time the words were different. I struggled to find a safe path through a verbal minefield that was impossible to navigate. Each time, the conversation ended up with the whole golf course on fire.

I got up earlier than I would have liked, but there was no help for it after rough sleep. I showered and dressed in the best approximation I had for golf course wear. Some khaki slacks and a pale blue polo shirt and wingtip shoes.

It was only six o'clock when I drove over to the police station. I was supposed to meet Cuevas and MacPherson at ten o'clock, so I had almost four hours to kill.

Downstairs, the evidence room was being manned by a former jarhead—a Marine—who didn't like me because I wasn't sixty years old with a buzz cut and facing retirement in five long years.

"Good morning," I said.

"What's it to ya?" he replied.

I had my computer in a bag along with other stuff. I fished around in the bag for a second and placed a list of robbery reports filed by jewelry stores between two and five years ago on the desk. I put my private investigator I.D. on top. "I'd like to see if there are any surveillance videos for these incidents please."

"There aren't."

I took a moment to nod and point at the papers.

"You want to take a second to look?"

"Not really."

I nodded again. I took my phone out of my pocket and scrolled through my contacts. I turned the phone around and put it on top of the papers.

"Do you know Chief Cuevas's cell phone number?"

"Nope."

"Here it is. Chief Cuevas is probably eating breakfast now. He and I have a meeting at ten o'clock at the Palmetto Golf Club. Sometime between now and then, I'm sure he can come down here and sign out the evidence boxes that he asked me to review. Could mean he misses his tee time but I know he's pretty patient when it comes to his day off." I put the phone down next to his hand. "Push 'call' if you want to."

Jarhead looked at me and shifted his jaw back and forth like he was chewing ten-penny nails. I gave him the most sincere and shucky-darn expression I could manage. "Look, I'm just glad Cuevas is giving me some work, you know. He has me doing a favor for his golf buddy. Lonnie MacPherson. Check if you want. I think Cuevas knows it's a dead end, but it means a lot to his friend. Cuevas doesn't want to waste the department's resources on a wild goose chase, so it's up to me to make a good show."

Jarhead finished chewing. He picked the sheets of paper up and started back to the vault.

I was glad he didn't push the button on my phone. He would have called my bank, which is closed on Sunday. Could have been an embarrassing moment when the call didn't go to Cuevas. Underneath my breath, I said, "Poker night's on Tuesday."

Six minutes later, Jarhead came back with a couple of boxes and my sheets. "Lemme know if you don't find what you're looking for in these. There's a couple more in the back."

"Hey, I appreciate your help," I said as I signed for the boxes. "This is really great of you."

Stupe.

I hauled the boxes to an empty desk and laid everything out. The first box had a layer of dust on the lid. I pulled a file out of the box at random. Jewelry store. Three years ago. There was a pair of DVDs in the file. Wish I'd brought some popcorn.

The DVDs played out on my computer screen in accelerated fashion. The security system at the jewelry store shot a frame every three seconds and the people moved around like they were in a Charlie Chaplin movie.

I wasn't analyzing every frame to catch somebody in the act. Mostly, I was just looking for people I recognized. While the DVD played, I skimmed the written report. The owner of the store stated that two necklaces and two rings were found missing after the store was closed on the day in question. From the corner of my eye, I could see when new people came into frame. Once or twice I paused the video or rewound to make sure I got a good look at a face.

Near the end of the report, there was a follow up. The owner of the jewelry shop had one employee who stopped showing up for work. The investigating officer noted that the theft was likely committed by the missing employee and the case was closed. I scanned through the rest of the security DVD anyway, which only took another few minutes on fast forward, pausing to examine new faces.

If nothing else, investigations required patience. I refused to be daunted. I reviewed six DVDs for more than two hours and failed to turn up anyone familiar. Yet I still maintained a full lack of daunt.

I wasn't sure yet what I was going to tell Cuevas and

MacPherson. It was possible I wouldn't have a lot to say. I could almost see myself just walking up to MacPherson and punching him in the face and then walking away. It would be an accurate summary of what I suspected about him, his relationship with Amad, and what his association may have done to ruin his daughter's life and end Barry Mallondyke.

Disc number seven had surprises.

The timestamp on the video was about eleven in the morning almost two years ago. The written report indicated that the store had lost a handful of loose diamonds that day. About fifty stones worth tens of thousands of dollars. Right at five minutes after the hour, Milly MacPherson—before she married—came into the store. She entered with a man. Milly was clearly framed in the security camera's field of view. She wore a business suit and silk blouse with oddly-matched accessories and carried an aluminum briefcase. Totally Milly. The man was either more aware of the cameras or just preferred to stay away from center stage and let Milly run the show. I couldn't see his face.

Milly was greeted by a man with closely-trimmed silver hair and a pinstriped suit. They shook hands and walked out of frame. About twenty minutes went by. A customer came in and was served by a tall, well-dressed clerk. Then a couple came in, holding hands, and was fawned over by a woman in a flowing blouse with pearls around her neck. Finally, Milly and her escort came back out, hands were shaken, and they left.

As they moved toward the door, I saw a glimmer. And a reflection.

The display cases had tilted glass fronts, angled so that the shelves with the jewelry could be arranged in stair-step fashion to let customers easily browse the items on every shelf. There was one place where the shelf behind the class was covered in black velvet and no items were laid out on the display. The man's face passed right across the spot, the overhead lights illuminating his features and for about two seconds. I rewound the DVD and went forward again, frame by frame. I repeated the process again and paused. The footage was in color, which made it easier to identify the red triangle of hair under his lower lip. It was Amad.

I watched the sequence again as they left the store. I didn't catch Amad red-handed. Blue-handed? Not exactly. But for a moment, I was sure, his hand was blue. To most, it might have looked like a glint of light hitting the camera lens, as when the front door was opened, sending morning sun streaking off all the glass in the room and catching the lens with a sparkling shaft that just happened to overlap Amad's hand. To me, it was clear: Amad was using magic.

As I drove to the golf course, I tried to figure out what kind of spell Amad had been using.

The morning had started out sunny, but now the sky was growing overcast and it could turn into a bad day for golfing—or having a conversation. I didn't have enough information to really know what Amad had been doing. All I'd seen was a flash of his power. I had no idea where Amad had directed that spell or what he had done. Maybe it had been a spell that let him steal fifty diamonds. That's what I suspected. I also felt that Milly didn't have anything to do with the theft. Not consciously. She was being used. Exactly how her father factored into the whole thing was hard to say.

But I thought of a way to find out.

I parked at the Palmetto golf course and sauntered up to the entrance. I let the guy at the desk know I was here as a guest of Chief Cuevas and Mister MacPherson. He directed me to the practice greens. I spotted the two men through the windows, wearing polyester and superiority in equal measure.

I took a quick, deep breath before going out. It was precisely ten o'clock.

"Good morning," I said.

"He's on time at least," MacPherson muttered. He didn't offer his hand and I didn't offer mine. I couldn't see any Stain on him. That scared me. I was confident MacPherson was working with

Amad. If he wasn't Stained, it suggested that MacPherson wasn't being controlled. He was helping Amad because he wanted to.

Cuevas got to the point. "Have you found anything worthwhile, Luck? Or have you just been wasting money?"

To confront MacPherson would just shut him down. As a businessman, he was accustomed to all kinds of pressure. Confront a guy like this and all you get is a letter from his attorney. Because he was asking me to report to him directly, he was a control freak. More than anything, he would be looking for ways he could turn the situation to his own advantage. Without knowing the degree of his involvement, I had to assume he would want me to fail so he could go to his daughter, pat her on the head, and tell her she had every reason to be concerned, but there was no sense spending money on a dead end. But his daughter was my client and I had to do the best job I could for her. Even if it pitted me against her father. MacPherson was trying to inject himself into the equation, and I didn't have a problem with that because I could make him work for me. I'd just have to come at him from a different angle.

The best thing to do was give the truth—or my version of it.

"I don't think your daughter is in immediate danger, sir," I began. That ought to get his attention. "But I'm concerned about certain . . . activities . . . that are going on around her."

"Activities? What is that supposed to mean?"

"As you know, your daughter worked for her husband at his company and is still employed there in an advisory capacity."

"It's that old goat Mallondyke, isn't it? Her father-in-law. He's keeping Milly around trying to get her into bed."

"Well, I don't know anything about that, sir," I said.

MacPherson turned to Cuevas and said, "I thought this guy was a hot-shot investigator. It's obvious to anybody who takes two seconds to look at this situation that there's something going on there. Mallondyke probably killed his own son so he could have a shot at my Milly."

Actually, the implication that Mallondyke the Third killed his son was completely implausible. From what I had found in research, Barry Mallondyke had learned fidelity and devotion from his father, who was, by my guess, several years younger than MacPherson himself. MacPherson's comment was interesting though. People will often project their own motivations onto somebody else without thinking. I was willing to bet MacPherson was sampling the interns at his own place of business.

I looked MacPherson in the eye and said, "Actually, my focus has been on Milly's associate. Goes by the name of Amad. Has white hair and a red patch on his chin. Do you know him, Mr. MacPherson?"

It took a second too long for Lonnie to cough up a lie. He blinked too often as he overdid the indignation and worked himself into a bluster. "Know who? Some guy who works with Milly? Why would I know him? Or anybody else at her office? What are you trying to say?"

"Nothing, sir. I just thought since they spend a lot of time together, possibly outside work, maybe she'd brought him around and you'd seen him. As a businessman, you must be a good judge of character, and I just wanted to know what you thought about him. But if you haven't met him . . ." I trailed off and let the compliment sink in.

MacPherson took the bait. "Well, if I'd met this . . . person . . . I certainly would have an opinion. I can tell the character of an individual right off. You're right about that."

Interesting that MacPherson wouldn't say Amad's name and just referred to him as "this person."

"Well, I have reason to believe this Amad person may be using your daughter."

"How so?"

I turned to Cuevas, speaking mostly to him. "Sir, I'll need a little more time to make some connections with what I've found already and what I think is happening." This would scare MacPherson a little and, at the same time, make him feel there was no clear-cut conclusion. "I'm sure, Chief, you will want to get to the bottom of this situation and I hope you won't mind my checking further into the evidence collected regarding these incidents."

From the corner of my eye, I could see MacPherson was growing nervous, but he hid it pretty well. I looked back at him and he gave me a squint and said, "What incidents?"

"Well, as I mentioned, I think Milly is being used. It's possible that Amad is going with her to various jewelry stores and—this is still just conjecture, mind you—stealing gemstones from the stores."

Both men were silent. This was their little party. I was just playing my role, knowing they had to stick with it.

I continued, "Like I said, I haven't made any real connections yet. I just have a set of circumstances that may lead to something concrete if I keep on it."

MacPherson recovered his voice. He was determined to hang on to his line of deflection. He stepped close and leaned in with his face only inches away from mine. From there I could smell his early-morning whiskey as he said, "You still need to look a little closer at her father-in-law. I don't object to you looking into other issues, but you're going to find there's something going on with that creep, I guarantee."

I'm glad he didn't object to these "other issues" because I wasn't going to stop looking anyway. I guarantee. "Appreciate the lead, sir. I'm surprised nobody mentioned it to me before. But I'll devote appropriate time to following up on that possibility."

"See that you do," MacPherson emphasized each word singly. Apparently, that was supposed to be intimidating. MacPherson shot a look at the gray sky and backed away. "What do you think, Juan? Can we at least get nine holes before it rains?" MacPherson walked off in the direction of the first tee without waiting for an answer, dismissing me.

Cuevas didn't say anything to me, but he glowered in my general direction as he followed MacPherson. He hadn't told me to stop, so if anyone asked about me looking at the evidence boxes, he'd have to say I had permission.

I suspected I'd also pulled the pin on a particular hand grenade and it would likely take a few hours for it to go off.

From the clubhouse window, I watched Cuevas and MacPherson climb into a golf cart and motor down to the first tee. I had my binoculars, so I could make sure they got started. MacPherson drove first and his ball sailed down the fairway a couple hundred yards. Cuevas went next. He took about ten warm-up swings and still sliced into the trees.

Yep. I had at least two hours to wait, unless it started raining.

CHAPTER 22

Boy in the Renaissance Shirt

I went to the men's room and then had some lunch in the clubhouse. After about an hour, I figured I'd stayed past my welcome. I went out to my car. The skies hadn't parted but the air was heavy and expectant. I sat in my car and pretended to take calls on my cell phone. I kept my eyes on the exits in my rearview mirror. Finally, after another hour, the weather broke.

It was almost twenty minutes later when I saw MacPherson and Cuevas coming out. They hurried to their separate vehicles, loading their clubs in a well-practiced routine. Cuevas took off first while MacPherson sat in his car for a few minutes. I wasn't able to really see what he was doing and the rain was covering the windows with streaks. Finally, he pulled out of his parking space and headed for the road. I followed right behind.

He turned south, and I was glad he was a careful driver. The rain pounded down even harder and visibility quickly became an issue. He wound his way south and west. I concentrated on keeping my quarry in sight. A van, moving faster than it should, nearly sideswiped me and I had to brake to avoid a collision. Oblivious, MacPherson kept going and cruised through a yellow light. I was forced to stop—traffic was heavy and unpredictable and it would have been too risky to run the light.

"Crap," I said. The rain was coming down in sheets now. The light changed, and I crawled through the intersection. I couldn't see MacPherson's car any more. I could barely see down the block. The taillights and headlights and lights from all the signs created muzzy stripes of color everywhere like an impressionist painting. I went for about a mile, changing lanes and scanning traffic, but

I decided I wasn't going to catch him. There was a convenience store on the next corner and I pulled into the parking lot and got out my list of MacPherson's properties. There were two in this area. He might be going to one of them. Unless, of course, I was entirely wrong and MacPherson had just gone to his office. Or a restaurant. Or maybe Build-a-Bear.

The nearest property on my list was a lot for parking storage containers. They were the same size as the ones loaded a few miles away on transoceanic transport ships, but the sides were painted with the name of a business that would bring a container to your residence so it could be loaded with whatever you wanted to store. Then the container would be brought here until it was needed again.

I drove around the block but didn't see MacPherson's car anywhere.

I hurried to the next location as the rain pounded harder.

I found an apartment building at the next address. There was nothing special about the building. Middle-range apartments. Probably eight units per floor. I didn't feel very optimistic about finding MacPherson here until I spotted his car in the rear lot. I picked a spot at the end of a row and parked. What I could see through the binoculars and the rain wasn't very impressive. The dark day had triggered the exterior lights, but they were few in number and not very bright. Minimal landscaping. No security on the rear entry.

Some of the apartments had lights burning inside them. Four of the floors were illuminated. But not the top floor.

"B-I-N-G-O," I spelled.

Great. Why does my brain do stuff like that? Now I'll have that song stuck in my head for the rest of the day.

I hustled from my car to the door, hoping that anybody who noticed would think I was one of the tenants. The rain in Florida was usually warm compared to other places I'd been, but this rain came down cold. Once inside the entryway, walking towards the hall, I brushed beads of water off my shoulders and when I looked up I was shocked to a standstill.

I saw a little boy, about ten years-old. He was standing in the dead center of the hallway. There was no rain on his shirt so it looked like he lived here. Then I noticed that his shirt was an old-fashioned linen shirt with laces at the chest. He had a circlet Stain of white.

I stayed where I was and said, "Hey. How's it going?" I kept my voice low.

The boy didn't move but he looked straight at me with eyes that were somehow familiar.

"Do you know me? Do you know who I am?" I asked.

The boy didn't respond.

"I think you might have been at my office. Right? Did you go to my office and leave a bullet casing? It was a little brass cylinder about this long?" I held the tips of my fingers apart to show him the length. "Was that you? Do you remember that?"

Again, nothing.

I took a step towards the boy. He immediately held up his hand in the universal sign for Stop.

I stopped.

He pointed up at the ceiling next and shook his head slowly from side to side.

"Do you know about the bad people up there?" I asked.

He nodded.

"You don't want me to go up there?"

He shook his head again.

"Well, buddy, I kind of have to. That's my job." I took another step towards him and he took a step back this time. Again he pointed up and shook his head.

"Okay," I said. "I promise I'll be careful. I'm just going to see if I can sneak in and listen to what they're saying. Can you stay right here? I need to talk to you, all right? But first I need to go upstairs." I took another step and the boy just vanished. There was no sound, no flash, no evidence to indicate that it had been something other than a mirage. Or maybe I was just losing my mind.

I tried to shake off the feeling that maybe I should follow the boy's advice. He had been helpful before, assuming it was the same kid. It had to be the same kid, right?

The building had an elevator, but I favored taking the stairs. Stairs didn't make noise and they didn't stop functioning in the middle of a rainstorm. The rainstorm was making noise to cover any creaks as well. As I climbed the first set of stairs, there was a flash and a boom as lightning struck. Not far away either. I wondered if the words "omen" and "ominous" were derived from the same root or not. Heh. That brain of mine.

There were no doors at the landings, so it wasn't hard to quietly scamper up the stairs. I didn't see anyone on the way up. I got more cautious at the fourth floor. The flight of stairs going up to the top was cordoned off with wide yellow tape that had "Under Construction" printed on it. I ducked under the tape and proceeded around the first half of the flight to get a peek at the top. Plywood had been nailed into place to cover the top of the stairs, but there was a makeshift entry covered in sheets of plastic. "Do Not Enter" had been spray-painted on the plywood. Through the plastic sheeting, I could see a shadow moving. Another lightning strike threw an exquisitely bright light across the plastic.

I heard a voice and knew my hand grenade at the golf course had paid off. It was MacPherson.

"I'm telling you, he knows things," MacPherson was saying. "He knows you and Milly were at jewelry stores where diamonds were stolen."

The voice that responded was both melodious and harsh. "He knows nothing," he said. I'd only heard Amad say maybe half a dozen words before, but I had to believe it was the same guy. He went on, "Of course I've been in jewelry stores. Part of my assigned duties. And, of course, some of those stores experienced losses. All stores do. Connecting the two events is an entirely different matter."

"He seemed pretty sure."

"Look, the one time we were searched, they didn't find anything, remember? Let Luck find that report and he'll give it up. Besides, I haven't stepped inside a jewelry store for two years.

It's a dead end."

"I still think you should take him out. As a precaution."

Jerk, I thought. First time I could remember overhearing someone planning my demise.

"We tried and it didn't work out. We can't try again. He's off limits."

"I don't understand why," said MacPherson. He sounded petulant. Childish.

"Trust me. It would cause more problems to kill him than it would solve . . . hold on."

I felt a sudden tingle as if I'd just been covered in a spider web and then the web was electrified.

"He followed you," said the voice who was Amad.

"What? He couldn't have!" MacPherson's protest was heated.

The plastic covering the plywood slid to the side.

"Would you care to join us, Mr. Luck?"

I stood there near the top of the stairs. I looked up. Off to the side. Behind me.

"Mr. Luck?" Amad repeated.

"I was hoping for some more lightning right then, you know?" I said. "The timing would have been perfect. You throw the plastic open like that, and say, 'Would you care to join us, Mr. Luck' and there should be lightning."

Amad looked at me like I was standing on the steps of the short bus.

I made a shooing motion at him. "Go back and try again. Maybe there will be lightning this time."

Amad brought his other hand through the plastic and I saw he had a gun. That's when I remembered I'd left my gun in the car.

I'm an idiot.

I showed my hands and followed Amad through the plastic. Amad had his serpent-headed cane hooked over his arm so he could hold the plastic with one hand and the gun with the other. I'd forgotten he walked with a limp.

The top floor of MacPherson's building was almost completely open. The elevator was in the middle and there were support columns but there weren't any walls. It looked like it was being renovated to make it a single living space. The view wasn't bad.

MacPherson watched me come in. "Hey!" I said, "Are you thinking about renting here too? Nice place."

MacPherson fixed me with a glare that was cold and sharp. "Cuevas told me you were worthless. And a screw-up. He said you wouldn't find anything and I'd be able to cut you loose. Looks like he was wrong."

"You're welcome?" I said it like a question.

MacPherson looked at Amad. "You're going to kill him now, right? Blow his brains out?" MacPherson was sure quick to violence. And he always volunteered other people to do the dirty work.

"No." Amad shook his head. "We don't really need to kill him anyway. In two days it will all be done. By the time he finds out what's really going on, it will be too late." The transformation was incredible. The Amad I'd met before had been halt and servile. This Amad was confident and strong and didn't really need the cane to walk.

I didn't want to mention what Keeper had revealed about the Jeweled Gate. Some pretense of ignorance would be prudent at this point. Let the bad guys think they still had their ace in the hole. Maybe provoke them a little. "So, Amad. Or should I say Camel Hair?"

MacPherson jumped to his boss's defense. "His name among the Fae is Caimiléir."

Nice. Even put the emphasis on the last syllable.

"A man's name is important," MacPherson stabbed the air in front of my face with a stubby finger. "You don't make fun of a man's name if you know what's good for you."

I thought about that for half a second. "You're absolutely right, MacPerson. My apologies. Hey! MacPerson! That fits you! Because you're cheap and you're made of questionable by-products!"

The stubby finger started to tremble. I ignored it. And the man attached to it.

"So, Camel Hair, how did you get the diamonds out of the stores?" I asked.

Amad smiled. "We don't have to kill him. But we don't have to let him go undamaged either. Perhaps a little pain will be a good reminder that he should avoid meddling in the affairs of others."

There was movement in the corner and Tiny the Tongan stepped out of the shadows. Then there was a flash and a boom, casting the big man in stark relief for the briefest of moments.

"See!" I said pointing at the Tongan. "That's a dramatic entrance!"

Actually, there was a lot of dramatic going on outside. It was really dark now, and the lightning was hitting every minute or so. I wish I had my gun. Maybe they'd let me go outside and grab it if I promised to come back.

Amad waved his hand and I felt the room change. He'd thrown up a ward of some kind. It wasn't as elegant as Max's ward and I could see the pattern across the exit from where I stood. Amad saw me noticing. "Just to make sure you don't leave prematurely," he explained. "And you seem to have a knack for problem-solving. So let's see how you are at multitasking." Amad rested his hand on the back of the Tongan's neck. There was a tattoo there. And I swear I saw the Tongan's Stain twitch. Was his tattoo temporary? Like Mayer's? Could I erase it somehow and set him free?

"Break both of Mr. Luck's legs," Amad said. "Then the ward will dissipate and you can go." His voice was soft and oily and commanding. Even without a tattoo on the back of my neck, I felt a compulsion to do whatever he asked.

I wasn't a big fan of pain, and two broken legs would hurt like hell. I moved toward the elevator while I could still walk. He had placed a ward there too. It looked like the ward was barring the windows as well. I remembered that I had Keeper's amulet. If I pulled the pendant, it would take me back to the safe room in *Corrchnámhach*.

Amad saw me thinking about an exit. I don't know if he could tell I was wearing Keeper's chain and pendant. He was prescient if not, saying, "If you are looking for a way out, there isn't one. I was very careful to craft just the right ward to keep you here for a while. There is no exit for you, Mr. Luck, magical or otherwise. Only through pain will you be free." Amad raised his cane to his brow and tipped it back toward me. A gesture of farewell.

Then he dropped the cane to the ground and the thing sprang to life.

The cane turned into a yard-long serpent that slithered across the floor, cracking and shedding its skin of wood. The cane was solid silver inside and its serpent's head was suddenly real.

"How Biblical of you," I said.

As the serpent crawled, it grew. I backed away as it came in my direction. It snapped and hissed at me. In moments, it had grown to an alarming size: as thick as my leg and twenty feet long.

I saw a pair of meaty hands coming at me and I ducked out of the way. The Tongan was already on the job.

"Can't you wait until the floor show is over?" I said. For the moment, I could easily outrun the big man. His hand was still bandaged from breaking against my shield. I kept him in my view and tried to see what was happening with the snake.

The snake slithered over to the feet of Amad and his minion, MacPherson. Once there, it curled itself into a circle, biting its own tail. Amad bent down and touched the serpent. Blue light erupted from his hand and cracked around the circumference. Sunlight exploded from the circle and I could see daffodils and butterflies in the other realm.

MacPherson gave me a quick look, filled with ego, condescension, and good, old-fashioned smarm. He tipped into the circle and was gone.

"Until we meet again, Mr. Luck." Amad said.

Then Amad fell through the gate as well. Gone.

I looked back to the Tongan and said, "Wow. That was cool."

CHAPTER 23

Battleground

The silver snake unbit itself, which broke the circle. The blue light flared out and the gate was closed. No escaping that way. I suspected I could stay away from the Tongan for a while. I didn't know how long he'd keep going. Maybe until he starved to death. When you're single-mindedly in thrall, you might keep going until your purpose is fulfilled. I knew from experience I'd have a hard time choking him out by myself. I could stop him from coming after me if I broke his legs before he broke mine, but that was about as likely as me chopping down a tree with my shoe.

I hadn't counted on the snake having another purpose.

Maybe it was part of the spell that had been cast on it, or maybe it was just bored now that its master was gone, but the thing came after me. The Tongan I could outrun—he didn't have me cornered this time around—but the snake was faster than I was. I caught it slithering toward me, hissing again, and I backed away. I could keep the elevator between myself and the snake, but sooner or later the snake would get me or the Tongan would. Then they'd both have their way with me.

I pictured myself alive, but with various puncture wounds from snake fangs, broken ribs from being squeezed in its coils, and all that on top of the broken legs I'd been promised.

Sucks to be me.

I looked around for a weapon. Some rebar maybe. A two-by-four. Or a stray sub-machine gun. For a construction site, the room was practically spotless. No weapons. Cripes. My heart flipped into my stomach. I was more comfortable with something physical to wield. My only option was magic. If only I knew what the heck I was doing.

Tiny the Tongan came doggedly in my direction, hands outstretched. I couldn't see the snake. It apparently stopped when it couldn't see me. The darkness of the day was useful then. But the lightning was more frequent. There was another flash, and before the sound of thunder rolled in, the snake spotted me. It was closer than I'd thought. It struck. My shield held up. The snake bounced away.

Dodging wasn't going to be a valid long-term solution.

My breathing was coming harder already. I thought about how ridiculous it must look to have me running around with a mind-controlled Tongan and a silver snake in pursuit. It would be funny if it weren't so pathetic.

I held out my hand and searched for a droplet of power. The Tongan took another swipe at me. Where had he come from? The power was hard to summon with so many distractions. To use Erin's analogy, I was trying to sneeze on purpose, but I was trying to do it with a giant and a snake chasing me. The wind and rain pounded the building. The Tongan's heavy steps were a drumbeat in contrast to the uneven, chaotic roll of the weather. I desperately tried to find my power. I had to be more worried about the snake because it was so fast and potentially lethal. What if it bit me in the neck? I still couldn't forget about the Tongan.

Another lightning strike cranked up the brightness. I saw the snake and it saw me. I stood my ground and focused.

"*TINE*!" I cried. Power surfaced as I cast the spell. The fireball that spat out of my hand was twice as large as the one I'd cast yesterday. It streaked across the room, spreading flame across the floor. It hit the ward on the far side of the room and splashed across the windows, blooming out into a wall of fire. It looked awesome and was worse than useless. I'd missed the snake completely but now I'd provided it with a constant source of light to find me.

The snake spotted me instantly. I backed away and tried to get around the elevator.

And ran straight into the Tongan. Stupid.

He got his arms around me, locking his good hand around his

other wrist. Then he squeezed. If he was planning on competing with the snake, he had a good start. Luckily, he was sweating, so he was having a hard time holding on. I started squirming to keep him from crushing my chest. Unluckily, he was sweating, so my back was now covered with his sweat.

The snake came straight for me.

I ducked as best I could and shouted, "*TINE*!"

The fireball flared up from my hands and the snake came through it headfirst. It hit my shield again and bounced off. The snake fell to the ground and slithered away. Some of the fire clung to it, like napalm. The fire didn't seem to be affecting the snake much at all. "Not hot enough," I told myself.

The fire was climbing to spread out across the ceiling. My casting was erratic. I'd need to be free to do it right. The Tongan was only vulnerable in one spot. I kicked my foot backwards and up into his crotch as hard as I could. I heard a grunt and thrashed as hard as I could. I got free.

Sorry Tiny.

I ran across the room. I'd noticed how the snake was so large and thick it needed to move away from me before it could turn and attack. Too close and it couldn't get an effective strike. So, crazy as it sounds, I ran toward it. The serpent saw me heading its way as it turned and instead of coming at me, it slithered sideways. I changed course as well and sprinted to get at its head. I thrust both hands in front of me, drawing a thread of power into each hand.

I chanted, "*Tine, Tine, Tine*!" Twin ribbons of narrow fire streamed out, hitting the snake in the head.

Holy crap. It was working.

"*Tine, Tine, Tine*!"

The snake rolled onto its back. I hit it with fire in its face. It opened its jaws, and I poured fire down its throat. The force of my power kept the snake from biting my hands.

The fire changed from orange to white as I willed the gouts, "Be hotter!"

The snake shuddered. Something inside it broke. It trembled, and I felt the heat coming from inside its body. Suddenly, it vomited a hot stream of silver.

I rolled to the side and brought my hands to bear again. "*Tine! Tine! Tine*!" White-hot fire shot from the center of my being through my hands, and the upper segment of the snake finally dissolved into a puddle of slag. The mass of the snake began to shrink and at the same time spread across the floor. The concrete beneath it was dissolving, decomposing. On the ceiling, where the serpent's convulsion of silver had struck, bits of concrete were starting to fall.

I half-heard, half-felt a heavy tread. I turned and dodged the Tongan as his huge arms tried to catch me again. Relentless. I dashed along what remained of the body of the snake. It was still melting, and incredible heat was coming off it in waves all along its length. I saw the tail twitch, and I jumped out of the way as eight feet of silver writhed and spasmed. The tail whipped through the air, visibly hot, and struck the Tongan in the face.

No.

The tail wrapped itself around the Tongan's neck. The skin of the snake's tail buckled and cracked under the pressure and silver magma leaked from its core. The air rippled with the release of heat. Then the Tongan's shirt caught. Flames danced as the snake quivered, the last of its energy being spent in the throes of death. The Tongan staggered under the weight and heat.

I looked around, the room bathed in flickering light, desperately searching for a fire extinguisher or a bucket of water or anything to stop the man from burning.

The Tongan stopped staggering, every muscle in his body taut.

I didn't want to watch what was happening. The Tongan was shaking. Fire covered him now from his head to his knees. The tattoo on the back of his neck had burned away, or the pain of the fire was enough to bring him back to his senses, because he moaned and then he screamed. It was the only real sound I'd ever heard him make, and it was deep and full of agony.

I was helpless to do anything for him.

The big man's knees buckled, sending him crashing to the

floor. Liquid silver splashed out and started chewing through the concrete. The screaming stopped.

I was inclined to let MacPherson's building burn all the way to the ground, but there were innocent people below so I had to do something. It wouldn't be right to let the building fall around them. More innocent people would die.

The superheated silver thrown up by the snake to the ceiling had continued to dissolve the concrete. A flash of lightning startled me and reminded me of the rain.

I softly said, "*Tine*," and directed a ball of flame at the weakened spot. The fire spread and chewed through more material. I repeated it several times until I punched through the roof of the building. Rain came in and hissed on the hot metal. Steam rose in little puffs that gathered into broader clouds. I widened the hole with more shots of fire. I was glad for the distraction. As long as I had another task to occupy my attention, I wouldn't have to look at what remained on the floor.

Once that section of the room was quenched of flames, I moved on to the area by the windows. I chewed through more ceiling with my fire. With practice, I was able to shoot flames that were hot enough to eat through the concrete but not so hot that they wouldn't be quickly extinguished by the rain when it came through. It took about ten minutes for me to completely douse the flames.

Without the light, it was easier to note the deep gray day outside. It was still midafternoon, but the sun was obscured and might as well have set already. It was surprisingly quiet outside. No more lightning. No more thunder. Just steady rain. Traffic was subdued. I was shocked to find there were no sirens sounding. No fire trucks were approaching although someone surely must have seen the fires burning inside the building. Perhaps the ward prevented anyone from seeing.

The dusky weight of the day outside perfectly matched my mood.

There was tragedy here. Enough for the sky to weep.

Soon, I knew, my sadness would turn to anger. There had been no need for the Tongan to die. In my mind, I could picture myself going to MacPherson's home with Nat and confronting him, fire in hand. Surprise him. Blow that smirk off his face. Figuratively. Maybe literally. It would be a stupid thing to do, and I'd never follow through on such a petty urge. Probably.

I kept the dark shape on the floor at the edge of my vision. Aware of it. Not looking directly at it. I didn't even check to see if his Stain was gone. I forced myself to think of the Tongan alive and stoic, as I'd seen him at the spa. Wearing that stupid Hello Kitty t-shirt. I'd force myself to bring that image of the man to the front of my thoughts anytime another image tried to take the stage. I'd force it.

There was rain on my face. It was soothing.

On the floor, splashes of silver, dappled with rain, cooled in the dark of the storm. The Tongan's hand, the one that wasn't broken, rested near a piece of silver. I focused on the metal, refusing to look any closer at his body. Refusing to feed my memory any more ugly images. The silver was shaped somewhat like a dagger with a wavy blade. A ceremonial knife. I touched it and it felt warm. I picked it up and held it. In it I could see my reflection as a darker shadow in a world of shadows.

I put the piece of silver in my pocket.

I stood again, turned away from the scene gradually being cleansed, and looked up. I looked closely at the edges of the ceiling. There was no shimmering ward covering the roof. Or maybe it had just expired. I couldn't see the ward along the wall any longer either.

The silver weighed especially heavy as I walked out of the building to my car.

CHAPTER 24

Invitation

"It was amazing. A portal and assault-snake in one creature. I had no idea how . . . awesome and . . . elegant magic could be. Of course, Amad is a complete psychopath. We have to stop him. And we only have two days. I'm just praying it's two days in this realm. Time goes slower here."

Erin was at my house and I was describing what had happened. It was almost midnight. I'd spent most of the evening brooding. I'd had a few drinks, and then I'd sat at the piano and played some Bartok and then Mahler's "Piano Quartet in A Minor," which was incomplete without the string parts, but that was okay because I felt incomplete myself. Then I'd had more to drink and then I'd called Erin.

She'd come over and we watched the late night news. There was a story about the fire and the reporter noted that the roof had collapsed in an "Act of God" and the rain had doused the fire, which had saved the building from total destruction. The building was evacuated briefly but the fire marshal had let everyone back inside after an hour. The reporter mentioned a single fatality but the identity of the victim was not released pending notification of the family.

After that, Erin listened to me. And listened some more.

"I called from a pay phone about the fire," I said. "The building could have been unsafe."

Erin replied, "You did the right thing."

"I don't know what they'll make of what they find. I guarantee they've never seen a crime scene like that before."

"A few centuries of contact between Eternals and mortals has taught us how adaptable human beings can be. They're very good at finding a rational explanation for almost anything. And if they find something they can't explain, they ignore it."

I laughed and the sound was bitter to my ears. "You're probably right."

Erin caught the emotion behind the words and put a hand on my shoulder. "You couldn't have saved him. If you had done anything else, you would have died too. I'd have been devastated."

"You would?"

Maybe she hadn't intended on revealing so much or maybe she just wanted to give me a hard time. "Of course. And Chief Cuevas would have been crying his eyes out."

Snort.

I laid the piece of silver on the table. "This is from Amad's cane. Part of the silver snake. I melted it. Foom. Call 9-1-1."

Erin looked at it like she expected it to bite her. There was a tightness around her eyes. "Is it possible to find out where Amad plans to construct the Jeweled Gate?" I asked. "Can you use this to find him?"

Erin took a dozen heartbeats to answer. "Maybe," she said. "Getting a reading from a common object is easy. Getting a reading from a magical object is more complicated . . ."

She trailed off and I filled in the blank. "And dangerous?"

Erin nodded. "It's like a bottle of liquid with a cork in it. It looks like water. But it could be vodka. It could be poison. Could be flammable. To find out, you pull the cork. You still may not know what it is, so you drink it. Once you drink it, you'll find out what it is all right, but if it's lethal, it's too late. Common objects are water for sure. Not harmful. Magical objects, on the other hand, could have all kinds of hidden properties."

I looked at my reflection in the metal and then I put the silver piece back in my pocket. "Not worth the risk then. We'll find out what we need to know some other way."

"We don't have much time. Keeper might be able to tell us more," Erin offered.

"That's all right. We'll think about it tomorrow. If Amad meant two days in the Eternal realm, it would be over already." I looked at the tightness around Erin's eyes and realized it was fatigue. "You're dead on your feet. You got up too early, and I kept you too late."

"I'll be all right," she said. She yawned.

Sandretta stood in the hallway. She already knew what I had in mind.

"You're staying here tonight." I said it with as much finality in it as I could manage.

"No, I'm . . ."

"Too tired to drive. You had some wine. The guest bedroom is in its own part of the house. You'll have the whole place to yourself."

"I can't . . ."

"You can't say no. Sandretta's ready to show you to your room."

Erin looked at Sandretta who raised a hand in gentle invitation.

Just then, Max appeared at the entry on the other side of the room. "Mr. Luck, there's someone outside asking for you."

"Outside?"

"At the end of the drive. I tried to coax him inside, but he won't come any closer. He has a letter. Addressed to the both of you."

Curious. "Who is he?"

"I don't know."

I had to wonder if it was Amad or MacPherson. Or an attorney. Or a cop.

"I think he is afraid of the wards," Max concluded.

Max didn't seem too concerned. Erin and I walked out to the driveway together.

It wasn't an attorney. Unless you can get a law degree by the age of ten.

It was my little friend in the Renaissance shirt.

I knelt in front of him. "Hello. What is your name?"

The boy held out an envelope almost the size of a pizza box. In a sickeningly ornate script, the envelope said:

Their Highnesses
Prince Goethe Luck
And
Princess Fáidh Bean O'Connell Luck

Whoever sent it was guilty of using royal titles without a license.

"Thank you," Erin said. She held out her hand and let the boy place the envelope across her palm. She put her other hand on top of the envelope so it wouldn't fall on the ground. The boy took a step back.

"Can you speak?" I asked.

The boy didn't say anything. He saluted. I'm pretty sure he was issuing a salute to sarcasm, not me. Then he disappeared. Blink. Gone.

Erin looked at me. "That's the boy you told me about? At your office and then at the apartment building today?"

I nodded. "Same kid. Keeps disappearing like that. You haven't seen him before, have you? In the Behindbeyond?"

Erin was examining the envelope but she heard me. "No. I haven't seen him anywhere."

We went back in the house and looked at the envelope some more. "Anybody think it's dangerous?"

"Don't think so," Erin said.

"No," Max said.

Sandretta shrugged.

I opened it. Inside was an invitation.

Dearest Goethe and Fáidh,
You are cordially invited to a dinner in your honor.
At Ail Bán Dearg upon the rise of the new moon.
Burn at the hearth to accept.
Love,
Béil

"Well, I will just have to check my social calendar," I said. "Oh shoot, I'm busy that night. What night is it again?"

Erin sighed. "It's tomorrow night. We have to go."

"We do?"

"Yes. It's the Fae equivalent of a wedding reception."

The surprises kept on coming. "Really?"

"Yes. New marriages are celebrated at the new moon in the Behindbeyond. It's traditional for the couples' closest family member or friend to have a dinner for them. People bring gifts. Leave their good wishes. Lots of blessings for, um, fertility."

"I'm good with all that except Béil being our closest friend."

"She's taken it upon herself. It's a chance for her to claim some honor. It's politics. It will make her look good." Erin touched my shoulder and led me back to the house. "I need to do a better job of keeping you informed. There's a lot to know, and I forget this is all new to you. You've had to adapt so quickly."

"You're doing fine," I said. "Do you know where this is?"

She read the invitation again. "*Ail Bán Dearg.*" It sounded pretty when she said it out loud. "That will be where Béil lives."

"Not lives. Roosts." That made Erin laugh. "Have you been there?"

"Why would I go there?"

"Good point. Betcha my raven can find it for us."

Back in the house, Max had a modest fire going in the fireplace.

We decided to drop the invitation in the fire together. We knelt on the floor. We each held a side and we counted to three and let go. The paper fell into the flames and was consumed instantly. Curlicues of flame and smoke rearranged themselves in the air above the fire and created a vaporous face. Béil. The face smiled and winked, then the fire flared out while the smoke rose up the flue and disappeared.

"Guess we're committed," I said. "Or should be."

Erin's wan smile let me know she was really exhausted now.

"C'mon, let Sandretta take you to your room."

Erin got up from the floor. She put one arm across her stomach and one hand on her hip. And she started chewing her lower lip, which was something I hadn't seen her do before. Not that I could remember.

"You okay?" I asked.

She glanced up at the ceiling for a moment. "I need to tell you something," she replied.

I stood up and reached out to her. "I'm sure it can wait," I said.

"No. I want to tell you now." She seemed ready to change her mind but at the same time didn't want to.

"Okay."

She retrieved her purse and leaned back on the table as she looked through its compartments. She produced a piece of paper, folded in thirds. She held it for a few seconds and stared at it. Then she extended the paper to me.

"Whatever this is," I said, taking the paper. "It doesn't matter to me."

She pressed her lips together and nodded.

I opened the paper and gave it a cursory review.

"Petition for presumption of death?"

Erin took a deep breath and let it out gradually. "I was married," she said. Simple. Direct.

"I'm guessing you haven't seen him for a while."

"Five and a half years now."

"What happened?"

"I don't know. The state police found his car down in the Everglades. He didn't tell anyone he was going there. Including me. No signs of foul play. The car was just sitting there. Keys in the ignition. There wasn't a note of any kind. There was an empty bottle of cranberry juice and a half-eaten sandwich sitting on the passenger seat. Nothing else. No wallet. No clothes. No body."

"I'm sorry." I hope she could tell I meant it.

"I was worried an alligator got him. Then I was mad and I hoped an alligator got him. For the last couple of years, I've tried to be . . . indifferent. But he's in my thoughts every day."

"Of course he is. You loved him. You'll always love him."

Erin looked the floor and nodded a few times.

"What was his name?"

"Blake."

"Did he have magic?"

Erin was still looking at the floor.

"None. He didn't have any idea about magic. He was just a sweet guy I met at a hotel while I was at medical conference. We went out for a year. Had the big church wedding. He traveled a lot. Commercial pilot. When he was gone, I spent time in the Behindbeyond, and when he was home it was just blissfully, boringly mortal."

"Sounds nice."

"It was." She looked up at me with her eyes all shot with green and dew.

"You want me to find him?" I asked. "I'm very good at that."

She laughed but it was more of a bitter-sounding burst. "See?" she said. "You're too sweet. And just plain dumb." She looked at the tips of her fingers, which were twining themselves together. "I don't want you to find him. It's time to move on."

She stepped in close and put her arms around me. I put my arms around her.

"I wanted to tell you before you found out from someone else. My marriage to Blake wouldn't mean anything to the Alder King. A mortal marriage is not recognized in the other realm. The Alder King only cares about the Behindbeyond. But my marriage meant something to me. Before I can even consider a serious relationship, I need to close that chapter of my life. Okay?"

"Okay."

"There will be a hearing. Ten days from now. I want you to come with me."

"Okay."

I could hear Erin's breathing. It was quicker than it should have been. The pulse in her neck was almost audible. Her heart was pounding so hard I could feel it. My heart was pounding too.

"Why are we so old-fashioned?" she asked.

I thought about it for a second. "Because we're fashioned old?"

Her giggle was soft. "I like that. I remember Queen Victoria ruling England. I was eleven when she died."

"Ah, the formative years," I said. "Lucky for you, I remember the Puritans." I felt Erin's fingers in my hair.

"No you don't," she said. Then, "I should go to bed," she said.

"I should let you," I said.

"Thanks for letting me stay."

"Yeah. Anytime."

We stood like that for maybe a minute. Our bodies calling to each other. I swallowed thickly. More pounding heartbeats. More breathing. Then she said, "I almost didn't come back."

I heard what she said but I didn't know what she was talking about. "Didn't come back? When?"

"In the forest. On your ten-thousandth dawn."

"Oh."

"When you were supposed to be picking a helpmeet. I almost didn't come back."

I didn't interrupt. I liked to hear her talk. She'd tell me what she wanted to tell me if I just let her.

"I almost didn't come back because I was afraid you wouldn't pick me. I was afraid you'd pick one of the other girls. I didn't have any right to expect you would want me. But it would have made me sad if you'd picked somebody else, and I wanted a chance."

"I did pick you."

"Yeah."

We were kind of swaying together. Like kids at a sixth-grade dance. She laughed, that bitter burst again. "If you'd picked one of the other girls, you'd be sleeping with her by now."

"Uh-huh."

With that, she backed up. She patted me on the chest but she wouldn't look me in the eyes. "Ten days. Then maybe I can think again." She turned and didn't say anything else as she let Sandretta take her off to the guest room to sleep.

CHAPTER 25

Lair of the Wild MacPherson

"What's your plan for the day?"

Erin and I got to eat breakfast together. Delightful. She looked well-rested, which I was happy to see. Somewhere she had gotten fresh clothes. Maybe Sandretta had procured an outfit for her. Or maybe she had somehow squeezed a complete blouse and skirt and different shoes into her purse. Or she had made a portal to the walk-in closet at her house. Didn't matter, I decided. She was here with me and it was a beautiful morning and she looked spectacular.

"I'm going to check the rest of MacPherson's properties," I replied. "If they're building a Jeweled Gate, we have to find it. Fast. I heard Amad say he's been stealing diamonds and getting away with it. They have to be stockpiled somewhere. If I have time, I might go work out at the Iron Foundry. How about you?"

"I have to finish my reports for the autopsies yesterday and try to catch up on the lab requests. Graves is taking the primary spot today."

That meant he would be the one examining Tiny the Tongan. My memories about him and the fight last night were still raw. I wondered with a flash of guilt if his family had been notified. If he even had a family. Erin was still speaking, and I pulled my attention back to what she was saying. "So, unless we get called out to a crime scene, I should be ready for our date tonight. About six o'clock?"

"Okay," I said.

We finished breakfast and walked out to our cars together. I followed her to I-95 and smiled as she waved at me.

The next property on my list was only a mile away from my house. It was a nice two-story office building with accountants, lawyers, a photography studio, and other assorted office types. Definitely one of MacPherson's profit makers. Definitely unlikely to have a gate to the Deamhan realm. The next two properties were farther inland. They were close to each other though, about four blocks apart.

The first one was a pile of dirt. Or multiple piles. It was an industrial parcel that hadn't been developed. Dozens of tall mounds of dirt had been deposited there, each one over ten feet high. Maybe it was topsoil for amending the dirt in garden plots or citrus groves. Nothing here to indicate a gate. The next parcel was better developed. Construction was in progress but no workmen were around. There was a building, of sorts. I drove up to it and got out of the car. There were trucks standing idle, including a backhoe and a cement mixer. The structure itself wasn't much more than a floor and four walls. No roof. Inside, there were some tall stacks of framing materials and a radial saw along with a few other tools. Everything except the aluminum was covered with sheets of plastic to protect it against the rain.

I went to three other locations before I ran into a warehouse in an industrial area that looked like it was used for raves. The warehouse was large, easily 25,000 square feet. I could see a bar and some overhead lighting through the roll-up doorway. There was a fence all around the property, and the gate was locked. I parked by the gate and got out to get a better look. If I didn't find any other leads, I'd come back with Nat and then we'd see what we could see.

It took two more hours, but I made it through most of the list. None of MacPherson's properties seemed likely places to build a gate for transporting deamhans into the world. Most were occupied by people with the usual lack of horns and the usual number of eyes doing their usual jobs. Two of the properties were developed but not occupied. They were relatively small buildings, three and four stories tall, partitioned into small rooms for small business use, but they were waiting for carpets and paint and finishing work. With nobody around, it was a quick job to walk through and see that there was nothing suspect to find.

As I sat in my car, I thought about how there appeared to be a lot of projects that MacPherson was leaving unfinished. Maybe when you're trying to put together a small apocalypse, you decide not to waste money on developing places that could just be destroyed or not needed. When humanity is decimated, it's hard to find renters.

I drove to a better-populated section of town and found a café that made pressed Cuban sandwiches. The radio was playing a jazzy song and it sounded like the woman was singing "prisoner of love" in Spanish. Aren't we all, señorita. The pork and ham were succulent, and the side of fried plantains went down nicely with a cold bottle of Malta.

The rest of the properties were nearer the coast. These were all well-developed commercial spaces full of tenants. One of the tenants was MacPherson's development corporation. I decided to drop in and say, "Howdy."

The middle-aged receptionist with the sensible perm in her hair tried to stop me. She really did.

"Heya," I said. "Is ol' Lonnie Mac this way?"

"I'm sorry sir, do you have an appointment?"

"I do. I'm Mr. MacPherson's psychiatrist. I'm here because he missed our session this week. I'm very worried."

"You . . . you're . . . what is your name?"

"Do you know if he has a couch in his office? It's very important for him to be relaxed. To keep the psychosis from taking over."

The receptionist glanced to the right, which told me where MacPherson's office was located. "Just a moment, sir." She started pushing buttons on her phone.

"No, this really can't wait," I said. "Could be an emergency. Last time, he thought demons were coming after him. Classic schizophrenic delusions. Possibly terminal psoriasis of the cerebellum."

I left the receptionist and walked up the hall. She was still mashing buttons on her phone when MacPherson's door flew open. His face was beautifully apoplectic. Without breaking stride, I put my forearm across his chest and shoved him back into his office and shut the door.

Wow. Was he surprised to see me, with two good legs no less. He retreated behind his desk where he stood, mouth opening and closing like a beached carp. His eyes were stunned wide enough to smooth out the crow's feet at the corners. Made him look ten years younger.

"Whassup, Lon?"

He finally remembered how to breathe. He leaned forward, putting his hands on his desk and almost made it look nonchalant. He looked down and took a few deep inhalations through his nose. I could hear the air struggling past his septum. It took a minute, but I heard the click in his throat as he tried to swallow, and then he said, "I heard there was a fire and they found a body. Would have been a real tragedy if it had been you."

I was up for that conversation. "Yeah. The tragedy is that man didn't have to die. You're going to pay for that one day."

MacPherson raised his head and looked at me with a feral gleam in his eyes. "It's not going to matter."

"Why? Because some idiot with a few magic tricks up his sleeve has convinced you he's going to build a Jeweled Gate and bring a deamhan into the world?" MacPherson's shocked expression told me volumes. "What? You don't think there are powerful people who know what's happening, Lon-nee? You don't think there are bigger and badder mages out there who are going to stop this, Lonnneeee?"

"The other Fae don't know or don't care," MacPherson said. "Unless it affects them directly, they can't do anything."

I noticed a silver ring in the floor of MacPherson's office. MacPherson was Amad's summoner. Or one of them. "Is that what Amad told you? Because I know a few Fae who are very interested in keeping this from happening."

MacPherson was gradually regaining his composure. "I'm not talking to you anymore." He sounded like a little kid again, caught pulling his sister's hair.

"Amad said two days. Is that when the gate will be finished?"

MacPherson glared at me.

"Where is it?" I asked, more insistently. "Where's the gate?"

"You're going to have to be a lot scarier for me to be afraid of you."

"Scary is for the weak," I shot back. "Scary is for people who don't have anything else to fall back on. It's the little yappy dog who bares its teeth and snaps at you, trying to scare you away because, deep inside, it knows it's small and weak and powerless and pointless and it doesn't want to have its scrawny little neck snapped in two."

MacPherson didn't have a ready reply for that.

"You can do the right thing, Lonnie. You can be a real man and help me stop this."

He thought about it. For half a second his eyes went to hopeful. He was a man trapped in a bad deal of his own making and a small part of him knew if there was a ray of light he should take it. Then the look went away.

"Get out of here," he said.

I didn't move. I just gave him a thousand-yard stare and made him repeat it.

"Get out of here!" He said it louder.

"Okay, Lonnie. I'll be going now. But know this: there will come a time when you'll remember this moment. When you had a chance to make it right."

I left the door open. Let the cowardly little monster shut it himself if he wanted to hide.

As I walked past the receptionist, I shook my head in her general direction and said, "Wow. He really hates his mother."

Mostly I was ticked.

The fruitless encounter in MacPherson's office just brought back feelings of helplessness and woe over the death of the Tongan. The biggest share of blame was Amad's, of course. MacPherson was to blame too, the weasel. The blame was theirs but all the guilt apparently belonged to me.

Rush hour hadn't got underway yet, so I made it to the Iron Foundry with enough time to work out. In an act of defiance, I went to the weight room to shove something useful around. The iron in the metal made me feel itchy and annoyed, but I went through every one of the stations with a determination and drive I hadn't felt in quite a while. When I finished, my muscles felt respectably torn up. I did a few laps in the pool and took a hot shower. The water sluiced over my skin and the heat soaked into me like a balm, soothing body and soul.

On my way out, I spoke to Nat.

"There's a place that looks like it holds raves," I said. I gave him the address. "I want to get in there and see what's going on."

"Legal? Or extra-curricular?"

"I don't know."

"I'll check it out. How's Erin?"

"Fine."

Nat nodded. "And?"

Sheesh. What a gossip. He didn't want to know if the raves were part of my case or anything official like that. He just wanted the juicy details about my love life.

"And . . . she's fine."

Nat just grunted.

"All right. We're going out tonight. Somebody's wedding thing." At least that was pretty close to honest. It was our wedding thing.

Now Nat gave a half-smile. "Wedding thing?"

"Sorry, Dad. Can't tell you more than that. Gotta be ready in thirty minutes. I'll have her home before midnight. Promise."

"You kids have fun."

What a gossip.

CHAPTER 26

Ail Bán Dearg

Erin looked completely gorgeous. I'd gone through my whole closet trying to find something good to wear, and Erin probably spent three minutes getting ready and she turned out certifiably drop-dead. Tonight she was in a rust-colored dress with a texture of tessellated geometric shapes that was eye-catching but still subtle. It was slit up the side to show off about a mile of leg, and the bodice featured décolletage so perfectly framed that any man who saw her would instantly wish he were me.

Awesome.

Her heels matched her dress and her cute toes poked out the front. Her hair was voluminous with rolling waves that trailed down her shoulders in a shiny, dark cascade. Her makeup was dark but tasteful, highlighting her cheekbones and setting off her glistening eyes with smoldering lines.

"It's okay if I stare at you, right?"

Max had led her into the great room where I was trying to decide between two pairs of shoes. They were the only dress shoes I had.

"You'd better stare at me," she said. "If you know what's good for you."

"Oh. I know what's good for me," I replied.

Erin pointed at a pair of shoes. "Those."

"Okay." I started putting on the shoes she had indicated. "These go better with the pants?"

"No. But they'll be better for dancing."

It took a second for that to register. "What? Dancing? We don't have to dance, do we?"

"Maybe. I don't know what they have planned, but it's traditional. You don't have to be good at it. Just hold me and go in a circle."

Dancing. Like I wasn't dreading this whole thing already.

"C'mon. We don't have to stay long," Erin said. "Just meet your princely obligations and we'll go."

Erin was at my house because Max and Sandretta were invited to the party as well, and we all wanted to go into the Behindbeyond together. It would be easier to coordinate that way since time behaved differently in the Faerie realm.

Max had also surprised me earlier that day with a wedding gift. He had converted one of the unused rooms into a portal room like the one Erin had at her house. Now I had gates to the glade near the Alder King's castle, Erin's house, and *Corrchnámhach* at my disposal.

The four of us stood at the gate, and I knelt down to touch the silver ring. I said, "*Oscailte*." The gate opened and together we fell into *An Taobh Thiar Agus Níos Faide*.

The glade looked much the same as it had the first time, except tonight there was a new moon cresting the horizon.

I called Midnight Dreary and she appeared after a few moments, soaring high above the trees. She dove like a hawk, pulling up at the last second. She lighted on a nearby branch and regarded us with sharp, shiny black eyes.

I said, "Show us the way to . . . what's the place called again?"

"*Ail Bán Dearg*," Erin said.

I pointed at Erin and said, "What she said."

Midnight Dreary crowed, which technically may have been against raven protocol. I think she was laughing at me. Then she dutifully took wing and led us toward the Alder King's castle.

We passed through groups of trees that I recognized, including the stand of willows where I had gotten my powers. Remembering that night made me feel queasy. We went on through the poplars and elms, and I marveled again at the cherry blossoms, which were still on the trees. The four of us didn't have much to say, but the walk was pleasant.

I didn't know if Max and Sandretta had different names here.

We arrived at a crossroads. To the right, a road led to the castle. It was the first time I'd had a chance to get a look at dad's house. It was impressive. There was an actual drawbridge and a moat. The castle's keep at the center was elaborate and very tall with multiple windows and balconies. Some of the balconies had long banners hanging beneath them. They had different artwork on them like colorful coats-of-arms, and I guessed it probably meant a duke or baron was currently in residence. In front of the keep was a bailey about the size of a football field, and also a gatehouse. The stone structures were impossibly clean and perfect, as if the castle had just been constructed and nothing had touched it yet to erode the edges or wear it down.

"It's like opening day at a theme park," I said.

Ahead, another road disappeared into the massive forest. The trees were towering and dense, and there were soft noises from within that still sounded dangerous. Like the purring of panthers.

To the left, the road climbed a short hill and that was where Midnight Dreary waited. We walked up the hill to find a wide circle of stones. There were thirty huge standing stones in the formation. Each one rose over twelve feet in height, and each had a different pattern carved into its face. The raven had landed on top of one and sat there shifting from foot to foot.

"Let's rock!" I said.

"You're more correct than you know," Erin said. "These are called *liagán*, which are different from regular stones."

She stepped up to the monolith under Midnight Dreary. When she pressed her hand against the pattern in the center of the stone, the familiar light flared and filled the pattern. Then the seams of a rectangle cracked open to reveal a portal.

Groovy.

"There are thousands of stone circles in *An Taobh Thiar Agus Níos Faide*," Erin explained. "The circles usually connect to other circles nearest them, but it depends on the ley lines and which circles are close. The ley lines give power to the *liagán* so that anybody can use the stones for travel without expending their own will."

Now I understood the need for a guide. Whether by experience or magic, Midnight Dreary could find her way anywhere in the realm. If this realm were as large as Erin said, it would take me years to understand and memorize all the places and routes. The idea of exploring this realm completely appealed to me, but I'd be lost in minutes without a guide.

Since we weren't going to a different realm, the landscape on the other side of the portal was parallel to the ground on this side. Going through was like walking through a doorway instead of falling around a corner. We emerged from another *liagán* in a different circle where the air was noticeably cooler. We were near the top of a mountain. After all four of us, and Midnight Dreary, had passed through, the portal closed with a hum.

Erin put her hand on my shoulder and pointed to a lighted area of the forest in the distance. "There's the King's castle," she said. We had just traveled about fifteen miles in an instant.

Cool.

Midnight Dreary picked a new *liagán*. We went through that one to another new circle and then through a third one to emerge near a lake with a delicate castle poised on top of a craggy peak. This castle was much smaller than the King's, but it held an air of grandness about it nonetheless. It was constructed of marble with a natural pink tint. Floating lanterns in a riot of different colors were set above the crenelated walls, giving the structure a festive air.

Midnight Dreary flew up to the castle and circled it once before flying away.

"This must be *Ail Bán Dearg*," Erin said.

The castle stood about two-hundred feet above the lake, but we didn't need to climb to get up to it. There was door at the base of the cliff across the sandy shore of the lake. Once we stepped through, we found ourselves in the entryway of the castle itself. The door maintained a permanent gate from the shore to the castle proper.

We had barely arrived before our hostess was there to

welcome us.

"Darlings!" Béil said.

She minced out and gave Erin a phony hug and kiss on the cheek. She was wearing a shimmery gold dress with a matching blouse that exposed her midriff. Her hair was teased out in wild loops that covered her whole back.

I stared at my wife instead. Always stare at the wife.

I got a phony hug and kiss as well and I was trying not to grimace. When I saw Erin looking at me with a bemused expression, I let the grimace out. She suppressed a smile with her hand over her mouth.

After that, Béil turned to Max and Sandretta and said, "Let me. Show you to. The kitchen. I'm afraid. You'll have to. Clear the dust. Off. I almost never. Entertain."

Apparently, my friends were here to work instead of relax, which annoyed me. On the other hand, they might be happier in the kitchen cooking instead of making small talk with strangers. I felt a bit jealous at that.

We surveyed the castle from the entryway. I was surprised to find it tastefully appointed. Not overdone or overloaded. The furnishings were simple and spare. In keeping with the scale of the building, the artworks on the walls were large but stylish. Besides the paintings, there were tapestries and a sculpture on a pedestal. There was plenty of space between the objects, lending a sense of open stillness and peace.

After a minute, Béil returned. Erin took my hand and we were led deeper into the tiger's den.

The reception room was almost Egyptian in style. It featured a sunken area in the middle of the room and the central rectangle was surrounded by several columns that held up the roof. The roof was open above the central space, and the stars were bright against the velvet sky. Around the perimeter, behind the columns, were open hallways so people could navigate around the room without passing through the center. In the sunken space squatted roomy couches with silk cushions. Clusters of guests were deep in conversation.

There must have been fifty people here, and I didn't know any of them.

There were a variety of hairstyles, although some of the swoops were unusual ears on second glance. A couple of guests had wings. One had hooves instead of feet.

A collection of ladies looked my way. I knew the woman with the dark hair flowing down to her ankles. She had been in the meat line on my first night in the Behindbeyond. I recognized the others as well. When the blonde flipped her hair over her shoulder I definitely remembered her. It took me a minute because tonight she had clothes on.

Around the sides of the room, built into the walls behind the pillars, were a modern bar and serving spaces with all sorts of finger foods.

"Mm! Shrimp!" Erin said.

"Mm! Pork rinds!" I said.

Erin laughed, and I followed her to the snack bar. I didn't mind watching her walk in that dress. When it came down to it, I didn't actually take port rinds. The comment had made Erin laugh, but the shrimp looked too good to pass up.

We added some fruit and cheese to our plates and then went to the bar. The selection of things to drink was even more impressive.

"Mm, champagne!" I said.

"Mm, beer!" Erin said.

She liked making me laugh too.

We picked up two flutes of champagne and turned to find ourselves face-to-face with a roomful of people studiously trying to look at us without looking at us.

I leaned over and whispered to Erin, "Vulcan or Alderaan?"

"Hmm?" she replied.

"I'm trying to decide which planet we're from because it feels like these people are capable of annihilation and they're orbiting our home world. So, Vulcan or Alderaan?"

"Vulcan," Erin said firmly. "The people of Alderaan never saw it coming. The people on Vulcan had time to realize they were doomed."

"Well played, princess. Well played."

Erin bumped me with her hip and hid her smile behind a sip of champagne.

Béil appeared from a hallway. "May I. Have your attention!"

Her smile was tight and strained as she spoke. "It's time to. Adjourn to. The dining. Room."

CHAPTER 27

Greim

There was a bottleneck at the entrance to the dining room. Whatever waited for us inside was unusual enough for everyone to pause at the threshold. Erin and I were the last to make it down the hallway so we were the last to see. The scene was definitely worth a stop.

The infamous Amad had crashed the party.

In this realm, I remembered, Amad was known as Caimiléir. Almost as shocking as his presence, Caimiléir was wearing blood-red armor. There was a helmet on the table, with bat wings and all the spikes an adolescent fanboy could ever want. The armor itself was the complete set, from greaves to breastplate to pauldrons. There were a lot of sharp angles and planes and edges to the armor, but Caimiléir wore it well.

Our collective shock clearly pleased him.

Béil tried to take it in stride. "Well. We are. All here. And dinner. Is waiting," she said.

Caimiléir raised his hands in supplication. "My dear Béil. Please forgive my intrusion. I just assumed you had forgotten to send my invitation. But, judging by the looks on all your faces, I see I was simply not wanted."

Béil refused to be drawn in to an argument or be made to feel sorry or intimidated. She stood with her hands on her hips and her chin up, and there was a torrent of fire in her eyes. She stopped short of asking Caimiléir to leave.

Caimiléir scanned the room and said, "Well, since we're all here anyway, let's have a little chat. Let's begin with the happy couple for whom we are gathered." Caimiléir limped in our direction and the crowd parted to let him through. Caimiléir stopped in front of Erin and she stood her ground. She didn't cooperate nor did she resist as Caimiléir reached down and took her hand. He raised it to his lips and kissed it. I clenched my fists and Erin felt me stiffen. She reached over to touch me to let me know she was okay.

I still wanted to punch him in the face.

"Thou art quite lovely and I wish thee much happiness," he said.

Erin nodded her head almost imperceptibly, but that was all the response she would give.

Caimiléir stepped to the side and addressed me next. "I wish thee a long and prosperous marriage," he said.

I couldn't help myself. "I thought you couldn't lie," I said, and I invested it with all the raw emotion I was feeling.

The temperature in the room dropped about twenty degrees.

Caimiléir leaned in so he could whisper his reply. "A wish can be anything," he rasped.

He pulled away and I saw something lurking in his eyes. Perhaps it was just my imagination, but to me it resembled insanity.

"Now, a little surprise," he said. "It's not a wedding gift because I'm going to be keeping it for myself. But I can get one for you—any of you—if you would like one." He indicated the open window at the far end of the room. "Greim! *Tar anseo*!"

Gasps of shock and cries of fear erupted from the guests as a small bestial deamhan scrambled over the window sill and hopped onto the table. Dishes scattered and goblets fell over and broke with a crash as his clawed feet shifted the heavy tablecloth. One wand came out and power sprang up from multiple hands, ready to strike. When it became apparent the little monster wasn't going to attack, everyone held still, keeping wary.

The deamhan had four rows of eyes, and when it squalled it revealed a mouth filled with a series of jagged teeth. The sound of its voice was like broken glass scraping on wrongness. A pattern of Stain roiled under its skin. Its eyes blinked in unison and a forked tongue flicked out of its mouth, testing the air like a snake. I didn't have a good recent history with snakes.

The deamhan looked at each of us in turn. As its gaze fell upon me, I felt a tremor of unreasoning fear—You are food! Be caught and slain! Cower now! Be prey!—but the feeling left me as soon as the deamhan looked away.

"Everyone, this is Greim," Caimiléir said. "Greim, everyone."

What was he expecting us to do? Shake hands and invite the thing to join us for dinner?

"Don't worry. He's completely harmless. As long as I want him to be." Caimiléir produced a slab of raw meat and held it in front of Greim's nose. The little deamhan's tongue flicked out and in again but he held still. Caimiléir said, "Greim! *Ithe*!" The deamhan moved in a blur. There was the sound of snapping jaws and the meat vanished from Caimiléir's fingers. Part of that sound included teeth on metal. The little monster's bite had left scratches on Caimiléir's gauntlet.

Having a small deamhan with razor-sharp claws and teeth would be sufficient reason to wear armor—but there was something else going on, I knew it. Why was Caimiléir dressed this way? And why had he made such a bold appearance with a Deamhan resident in tow?

I wasn't the only one whose curiosity had been pricked. "Why art thou. And this creature. Interfering. With my. Dinner party?" Béil demanded.

"Ah, excellent question," Caimiléir replied. "The reason is really two-fold. The second reason will become apparent following the first. We only need to wait." Great. Cryptic comments from the crazy guy.

Caimiléir pulled a chair out from the table and sat down, his armor making metal sounds as their parts scraped against one another. Then there were shredding sounds as the exquisite upholstery of the chair was ripped by the armor plates. Greim curled up on the table by Caimiléir's arm, sniffing the fingertips of his gauntlet for more meat. There was bread and wine at the table and Caimiléir helped himself, pouring the wine sloppily and staining the table cloth a bloody shade of purplish red. He ignored us after that.

The group didn't know what to do. Nobody wanted to be rude and leave the room and nobody wanted to sit at the table with the lunatic. So we stood around awkwardly looking at each other for what seemed like the first millennium of a slow eternity.

Béil was understandably put out. She crossed her arms and stood by herself. I almost started to feel sorry for her again.

Though it felt like forever, only a few minutes passed before Caimiléir looked up from the bread crumbs on the table. "There!" he said. "The first reason for bringing Greim approaches!"

A moment later, I heard a double note from a horn sound in the distance followed by a heavy barrage of drums. It was the same call that had preceded the entrance of the Alder King a few days ago. Shortly thereafter, we heard the sound of hooves from a dozen horses.

The Alder King appeared at the end of the hall. He arrived alone, with no guard or retinue. Everyone in the room knelt and bowed their heads, including me, thanks to a quick grab of my arm by Erin. The King—father—was dressed simply, but was resplendent in a cloak and a doublet that bore our crest. His feet were shod with exquisitely-tooled leather riding boots and his crown sat on his head as if it had grown there.

As we knelt, I noticed how Caimiléir was the last person to touch the floor.

I looked up at the King and again felt a wave of charisma emanating from him like an intoxicating cloud.

"Rise," the King said. "Please do continue with your repast. Caimiléir come with me. We have imposed upon these good folk unduly."

"We'll stay here, your majesty," Caimiléir said, suicidally. "These good folk need to hear what we have to discuss."

I looked at the King. A dark shadow fell over his visage and his eyes were bright with lightning and danger. He wasn't accustomed to being countermanded. He looked sharply at Caimiléir and said, "Thou wast iron-scarred once before because thou lackest obedience, nephew. Is it time I gave thee another reminder?"

Caimiléir stood defiant and unmoving. Now I knew why he had the limp.

To Béil, the King said, "With thine indulgence, milady."

Béil nodded.

The King returned the storm of his attention to Caimiléir and he pointed at the little deamhan. "Briefly then, knight. Begin with the reason thou hast for polluting my realm with this creature."

I had a feeling we were now about to be treated with the second purpose for Greim's presence. The first having been to bring the King out of his castle.

"Your majesty, I do feel ill at ease for my gaffe. I really do. I did not mean to offend any attending here. But thou hast refused to give me an audience and now, behold, here is an audience ready-made."

The King sighed but there was anger there, not resignation. "Get on with it," he replied.

Caimiléir clapped his hands together and the sound of metal striking metal was stunningly loud within the echoing walls of the room. The sudden gleam of eager delight in Caimiléir's eyes was anything but reassuring. "Splendid! So what is the one problem that has been responsible for the decline of our people?"

Insanity? Stupidity? Over-inflated ego? I didn't say anything aloud, but I came up with a pretty good list in short order as it applied to present company.

Caimiléir gave his own answer, "It is a religion known among the mortals as Science." Caimiléir paused for effect and then went on, "Make no mistake, Science is a religion, studied and given adoration in equal measure. At one time, our people were gods and demi-gods, worshiped and feared the world over. Glorious days! Our realm was vibrant and thriving. We had children. We had power. The mortals kept us eternally strong through their belief in myth and legend. We were myth. We were legend. We were fed by the strength of their superstition. We built the great civilizations of the Phoenicians and the city of Babylon. We shared in the dazzling glory of Atlantis and basked in the power of the great Egyptians. There was no corner of the world where our influence was not felt.

"Then came Science. The Greeks opened the door. The Romans threw it wide. We closed the door for a time, but the human Renaissance cracked it open again. We fled and had momentary rest among the Aztecs and the Chinese. It didn't last. The Industrial Revolution accelerated the growth of rational thinking and our strength began to fade. Then more discoveries were made to explain away the mysteries of the world that had sustained us for so many centuries. Now we are so weak and so impotent we can't maintain our population. We are on a long, slow, inevitable slide toward death and oblivion."

Having captured the attention of the group, he looked from face to face, measuring their responses. Some were just shaking their heads and others were wearing expressions of disgust. Several of the ladies had covered their mouths with their hands or handkerchiefs. Erin slipped her hand into mine. Whatever Caimiléir proposed, it was going to be bad.

Caimiléir held an armored fist in the air, staring at it as if he had the answer in his hand. He said, "We can change everything. We just need a little hint of something that can't be explained or analyzed. Something that will return a measure of uncertainty and chaos into the mortal realm. Give the mortals a reason to look away from science and they will look back to myth. Back to us. Is there anyone among us who does not yearn to be strong? Is there anyone among us who does not feel the need to leave weakness behind? To resume our rightful place? To hold sway again over the lesser creatures as we are intended? Who would not want this? How can this not be the correct action to take?

"My friends, we need to introduce the Deamhan realm to the mortal realm and there will be a shift. A shift in our favor. And there can be only glory in that."

I noticed Caimiléir didn't say how he intended to accomplish this. He didn't mention the Jeweled Gate. Of course, I had no proof either. Yet.

Caimiléir went on, "And I can ensure the safety of the mortals.

As you have seen, I have complete control over this creature. He obeys me in every way. If I command him to come, he comes. If I command him to eat, he eats. My control is absolute. Behold."

The little monster had not moved from the table. He looked up at Caimiléir and blinked all his eyes.

"Greim! *Maraigh tú féin*!" Caimiléir commanded.

The deamhan shuddered. He put his front claws on the side of his head and then plunged his claws into his eyes. He opened his mouth in a silent scream and continued to tremble as if having a seizure. He fell onto the table and then onto the floor. He stood and bashed his head against the wall. The stone cracked. Greim slammed his head into the cold marble until his inky blood ran down in rivulets. Nobody tried to stop it, but women began to cry. In stunned, nauseated shock we all watched the scene before us playing out its nightmare. The sounds of impact went from hard and bony to soft and wet. A gurgling sound rose from Greim's throat. Finally, the little monster reached the end and lay on the floor, still and silent.

Caimiléir, the bigger monster, smiled and held his hands out as if expecting applause.

"Complete control! Do you see? Thousands will witness the deamhan emergence! We will give the mortals something new to believe in. Something they cannot explain away. The mortals will set aside their science and renew myth. Renew us! We can become strong again and nobody will be harmed."

"Nobody but the deamhans, you mean." I found myself speaking before I'd even thought about it. "I'm new here but I thought one reason the realm of the Fae existed was to keep the mortal realm and the Deamhan realm separated."

"A good point, fairly taken, dear prince!" Caimiléir stepped forward to accept my challenge. "The deamhans do so love the taste of mortal flesh. They don't mind having an Eternal to snack on either—but oh! The sweet flavor of mortal meat is a true delicacy! Let's face it, a mortal in the hand is worth two Eternals in the bush. Ten even! So, thou art correct. We keep the deamhans away from the mortals for good reason. The deamhans would gladly go to the mortal realm, if we allowed it, in order to feast. But the deamhans have no restraint whatsoever. It would just be nom-nom-nom all night and all day. That is why we must control them. And we can."

Caimiléir went back to the corpse of Greim, which looked very small and very sad now. He held his hand above the creature's head and invoked his will. The light flared for a moment and there was a sound of stone-on-stone.

Diamonds.

There must have been a dozen or so. Caimiléir picked them up with the tips of his armored fingers and placed them in his palm. He returned to me and grabbed my hand—his strength was instantly obvious—and he let the gemstones trickle from his hand to mine.

"Here. These are more of the things the mortals believe in. These unremarkable stones are given incredible worth by the mere belief of value in them. These stones have power and I have found a way to harness that power and use it. As you have seen, I can control even the wildest, fiercest creatures in existence with these."

The stones sparkled in my hand, no blood on them, and they were large. Each one several carats in weight. I must be holding tens of thousands of dollars in my hand. Then I realized that my thoughts had just proven Caimiléir's point. And I finally had an admission from Caimiléir that he was using diamonds for power.

"The mortals will kill the deamhans, if they can," I said.

"Ah, they will indeed. After they have recovered from the shock, and argued and fretted, they will find a way to annihilate what they fear. But here's the secret: deamhans don't really die. Greim will be remade. It may take time—decades perhaps—but its essence will return to its realm and find a new physical form."

"So a little pain and suffering. A little fear and slaughter and resurrection. That's all it takes to realize your vision?"

Caimiléir clapped his gauntlets together again. "Now thou art beginning to catch on, dear prince."

I probably shouldn't have, but I said, "Let me say this slowly and clearly so you can understand: speaking as a mortal, you are completely out of your mind."

Through the entire speech, the Alder King had remained patiently silent. Now, he brought the thunderclouds of his attention to bear. The resonance of his voice made the floor rumble.

"Thou knowest the law, Caimiléir. The courts are all agreed on this one thing, if nothing else. We cannot interfere with the mortals."

Caimiléir started to protest and the King raised his hand to cut him off. A wave of controlling power swept through the room, and I felt myself wanting to kneel again.

"Thou hast attempted to create an exception to the law, Caimiléir. The law states that the Fae may not take action that would change the course of human events. I see thou dost want to have the deamhans do it for us. That is a fine line to walk, and thine actions, though indirect, still violate the law.

"The courts do not forbid interaction between us and the humans. Some conduct that would be considered harmful to mortals has always been tolerated. Toying with a farmer's livestock or dallying with his daughter can be amusing, I'll admit, but such actions do not change a species. Removing deamhans from their realm is a breach of the law in itself, and thou art forbidden from doing so again. Putting deamhan in the mortal realm is cause for banishment.

"Remember, knight, we do not rule the mortals. We protect them. We are not their masters but their servants. The growth of their species must be allowed to follow the path that they determine. To do otherwise does not strengthen us but makes us weaker."

The King indicated Greim's little body with a sweep of his hand.

"As for this one, thou hast not exhibited control or discernment. Thou has taken the agency of the creature away from it and robbed it of the ability to choose. This has brought dishonor. For that there must be a payment. From this time forward, thou, Caimiléir,

Knight of the Alder Realm, art Uncourted and Unblessed. Thou wilt hereafter be known as a Knight Solitary with no land, no host, and no master.

"Furthermore, thou must repay the lady Béil a debt of honor, and she will have claim upon thee for one hundred years."

The King had a short sword in a scabbard on his back. He reached behind and pulled it free.

"Upon our land these decrees are sealed," he said. He tapped the sword on the floor and Béil's castle quaked on its foundation.

The Alder King nodded in Béil's direction and she curtsied with her head bowed.

Then the King turned on his heel and departed.

CHAPTER 28

Broken Child

There was no salvaging dinner.

Caimiléir left first. He gathered his helmet and turned to give us a sneer before he stormed out of the room, leaving the body of Greim on the floor. That crazy look passed over his face again, and I wondered if the events of the evening had gone more the way he had wanted than we could guess. I wondered what all the Uncourted and Unblessed pronouncements meant. I'd have to find out later.

The remaining guests didn't precisely make a run for it, but they made little effort to linger. They gave Béil their sympathy, wished Erin and I well, and headed for the exits in small, embarrassed groups.

I wasn't all that excited to hang around either, but I had a question I really wanted to ask our hostess. And it seemed disrespectful to leave Greim's body on the floor and just walk away. I knelt down by the side of the little corpse.

There was a surprising amount of heat coming off the body. I could see a few holes on the back of the creature where the diamonds had been. They had been buried under the skin somehow. I couldn't hazard a guess regarding the method Caimiléir had used to control the creature while the stones had been put in place. Perhaps he had a spell that put deamhans to sleep.

There was a tremendous clattering, and I turned to see Béil pulling the tablecloth off the table. She wasn't bothering to clear the dishes first, so they were tumbling to the floor. The dishes and goblets shattered on the stone and the silverware rang out musically and loud. Her lack of concern over the breaking china and crystal stunned me for a moment. She handed the corner of the cloth to me, already stained with wine and I spread it out for Greim's shroud. The body was very dense and weighed a surprising amount. I laid Greim out on his back and folded his arms across his chest and proceeded to wind him tightly in the cloth.

We held an impromptu funeral of sorts. I carried Greim outside to a spot under the cliff. Béil drew a rectangle on the ground and the dirt rolled out of the way. I laid Greim on top and jumped down into the newly-formed grave. It was comforting to feel the earthen walls around me and the smell of the freshly-opened ground spoke of rich and fragrant soil. And there was power. Like a thrumming wall of electricity just behind the dirt. So much power there, just beyond reach. So much power calling for my touch. But touching would be lethal.

The grave was deep enough that I could barely reach the little bundle, but I was able to get hold of him and put him gently to rest. I clambered out of the grave and we stood for a minute, me and Erin and Béil, looking at the black opening in the dirt in silence. Then Béil waved her hand over the dirt and it rolled itself back into place. Erin collected a small bouquet of flowers from near the shore and put them on top of the dirt.

I couldn't think of anything to say.

Finally, Béil whispered. "There will be. All that food. Inside."

"Dinner would be nice," I replied. I was actually starving.

Erin put her arm through mine as we trailed behind our melancholy hostess.

We looked in the kitchen to find Max and Sandretta had prepared a royal feast. There were six kinds of soup, mounds of roasted beef and ham, chickens on a rotisserie, potatoes with rosemary, rice scented with saffron, loaves of bread, baskets of rolls, beans, peas, carrots, turnips, spinach, and enough cakes, puddings, and pies to feed a party twice the size of the one that was no longer present upstairs.

Béil looked at all the food, in shock, for a long moment. Then she just shrugged her shoulders and laughed.

I tried to break the tension. "Well, there's my dinner. What're you ladies going to eat?"

Béil laughed harder. "We will. Have enough. Leftover. To celebrate. Your anniversary!" she said.

"Which one?" Erin replied. And we laughed together.

Béil's sadness returned like a sudden summer cloud. She patted Erin on the arm. "Come. We'll eat. And talk."

There were serving platters nearby with nothing better to do, so we used them as trays to load up on bowls of soup with slabs of meat and vegetables and potatoes and rice and breads on the side. Instead of leading us upstairs to the dining room again, Béil took us to a room adjacent to the kitchen where there was a small table and some chairs. She got us seated comfortably and excused herself. She returned with two bottles of wine and two glasses, which were all her hands could manage.

"I begged. Stail and Láir. Whom you know. As Max. And Sandretta. To take. Some food. And go home."

"That's very thoughtful," I replied.

Béil opened both bottles of wine and poured a glass for Erin and me. She left the opened bottle between us. The other bottle she kept and drank right from it. Couldn't blame her.

She picked at her food, but Erin and I dug in. Delicious and filling comfort food—and some comfort was surely called for.

"Thou wast. Supposed. To be mine," Béil said suddenly. I looked up at met her eyes. She was talking to me.

"What was that?" I asked.

"Thou wast. Supposed. To be. Mine," she repeated. Then she looked at Erin and said, "Worry not. I want. Thee to hear."

Erin nodded.

Béil took a deep breath. "Goethe. And I. Were born. In the same. Month. The only. Children born. That entire year. Can you. Imagine? Many thousands of. People. And only. Two children. Born."

"I think it was a good year," Erin said.

I smiled at her.

"We played. Together often. As children. You, Goethe. Don't remember."

She was right. I didn't remember anything before I was eight years-old. For all I knew, we ran barefoot together through the autumn leaves and shared a baby bottle. Or, considering the times, a wet nurse. Bosom buddies.

"Thou was. Just called. Laoch then. Our parents. Always talked. About us. Getting married. Someday."

"Did you know my mother?" I asked.

"I did. She was. Very beautiful. Young mortal. Dark hair. Dark eyes. Carried off. By the King. She lived. In this. Realm for. A while." Her brow furrowed, remembering. "Then thou. Wast kidnapped. The King. Found thee. Brought thee back. Didn't tell. Thy mother. Let her. Think thou. Wast dead. She died. Of a. Broken. Heart."

I remembered Keeper's telling of the story. He said the King was afraid to trust anyone. Still sucked for my mother.

"I was sad. As well," Béil continued. "I was. Curious. I wanted. To know where. Thou wast. Buried. I followed. The King. Although it was. Forbidden. He went. Into a crypt. Beneath it. Was a room. Thy body. Wast there. But thou wast. Not dead. The King. And his. Priests. Talked about. Thy condition. They said. Thou wast. In between. Places. Not alive. But not dead. I was so. Scared."

Béil took another drink from the bottle. A long one. She smiled ruefully.

"After that. I went. To visit thee. When I could. Manage. My parents. Never knew. Why. But they thought. Me morose. Going to. The crypts. As often. As I did. And I would talk to. Thee all. The time.

"Then. One day. I heard thee. Thou hadst mater . . . materialized. As a. Spirit."

I had no idea what to think about this. The hairs on the back of my neck came to attention nonetheless.

"Thy body wast. Lying still. But thy voice. Wast coming. From this. Other image. At first I was. Too afraid. To speak. After a while. I found. My courage."

She had almost finished the bottle of wine now. She was often a mean person, but as she drank, she grew mellow.

"We talked. Thy spirit. Could not leave. The crypt. Thou saidst. Thou wast in. A place. That was. Bright. At least. A place. Of beauty. Trees. And rivers. And animals. Of every kind. But no. People. Thou wert. Alone. In paradise.

"So. I would visit. Often and. We would. Share stories. I grew. Thou remained. A child. Thou wast. My best friend. And. I fell in love. With thee. My powers. Had always. Been strong. As I became. A woman. I tried. To find a way. To bring. Thee back. My search. Was long. And difficult. I read. All the books. And scrolls. I could find. For decades. I searched. For an answer. At last. I found. The means. To reunite. Thy spirit. And body. Or so. I thought.

"I had. To summon. A deamhan. His name. Was Brón. We made. A bargain."

"Oh, Béil," Erin said. She moved her chair to be next to Béil and wrapped her arms around her.

"It was. Simple really. Brón would create. A vessel. For. Thy spirit. The deamhan. Would let. Us live out. Our lives. And. When I die. My soul. Will take. Deamhan form. And I will. Serve Brón. Forever."

I was amazed how controlled Béil was. She didn't cry or get angry. I suppose she had come to terms with the consequences of her decision a long time ago. She was like Milly Mallondyke in that way. She had already given the allotment of tears necessary to pay the bill on the pain. On the other hand, Erin was a basket case. Tears ran down her cheeks and she wiped them away before they could fall and stain Béil's dress.

"I also. Had to give. Offerings. From inside. Myself. Since that. Day. I have. Had trouble. Speaking." Béil gave that rueful smile again. "But. It worked. I passed out. After the. Ceremony. When I woke up. My friend. Had returned. Body and spirit. Together."

Béil put her hand on Erin's cheek for a moment. Then she stood up and left the room.

Erin and I looked at each other, not really knowing what to

think or what to say.

Béil was only gone for a few seconds. When she returned, she was holding the hand of the little boy in the old-fashioned shirt.

"This is. My friend," Béil said. "This is. Laoch." She turned and looked at the boy, "Can you. Say 'Hello.' Laoch?"

The boy stared at us for a long moment and then shook his head.

"Laoch. Rarely speaks. To anyone. But me," she said. "Please don't. Take offense."

"Of course not," I replied. This was the answer to the question I had been meaning to ask. I stood and went over to the boy and held out my hand. With a measure of defiance burning in his eyes, he shook my hand. "You gave me a warning the other night. I should have listened to you," I said. "And you brought that bullet casing to my office. It helped me find out some very important information. You may have helped save a man's life. Maybe even my life. For that you should be proud."

The boy Laoch didn't move to respond. He just looked at me and I realized where I had seen his eyes before.

Every morning in the mirror.

"May I look at your hands for a moment?" I asked.

Laoch stuck his free hand out, but he didn't let go of Béil with the other. My new vision was more than good enough to see the fingerprints on our hands. They were a match. "That explains a lot," I said. "We have the same fingerprints." I turned to Erin. "That's why you found my fingerprints on the bullet casing." Back to Laoch, I said. "Do me a favor, okay? Don't rob any banks."

I stood and looked Béil in the eyes. She was calm.

"He does. Tasks for me. Without fear. He is very. Strong. And brave. As thou art."

But he's not really me. He's a facsimile.

"When I. Need to go. To the. mortal realm. I send him. And he. In turn. Summons me there."

That explained a great deal.

Béil knelt and gave Laoch a kiss on the forehead and ran her fingers through his hair. She whispered something to him and he left the room. Before he turned the corner, he gave us all a quick stare.

Béil watched him leave. I couldn't tell what she was thinking, but her expression would be best described as mixed. We went back to the table. "He never. Ages. He never changes. This is why. You are. So broken. And so. Am I. There are. Other things. Missing. From inside me. This is. Why I. Have treated you. So cruelly. I have. Been like this. For so. Many years. I now. Have. A reputation. To uphold."

She smiled again, but it was more sad than rueful.

She turned to Erin. "The other. Night when. There was. The choosing. For the. Helpmeet. I thought. Got would. Remember me. Or at least. Remember the. Pleasure I. Showed him. It never. Occurred to me. That he would. Choose. Someone else. I thought. Destiny. Would bring. The two of. Us together. Again. I was wrong."

Béil turned to me again.

"Because I. Thought I. Had thee. I never. Went back. To the crypt. I did not. Realize. Thou wert. Still there. After a while. I realized. Laoch was not. Growing older. Still I. Never went. Back. I thought. It was. Brón's doing. Decades passed. Instead of. Laoch's lover. I became. His mother. Then. The Alder King. And his Priests. Found a way to. Heal thee. Thou wast taken. To the Mama. Thou grewest. Into the man. I expected."

She looked at me as if she was comparing me in the flesh to what she had envisioned in her mind. I wished then that Laoch hadn't gone from the room. If he and I were different pieces off the same soul, how would it feel to look into his eyes now? My eyes?

"I visited. The Mama. From time to. Time. You know. To see. How thou. Wast growing."

I had a flashback. Peeking out from my hiding place in The Mama's house to see a hooded figure who came in the middle of the night. It had been Béil.

"I became angry. At the King. His priests. At Brón. At thee. But mostly. At myself."

"You couldn't have known how things would turn out," I offered.

Béil shook her head. "I knew. The bargain. With Brón would. Be a trap. Of some sort. Deamhan bargains. Are ever thus. But never. What you think."

I looked down at my platter and found most of the food was gone. I hardly remembered eating it. I had been listening to Béil intensely and hadn't paid attention to the task of putting food in my mouth—but I had certainly had my fill.

"I am. Concerned thou. Wilt be. Unable to. Defeat him," Béil was saying to me.

"What do you mean?"

"I mean. Caimiléir. Thou must. Defeat him."

"I get that. I'm the prince, and the task falls to me because the Eternals have to be summoned to the mortal realm to do anything. And Eternals won't take action if it doesn't affect them directly. Caimiléir knows that," I still wasn't prepared to mention the Jeweled Gate, but it was pretty clear that Caimiléir had designs to keep the Eternals out of it. "If I'm right, he's bypassing this realm altogether and skipping straight to the big show in the mortal realm. I think that scene he put on tonight was just to make sure the King had one last chance to get on board Caimiléir's crazy train. By the way, what does all that stuff mean that the King said about Caimiléir being Uncourted and Knight Solitary?"

Erin offered an explanation. "Uncourted means that he belongs to no faction. That's both a good and a bad thing. On the one hand, he won't be able to ask for support to back him up."

"I don't think he wants any," I replied.

"I agree," Erin replied. "It also means that he cannot dishonor any of the houses of the host. Any dishonor belongs to him and him alone."

"So if there are consequences, he has to pay them—but he's almost free to do what he wants this way because he's not bound by any court rules. Is that it?"

"Exactly."

I sighed. "It's almost like the King wants him to try this insane plan of his."

"If so. Then only. That thou. Mayest stop it," Béil said. "Thou art. Halfling. Thou hast. A vested. Interest. In both realms. Especially the. Mortal. But thou. Art reckless. Ignoring the. Warnings from. Laoch and I. Almost killed thee. This begs. The question. Canst thou make. The choices. That will. Be required?"

I didn't answer. Béil turned to Erin. "Time. Is short. Will he. Be prepared?"

Erin didn't say anything, but I saw her clench her jaw.

"Be vigilant. Be wary. Caimiléir. Will use thee. For his. Own purposes. Don't be fooled."

I nodded.

"Lastly. Remember this," Béil continued. "It's no secret. I will. Want my. Share of the. Glory. When the. Time comes. Find. The place. Where Caimiléir. Will be. Summoning. The deamhan. I will. Help thee. Kill. Him."

"I already have a pretty good idea where that will be."

"Do you?"

"It's what I do. I investigate."

Béil looked at me intently. Her words were as cold as an iceberg. "Caimiléir too. Must die."

Suddenly, Béil went from lecturing me about how to do my job to rolling her eyes up into her head. She was as immobile and silent as a statue.

"Béil?"

She didn't move. Her lips didn't move. Her throat didn't move. But there was a voice. It sounded like Béil, but it didn't speak like her. The syntax was elegant and smooth.

What was once above is below,
What was below, above.
What was once in is out,
What was out is in.
Call the inside out,
Not the outside in.

What the heck was that?

Her eyelids fluttered and Béil stirred. Only a few seconds

had passed.

"Are you all right? Béil?"

I dipped a table napkin in a goblet of water and brushed Béil's forehead and cheeks. Erin rubbed her hands. "She's cold," Erin said.

Moments passed with no change. I shot Erin a look wondering if she knew what to do and she looked back at me. Finally, Béil shivered. Her eyes rolled back down and focused on us, seeing the concern in our faces.

"Oh," she said. "Was I. Gone?"

"Just for a minute," Erin replied.

"What did. I say?"

I repeated the words.

Béil listened and nodded. "Another. Gift from. Brón. A side effect. I can't control. It happens. From time. To time."

"Is it prophecy?" Erin asked.

"I'm. Never sure. Sometimes it. Seems to be. Prophecy. If one. Can understand it. It sometimes. Comes true. Sometimes it is. Just. Bad poetry."

That made me laugh.

Béil laughed too. She said, "I'm like. Cassandra. Except instead. Of being. Cursed with prophecies. Nobody believes. I'm cursed with. Prophecies that. Aren't worth. Believing."

"Maybe it will be useful," I said.

Béil waved her hand wearily. "You two. Should go. I'm tired. And. You have things. To do."

We took her at her word. As we left, we told her that the evening had been memorable and the food delicious and she was thoughtful to have put all the arrangements together. She sort of nodded her head and that was it. For the first time, I thought of Béil as a real person.

Erin and I walked down toward the lake. The new moon had made some progress in its climb up the sky and its light shimmered on the lake like silver ribbons cast on the water. Behind us, there was a new grave for a dead deamhan. There had been another death in my realm, the mortal realm, with the Tongan. The blood of both was on Caimiléir's hands, and he needed to be stopped before more blood was spilled.

"I have a question for Keeper," I said, breaking the stillness of the twilight. I regretted doing it. "First I have to check out the place where Caimiléir may be building the Jeweled Gate."

CHAPTER 29

Warehouse Rave

It was late. Erin and I were waiting for Nat to pick up the phone. He wasn't at work and he wasn't home either. I'd left a message on his cell phone and he hadn't called back yet. It had been an hour. I wasn't worried. Maybe a little.

"One more day," I said.

Erin replied. "I just hope I'm giving you what you need. I'm teaching you what I know and I hope it will be enough. Realistically, the best preparation is information. You're using your training to find the gate."

I nodded.

"You already know how to make and recharge a shield. That was three days ago. You learned the fire spell and then actually had to use it yesterday. Your magical power needed time to return. So we're going as fast as we possibly can. Your fire spell is as strong as anyone's. You do know that, right? Because magic isn't really something you can make more powerful with practice. In this one regard, at least, you're as powerful as you will get and that is more powerful than anyone I know.

"You can really only do one thing at a time, remember? Spells on top of spells just tend to cancel each other out. So the main thing is your will. After that, it's a question of capacity. Survival in a mage fight often comes down to who runs out of power last. That's the winner. Let me ask you a question: how do you prepare to deal with a psychopath? One without magic? You really can't, right?"

She had a point. "Not realistically," I replied. "You analyze the best ways to find him, try to anticipate his moves so you can predict what he'll do and then you stop him by whatever means necessary."

"Exactly. It's the same thing with Amad, okay? A murderer could come at you with a gun or a knife or a flamethrower."

"Flamethrower?"

"I'm exaggerating. But you don't know, right? You use your skills and your tools to stop him, right? And you're careful. Same with Amad. He has some fancy spells, but if you're careful, if you're smart, he's no better than your average killer. And you may not have a lot of spells, but your spells are strong. Strength doesn't come from the spell but from the heart of the caster."

"You'd make a good chief of police with a speech like that," I said. "Yes, I've gone after killers before. Amad just has different weapons. I can work with that. What about counterspells?"

"We can work on those all right," Erin nodded, thinking it through. "We should. That will be tomorrow's lesson."

"And wards. I want to know more about wards."

"Okay, but like I told you, wards are usually tied to a location or an object."

"But they don't have to be?"

"No."

"Okay. There was something you told me the other day that made me think. It may apply to anticipating our favorite psychopath's next move."

Over the next few minutes I outlined what I was thinking.

In the middle of it, finally, my phone rang.

"Nat?" I said.

No hello. Nat just said, "Got passes. We going?"

"To the ballet? Finally! Giselle? Swan Lake? Cinderella?"

Silence.

"Symphony? Beethoven? Mozart? Shostakovich?"

Nothing.

"I know! Opera! Carmen? La Bohème? Tosca?"

Crickets.

"Okay. When do you want to go?"

"Midnight," Nat said.

"Pick me up. They might know my car."

Nat hung up. His word count on that phone call: five.

Erin appeared at my elbow. "Where are we going?"

"Um. Nat and I are going to one of MacPherson's properties. Could be the place where they're building the gate."

"Great. I'll go with you."

"You don't even know where it is."

"Okay. Where is it?"

"Dance club."

As soon as I said it, I knew I'd just given her more reason to go. She put her hands on her hips and gave me a snarky expression. At least she was kind enough not to insult me by verbally pointing out the obvious.

I sighed. "Yeah, I know. Hot girl, underground dance club, perfect match. I'm just thinking it might be dangerous."

"There will be other people, right?"

"Should be. It's a Monday night though. Probably not as busy as a weekend."

"Good. I don't like it jammed wall to wall. Besides, this is Miami. There's a crowd ready to party every night."

"And how would you know that, exactly?"

Erin gave that wicked half-smile. Right. Second stupid thing I'd said in the same minute.

"We do have one problem, however," I said.

"What's that?"

"This place is pretty exclusive. Nat might only have two passes."

Erin spoke really slowly in response. I mean really, really slowly. Embarrassingly slowly. "How about I go put on a dance club dress, and then you can guess how many times I've needed a pass to get into a club."

Three strikes. I'm out.

So very out.

Having never been married before, I didn't know if Erin was

the best wife ever. I did have a pretty good idea what a great girlfriend was like, however, based on my own years of experience and the empirical data gathered from observing a broad selection of my friends' girlfriends.

In my humble opinion, even though she wasn't sure we'd make it as a couple in this realm, Erin was a fantastic wife-slash-girlfriend.

I don't know if anyone else had ever tried the accidentally-married-and-abstinence approach before. It was strange in concept at best. There had been women in my life in the past and I wasn't qualified to talk about virtue without being a hypocrite. But we both remembered very clearly an earlier time when people didn't sleep together before marriage—at least not so blatantly. Erin couldn't open herself to a real relationship with me until she could get closure from her last relationship, and I wanted to respect that.

In the meantime—and the time was mean indeed—I was getting to know Erin as a person. She was as smart and funny and accomplished as I had ever expected, and the time we were spending together had a certain kind of closeness and gratification I hadn't experienced in my life before.

It was its own kind of nice.

We sat together in the front seat of Nat's SUV. As expected, Erin was wearing an eye-popping dance club dress that would have any doorman in the country throwing down the welcome mat on first sight. Bright red and tight in all the right places, with shoes to match. Her hair was fluffed out so it would bounce when she danced, and her makeup was on the dramatic side. And she smelled amazing. Feminine and fresh.

I noticed our hands weren't touching, but they were next-door neighbors. My hand was on my leg and Erin's was on the seat between us. I just left it at that. Nice.

The gates at MacPherson's property were open. There weren't any searchlights or other attention-getting devices to attract a crowd. They didn't need to promote the place at all. Even for a Monday night, the dark parking lot was more than half full. With the sun gone down for hours and a heavy darkness shrouding the sky, the blacked out windows meant the building was almost completely dark except for the roll-up door I had seen before. The door was raised high enough for people to walk under, and from there a flood of colored light poured out across the ground.

We parked and the three of us went up to the entrance. I was wearing a polo shirt and slacks but Nat was wearing ripped jeans and shades and a black t-shirt. There were two women waiting for us. As it turned out, they had the passes for us to get in. Nat hadn't mentioned there would be a pair of girls or if one of them was meant as a date for me. He also hadn't said anything when Erin got into his truck for the ride over. He didn't know Erin and I were magically married and had just brought us all together in his customary silence.

The girls smiled at us and Nat introduced them. Brandy was a blonde and Carlene was a redhead. I introduced myself and introduced Erin and put my hand on the small of her back to show we were together. Nat smoothly put his arms around both girls, one on each side. The girls were happy to settle in under him and give Erin sideways glances. They were dolled up to the nines with short skirts and heels.

Sorry ladies. Erin's the prettiest girl at the dance tonight.

We went up to the doorman. He paid no attention to Nat or me but he looked at the girls with official thoroughness. His review of Erin started at her toes and went up from there at a pace that I found more lingering than necessary. Then he marked his clipboard and gave us the thumb in. He didn't even check our passes. Twerp.

The music was loud with a pounding beat synchronized with the lights. The aesthetic of the place was entirely built around an industrial manufacturing theme with lots of steel beams and metal walls and oversized machinery. The main dance floor stood in the center of the warehouse and featured what appeared to be, at first look, a catwalk, about forty feet long, but turned out to be a working conveyor belt. Dancers took turns boarding the conveyor belt to do their thing as it carried them slowly down to the other end where they disembarked. There were handrails down the length of the conveyer and they were crowded with observers who expressed their appreciation of the dancers with applause and whistles and outstretched hands. There was too much distance for the watchers to touch those who were dancing, but the dancers could reach out and exchange a high five or a fist bump. One of the several bars was situated a few feet behind the belt on one side so that the customers could get drinks without losing sight of the action.

Above and surrounding the dance floor was a wide balcony, accessible by stairs from the main level. Sections of the balcony were being used for dancing and were lit for that purpose. There were additional bars on both sides as well. The place had a spacious freight elevator, situated next to one of the stairways, which was also filled with dancers. The elevator appeared to be constantly and slowly going up and down with a pause for a few seconds at the top and bottom in case people wanted to get on or off. Opposite the elevator was the DJ booth and it looked like almost a full circle of equipment suspended over the crowd. Below the booth was a set of huge metal gears, lazily turning. The largest gear was eight feet in diameter.

The far end of the warehouse was glassed off from floor to ceiling. There was another stairway going up which was flanked by a pair of oil pumps. These were also in motion and seemed to be nodding in solemn worship of whoever was walking up. The stairs undoubtedly led to the VIP rooms. Overall, the effect was an intoxicating mélange of movement, sound, and light.

Party paradise.

The women loved the place. Erin clapped her hands together and all three of them started moving their hips, responding to the music without being fully aware of the rhythm affecting them. Nat remained opaque behind his shades and granite-chiseled expression, so I had no idea what he was thinking. I thought the place was cool.

Brandy gave Nat a pat on the shoulder, "Champagne's on you," she said. Nat pulled out his wallet and handed her a pair of hundred dollar bills. She took them and said, "Ladies, let's go."

I was glad to see them include Erin. Brandy hooked Erin's arm and led her and Carlene towards the bar in the corner.

"How'd you meet those two?" I asked Nat.

"Iron Foundry," he replied. "Carlene teaches aerobics and kickboxing. Brandy's her roommate."

"And they knew how to get into this place?"

Nat shrugged. Eloquence in shoulder movement.

"Which one are you dating?" I smiled.

Nat didn't respond.

"Unless you tell me otherwise, I'm going to assume you are going out with both of them."

Nat turned his head just enough to look at me dead on.

"Dude!" I said, just to mess with him. Knowing Nat, he would have reacted the same whether he was dating them or not, so I still had no idea. Curse his wall of stone.

"At some point, we need to have a look around," I said. "I especially want to see if there's a back room."

"Okay," Nat replied.

"Or maybe a basement."

"Basement? In Miami?"

It was my turn to shrug. "Elevation here could be twenty or thirty feet above sea level. It's not unheard of."

"Okay."

I was thinking about Béil's words. What was once above is below. What was below, above.

I couldn't really be sure what it meant, but maybe I'd know it when I saw it. Might be a basement, right? I scanned the crowd trying to identify security. I didn't see anyone who stood out. There were a few obvious cameras in the ceiling. There would be other cameras as well that would be hidden.

The girls came back with champagne for everyone. We walked down the length of the warehouse sipping and watching people gyrate. Erin pointed at the stairs between the pumping pumps. "What's up there do you think?"

"VIP rooms," I said. "Offices."

After we finished our champagne, the most horrifying monster reared its ugly head.

"You owe me a dance."

Erin was already pulling me out to the floor as she said it. Nat gave me the half-smile. He'd seen me dance before.

The music was booming and I could feel big bass waves hitting my chest. I had to yell for Erin to hear me. "All I can do is a Bob-and-Sway," I confessed. Loudly. "At one point, I had a special move called the 'Flailing Octopus,' but I was asked to retire that for reasons of public safety."

Erin smiled and shook her head and started to dance. She was graceful and sexy and she bounced smoothly in time with the music, swinging her hips while making elegant motions with her arms and hands above her head. Captivating.

Meanwhile, I made do with a three-inch side to side motion that put every ounce of grace I owned on full exhibit. I also bobbed my head up and down, trying to find the beat. Nobody was looking at me anyway. Erin looked good enough for the both of us.

Nat brought both Brandy and Carlene with him and they danced adjacent to us. Unlike me, Nat was capable of actual moves. They were mostly a variation of my patented B&S, but he actually put some masculine strength into it and looked cool.

The music never stopped but flowed from one bass-heavy throb to another. Some of the songs had waifish, breathy female vocals, and some sounded like German men singing in English for the first time in their lives. Most of the songs had no vocals at all, and they changed every two or three minutes.

After a while, the girls wanted to try the conveyor. Nat and I didn't object, but there was no way we were getting on that thing ourselves. We strolled down the walkway and watched as the three of them put on a show. There were plenty of whoops and whistles from the male observers lining the handrails. Brandy and Carlene brushed their hands down their bodies as they shimmied and Erin bounced and turned in a blur. It took a full minute for the girls to be carried from one end to the other and by the time they stepped off the belt, the crowd was in a lather.

Erin half-fell into my arms, losing her balance for just a moment as she went from the moving belt to the stationary platform. She laughed as I caught her, and I said, "You are amazing."

"Whew! That was fun!"

We decided to go to the bar and get another drink. This time we just got fruit juice except for Brandy, who didn't get a brandy, which would have been poetic, but an appletini.

It looked like the evening was at its peak. The music and the people were as fevered as they were going to get.

"Take a look around?" I asked Nat.

He nodded in response.

"We'll be back in a few minutes," I said to Erin. "Stay here, okay?" I said the second part to all three women.

Erin understood what Nat and I were up to. Brandy, who didn't, said, "The men's room is behind that stairway."

I thanked her and we walked away.

I wanted to start on the main level. The VIP rooms were probably too busy and too valuable to use for another purpose like a hidden lair. Most likely, we were looking for a room on this floor or possibly a basement. If anyone questioned us, we'd tell them we were looking for our dates.

We found the restrooms. The first was for the women and the next was for the men. We looked inside the men's room to verify it was nothing more or less than expected. Beyond that, there was a locked door that said "Employees Only." The door was cheap and so was the jamb. I gave it a hard pop with my shoulder and there was a satisfying snap. Thanks to the cover of the thump-a-thump-a from the floor, I was the only person who heard it. My pocket-sized flashlight showed me that the room held janitorial supplies, and in the back was the machinery that operated the elevator. There wasn't space for anything else.

We backed out of the room and pulled the door closed. It didn't stay shut, but it would go unnoticed for the time being.

The hall continued on and we found ourselves in a storage area. Access was blocked by a chain link fence and a gate that was held shut with a heavy chain and a padlock. With the flashlight

I could see shelves with everything from paper towels to cocktail onions, along with machines on standby like a wet/dry vacuum and window washing equipment. There was a whole lot of booze back there too, which explained the chain and padlock. The room was long and appeared to go all the way to the corner of the building. We emerged again onto the dance floor

There were only two other rooms on the main level. Both were too small to be of use. One was blocked by a sturdy door with a sign that said "Machine Room." Since it was right behind the area with the gears and below the DJ booth, I expertly deduced it was a room with machines in it. All the electrical for the sound equipment appeared to be in there too. The last room didn't have a sign on it, but it had a little window in the door. Through it, I could see the building's heating and air-conditioning equipment.

No room here for inter-realm shenanigans. No access to a basement either. It was possible, though extremely unlikely, that the basement, if there even was one, could only be accessed from the upper floor. Such an arrangement would require a hidden stairway behind the walls somewhere, but there wasn't any place where one could be hiding from what I could see.

"Looks okay," Nat said. "Upstairs?"

"Maybe," I replied. We'd been gone for about ten minutes. "Let's check on the girls first."

We went back to the bar where we'd left the ladies. None of the three were there and for a second I felt a rising panic that tripped the beat of my heart. It must be the feeling parents get when their child gets lost in Wal-Mart. It didn't help that the lighting was darker near the bar and a dozen more people than before waited for drinks. I started scanning the crowd and felt a hand on my shoulder. Erin.

Relief. Cooling and sweet. But there—Erin stepped in close and kissed me. Her mouth was soft and warm and I again caught the scent of her perfume, lightly-sweetened now with her perspiration. Her tongue flicked between my lips, which was even more unexpected.

Holy wow.

She broke the kiss. I wanted another.

"Brandy and Carlene are in the ladies' room," she said.

"Okay," I replied.

"Be right back." Her voice was husky. And soulful.

As quickly as she'd appeared, she was gone, lost in the crowd. She was extra-tall in her heels and once, for a moment, I saw the spectacular fall of her hair over the press of humanity and then she dissolved into the light and shadow.

I looked at Nat who was standing immobile like he was carved in marble. I responded anyway.

"A little champagne and a little dancing gets her worked up, I guess."

I couldn't wait for her to come back.

She didn't come back.

I waited for ten minutes before I started to wonder. Five minutes more before I really got worried. Like every guy, I'd had to wait for a woman to come back from the restroom before. Sometimes it took a while but this didn't feel right. I gave Nat a shake of my head and we headed back over to the restrooms. There was a group of girls standing outside the entry shifting back and forth in their heels and staring at their cell phones.

"Hey, can you check on the people that went in there?"

I found myself accosted by a skinny blonde chick in a striped outfit that looked like it had been designed by Tim Burton. She was standing nearest the bathroom. Maybe it was the latest dance move she was doing, but I guessed it was a standard pee-pee bounce in a black and purple dress.

"Who went in there?"

"Some freaky-looking guy and a woman in a red dress. He kicked us all out and said we had to wait here until it was all clear."

"All clear?" I asked.

"That's what he said. Until it's all clear."

"How long ago?"

"Like forever." The high-pitched whine of her voice indicated her bladder had taken over her larynx.

"The woman, was she about five-foot ten? Long, dark hair. Beautiful?"

"Yeah. Totally."

"And the guy?"

"Light blond hair. Red soul patch. Creepy."

I pushed my way past the group and went into the ladies' bathroom with Nat right behind me. There was nobody inside. We banged open the doors to the stalls as we worked our way to the back. Empty. Facing the stalls were some tall mirrors and a row of sinks. The two guys in the mirrors looked big and mean and the shorter one looked worried. Like his girlfriend/wife was missing. In the rear was a small alcove with another mirror and a vanity about eight feet wide. The mirror here had a series of warm lights so that the women could repair their makeup in a more dramatic setting.

On the floor was a gauntlet. From a set of red armor.

Nat took in the scene in about two seconds.

"Somebody's calling card?" He asked, jutting his chin at the gauntlet.

"Yeah," I replied.

There was a circle of gray ash on the floor but it wouldn't mean much to Nat. I knew it was a place for a portal. There was no pattern on it that I could see, like when the silver snake had made itself into a circle. This must have been the same kind of thing.

Nat was checking the walls and ceiling as well as the floor. "Secret exit?"

"Must be," I said. That was as close a guess as anyone could get without knowing about the other realm. "No time to figure it out."

Nat followed me back out of the restroom the same way we had come in.

"Were there any other girls in here?"

The pee-pee dancer shrugged her shoulders.

"Two girls, maybe? Blonde and redhead?"

The women gave us a variety of non-committal grunts, which apparently passed for communication in a dance club crisis.

My heart had fallen somewhere near my gut and I was feeling nauseated. Amad had Erin and could be anywhere in the world by now. Or another world. I waded into the girl-ball that was pressing closer and said, "All clear now. You can go in."

Pee-pee dancer led the charge.

For a panic-filled moment I was swimming upstream. Shouldering like a bull through the mass of women earned me a couple of expletives and a well-manicured hand pointing an accusatory finger in my face.

We moved up the dance floor at a steady walk, even though I wanted to run. We climbed the stairs between the pumps at the far end of the room. To the left was a short hall with a door marked "Management." If nothing else, this place did a great job of labeling. The door looked like it was set in a reinforced steel frame and it had a deadbolt along with a door handle lock. I tried it but it didn't move at all. I looked at Nat for the space of a heartbeat and pointed at the locks on the door. He nodded and reached into his pocket. He pulled out a set of lock picks, and I turned up the hall the other way. We would stay quiet as long as we could, but there was an undercurrent of urgency now pressing us forward.

There were four doors up the right side of the hall. VIP rooms. The first one was open and empty. Inside was a couch, a private bar, and a couple of overstuffed chairs with a short table between them. On the wall was a television with a feed showing the dance floor below. Across the back the glass was frosted, so no details could be seen at all, but the lights bled through and painted moving colors across everything in the room. The sound was muted enough for conversation.

The second room was closed, but none of the doors had locks. I opened the door and saw six people inside. Everybody froze when I came in. I didn't know any of the women so I left.

The next room had a guy in a fifty-dollar suit with a couple of girls who hadn't got their party going quite yet. Small favors.

I burst into the last room. There was a guy making out with a woman old enough to be his mom. Maybe it was his mom. I went back down the hall. Nat was coming out of the office.

"Anything in there?"

Nat shook his head. "Computers. Cameras. Take some time to find footage."

I took a couple of deep breaths, thinking. "I may know who has Erin," I finally said. "He might have Brandy and Carlene too."

"You know where?"

"I wish I did. There's a place. It's important to this guy. I've been trying to find it but I haven't had any luck yet. I've got no other lead."

"We should go."

On our way out, we searched the dance floor and the conveyor just in case. No sign of the girls.

We made it to the exit. I made a mental note to chastise MacPherson for operating a club with no discernible security. Cheap and stupid. But this was really all on me. I'd lost Erin and Brandy and Carlene. Me.

We went out to Nat's SUV and rode home. It was the longest, most silent ride of my life.

CHAPTER 30

Halfling Ninja

Nat dropped me off at my house. As I got out he said, "Carlene introduced me to Brandy. We've been dating for five weeks. They're both important to me. When you find something, call me." I closed the door and he drove away. It was the longest string of words I'd gotten out of him in two years.

He had every right to assume I'd let him know. But if I found the girls where I suspected I might find them, I couldn't tell Nat anything. I hated this situation. I'd brought Nat in to help, and he'd brought in the girls, and now they were missing, and I could lose Nat's trust in the bargain. But there was precious little that I could tell him about any of this.

I ran inside the house. It was after 3:00 a.m. but I got Max out of bed anyway. I told him very quickly what was happening. Then I asked him if he would make sure to take Sandretta with him someplace safe if everything went sideways. And find Nat and take him with them, too.

I've been afraid for myself before plenty of times. I'd been afraid for combat buddies. I'd been afraid for fellow officers. I had never, until now, been afraid for another person quite the way I was afraid right now for Erin and the other women. The fear in my veins was like an electrical wire running down every branch of my system. The feeling galvanized me like no feeling I've ever had before. I should have been exhausted, but I was energized because people needed me and I had to come up with a plan. I had to believe that events were nearing their culmination and I had Amad worried if they were taking Erin. I was getting close.

From my house, I activated the portal and went to

the Behindbeyond.

Corrchnámhach was just as busy as before. It took me only moments to find Keeper.

"The look on yer face tells a troublesome tale," he said. "Come with me."

We went to a quiet room and there was already food and drink. Water. Exactly what I needed.

"You heard about Caimiléir and the little deamhan he summoned?" I asked.

"Aye. He claims he can control them and wants to summon one to the mortal realm. He thinks it will return the human world to a belief in myth again, and by their belief, increase our power. And fertility." Keeper was shaking his head. "Controlling a wee deamhan for show is not the same as controlling the monstrous one he'll need to summon next."

"He was rebuffed by the Alder King," I said.

"As he shoulda been."

"My father made him Uncourted and Unblessed and I think that's what he wanted. I think he's ready to open the Jeweled Gate. It's been a huge undertaking and I've been wondering what else he hopes to gain. I mean, he doesn't strike me as a person who would do all this just for the good of his people, I don't buy it."

"'Tis simple lad," Keeper replied. "If Caimiléir's ploy comes to fruition and proves the King wrong, Caimiléir dethrones the King."

The import of Keeper's words stunned me.

"How do you mean?"

"A king is only as powerful as the number and strength of his followers," Keeper replied. "'Tis the same for us Eternals. The greater a king's holdings, the more subjects he has, the greater his power. For Fae Kings, the belief of the followers is just as important as any land or money or hereditary right. Our lords are rulers of the metaphysical just as they are rulers of the real."

Now it made sense. Caimiléir wasn't just concerned with returning his people to their former glory. He wanted to be their king. That's why he was willing to be so patient. He wanted to be the lord of this realm and the mortal realm as well.

Oh man.

Not good.

"I don't think there's much time now. He's taken Fáidh and at least two other women."

Keeper was all business.

"Well, lad, we were hoping to find the gate before he completed it. Now, if he's got it done, as ya think, he'll be wanting to open it. That said, there are things ya must know. The gate requires a lengthy ritual to open. He has to start at moonrise and continue until moonrise tomorrow. Depending on location and time in the month, that's usually more than twenty-four hours but less than twenty-five. There will be blood required at the last stage. Blood to power the gate and blood to feed the deamhan."

"If the gate is big, that's a lot of blood."

"Aye. How long has it been since Caimiléir was seen?"

"Two hours at least."

"Then time is growing short."

The knot of dread in my gut was growing larger. If the blood wasn't needed until the end, the girls had only a few hours to live.

"I need to know more about wards."

"Dinna Fáidh teach ya?"

"She taught me enough to come up with a plan."

I told Keeper what I wanted to do and how I thought it could be accomplished. As I spoke with him, he repeatedly ran a stocky hand from the crown of his head to the tip of his beard, rubbing his face and scratching his whiskers.

When I had finished my explanation, he squinted at me and bobbed his head to the side. "'Tis a very dangerous game to play," he said. "Even if it works, there's a chance he'll best ya. Or the deamhan will best ya both."

"Do you see an alternative?" I asked.

"Can't say I do," he replied. "But keep the risks in mind if ya would follow this path. Once ya have set foot upon it, there's little choice but to see it to the end. And that end may be very bitter to ya."

"I know."

Keeper nodded. "Then we'd best get to work."

It took almost two hours of painstaking effort, but it was all I could ask for.

I looked at the results. "It'll work," I pronounced.

"It'll have to," Keeper replied. "I'm glad I could help this much. I wish ya good luck."

All I could do was nod. I didn't have any words.

Keeper sensed the reason. "Go save her lad. And if ya can, save yer realm as well."

I choked out two words: "I will."

I departed *Corrchnámhach*. Just outside the door, I looked up into the open sky and admired the patriarchal oaks. Dawn was not far off in this realm. The clouds were edged in a pale pink, and the first swallows took gliding swoops over the quiet places in the nearby stream, catching bugs and leaving circlets on the surface of the water with the tips of their wings. I stored a mental image of this winsome place, cementing it inside my brain so I could recall it in detail.

In case I never saw it again.

I took a deep breath and went back home. Home to the mortal realm.

I showered and changed. The scalding water was purifying and fresh clothes made me feel ready for battle. Black jeans, black shirt, black running shoes. Halfling ninja. I took a flashlight that clipped onto my belt. In my pocket I put the silver shard from Amad's serpent, along with the healing medallion and my shield coin, which I had recharged. I had Keeper's chain and pendant around my neck. Atypically, I actually made sure I had my gun and even an extra clip.

Before I left, I called Milly's number and left a message telling her I had a good lead, I needed to follow up on it right away, and I would get back in touch with her as soon as I could. That way, if she never saw me again, she would know I had been trying to complete my task.

Erin's house was empty. I went there not expecting to find her but more as a way of reassuring myself that I was being thorough and diligent. And confirm my worst suspicions. She hadn't gotten amnesia or something and been brought home by the police. She was gone. The space was empty of life and warmth. I dutifully went through every room, checking for anyone or anything out of place, before going back to her portal room. Her stack of gate sigils sat there on their shelves. I could drop one onto the silver circle and be gone to a far-off place where there were no lunatic knights summoning deamhans. No kidnapped friends. No impending doom on a city that had been good to me.

I wasn't tempted for even a second.

I'd been thinking about MacPherson's properties. The two that were near each other with the piles of dirt and the unfinished building bothered me. Where had all that extra dirt come from? What if there had been a huge excavation project on the one property and they had hauled all the dirt away to the second property? Had they then built a structure over the hole in the ground?

What was once above is below. What was below, above.

The surface of the land had once been above ground but now it was below. And the dirt that had been below ground was now sitting above. Could it be that simple?

Maybe.

One way to find out.

When I'd been to the site before, I had only given the place a cursory examination because it seemed to have been abandoned. There could easily be a way to get belowground that I hadn't noticed. But now I'd know what to look for. And the excavation could be fairly deep since that land had to be at least thirty feet above sea level. Not a problem for a contractor like MacPherson who had an army of workers and a fleet of equipment at his disposal.

I drove over to the property, parking two blocks away. The sun was about three hours from rising here so the night was full and deep.

The structure sat on the property like the skinless skull of a giant prehistoric animal, faintly gray and empty with open eye sockets and an attitude of neglect. Looking at it from a distance, I could imagine the rest of a skeletal body going for a hundred feet or more beneath the dirt. I really should avoid giving myself the willies. There are enough terrible things in the world that are real.

There appeared to be no activity. If I was wrong, I would have to scramble to find the right place before it was too late.

I checked the sky, remembering Keeper's words about the timing. The moon showed a sharp, curved edge just setting. It would have to make its way back around to the eastern horizon before time would be up. Somehow, that realization didn't do anything at all to ease my fears.

I crept closer, taking cover behind a stand of trees at the edge of the property. If I was lucky, I'd be able to find the girls and get them out. After that, once they were safe, I'd deal with Caimiléir and his gate.

If you do stakeouts long enough, you get a feel for places and their character on the outside, which can tell you a lot about what is happening on the inside. I sat for thirty minutes behind the trees waiting for something to reveal itself and I got nothing. Usually, that meant that there was nothing there to see after all, but in this case—here in this place—it made me more nervous instead of less. A ward could be set so that nothing could be observed behind it. I knew that from the fireball lesson at my own house. And the fire I'd caused on top of MacPherson's building. The flames had gone unnoticed outside until the ward had collapsed.

This place had been built by human beings and existed in a world where things constantly changed. Sometimes it's subtle, but something will be different over time. A leaf will shudder with the invisible passage of air. Shadows will shift with the changes in the surrounding light. Looking at the building was like looking at a painting. It was too perfect. Too immune from influence. Too set apart from the world around it.

This had to be the place. I crept closer and finally saw it. The pattern of the ward. I touched it, in case it was meant to keep me out, but my hand passed right through. It was just a ward to keep the place looking innocent. Yay me.

I entered the empty husk of the building. My senses were on high alert, and I hurried from the shadow of the wall to the space behind a stack of lumber without trying to identify a ward. In moments, I found what I was looking for. Stairs. A forklift sat conspicuously nearby, burdened with building materials covered in plastic. The stairwell had been underneath.

The stairs went down about eight feet to a hallway that went straight. I couldn't see where it led, although there was a utility light on the floor at the bottom of the steps to light the way. The stairs were on the narrow side and steep.

I knelt at the edge of the opening, opposite the top steps. Then I laid on the ground and eased my head down into the opening. I got a quick look, upside-down, at the hallway. All I could see was the area illuminated by the utility light and, beyond that, a pool of darkness.

I was going to be entering a tunnel, basically blind.

If I needed to see in the darkness, I had my flashlight, but I didn't want to use it unless I had to. My heartbeat threatened to explode through my eardrums as I descended the stairs. This all felt bad and wrong and stupid in every way conceivable. I had no choice but to press on. The hall felt ridiculously long and I must have gone about a hundred yards before stopping, leaving the comfort of the utility light far behind.

I put my hand on the wall, trying to remain silent as I felt my way into the blackness. Somewhere, echoing up through the black, I heard a man's voice and then a woman crying.

That's when the world erupted in painful, blinding light.

CHAPTER 31

Béil

It was morning now. We were lying in bed, enjoying the quiet. She was wearing the satin nightgown with the little bow in the small of her back that I'd bought her for our fifth wedding anniversary.

"Want some breakfast?" I found myself asking.

"Are you cooking?"

"Pancakes. Bacon. Eggs. Anything fancier, you'll have to go elsewhere."

"That sounds absolutely great."

I got up and donned the world's most comfortable bathrobe. The pink marble floors were never too cold, so I went without the matching slippers and padded down to the kitchen barefooted. Saturday was always Stail and Láir's day off. It was my job to make breakfast and I loved doing it. Soon the bacon would be frying and the pancakes would be golden and the eggs would be fluffy and the kids would come down and join us.

I was pouring a third round of pancake batter into the griddle, making Mickey Mouse shapes, when I felt a pair of hands slide around me. Her hands were small and warm on my chest. I turned around and kissed her. "Minty," I said.

She smiled and took a step back. She moved her hair out of her face with her fingers. Her hair was long and straight and shiny and somehow managed to be perfect even first thing in the morning.

"You are so beautiful, Béil," I said.

And she was. All soft and sweet. A kitten who'd retired her claws.

I was still married to Erin of course. But she and I had not been able to have children. Béil was my courtesan, which was all she ever wanted. We had been lucky enough to have twins, a boy and a girl, who were the absolute apples in Grandpa Alder King's eyes.

"What are you thinking, my darling?" Béil asked. Her speech pattern was smooth. I was glad for her.

"Honestly?"

"Sure."

"I'm thinking there's a good chance I'm dead. Or dying."

Béil sighed and folded her arms. "Why do you say that?"

"This is all an elaborate fantasy."

"What if it is?"

"I don't know. I can remember things from the past several years that are impossible. The Alder King granted permission for you to become my courtesan. We traveled to some of the most beautiful places in *An Taobh Thiar Agus Níos Faide*. We had two children and their names are April and Alex. My father asks for my advice about running the kingdom. I make breakfast every Saturday morning. I just correctly pronounced *An Taobh Thiar Agus Níos Faide.*"

"It's wonderful, don't you agree?"

"Sure. It's great. But these are all things you want. I have all these memories and I'm feeling all these feelings. I love you and I love the children, but I know that something terrible just happened to me. I'm in the mortal realm right now—or my body is. And this existence, all this stuff, isn't any kind of thing I'd come up with on my own. It feels real but logically, this can't be happening."

Béil stepped into me and wrapped me up in her arms. "But it all could happen. All of it. I can make it happen."

"Even children?"

Béil smiled. "If you roll the dice often enough, you'll hit the jackpot."

I had to pause. She had abilities and powers that I might never understand. I believed that she probably could make things happen as she wanted somehow.

"All this could be yours," she continued. "More. But you're right. These are all the things that I want. I've made them real for me because I know what will make me happy. I know what I've always wanted. Since we were children, remember? So talk to me. Tell me what you want. I can make it real for you too. Not just in a dream."

She raised her arms over her head, her fingers describing intricate patterns, and the entire scene changed. Béil was joined by a dozen beautiful women. "All yours," she said.

"If you think that's what I want, you haven't been paying attention at all," I said.

Béil smiled and snapped her fingers. All the women, except her, were now Erin. A dozen of her.

"No," I said.

She gestured again and I was standing knee-deep in gold. There were coins and bars and chains and cups and knives and crowns. The women changed to high-ranking nobles of various courts. They were all in their finest dress and they were applauding me and shouting my praises.

"Bravo, Prince Goethe!"

"Well done, your highness!"

"Congratulations!"

"Not even close," I said.

Béil stepped up to me and waved her arms some more.

We were suddenly on a mountain peak. McKinley. I was holding Béil in my arms. The air around us was thin and crisp and invigorating. The afternoon sun brilliantly lit the snow and rock where we stood. In the distance, far below, the pines were dense with fragrant shade. In my heart, I was content. All the people I knew and loved were happy and well-cared for. I knew no worry. I had no conflict to disturb my heart. I knew that all was well.

I had no idea how she could make me feel these things. Magic Prozac? She was getting closer.

"Enough," I said.

With a disgusted twist upon her lips, she snapped her fingers and we were back in her kitchen.

"Thank goodness," I said. "The pancakes aren't burning."

She pushed me away and waved her hand and the food disappeared.

"Stupid Halfling. I can give you whatever you want," Béil said. "You only need to name it and I will make it real."

"The price is too high," I replied.

"Idiot," she snapped. "You'll be waking up soon. There will be unbearable pain. You have been sedated for hours now and the moon is about to rise. Caimiléir is nearly finished with the ritual and he will want you to be awake to witness the end. Fáidh has been unable to teach you what you need to overcome him. You won't be able to stop him from summoning the deamhan.

"Then you will die and Fáidh will die and the other women will die. The deamhan will emerge and lay waste to the land you hold dear. Caimiléir will let it kill thousands of the mortal herd you care so much about before returning it to the Deamhan realm. Caimiléir will have made his stand, and mortal belief will make him more powerful than the Alder King. He will reign over both realms with death and terror. All because you are stupid."

I tried to remain unmoved by her plea. It wasn't easy.

I said, "Do you know all this for a fact? Or are you guessing? You must answer honestly."

Her expression fairly curdled with sourness. She didn't answer directly. "With my help, you stand a far better chance of prevailing," she replied. "Without my help, you are almost guaranteed to fail. And I cannot understand your stubborn refusal to let me help."

"At least that was honest," I said wryly. "In exchange for your help, I must take you as my courtesan then. And you need to be present when the deamhan is defeated so that you can claim a share of the glory. And you want to kill Caimiléir as well. Is that it?"

Béil was growing petulant again. She didn't want to answer. I looked at her with a stone face and waited. Finally, she said, "Most of it."

"Well, I don't really want a courtesan. I couldn't care less about who gets credit for ending the deamhan. Or stopping Caimiléir. But what's so almighty important? You need this so much. What else is there?"

She turned her back on me then. "I can't say," she replied flatly.

"Can't? Or won't?"

There was no further reply forthcoming it seemed. She held her tongue for a full minute. I decided she couldn't tell me after all.

I groaned. Something was happening to me. I was starting to hurt. I bent over, putting my hands on my knees as my breathing grew short.

"You're waking up," Béil said. Her voice was suddenly tense and urgent. "You have to summon me. As soon as the deamhan appears, trace a circle on the ground and say my name. Say 'Béil, I summon thee' three times. It'll even work in English. I'll hear you and do the rest. Remember! Three times! Summon me! Summon me!"

I was consumed by the white light. It ran through my body, filling me with pain. Then the light went out and all was blackness.

I gasped.

I opened my eyes.

I saw only darkness.

I couldn't move.

I felt my eyes close and open again.

I saw only blackness.

I heard a voice.

I tried to breathe but it hurt.

I tried to move my hands.

I tried to move my feet.

So much pain.

It felt like my arms and legs were restrained and something covered my eyes. I took short breaths and suddenly coughed. A wellspring of new agony came up through my chest. I had broken ribs. Again.

Something was going on at the back of my head. Someone

untied the blindfold that was covering my eyes and then I could see. There was a wall of concrete in front of me. Or rather, a concrete floor. I realized I was lying face down looking at the ground. I saw a pair of shoes. Expensive.

"Welcome back," said a voice.

Lonnie MacPherson. Son of a monkey.

I was about to attempt a smart-aleck reply when he pushed on my ribs and another wave of pain flourished along my side.

While I groaned, MacPherson started holding things in front of my face where I could see them.

He had my shield coin along with the medallion for healing and the Kris-shaped silver piece from Amad's serpent. "Found those on you," he said. He put them in his pocket. Then he showed me my flashlight. And my gun. "You won't need these anymore," he said. He kept those too.

Next, he dropped a stun gun on the floor where it clattered.

"These things are beautiful. The electrical charge goes right through magic shields. Did you know?"

An empty hypodermic landed on the floor beside the stun gun.

"This little number kept you out for the last twelve hours. While our friend Amad and I made final preparations."

He leaned into my side again. I groaned again and hated the sound. Hated giving my tormentor any satisfaction.

When he eased up, I said, "Pretty brave. Beating a man who's unconscious. What do you do for an encore? Pull the wings off butterflies?"

He didn't attack me again, although I expected him to.

"We did a lot more than beat you up," MacPherson said. There was certain gleeful malevolence to his voice. "This will be payback for coming to my office. Embarrassing me in front of my employees."

"Yeah? How about you help me up and see if I can embarrass you again?"

MacPherson actually laughed at me, but there was no mirth in his voice at all. I was lying on a table of some kind and it rotated. MacPherson unlocked it and pivoted the table so I was upright and able to face him. My weight shifted and the pain was enough that I wanted to pass out.

"Tell me, Mr. Luck, have you ever had a tattoo?"

A shaft of cold plunged into the center of my being. It wasn't hard to guess where this was going.

"Your luck has finally run out, Luck. We didn't have time to give you the full treatment, with the needle, but we've found that a painted tattoo works just as well. You know what I'm talking about, don't you?"

Of course I did.

"You think you can control me?" I snapped. "Like you controlled the Tongan?"

"I know I can. Works every time. So the only way you're going to do anything to embarrass me is if I tell you to."

Bits of information clicked in my head like magnets rolling together. When assembled, they formed a complete and terrible truth.

"You made her kill him." It was a statement of fact and I could hear the sadness in my own words. "You forced your own daughter to kill her husband."

He didn't deny it. He didn't expect I'd live long enough for him to be worried.

"Like I said, works every time." All smiles. He was actually proud of it.

"You're a spineless coward and a sycophant," I said. "The magic comes from Caimiléir and you can't take any of the credit for that. You're a sadist, but all you can do when faced with actual killing is try not to pee your pants. You can neither create nor destroy. You're nothing more than a parasite."

I was finally getting to him. His jaws were clenched along with his fists, and his eyes were starting to bug.

"I made all of this possible," he said, insistent.

"Sure, you provided a location. You have people who can build for you. And you're willing to let your daughter be used. You're a tool, in every sorry sense of the word."

MacPherson was losing it. He wanted to hit me. I could feel it. I was trying to get my arms out but it was slow going. Every movement hurt and I was nowhere close to being free. If I could get him close enough, I could hit him with my patented, clock-stopping head butt. That would hurt both of us, but if I could knock him out, I could get away.

He fumed, "I have made important contributions here." He said each word slowly, emphasizing each one, spitting out the syllables. "I will have a throne at his side."

"Is that what he promised you? Your own little corner of the new kingdom? Don't kid yourself. Duke MacPherson? What a joke. Duke MacDumbdumb is more like it."

MacPherson's face was red, and veins stood out on his neck like worms under the skin.

I kept on him. "As his personal tool, he'll discard you the moment he doesn't need you. As soon as he's done blowing his nose on you, he'll flush you like the used-up wad that you are."

"You're dead," he spat at me.

"Maybe, but not by you, limp noodle. You don't have the spine to kill me. You only do what Caimiléir tells you."

He pulled back to punch me. I wasn't free yet but my shoulders were loose enough I could dodge and maybe—

"Stop."

Dammit. The command came from the shadowy corner of the room.

"Calm down, Lonnie. He's provoking you."

MacPherson backed off. He lowered his fists and looked at the floor like a kid caught stealing candy from his baby brother.

"See that?" I said. "You just did what he said. You proved my point and you're too blind to see it."

Caimiléir slowly walked into the light. He looked tired. There were dark circles under his eyes and his hair had lost its usual perkiness, sitting on his head like a wet poodle. He was far removed from the limping and hesitant man I'd first met. Now he looked very dangerous and very much in charge.

"How are we feeling, Mr. Luck?"

We are feeling like crap.

"Hey, Lonnie," I said instead. "Remember that day in your office? When I told you there would come a time you'd wish you'd done the right thing. It's almost here, pal. Won't be long now."

MacPherson backed farther away as Caimiléir walked up to me. There was a look in his eyes that was part pit bull, part inmate, and entirely psychotic.

"Been busy?" I asked.

"Mr. MacPherson," he said, ignoring me. "It's almost time."

CHAPTER 32

Chamber of the Jeweled Gate

The next part was quick and simple. Like lopping the head off a fish or snapping the neck of a chicken.

Caimiléir touched the top of my spine. I instantly felt a tingle of power as he activated the design I knew was there. A trembling wave of shock swept through me, like a bucketful of cold water.

"Obey me," Caimiléir said.

I felt my will leaving me. I tried to hold onto it. I needed to maintain control.

"Stand still. Don't move."

I did what I was told.

Caimiléir gently undid the restraints. I was surprised that he was so careful about it.

"Are you in pain?" he asked.

"Yes," I said.

"Mr. MacPherson can be very enthusiastic about pain. However, you are not to be killed. Lonnie, do you understand?"

"No, I don't," he replied.

Caimiléir sighed. "We need a witness to carry word of our victory to his father, the King. He will tell the Alder King that you, Mr. MacPherson, a mortal, were instrumental in completing our mission. Having those words coming from his own son will be exquisitely embarrassing, don't you think?"

MacPherson grinned. Caimiléir certainly knew how to motivate his minions. I wasn't worried about MacPherson killing me anyway. He didn't have the manhood.

Caimiléir finished with the last buckle. I was freed from the physical bonds that had held me and able to move at last. But I hadn't been told to do so.

"Walk with us," Caimiléir said smoothly. "You may not speak."

In silence and suffering I walked behind Caimiléir. MacPherson followed after me, an oily and smug presence. With my hands free now, I wanted to wrap my fingers around his pathetic neck and squeeze the life out of him.

But I couldn't. Not now.

We walked down a hallway which turned a corner and emerged into the craziest room I'd ever seen. It was far more vast than the fake structure at the surface indicated. There were sections of the floor that were elevated or just had concrete slabs laying on the floor. The main area was enormous, like one football field laid at a right angle on top of another in a cross. The center of the room was dominated by a deep pool of water. In the center of the pool was an elevated dais of concrete. The diameter of the circle must have been fifty feet across. This was where the Jeweled Gate had been inscribed. There were five layers to the gate. Four of them were already glowing black. Sickly purple lights, like a stack of bruises, emanated from these layers, and even though the top of the slab was solid, each ring appeared to penetrate deeper level-by-level into the concrete. Reaching down to the Deamhan realm.

The designs were even more intricate than pictured in the illustration Keeper had shown us. Each ring had its own filigree pattern. Each successive ring added to the complexity and beauty of the whole. At the same time, the potential it represented was terrifying.

We passed over a threshold, and I suddenly felt the heat of the room. There had to be a ward of some kind. A ward that kept the heat inside. The air was dank and foul and stifling and swampy, and I understood now why Caimiléir was so disheveled. He had been working in this room for almost twenty-four hours under conditions that rivaled the worst jungles I'd seen. There was a definite rhythmic thrum here as well, like a thousand bass drums played in unison as a dirge. With each beat, one of the rings pulsed with purple illness. Every fifth beat was quiet because the final ring was dormant still.

The height of the room was also surprising. The roof overhead—the underside of the structure at the surface—was at least five or six stories up. Six massive columns, surrounding the pool, supported the ceiling. Runes were carved into the concrete along with scenes of deamhans cavorting under the moon. The water in the pool had to be from the natural groundwater here, and MacPherson must have worked hard to build a place where the water could be controlled and channeled toward some purpose I didn't yet fathom.

I didn't see Erin or the other women.

I did see a whole lot of diamonds. The outer edge of the gate was overwhelming; brilliantly dazzling with a circle of diamonds completely surrounding it. The band of diamonds was six inches wide. It captured the light in the room and fractured it into zillions of sparkling colored lights.

There are billions of dollars on the floor. Trillions.

I couldn't help thinking it. And then I couldn't help that it bothered me because I was fueling the strength of the ring and Caimiléir's plan by giving a new measure of belief in the value of all those tiny stones.

An engine of evil driven by innocent faith.

More diamonds waited on a nearby platform in an oversized concrete receptacle that would keep them from spilling into the swamp. There were so many it would take a lot of shoveling to move them.

How many carats are in a shovelful?

"Tell me, what do you think?" Caimiléir asked.

I felt a tingle on the back of my neck and the compulsion to reply.

"You're cutting out the burning heart of the world and breaking it into a million little pieces," I said.

Holy crap. The heat and pain must be getting to me.

"Very poetic, Prince Luck," Caimiléir returned. He gave me the slow applause. One. Two. Three. Four. In time with the thrumming of power in the room. "It has taken more than fifty years for me to collect the fortune you see before you. A few stones at a time, here and there, from my realm and yours, to avoid attracting attention. Until it was time. And I knew I would be successful. I knew this day would come. I'm a very, very, very patient man."

"Six years building this place," MacPherson said. "Millions of my own money. That's what I've put into it."

Atta boy, Lon. Make sure you get your slice.

Sweat was running down my face and into my eyes. The stinging made me want to wipe the perspiration away, but I couldn't do that without permission from my captors. I couldn't even ask if it was all right to move.

"It's time to reunite you with your friends, Mr. Luck," Caimiléir said. He strode lightly to the receptacle of diamonds. He was so elated his limp was almost non-existent now. He waved his hand over the stones and released a little trickle of power. Light flared up from the stones. Scraping, concrete slabs moved under unseen forces, revealing an oubliette deep within the floor. Finally, I heard women's voices. More scraping. The floor itself was rising, bringing the women up from the dank, musty hole beneath the concrete slabs. The women had been in the dark for hours. Brandy and Carlene were trying to see while protecting their eyes from the sudden change in light by putting their hands up over their brows and squinting. Caimiléir's Stain encircled each of them. I could see plastic ties binding their wrists and ankles so they couldn't fight or run. Their mouths had been gagged with pieces of cloth torn from their own dresses. They both made hoarse sounds that weren't like any language I could recognize. They'd been screaming and they were traumatized and shaking. Their dresses were torn and ragged, and they were wilting from the heat and from crying.

Erin stood beside them. She didn't have the benefit of using her arms and hands, so she stood with her eyes closed, in silence. I knew now that there was a tattoo on the back of her neck, hidden beneath her flowing hair. She would be unable to move until she was told to do so. Worst of all, Caimiléir's ugly Stain now flowed among her own beautiful ribbons. I rolled my eyes down.

A writhing black ribbon turned on top of my white Stain. My cousin had Stained me too.

More mental magnets clicked into place. I'd been so stupid.

At the dance club, when she had kissed me, I'd been pleasantly surprised. And duped. She'd kissed me so quickly in the dark, among the crowd. I might have caught a hint of her new, dark Stain if I hadn't let myself get distracted. Besides, it wasn't at all characteristic of her or the relationship we had. I should have recognized that moment for what it was: what Caimiléir thought our relationship must be like. Somehow, while Nat and I had been looking around the club, he'd spirited Brandy and Carlene off. Then he'd caught Erin by surprise. He'd applied a tattoo and then he'd told her what to do. He'd told her what to say and how to act. Forced her to kiss me and tell me she'd be right back. All to keep me from looking for her in the bathroom for as long as possible while he stole his prizes away.

If I'd given it one non-hormonal thought, I'd have realized Erin hadn't been herself. I'd have realized the reason for her behavior, so much out of character, and I'd have known she was being controlled. Realizing that, I might have kept her safe.

She was the one person I would trust completely. Caimiléir had used her against me, and now I was about to find out the price of my stupidity.

I had found the women all right and they were alive. But now it may be too late.

Caimiléir stood between me and the girls. It was safe to assume that Caimiléir was determined enough, after all this time and effort, to kill them without hesitation. He'd been ruthless and cavalier with lives before, and I suspected we didn't mean anything more to him than Greim had. I have to get them out of here.

Two glass daggers appeared in his hands. One moment his hands were empty and the next, they held a pair of wicked-looking blades. Caimiléir grabbed Carlene and yanked her to her feet. She screamed and tried to pull away. Even though he looked exhausted, Caimiléir was a knight and more than strong enough to control her.

"Pick her up and follow me," he commanded.

I did as I was told. I lifted Carlene off the ground. She fell over my shoulder. Her weight reignited the pain in my ribs but I could only groan inwardly. She tried to hit and kick but she was so wrung out she barely had strength to fight. My heart ached. To what doom was I carrying this innocent girl?

We walked around to the other side of the ring. Caimiléir had probably chosen Carlene first because she was the smallest. Because they were Stained, I knew he'd used magic on them, but I wondered why Caimiléir had not tattooed them as well. Not enough time? Or because the girls were mere Mortals? Or maybe he knew that having them struggling and crying would entertain the sadistic side of MacPherson's warped personality. And that would amuse Caimiléir.

I hated both of them.

"Drop her here," Caimiléir commanded.

With her hands and feet still bound, I dumped Carlene unceremoniously to the floor. She crumpled to the hard concrete and it looked like it hurt. She was crying again. Caimiléir remained unmoved. I regretted every moment.

We were at the edge of the ring, adjacent to the glittering circle of diamonds. Now that I was closer, I could see a faintly-glimmering spider web of power over the diamond circle. A ward had been placed over them, but I couldn't tell what the ward was doing. Next to the circle, there was small receptacle of some kind that fed into the diamonds.

Caimiléir grabbed Carlene's hand and slid the blade across her palm. Blood welled from the wound and she cried out again. Caimiléir squeezed her hand and the receptacle quickly filled with Carlene's blood. I could almost hear the beating of Carlene's heart matching the rhythm of the beating gate.

The shock of watching this happen turned my heart to ice. I wanted to scream for her. I wanted to wake us all up from this horrible nightmare. But I couldn't.

"Take your medallion!" Caimiléir shouted at me. He held my

healing coin. He must have gotten it from Lonnie while I'd been looking elsewhere. I took it.

"Heal her," Caimiléir commanded.

I knelt so I could reach her. I put the medallion over her palm and said, "*Leigheas*," as I released a flow of my power. The wound started to close itself. I had to move the medallion along the cut to heal it completely, so I repeated the word and my will continued to flow. The wound was about three inches long and my stomach roiled on Carlene's behalf. The poor girl must have felt the easing of her pain because she raised her head off the ground. She looked at me with fearful sweetness and tried to say something. I couldn't discern the words but they sounded like hope. I prayed it wasn't misplaced.

We went after Brandy next. She cried and shook her head repeatedly. She had seen what had just been done to Carlene and her fear was palpable from the other side of the room. She tried to squirm away, but of course Caimiléir commanded me to snatch her up and carry her toward the next spot on the circle. She was a bigger girl than Carlene and continued to thrash in my grip, trying with everything she had to avoid Carlene's fate.

I almost dropped her. The pain in my side is getting worse.

"Hold on!" Caimiléir said. "We wouldn't want her to bleed where it won't do any good."

She continued to fight me. Short, explosive sounds came through her gag. It wasn't hard to guess at the words she was throwing at me. She was tough, and I could see why Nat liked her.

"Put her here, Goethe," Caimiléir commanded. I hoped Brandy would be able to endure what was coming, knowing that Caimiléir would command me to heal her after a minute. Caimiléir cut her and the fight flowed out her as fast as her blood. The receptacle filled with crimson.

"Heal her."

I saw MacPherson on the periphery as I closed Brandy's wound. "Why are we healing them?" he asked. He sounded like a four year-old whose parents had shelved his favorite toy.

"All we need for now is blood," Caimiléir answered. "And we need to make sure Prince Luck has used up his power reserves. When our guest arrives, there will be a surge of wild magic. It could undo the wards and spells we have cast. So, if Luck is released from our control, we want him weak and unable to use his magic."

Caimiléir fixed his eyes on me and smiled. It almost seemed genuine. "I understand he is fond of fire spells. It would be better if we take away his fuel now lest we regret it later."

MacPherson remained doubtful. Caimiléir took notice. "Everything has a purpose, mortal," he said. "I waste nothing when it matters and everything I do is necessary."

Give him a break, Lonnie. He's killing people as fast as he can.

"My prince. Follow me," Caimiléir said. I followed, feeling like a pet dog. We stopped at the third receptacle. I realized now that the receptacles were at the four points of the compass. North. South. East. West. I wouldn't be surprised to find out that we were on at least one ley line as well, and I wished I could ask if we were. A ley line would provide more power to the gathering magic.

"Are you screaming in there?" Caimiléir asked. He looked directly into my eyes and peered at me as if trying to see behind a mask. All I saw in return was a whole lotta crazy. "If you were unbound, would you beg for your life? The lives of these women you're so fond of?"

Beg? No. Take your head off? Yes.

I was ready to suffer being cut. The women had survived and done so courageously. I just worried I wouldn't be able to heal myself. Erin had said it worked better to be healed by someone else.

"Fortunately for you, my prince, I am a terrible healer. My talents lie in the opposite direction. I imagine your little wife has a talent for it, but sadly she has been drained of her power already. She opened the first four rings. Such a helpful girl."

Caimiléir held out his own hand and cut himself. I noticed he didn't do so with as much enthusiasm as he'd shown previously.

His wound was shallow and it took more time for his blood to fill the cup.

MacPherson had moved to the other side of the circle to stand next to Erin. He watched us with a mixture of disgust and anticipation. He had produced his own knife—made of steel—and was holding it so hard his knuckles were turning white. He stared at me like he could read my thoughts. Like he knew I would kill him to make sure Erin was all right, if I could. He might be unable to actually murder Erin on purpose, the coward, but I worried he would hurt her for the thrill of it.

When no more blood could be contained in the bowl, Caimiléir stood. "Heal me," he said.

What I wanted to do was wrestle the knife from him and plunge it into his heart.

Instead—and it galled me—I healed his wound.

When I was finished, there wasn't even a trace of a scar on him.

"Nicely done," Caimiléir said. "Follow me."

I knew where we were going. There was only one receptacle remaining and Erin was standing next to it. She had to know what was going to happen. My stomach churned and my heartbeat skipped. She had to be dying inside. I know I was.

As directed, I followed Caimiléir until I stood in front of Erin.

Our resident psychotic commanded her to open her eyes and she did. They were brilliantly, deeply green.

I wish I could talk to you right now. I wish I could tell you everything will be all right. Look at me, Erin, and trust me.

Caimiléir spoke to me, pulling my attention away from Erin. "Prince Luck, you will do exactly what Mr. MacPherson tells you to do." Caimiléir rubbed his hands together. I think he was maybe a little nervous or excited or both. Maybe it's just what bad guys do.

"It's almost time," he said. "I will cast the last incantation. Mr. MacPherson, we will need a little blood."

"I know what to do," MacPherson said. He was put out, like being told to clean his room when he was already planning on doing it.

Caimiléir moved to his platform with the box full of diamonds. With his hand extended, he threaded power into the diamonds.

He started the incantation.

The words were mostly unintelligible and most of the bits of sound I caught, I couldn't begin to interpret. The incantation was long, but one section Caimiléir repeated.

Ríoga-Brón, tagann ó i bhfad i gcéin,
Ríoga-Brón, tar níos congarach,
Ríoga-Brón, tar chun deifir,
Ríoga-Brón, tar duine le duine liom.

He sang other sections in between, in a surprisingly strong baritone, but I heard those four lines over and over. As he chanted, the drumbeat in the room pounded harder, ramping up.

I looked in Erin's eyes. If I could tell you what Keeper and I had planned, maybe you wouldn't be so scared.

"Won't be long now," MacPherson said. He was gloating already, but I didn't see any deamhan yet. "Take this," he commanded. He held his steel knife out to me. I had to do as he asked. "I can't kill you but there's no reason I can't have a little fun."

I took the knife by the handle. The iron in the knife made it feel like an electrical wire. My hand clenched and I felt pain shooting up my arm. My head started pounding. I wanted to drop the knife but I couldn't. The pain aggravated my sore ribs as well and my breath caught in my chest.

Caimiléir's voice was getting ragged around the edges. Five rings in the circle, five chants to wake them. He went on while the pain in my hand deepened and my head felt ready to explode. It was starting to burn now, as if the knife were an ember. MacPherson grinned at me. He knew the knife was hurting me. He knew the dread I was feeling and the fear gathering around Erin.

The anticipation now was torturing MacPherson too, but in a different way. Keeper had told me that there would be a point of no return. A moment where, if Caimiléir stopped, the whole ritual would fail. It felt like that moment had to come soon. I prayed that it would. There was a pealing bell, low and deep and resonant. Caimiléir's fevered chanting rose to a climax.

"Moonrise," MacPherson said, smiling a gleeful, toothy rictus. "Now slit her throat."

CHAPTER 33

Blood and Summoning

MacPherson took a step to the side. He wanted a clear view for what would happen next.

I moved the knife to Erin's neck. Of course, she didn't flinch. She couldn't.

Don't be afraid! It was time for the next step of my plan. The plan that Keeper and I had forged to keep me from being controlled. Now I could stop pretending. Stop faking. Take action.

I turned my wrist so that the flat of the blade pressed against the back of her neck.

The steel knife, given to me by MacPherson, shattered the spell fueling her tattoo. The release of power trembled through the knife into my hand.

Erin blinked and I pulled the knife away and she gasped. In reflex, her hands went to the back of her neck. I turned and threw the knife at Caimiléir. He didn't see the knife coming, but my hand was numb with pain and my throw went wide.

MacPherson, expecting blood, growled like an animal. He jumped and grabbed Erin around the stomach, lifting her off the ground.

She whipped her head back and nailed MacPherson's face with an audible crunch. His growl turned into a scream as his nose erupted in blood. She kicked back with her foot and caught his knee with her heel, which made him drop her. She landed on her feet and turned. She kicked from the side and connected with the knee again. It buckled inward and MacPherson went down.

His scream rose higher as he clutched his knee with both

hands and then the sound went too high to hear. Not for the first time, I wondered how this walking bowl of pudding had managed to father an intelligent, competent woman like Milly.

Different deal when you're on the receiving end, huh, Lonnie?

Erin stepped back and left him in agony on the floor. I caught her by the shoulders and she turned to throw her arms around my neck.

"I knew you wouldn't do it!" she said. She buried her face in my shoulder. "I knew somehow you wouldn't hurt me."

There wasn't time for explanations. "Good job," I said. "You remembered your training from the gym. I'm proud of you." Erin looked into my eyes and then she started to kiss me but she felt me take her necklace in my hand.

"Hey, what are you—" she said before I yanked the pendant off the chain. She disappeared. Blink.

"Following my plan," I said to the empty air.

A rumble took over the whole complex. The drumming sound had increased tempo and now beat a heavy staccato that raised the dust and rubble off the floor. All five rings in the Jeweled Gate were spinning in alternating directions. Caimiléir continued his chant. He looked over at me, wild-eyed. He needed blood in the last bowl but Erin was gone.

I broke for Carlene as she was closer. My ribs complained as I sprinted towards her. I had extra necklaces from Keeper. I told Carlene she was going to be all right now. She was in shock and couldn't even focus on me. I put the chain around her neck and pulled the pendant. Blink. In my mind, I thanked Keeper for his help.

Caimiléir leaped from his pedestal, running too. Running toward MacPherson.

My priority was to save the innocent. Until that was done, I had no other purpose. I went to Brandy and put the chain around her neck. She said "Thank you" as I pulled the pendant. Blink.

I spun around.

MacPherson was still writhing in pain on the concrete and Caimiléir stood over him. I'd never reach him in time.

Caimiléir kept his song flowing uninterrupted as he raised MacPherson's head by the hair. Caimiléir's glass knife flashed, and the cup filled in a literal heartbeat.

No corner of the kingdom for you, Lonnie.

The drumming struck five beats in a row as Caimiléir's chant came to a climax. Finally, he fell silent.

Underneath the drumming had been a second sound: a keening whine. Now it grew as the five rings of the Jeweled Gate accelerated. Red lightning filled the space in the center with crackling energy like a tornado made of electricity. The accompanying thunder added fresh booming sounds to the symphony of the summoning. The ritual was completing itself now. The machinery was running away on its own, and I had no idea how to stop it. All I could do was watch. Lightning bolts flashed from the vortex, striking the pillars overhead. The smell of sulfur and charred concrete suddenly filled the air. The temperature jumped up noticeably. I was already sweating through my shirt.

Caimiléir watched the unfolding release of elemental power, transfixed. He moved back to stand on his elevated platform, never taking his eyes off the spinning dance of light. I crept toward MacPherson's body, trying to stay out of Caimiléir's view. I wasn't in the habit of rifling through a dead man's pockets. Desperate times.

I took everything. MacPherson's wallet. Car keys. A pair of reading glasses in a hard case, and all the things he had stolen from me, including my gun. I checked the clip and it was still full.

For all the good it will do. This is shaping up to be a really lousy gunfight.

Worth a try.

I fired past Caimiléir. I intended to get his attention and order him to stop the gate. The pop was barely audible over the roar of the portal coming to life. Caimiléir slowly turned in my direction, giving me half a smile. He reached inside his shirt and pulled out a silver disc on a silver chain.

"Shield," he yelled at me. Then he flicked his finger, and my gun went flying into the dark perimeter of the room. I wanted to ask him how he did that, but I had the feeling he wasn't in a mood to share.

The whirlwind was collapsing in on itself. Not like an implosion so much as a supernova, drawing all the energy into itself before flinging all the force it had out into the void. The gathering power made my skin itch and my instincts told me to find shelter. Now.

I hid behind a pillar and sat down. The whine of the gate had grown so loud and piercing that I covered up my ears. Long moments passed and I wanted to add my protest to the wail of the machine. Then the sound stopped altogether. For a heartbeat there was silence. I felt the pressure wave a split-second before I heard it. Wild magic, Caimiléir had called it. It came through the concrete pillar like it didn't exist. I felt the magic of the tattoo on the back of my neck peel away and the magic of the ward Keeper had put on me get stripped like the top layer of skin in a sandstorm. The magic of my pendant fled in a ping sound—I wouldn't be using it to escape my situation like I'd done for the women. At least they were safe. My shield and my healing medallion also jumped in my pocket and I knew they had been stripped of their power too.

Great. Caimiléir's shield was probably gone along with mine, but I didn't have my gun anymore. Son of a gun.

Excuse me. Please hold the apocalypse while I poke around in the dark for my weapon. Love ya. Be right back.

I ventured a look around the pillar. The gate was open now. Almost placid with a shimmering surface of crimson light. The heat and pressure had been absorbed by the water in the pool, protecting the structure around the ring. Now steam rose from the water, shrouding the gate in patchwork ghosts.

In terrible majesty, the deamhan rose from the gate. His features were chiseled and strong and he oozed charismatic power that washed over me like a metaphysical bath riveting my attention. He had a row of eyes over the slits of his nose and more eyes below the jaw, which was shaped like the prow of an icebreaker ship. He had thorny spikes down his neck and on his head with a circlet of taller horns like a crown.

He opened his mouth in a soundless roar that shook the earth, making it feel like the ground was shifting out from under me. He had three rows of sharp teeth like a shark's that clacked shut individually. His head swiveled around to take in the room, settling first on Caimiléir and then on me.

The power of his will was almost a physical blow. No actual words came from his mouth but there was clear and controlling weight in his gaze. The massiveness of his stare was crushing and blasted my resistance. Succumb! Be subjected! My playthings. Souls to feed me.

He continued to emerge. His Stain covered him, but it moved just beneath the surface of his skin. His shoulders and torso were decorated in scars with runic shapes. His arms were like trees, with flesh instead of bark, and hands that ended with stiletto-shaped talons. Around his neck he wore a priestly stole, decorated with profane symbols in a bloody script. The stole was fastened in place with spikes the size of my arm driven into the deamhan's pectoral muscles. The ends of the stole were tattered and the article gave a clue, perhaps, at the deamhan's mortal history from his prior life.

The behemoth continued to rise. His muscles were so powerfully toned they looked like the bony plates of a beetle. More of his body appeared as a dozen long, probing legs came over the edge of the gate. Below the navel, the deamhan had segmented body parts with legs in the form of a millipede.

He rose forty feet in the air before pausing, his multitude of insect legs lifting him up.

He roared again and this time there was an audible component to his voice that went along with the subsonic bass.

He found MacPherson's body. The talons closed around him and lifted him into the air while the deamhan's many eyes scanned his acquisition. MacPherson had passed out. He woke up just in time to look into the deamhan's otherworldly face. Just in time to see the deamhan open his jaws.

I looked away. I didn't want the image of what we all knew would happen next to haunt my nightmares, assuming I lived long enough to have any. I still heard MacPherson's shrill scream, which suddenly ended with a wet snapping sound.

I'd never bite the head off a cinnamon bear again.

I grimaced, catching a glance of the deamhan pulling off MacPherson's shirt, like taking the wrapper off a candy bar. The deamhan took another bite then and the crunching and smacking of MacPherson being consumed was a new sound I never wanted to hear again. The serial progress of the deamhan's three sets of teeth coming down in sequence, chunk, chunk, chunk, was as efficient as a wood chipper. In moments, MacPherson was gone.

Art thou there?

I heard the voice and flinched. Searching the shadows, I tried to find the person who'd spoken to tell them to get out of here. I found no one.

What's going on? I've been. Trying to find. Thee.

The voice was Béil's. And it was inside my head.

Go away.

I will. Not. Go away!

Crap. She can hear me! She was in my head like Erin had been at my Quickening.

Summon me!

The deamhan bent down and drank from the pool. He took huge gulps of water, his face buried in the pond. It would be a good time to cut the deamhan's head off, if there was such a thing as a fifty-foot sword.

Draw a circle! And. Summon me!

I'm a little busy right now.

Is the. Deamhan. There?

Deamhan? What deamhan. No deamhan here. Oh. That little guy? That's a deamhan? Why else would I be busy?

Summon me! We must kill. The deamhan. And Caimiléir.

I don't think so. Too many strings attached.

Caimiléir was bowing to the deamhan now. The wild magic had blown away whatever wards he had used to hide his Stain. It billowed out behind him like a majestic cloak of deadly vipers. So many ribbons. He was speaking again, but the words were alien to my ears.

The deamhan towered over him, arms outstretched, accepting whatever praise or promises Caimiléir was showering him with.

Has the. Deamhan. Had anything. To eat? Or drink?

The deamhan ate . . . someone . . . and drank water.

Good. Now. He is part. Of the mortal. Realm.

That's not good.

Before. He could. Not be. Killed. But now. He can.

Ok. Good then.

Summon me! We will. Kill him. And Caimiléir. Together!

I tried to tune out Béil's voice. There was no way I was going to invite her to this party. And her interruptions were wreaking havoc on my ability to pay attention.

Leave me alone, Béil.

Caimiléir was getting more animated. The deamhan was bending closer. I wasn't able to hear their conversation at all from here. If I moved, the deamhan might focus his gaze on me. I feared I would give in and surrender myself as his next jerky treat.

If thou diest. Thy realm. Ends.

The deamhan pointed a talon in Caimiléir's face. Caimiléir fell to his knees. Something was going on and it was bad. If I had to guess, the deamhan was complaining about the lack of snacks. He was promised a full plate of goodies, including a few tender female morsels, and all he'd gotten so far was one wrinkled old cocktail weenie.

Thou art. A fool. Not to. Use all. Thy tools.

I know.

I want to. Tell thee. Something more.

Caimiléir was holding diamonds in his hands. I couldn't see what he was doing but there was a flare of power.

Diamonds materialized in the forehead of the deamhan. Caimiléir threw another gout of blue power and the deamhan didn't seem to care.

Or maybe he couldn't care.

I remembered how Caimiléir had controlled the little deamhan Greim and how he'd forced him to bash his own brains out. Afterward, Caimiléir had taken diamonds from his head.

More mental magnets realigned and clicked into place. I knew how the diamonds had been taken out of all those jewelry stores in all those robberies. I also knew why Barry Mallondyke had been cut open after he had already been killed. I finally had the answers I needed for my client. I just hoped I would live long enough to tell her.

I must. Tell thee. Something more.

I really don't care.

The deamhan. Is Brón.

CHAPTER 34

Betrayal

It took a few moments for me to assemble her words and realize their meaning. Revelations were coming at me too fast now. And as soon as I realized the implications of what she had said, I remembered Caimiléir saying "*Ríoga-Brón*" over and over again during his summoning song.

The same deamhan you bargained with? The one who owns your soul?

The same.

Wow.

If I failed here, she was completely screwed. It was clear why this was so important to her. Why she would want to fight this deamhan in the Mortal realm, where he'd be vulnerable. If he gets dead, she gets free. And she very much wants to make sure he gets dead. I couldn't blame her.

I can make. Sure thou. And Fáidh. Are. Together.

What? What did she say?

Forever.

She was distracting me. Something was going on. Caimiléir was talking again.

He was sending a ribbon of blue into the diamonds in the deamhan's head—Brón's head. Brón leaned down and extended his taloned hand. Caimiléir used his glass knife to stab Brón's hand with such force that it went to the hilt. The knife must have gone to the bone. Maybe Caimiléir needed some of the deamhan's blood. No, it was a test of Caimiléir's control over the deamhan. I badly wanted to understand what he was saying.

Whatever the motivation, the deamhan didn't bat an eye. And

he had plenty of eyes to choose from.

Credit where credit is due: it took a lot of guts to double-cross a deamhan.

The gleam of insanity in Caimiléir's visage was full-blown, and his face glowed in victory. He threw back his head, flinging sweat, and yelled—a primal shriek—that split the air with enough strength to be heard over the whine of the Jeweled Gate.

This was getting really bad.

Caimiléir almost danced as he went back to his collection of diamonds. A thread of blue power trickled into the stones and there was a huge rumbling sound. It sounded like it was coming from everywhere at once. I noticed bits of stone and dust falling from the ceiling.

Something was moving again.

The entire building above ground was sliding, opening the pit down here to the sky overhead. Cool air billowed in and I nearly swooned as the fresh air swept over me.

Caimiléir climbed aboard Brón's back. He had successfully enthralled his deamhanic millipede. Now the lunatic was planning to ride the monster up and out of the pit. His plan was moments away from fruition.

I had to do something.

I can. Give thee. Fáidh. Summon me!

Go away, Béil!

I will. Make sure. A body. Is found.

No!

The body of. Her husband. That's what. Thou needest. Is it not?

Tears started to burn my eyes. Béil's promise struck directly into the center of my being. She'd finally figured me out.

Summon me! And tomorrow. His body will. Be found. And Fáidh will. Be. Thine.

I found myself running. If I broke the circle, the gate would close. I fell on the diamond ring. The deamhan's wild magic had erased the ward. I could reach the diamonds now. I swiped at the stones, dislodging hundreds. There were more stones beneath. I shoveled diamonds out of the way with both hands—but the ring was deep and I wasn't breaking the circle.

Overhead, the way out was almost open.

How deep was this ring?

I pushed my arm into the diamonds as far as I could reach and couldn't find a bottom. The power surged around my arm. Even if I could interrupt the circle here, it continued below where I couldn't reach.

Holy Mother . . .

There were too many diamonds. The ring was too deep. I pulled my arm free. There were dozens of scratches on my skin.

Caimiléir was on the back of Brón's shoulders and saw me digging. He smiled and nodded. He knew what I was trying to do. He knew that the ring was too deep and I'd never be able to break the circle. The exit overhead was nearly open and in a few seconds Caimiléir and his deamhan would be free.

I couldn't give up.

Caimiléir had drained some of my power, but not all of it. I woke it up and threw it at the diamonds. "*Tine*!" I cried.

A pillar of flame erupted from my hand. Diamonds were the hardest substance in the world, but they had also been born in fire. I prayed they could be destroyed by fire as well. How hot is magma? I didn't know. I just cranked up the heat like Erin had taught me and begged the diamonds to burn.

The flame from my hand shifted from orange to blue to white. The diamonds were almost blindingly brilliant. The light shattered in sparkling colors and shattered again a million times over. I looked up and saw the deamhan reaching to grasp the edge of the opening. He was carrying Caimiléir into the open air and they were almost out. I looked down again, intensifying and focusing the flame, and saw diamonds falling in on themselves. I wasn't sure what was happening—just that something was. And I needed it to work.

I moved the flame, widening the hole.

Brón bellowed. Maybe it was the glimpse of the Mortal realm he was seeing as he emerged from the pit. Maybe it was the sense that something was changing with the gate.

Then Brón bellowed again. This time the sound was pure pain.

The gate slammed shut.

The orange light of the Deamhan realm went out.

The whine of the engine started to slow.

I stopped the stream of fire.

Brón and his passenger fell back into the pit.

The millipede part of Brón was curling in on itself, and the meaty, severed end of his body convulsed.

Caimiléir jumped from Brón's back to keep from falling into the pit where he would be crushed, but he was turning sideways and didn't have enough distance to make the gap. Instead of landing on flat ground, his legs slammed against the edge of the diamond ring and it sounded like a baseball bat being snapped inside a bag of sirloins. He cried out and started to slip back into the pit. His fingers scrabbled for purchase on the concrete, which was slick with Brón's blood.

I considered letting him drop. He'd be good company for all those sharp, chitinous legs that were thrashing in the pit like the blades of the world's biggest blender.

But I might need him.

And I'd have a hard time living with myself if I had the chance to save someone—even someone who didn't deserve it—and let them die. The Mama had taught me too well. I staggered over and grabbed him by the wrist and pulled him up.

"I underestimated you," he said. "You still have power. Heal me. My leg is broken."

"Help me kill Brón first," I replied.

Through the pain, Caimiléir managed to look surprised. "You know the deamhan's name?"

"Béil invaded my thoughts," I explained.

Caimiléir managed a weak laugh. "Of course she did."

"Until Brón's dead, nothing else matters."

Caimiléir turned to look in the direction of the pit, concentrating. "He has shaken off my control. I can feel it. He is stronger than the other deamhans I have summoned and he is wounded. The diamonds I used for the focus are useless now. I have betrayed him and I must agree. It will be exceedingly difficult. I have used nearly all my power."

"Brón is cut in half. He's dying, right?"

"He could survive. If he heals, he will regenerate. Then he will kill us and escape."

Why couldn't he just die? I thought bitterly. Then I remembered something Keeper and I had discussed. While Caimiléir continued studying the deamhan, I used a small supply of will and transcribed the symbols Keeper had shown me in the middle of the air.

Brón bellowed again. I'd cut the deamhan in half but it wasn't enough. There was still a wealth of agony in his voice but now there was also anger.

Caimiléir looked back at me. Every time he moved, the pain made him grimace. I was having a hard time feeling bad about that. "I could just use my power to leave this place. You could follow me."

"Bad idea," I replied. "First of all, I don't trust you. Second, this place is warded now. Keeper taught me how. None of us are leaving."

Caimiléir looked around and sensed I was telling the truth.

"Then it seems we share a common purpose," he said. "Though I am Uncourted, it is the duty of a Fae to return a kindness swiftly. In exchange for pulling me away from the pit, I vow with an oath on my life that I will cause no harm to thee or to thy wife or thy progeny for one hundred years. Do you accept?"

"Throw in a bag of chips and you got a deal," I replied.

Caimiléir nodded and said, "It is done."

Thou livest!? Béil's voice came again into my mind.

Nope. I died.

There was silence and I took advantage of the moment. "How do we kill him? Permanently?"

"It is a challenge. A deamhan is rarely killed entirely, but it can be eliminated for a very long time."

"What do we have to do to kill it forever?"

"We have to eat his heart."

Béil's voice came back to me.

Thou art. A liar.

Sue me.

Brón roared and it appeared that he was no longer leaking.

Only a minute or two after being sliced in half and he was healing already. I suppressed a laugh but it came out anyway.

Through gritted teeth, Caimiléir asked, "What is so funny?"

"Somewhere in the Deamhan realm, there's a chunk of Brón's butt!"

I laughed some more.

"Prince Luck, I envy your ability to find humor in such a circumstance."

The deamhan. It lives?

Yep. We're having tea and crumpets.

Summon me!

Can't do that. Caimiléir and I are busy killing Brón.

No! Béil sounded desperate. I must. Help thee!

You also want to kill Caimiléir.

For his crimes!

I can't allow that.

It is our law!

But it's not human law. You can't be judge, jury, and executioner.

Thou deniest me. My vengeance. I have. Waited. For centuries!

This is my realm.

And all. I have. Offered? Does. None of it. Appeal to you?

Of course it did. Not so much the courtesan part. Maybe the part where I'd be wealthy and contented and be needed by my father. Certainly the part that would allow Erin and I to be together.

No.

Thou art. Stubborn. And stupid.

Yes, I am. Goodbye, Béil.

Caimiléir looked at me, waiting. His face was ashen and his skin was clammy. He didn't look well at all.

"Is Béil communicating with you?"

"Yes. She might give up now."

"Don't count on it," Caimiléir said feebly. "I have known her for hundreds of years and she is nothing if not persistent."

"She wants both you and Brón dead."

Caimiléir nodded. "I know." He looked over at the deamhan who seemed to be gaining strength. "I have recovered a little more power. But it seems that Brón is healing now. We will need to strike before it is too late."

"What do we do?"

"In a moment. First, tell me, how did you defeat the tattoo?"

I hesitated. To explain, I'd have to tell him that I could see Stain. Then I'd have to tell him that I figured out he used a ward to hide his magical power. Then Keeper had placed a ward on me to make sure I'd be able to resist his tattoo. And Keeper had suggested my left buttock himself as a place to hide it and hadn't hesitated at all when painting the sigil. It would be satisfying to point out that I'd used Caimiléir's trick against him but I couldn't forget that he was an extremely dangerous man.

All those thoughts went through my head in the space of a second.

"Sorry," I replied. "That's going to have to be my secret."

"Ah," Caimiléir nodded. "But you did defeat my tattoo, which means you were only pretending to obey?"

It was my turn to nod. "I had to pretend to be under your control until I could help my friends. After that, I hoped to keep the deamhan from being summoned. Now I have to kill him."

"In the next few moments, you will either succeed and become a hero or you will die."

I didn't really have a response for that.

"And what of me?" Caimiléir asked.

I thought about it. "Did you have anything to do with Barry Mallondyke's death?"

"I put him in harm's way," he replied. "But MacPherson was responsible for his death and mutilation."

I had to believe what he said because he couldn't lie. I replied,

"It's not my place to judge or condemn you. You've promised not to harm me or the people I care about for one-hundred years, and I also agree not to harm you for the same period of time."

"Very well. We attack then. You will need to collect the heart and bring it back. I cannot walk. Keep in mind that the deamhan will live as long as the heart is intact and while he lives he will try to bend you to his will."

CHAPTER 35

Heart of a Deamhan

"I will keep Brón off-balance as long as I can. Your fire will be effective enough if you can tighten its focus. Make it as hot and sharp as you can. In this realm, a deamhan has fewer defenses. Something like a fish out of water."

I pulled the silver piece out of my pocket. Erin had told me I could use it to concentrate my power. I hoped it would do the job I needed.

Caimiléir looked at the piece of silver and recognized it. "Souvenir?" he asked.

"Something like that."

"Carve out the deamhan's heart," Caimiléir said. "Do it quickly."

Brón was watching us with his many eyes. He had to know something was coming. We weren't conspiring to throw him a birthday party. His gaze followed me as I walked around the perimeter of the ring, out of reach. His body was growing new sections now and little legs were sprouting like saplings.

There were no words spoken but the deamhan's command was clear. Surrender to me.

Caimiléir hit him at that moment with a bolt of lightning. It seared the side of Brón's face and several of the deamhan's eyes exploded. Brón roared in fresh agony. I was caught by surprise as well.

"I knew there had to be a zap spell!" I said.

I held the silver shard and channeled a surge of power into it. "*Tine*!"

A tight beam of white fire lanced from the point. It hit Brón in the chest. Brón was stunned for the moment by Caimiléir's spell. I was worried my fire wouldn't burn through the deamhan's hard-plated flesh but, after a long moment, the light emerged from his back and burned into the concrete wall on the other side. The shard allowed me to control the power I had to maximize its efficiency. I felt a boundary within the shard. There was a limit to the amount of power it could accept no matter how hard I pushed—but the control was precise and the power it emitted was more than enough to cut through the deamhan's hide.

I carved an arc into Brón's chest. Brón suddenly shook his head and roared. The effects of the Caimiléir's spell were short-lived. I made the mistake of looking into the deamhan's eyes.

Kill the other.

The thought was so clear. It made so much sense. Caimiléir had started this. He had been responsible from the beginning. It wasn't the deamhan's fault that he had been summoned, was it? The deamhan hadn't even wanted this.

It was Caimiléir's fault.

He couldn't be trusted.

Caimiléir must die.

I turned my silver shard and aimed it at Caimiléir.

Another blast of electrical energy slammed into the deamhan's head. Brón howled.

Wow.

I pressed my hands against my temples and blinked a dozen times. The influence of the deamhan's mind was incredibly hard to resist.

I had almost tried to kill Caimiléir after I promised not to.

I gritted my teeth and returned to carving Brón's chest. I walked closer to the ring to better control the power of the silver shard and the pencil-thin shaft of flame that was mine to wield. I made it most of the way around the circular cut before Brón shook off the effects of Caimiléir's spell again. This time the deamhan leaned down toward me and reached out one long-taloned hand to crush me. It was close. The deamhan's hand slammed down and his talons stabbed the concrete and caught there. Brón had to try a couple of times to extricate his talons before the concrete broke apart. Brón raised his hands in a defensive gesture. I cut through his hands, removing some fingers and then Caimiléir hit him again with a third bolt.

My heart was pounding hard and my breathing was becoming labored. My whole body ached. How much adrenaline can one person's body produce? Or survive? I felt my own heart might leap out of my chest before I could get Brón's heart out of his.

Brón was losing the fight. He had lost a lot of blood now, which colored his chest and ran into the pit. Caimiléir's spell had stunned him again and I had maybe a minute to finish the job. Brón had tilted backward and was lying half outside the ring on his back. I ran as fast as I could up the monster's body, slipping twice on the blood.

I held the silver shard in my teeth and grabbed the incision I had made with both hands. The muscles were heavy, and I grunted as I pulled Brón's chest open. My fire had cut through Brón's ribs in a couple of places, and I pulled the pieces of bone out and threw them down.

The creature's heart was there for the taking.

A few quick cuts and I had it. The heart was bigger than my head and must have weighed fifty pounds. It was slippery and awkward to manage but I wrangled it out of the cavity.

It was still beating. The force of the muscles contracting nearly made me lose my grip. I'd never be able to carry it down so I threw it in Caimiléir's general direction. It plopped onto the concrete with a wet smack.

Brón snapped back to his senses as I slid down his belly and landed on the ring, dangerously off balance. I almost fell into the pit before catching my balance and jumping. I landed in the swamp. My body begged me to stop and rest in the cool water.

Brón curved his body and made a leap for the opening overhead. His hands caught the lip of the concrete and he started to pull himself up. We had his heart but he was still getting away. The hole above was the only place my ward didn't cover. The gap there was too big.

I yelled at Caimiléir, "Hit him!"

Caimiléir looked exhausted and waxy and pale. "Can't," he said. "Nothing left."

Really?

I focused the flame at Brón's remaining fingers. I cut through enough of them that he lost his grip. He swiped at the concrete anyway and broke off huge chunks of it. Brón landed halfway out of the pit and the impact felt like an earthquake. More concrete fell from the ceiling, crashing onto the floor and splashing into the pool.

Brón stopped moving.

I scrambled to the deamhan's heart and dragged it over to Caimiléir.

For a minute, it was all I could do to stay upright and pant. Finally, I was able to ask, "How much of this thing do we have to eat?"

Caimiléir's eyes were closed and he opened them halfway and barked in a laugh that was curt and bitter.

"It's much larger than I thought," he said.

"What did you expect?" I replied. "Huge deamhan, huge heart."

"I didn't give it much thought, I admit. I was not prepared for a change in plans."

Great. Spiffy.

"Well, there isn't enough steak sauce in the world to make this taste any better, so . . ." I bit into the end of the deamhan's heart and tore off a piece.

"Nasty," I said. "What kind of wine goes with this?"

Caimiléir chuckled. I felt sick.

Brón woke up.

His bellow was the longest and loudest one yet and it shook the ground. More chunks of concrete fell from the ceiling. Some of them fell too close for comfort.

"We better move," I said.

COME TO ME.

Without even looking in Brón's eyes, the compulsion swept over me.

I resisted though. Even though I was standing up and my feet were moving slowly in the direction of the pit, I resisted.

I was rather proud of myself, in fact. The deamhan couldn't make me do anything I didn't want to do. I'd just go stand over by the pit and then he'd see how well I resisted. That would show him.

I am my own master. And I am a genius.

Of course, if I were closer to Brón he'd be able to see that. Not that I had any plans to be getting anywhere near . . .

I fell into the swamp.

The water got up my nose and into my eyes.

I stood, coughing and spitting.

Somehow, I'd walked thirty yards unaware.

What am I doing?

Maybe it was the practice I'd gotten with Madrasceartán, but my reflexes were quick. I barely saw the blow coming. Brón's maimed hand missed my head by a fraction of an inch as I ducked beneath his swing. I backed up, tripping over my own feet, and tumbled back into the pool.

Brón was looking pretty spry for a beast without a heart. I sloshed to the side of the swamp and turned. Miraculously, I hadn't dropped the silver shard and I aimed it at the center of the deamhan's forehead. He saw the light bursting from my weapon and dodged. My silver fire hit him between the eyes, but his movement made the beam rake across his brow. Brón howled. He struck at the ring around the pit with what remained of his fist. Diamonds flew, glittering fire cascading in all directions.

I'd had enough. I'd blind him first and then I'd remove his head and then I'd sever his arms. We'd see how long it took him to regenerate a brain. I took aim at a row of eyes and . . . nothing happened.

I had no more juice.

Poodles.

It would only take a moment for Brón to realize I'd exhausted my power. Then he'd chase me down in a corner of this chamber and I'd be toast.

What could I do?

I couldn't use my pendant. Its magic had been obliterated.

Great. I could summon Béil. She'd be able to come through the ward since I'd only learned to make one that kept everything in. Not out. I believed her when she said she would be able to kill the deamhan. All it would cost would be my integrity and Caimiléir's life. Neither of those things was looking too worthwhile at the moment.

I couldn't bring myself to do it.

All these thoughts flashed through my mind in the space of a breath.

At the edge of the pool, the water was only a foot deep. I was standing in the water with my feet buried in muck. But it was good muck. Rich, earthy muck. Muck of the land I had learned to love. The only land I really knew. This realm, the mortal realm, my home.

The home that was blessed with life. And power.

It was there, just beneath the surface, calling to me.

Erin had warned me. To touch the power of earth was to open myself to annihilation. I'd make a great firework though. If I could be sure the explosion would turn Brón into kibble, I'd do it. Although if it worked, Caimiléir would die as well.

I looked down. The only tools I had were my mind, my body, and a silver shard.

A shard that controlled power.

A whole new set of mental magnets lined themselves up and clicked together.

If the silver regulated output, why not input?

Brón had cocked his wounded head and was looking in my direction, thinking. I had to act fast or I risked falling under his will again.

My hands were shaking. I was desperately weak and afraid. If this didn't work, I would die. I couldn't see Caimiléir from here. I was alone. Just me and Brón.

And the land I loved.

I thrust the silver into the muck and hoped.

The power of Earth was eager to join with me. The silver shard was of the earth herself and the earth had to work with it. But the power behind the shard was massive. And it wanted to surge up all at once instead of being drawn in a sip. After what seemed like forever, the earth conceded to the connection. Power leapt up in a line through the silver point and I felt myself being pulled down at the same time, anchored to the land beneath me.

I looked up. Brón saw I was stymied. He opened his mouth and his rows of teeth clacked against each other in anticipation.

I let the power in.

Several things happened at once. First, I did not explode in my own personal supernova. Second, Brón came at me like a freight train with a hundred knives in front. Third, I extended my free hand and the power that erupted from me was a column of purest flame, an incandescent searchlight.

Brón's head evaporated.

No ash. No flying gore. In one moment, Brón was roaring and full of teeth and horns and eyes and in the next moment there was nothing.

I felt so justified.

The earth's power illuminated every corner of my being. I was full of light. I cast the light on the deamhan and more chunks of him burned away in righteous flame. The fire consumed the deamhan, erasing it, transforming wicked flesh into holy oblivion. I stood and the tether of power followed me as I walked. The silver point remained down, pulling the earth's power up into me. My open hand swept around the room. Brón's shoulders and arms and torso ceased to exist. I climbed to the edge of the pit and burned away the insect body, cleansing every trace from the depths of the vile pit at my feet.

Diamonds, symbols of greed. Diadems of lust and oppression and dominion. Those were next to go. I burned them out of the ring. Every glittering facet was anathema to me for what they represented, what they had been used for. They were tainted by evil magic and had to be cleansed in the fire that had made them. When the ring was empty, I ascended the platform with its box of sparkling sins and I cleansed those too.

More concrete was falling. My fire was too much for the ceiling to withstand, and the stray light had turned patches of the room to dust. There was rubble around me and more was falling, but I was not afraid.

I cast about, searching for more wickedness to purify. Caimiléir! Servant of evil! I could not find him. Perhaps he was buried now, beneath the fallen roof.

I was so tired. The light inside me had burned away all my impurities. It was too much. I was filled with holy fire but my flesh was growing weak. I had not been consumed in an instant, but I suddenly felt that the power coursing through me was stronger than I could bear. With great effort, I unclenched my fingers and dropped the silver shard. The connection between the silver and the earth winked out.

I was falling.

As I fell, I saw several beams of light catching the motes of dust.

The light was coming from my eyes and my mouth. The light stored within me had to escape. I had to let it go. It gradually drifted away, and I watched it leave me with a feeling of wistfulness. It was so beautiful.

Then there was no more light except the stars and sky. A solitary cloud directly above me showed traces of pink.

Dawn of a new day.

CHAPTER 36

Survivor

I don't know how long I lay there, but I knew I was dying. I faded in and out of consciousness. Each time I awoke, the sky was a little brighter. Too weak to move, I was content in knowing that Brón was no more. Erin and Brandy and Carlene were all alive. Max and Sandretta and Nat wouldn't need to hide. Keeper would check on them for me. My father, the Alder King, would remain on the throne.

It all felt good and right.

I heard scrapes. Perhaps it was the earth, moving to take me.

"Thou fool," said a voice.

Béil was with me. She walked around toward my feet so she wouldn't have to look at me upside down.

"Thou fool," she repeated.

"You said that already," I replied. And then, "Brón is gone. You're free from him, Béil. Caimiléir told me how to make sure he couldn't return. He will never come back to claim you."

She continued to look at me with a sour expression.

"I know you wanted to be here for it," I said. "But you could still say 'thank you.' Nobody will know, and I'm dying so it won't matter anymore. In fact, you owe Caimiléir, too."

She looked me over and I think she was probing me with her fingers. I grunted a bit when she found my broken ribs, but I really wasn't feeling much of anything.

"Where is. Caimiléir. Then?" she asked.

"Under a slab of concrete. Maybe. If you find him, don't kill him."

I watched her as she looked around. She remained kneeling

over me as she scanned the scene in every direction.

"I don't. See him. Here," she said.

"Huh," was my eloquent reply. It was possible, I supposed, that I had destroyed the ward with my silver fire and Caimiléir had gotten away. I wasn't sorry.

"Is the deamhan heart still here?" I asked.

"Deamhan heart?" Béil replied.

I told her how Caimiléir and I had attacked Brón together. How I had carved out Brón's heart. How I had eaten a piece of it and then I stopped Brón for good. I didn't tell her about the silver shard or my discovery in connecting to the earth's power, but I assured her that I had been able to burn the deamhan's remains completely.

As I spoke, Béil grew more grim and her features hard.

"The last. Thou sawest. Of the heart. Was with. Caimiléir?" she asked.

"Yes. Is that a problem?"

She didn't answer that question. Instead, she said, "We must. Get thee. To a safer. Place."

"It doesn't matter," I said. I was starting to go under again. Maybe for the last time. "Tell Erin—I mean Fáidh—I, uh," I cleared my throat. There was a catch in it that wouldn't budge. "Just tell her I wish we could have had more time. Tell Nat he's the best friend I ever had."

"Thou fool," Béil said.

"You keep saying that. I might start taking it personally."

"So. Thou didst attack. Brón. Thinking. Thou. Wouldst die?"

I laughed a little. "You're the one who told me I was going to die."

"To frighten thee. To make. Thee want. To summon me."

"Well, you accomplished half of that. I was frightened."

"And yet. Thou didst keep. Fighting?"

"Of course."

"Even though. Thou wouldst. Die?"

I was too tired and weak to open my eyes again. I let the moment be. I felt a few drops of water land on my face. It seemed to be raining. The drops were warm and ran onto my lips. They tasted salty. Funny. Rain didn't usually taste salty.

I heard Béil sniff. "What fools. These mortals. Be."

"See. Shakespeare said it better."

I felt her fingers on my face. "I can. Save thee," she said.

"No more deals," I replied. "You already owe me."

"Yes."

"So. Do what you need to do." She would either save me or not. My mind fell into a pool of white.

I guess she needed to save me.

Images and noises floated through the white for a while. A female voice. Urgent whispering. A child's face drenched in sweat but determined. I struggled to recognize the faces. I tried to speak. But I couldn't move or make a sound at all.

Then I woke up at the pink castle. Jon Bon Jar-Jar or whatever it was called. Béil and Laoch were there when I finally cracked open my eyes. Turned out I'd lost a whole day. I could tell when I did a bit of sleuthing, which is, after all, my profession.

"How long have I been out?" I asked.

"A day," Béil said.

See? Sleuthing. My profession. I only moonlight as a deamhanslayer.

"I'll live then?"

"Thou shalt live."

I was filled with gratitude upon hearing those words. If I weren't such a man, I would have cried. More than a couple of tears. A couple of tears are still manly. I was entitled to shed a couple of tears. One for each "X" chromosome.

"I wish I could express my feelings to you in words," I said, remembering to avoid the words "Thank you."

"Ironically. Credit. Goes to. Brón," Béil said.

"How's that?" I asked.

"It was. Brón who. Enabled me. To have. Laoch."

I was confused.

She went on, "And Laoch. Is a part. Of thee. Ye are. Part of. Each other."

I tried to grasp what she meant.

"It would. Be unwise. To. Test the limits. But. With Laoch. Thou hast. Two lives. In a way. Ye are. One person. In two bodies. Together. It's possible. Thou mayest. Never. Die. But I fear. If thou diest. So will he."

Her words were sobering. And amazing. And in my mind, I had to review again all the reasons Béil had for wanting to help me.

Those images and noises came back to me in a flood. They had healed me together, Béil and Laoch. But the boy had made the greater contribution. I found myself very concerned about Laoch.

Does any of this harm the boy? How does it work? Is there anything I need to do for him?

Béil didn't offer any further information. She fixed a cryptic expression on her face and put her hand on Laoch's head, stroking his hair with a gesture that was comforting and motherly. Laoch hadn't said anything at all, which wasn't odd for him. He looked at me with solemn eyes and an awareness that Big Things had been happening and he had been a part of them.

I decided that the way they quietly related to each other was sufficient answer. I didn't need anything more.

Not right now. I was here and alive and it was enough.

"Madrasceartán. Arrived. And carried. Thee here. Thy father. Asked me to. Tell thee. 'Well done.'"

Wow. Two whole words from dad.

But my sarcasm was unfair.

At least he cared enough to try. How many people had fathers who didn't care at all? I was still living, and I had a father who cared enough to send his special liondog assassin to haul my unconscious keister to a relatively safe place. And he even left a message.

Well done.

"Has anyone else come to see me?" I asked, hoping for a certain answer.

"Yes," Béil replied, rolling her eyes. "She came. Fáidh helped heal thee. Too."

Nice.

I felt a measure of added relief that had nothing to do with the physical state of my injuries. There was no pain to speak of, but I felt extremely weak. Probably explained the extra leaking chromosomes. Stupid chromosomes.

"I can't apologize for how things have turned out," I said. I pinched my eyes with my fingers to dry them. "Remember, the words you spoke?" I quoted the prophecy she had given:

What was once above is below,
What was below, above.
What was once in is out,
What was out is in.
Call the inside out,
Not the outside in.

"The first two lines referred to the location, I decided. There were two parcels of land near each other and dirt had been excavated from one place and dumped in the other. The next two lines referred to Caimiléir and Brón. Caimiléir was once in the Alder King's court but he was kicked out. Brón was out of the Mortal realm but Caimiléir brought him in."

Béil was skeptical but she had a pretty good idea what the ending meant. "And the. Last lines. Are the. Two of us. I suppose?"

"I think so. Maybe I'm just interpreting the words to fit what happened. Maybe it's just bad poetry. But I called the power inside me to defeat the deamhan."

And the power inside the earth.

"And I don't think bringing you in from the outside was meant to be."

"You have. More power. And capacity. Than any. Halfling should," she said ruefully.

I had the earth. I am a . . . Conduit.

"I had Caimiléir's help," I countered. "If I hadn't

convinced him—forced him—to help it might have been a different outcome."

Béil's expression did not soften.

"I don't blame you for being angry. I know what it's like when you want something and you don't get it."

Béil looked at me with her eyes half-closed. After a long moment of frozen silence, she finally nodded. That's what passed for understanding and gratitude among the Fae.

"I'm glad you are free from Brón's promise," I said, trying to be magnanimous while still venturing to remind her how some circumstances that were quite important to her had turned out in her favor.

She looked at me for a moment and then turned her head away while she pretended to be interested in something on the far wall. I guess that debt was paid by her caring for me in the last day or so. Although, from what I had just learned, saving me was also saving Laoch, and I knew he was definitely important to her.

I let it go but had a different question.

"Has Caimiléir been seen?"

That question brought half a smile to her lips.

"He has made. No appearance. In this realm. As thou saidst. There was. So much. Rubble. To sift. Through. He either. Escaped. Or is. A puddle."

Laoch actually giggled. The sound was creepy.

For better or worse then, the fate of the deamhan's heart was the same as Caimiléir's. I was pretty sure he was still alive. I still carried his Stain.

Keeper would know more about the deamhan's heart, I bet. If anyone knew—or could find out—it would be Keeper. I'd go track him down as soon as I had the chance.

I didn't have to track Keeper down.

When my stomach decided it was tired of being empty, I walked stiffly down to the kitchen to find my friends Stail and Láir had allowed themselves to be recruited to cook again. Everything they had prepared was fresh and light and easy on my stomach. Consommé. Salad niçoise. About a dozen different tapas dishes, each more delicious than the last. The food nourished and comforted in bits and pieces.

As I sat at the table, I caught Láir looking at me and beaming. "So good to see you," I called. Láir nodded and Stail raised an eyebrow in my general direction. They were glad to see me too.

Keeper's voice came booming down the marble halls, telling Béil what a beautiful residence she had and how he needed to visit more often.

He came around the corner and spied me, and a wide grin erupted from beneath all those whiskers.

"There ya are, lad," he said. He was carrying a bottle of something.

He put his burden on the table and held his massive arms outstretched. I stood and received a rock-like embrace that just about crushed the wind out of me. He smelled of wood fire and baked bread and brotherhood. With tenderness, he said, "Ya won a victory for the ages, my boy." I caught a sentimental glimmer in his eyes when he let me go.

He clapped me on the shoulder, which was like being hit by a linebacker. Then he handed the rather dusty bottle to Béil.

"Don't ask where I got it," he said conspiratorially, "If we're lucky, it won't be missed until savored and all evidence destroyed."

Béil smiled and accepted the gift with a polite curtsy.

Keeper half-whispered to Laoch, "I haven't forgotten ya." From thin air, as far as I could see, he produced a tall mug with froth on top and a spoon. "The mortals call this 'root beer float' and I can tell thee from personal experience that its contents are a marriage made by the gods."

Laoch took a sniff, then a sip. A huge smile spread across his face.

Having completed his duties, Keeper turned his attention back to me.

"How are our friends?" I asked.

"Fáidh is well. She came to see ya," Keeper replied.

"I've been told she helped patch me up. Again." I said. "I'm glad to hear she's all right."

"She is and she'll want to see ya now yer awake."

"That's great. What about the others?"

"The one called Brandy suffered less and recovered quickest. The one called Carlene needed some care. The ordeal frightened her greatly and she was ill-prepared to deal with deamhan beings from another realm. The night was long for both, but we set them to rights. I'll tell ya that they neither remember nor bear any sign of their misfortune. They've forgotten all from that night and believe they had a wee bit much to drink and fell asleep at Fáidh's house where they found themselves when they awoke. 'Tis best if they are not reminded of the truth."

Oh, they bore signs of their misfortunes all right. They had Caimiléir's Stain on them as well. I just replied, "Of course."

Keeper put a meaty hand on each of my shoulders, and it felt as if I were carrying a full pack on a fifty-mile hike. He looked into my eyes with probing intensity. "Ya defeated one of the seven Lords of Deamhan, lad."

"Really?"

"Oh, aye. Brón was no common deamhan. Caimiléir bargained with him to gain his service and all his followers. Are ya certain he's gone?"

I returned a steady gaze. "Brón's annihilated," I replied. "Burned, except for the heart."

Keeper nodded. I didn't mention my finding the means to become a Conduit to him either. First, because it was too important to discuss in mixed company. Second, because it had nearly killed me and I had no plans to try it again. Ever.

"And Caimiléir?" Keeper asked.

I shook my head. "I can't be sure. I didn't see him escape, but it's possible my ward was broken when the ceiling started coming down, so he probably made it free. I plan to find out what I can as soon as I return to my realm."

"Your realm?" Keeper chuckled. "Lad, yer only a few days past

10,000 dawns, but ya served us all well—better than most who have lived centuries—and yer already one of us. This realm is yours now."

I smiled and said, "I stand corrected."

"Indeed ya do."

"May I ask you a question, Keeper?"

"Always."

"What about Brón's heart? If Caimiléir lives and has the deamhan's heart, is that a problem? Everything happened so fast. I got Brón's heart and I ate a little bit of it and then I had to kill him. Now it may be gone."

Keeper took a step back and stroked his whiskers while he thought. I was relieved to have the weight of his hands off my shoulders. "So thou has tasted the heart of a deamhan, eh?"

"Yes. Caimiléir said that if the heart was eaten, the deamhan could not live again."

"Then it is true. An Eternal cannot lie. The heart cannot be restored if thou hast eaten a part of it. And the deamhan is gone."

"Is it a problem though if Caimiléir has the rest of it?"

Keeper's thick eyebrows knit themselves together as he frowned. "'Tis a problem indeed," he said. "Ya want to cook a heart with young green leeks, and those are out of season right now."

There was a silent moment while my overtaxed mind tried to worry about the horrible consequences of Caimiléir taking the deamhan heart while half-listening to the words Keeper said. Finally, my mind caught up to what I'd heard, and I realized Keeper was putting one over on me.

"Ha-haaah!" Keeper roared. He grabbed me by the shoulder and leaned over.

I laughed in return, in part because Keeper's laugh was so over-the-top. And it struck me funny to see how he was killing himself with his own joke. And also because I was finally able to know it was really over. Relief equals laughter. The doctor tells you your disease is in remission, or the cops find your lost child, or the deamhan is truly dead and gone—you laugh. Keeper and

I laughed until my sides ached and then he put his arms around me again.

"Thou hast naught to fear," Keeper said. "Be well and visit me when thou returnest to the realm."

In my heart, I vowed I would.

Keeper was the father I wish I had.

CHAPTER 37

A Woman and a Lie

I wanted to sleep in my own bed that night. As soon as I felt strong enough for a walk, I descended from Béil's castle and went down to the lake. I called "Midnight Dreary!" and within minutes, my friendly neighborhood raven had found me. "I need to find the quickest way to my home in the Mortal realm," I said. The raven led me gate-by-gate to a stone that was only a jump from the Alder King's castle. When it opened, I saw the inside of my own house.

Huh. Got my own stone now, it seems.

I gave Midnight Dreary a nod and said, "You are a good and faithful friend." She croaked once and flapped away.

I wanted to check in with Nat—and Erin—but the coincidence of days and nights was not in my favor. When I stepped through the portal into my house, it was the middle of the night in the mortal realm. I was curious to see if there was news about the building over the pit—the second building of MacPherson's I had destroyed. The middle-of-the-night rebroadcast of the evening news devoted a whole sixty seconds to the story. The reporter on the scene stated that the building was being constructed as a movie set for an upcoming blockbuster. The site wasn't finished yet, but some work being done to prepare for some special effects had gone wrong, and according to company officials, the test had gone badly, resulting in the building's collapse. Lonnie MacPherson, the company's CEO, could not be reached for comment.

Well, that's a good cover story, I thought.

I considered sneaking out to the site at some point to see if I could find anything useful and decided it would be a waste of time. I had developed an allergy against diamonds in particular, it seemed. They had no value for me anymore.

And guess what? After a quick search online I found out what happens when diamonds burn. They turn into carbon dioxide gas. No ash, no residue, because they are pure carbon.

There had been one thing missing from the news report. No bodies found. Brón and MacPherson had been obliterated. It bothered me a little that Caimiléir had made his escape. Where could he have gone? If it was me, I'd remain in the mortal realm and stay under the radar. Going to the Eternal realm would be stupid, unless Caimiléir had a secret hideaway where he could lie low in safety for the next hundred years, give or take a millennium.

Final confirmation that he was alive came the next day when I received a case of bagged potato chips. It took a minute of thinking, but I remembered that Caimiléir had offered to take assassination off the table for an entire century. I'd agreed by saying, "Throw in a bag of chips." Here they were. He was keeping up with his end of the bargain completely. Those Eternals were sticklers for detail. I'd have to remember to ask for something better than chips next time. Although, really, what was better than chips?

I called Nat at the gym. He answered with typical verbosity.

"You okay?" he asked.

"Fit as a fiddle and twice as stringy," I replied.

"Kay," he replied back.

"I would've called you. I didn't have a chance."

"I know."

"You talk to Brandy? And Carlene?" As far as they knew, they'd slept off a drunk at Erin's house.

"Yes. They're fine." Nat paused. "You find what you needed?"

"I did," I replied.

"Good." Then he hung up.

I guess we were good too.

I tried calling Erin, but it went straight to voicemail. I left a message.

I went to the police station. I needed a story as quickly as possible. It needed to be believable for both Milly Mallondyke and the Chief. It took time, but I found a few facts I could work with.

I was on my way out of the police station when I felt someone watching me. I turned around and saw Erin. Her eyes were aflame in emerald shades. She was wearing her lab coat and she had her purse over her shoulder, but she was in the wrong building if she was going to work. We stood and looked at each other for a dozen heartbeats. In a movie, she would have rushed at me and slapped me for sending her off to Keeper and making her worry. Or maybe kissed me hard enough for my lip to bleed in barely-constrained passion.

Instead, she put her hands to her mouth and just looked at me as she walked into my arms. I held her for a long moment, neither of us saying a word. When I looked down, her face was right there and she pressed her lips to mine with a tenderness that filled my soul. Better than the kiss at the club because this was completely her.

Holy. Wow.

Her voice was deep and quiet. "Don't do that to me again. Promise?"

"You mean, don't get you involved in a plot to summon a deamhan that results in you being kidnapped by an insane and disgraced Fae knight who forces you to use your power to open a Jeweled Gate while you could possibly have your throat slit at the whim of a sadistic mortal before being transported to safety in the Eternal realm while I battle said deamhan, human, and disgraced knight, leaving you to wonder what happened for a desperately lengthy amount of time?"

"Yeah, that."

"Never again. I promise."

We stood there in the lobby of the Miami Police Station, holding each other long enough to draw some attention and then long enough for everyone to lose interest.

"Come over tonight for dinner?" I asked.

"That'd be great."

That was the moment when Erin's phone rang. She answered

it and her eyes grew wide. For the longest time, all she said was, "Oh" again and again and again and again.

I asked Milly MacPherson Mallondyke to meet me at my office. We sat in precisely the same places on opposite sides of my desk. We wore different clothing, of course, and we both had black Stains now. Instead of a sunny day, it was overcast and raining. If Nature had ever sensed a mood and provided a setting to match, this was it.

I'd thought long and hard about what to tell Milly. I had to lie to her, there was no way to avoid it, but the troubling questions I had to answer were how much to lie and for what reason. First, I would need to satisfy her concerns about the murder of her husband since that's what she'd hired me to do. But I'd also need to explain the disappearance of her father in a way that was final and convincing. There was no chance she'd ever see him again. In my opinion, no daughter should remember her father as a bad guy, even if he was one. I couldn't paint him as too much of a hero either. As an intelligent woman, she'd know on some level her father wasn't a saint.

So, I approached this conversation filled with angst.

"This is my fault," I began. "As much as anyone's."

Milly nodded, patient, knowing there was bad news.

I stayed as close to the truth as I could. It wasn't easy.

I pushed a matchbook across the table. In bright green letters it read "Voodoo Kitten." It provided a concrete piece of reality upon which I could hang my lies.

"What's this?" Milly asked. She picked up the matchbook and looked at both sides. She opened it and looked inside. On the inner flap, in a bold hand, I had written the address of a warehouse that had burned down in West Palm Beach on the same night her father had died.

"Have you seen Amad lately?" I asked.

"No. Not for a few days."

"I believe he has fled the country," I said. "He was using you and your family to smuggle diamonds. Or at least, he was trying to."

"He couldn't," Milly said. "There's too much security. There's no way to get diamonds out of the facilities undetected."

I nodded, trying to look resigned. As a point of fact, there was a way and Caimiléir had used it. He had smuggled undocumented diamonds out of the Mallondyke facilities in all kinds of large quantities. He had smuggled them inside the bodies of Barry and Milly and who knows how many others. Caimiléir had the ability to teleport diamonds in and out of people. I'd seen him do it to Greim first when he pulled the diamonds out of the little deamhan's body. And I'd seen him do it again when diamonds vanished from his hands and reappeared embedded in Brón's forehead. That's what Caimiléir had been doing in all those jewelry stores. That's why I had seen Caimiléir in the video using his magic. But the stores were tiny potatoes compared to the treasure trove of the Mallondyke stockpile, which was lightly-guarded and never inventoried because Barry was one of the very few people who had access to it.

And how do you get diamonds through security? The old shell game. The first person to go through has no diamonds. After that person is cleared, the diamonds are instantly teleported from one carrier into the person who is cleared. Probably sealed in small bags for safety. Caimiléir could have done it with his hands tied behind his back, which is probably where his hands were the whole time, to hide any telltale signs of magic.

I didn't tell Milly any of it. "You're right," I said. "Amad finally realized that he couldn't get the diamonds he wanted from your family's company. The problem was, Barry had figured out what Amad had been trying to do."

Milly interjected, "Did Amad kill my husband?"

"No," I replied with painful honesty.

You killed your husband because your father made you do it.

Somehow, a part of her had known there was more going on with her husband's death than she'd been told. Her subconscious needed more information, so she'd hired me to fill in some of the holes. I wished I could fill them with something better than lies.

I pointed at the matchbook. "Amad was working with an international ring of criminals out of a warehouse at this address. One of the people working at the warehouse made an appointment with Barry. He lured Barry to the hotel and killed him."

"Who? Who was it?"

"I didn't get close enough for a name. But I believe the killer is dead. Burned in the fire at the warehouse. You probably heard about it on the news."

Milly nodded. It had been the more noticeable of the two fires that night, getting a full two minutes on the broadcast news because the area was more populated.

"What about the wound in Barry's stomach?" she asked. "Why cut Barry open like that?"

I had prepared an answer for that particular question. "The criminal organization responsible is known to cover their crimes by making them look like the work of a cult. Disembowelment and Satanic symbols and things like that. I'm certain the killer simply didn't have time to finish what he started. He made the first cut and then he heard something or saw something that spooked him and he ran. If he'd had time to finish what he intended, it would have made more sense."

Milly was nodding. I hoped she believed me. The truth was far more disturbing and it was vital that Milly never know it.

Barry had to die. Somehow, your father found out that Barry knew too much. He couldn't go to Caimiléir. Couldn't ask him to just teleport the diamonds out of Barry's body. It had gotten bigger than that. Caimiléir would have cut your father out of the deal. Your father forced you to kill your husband before he could talk. And to indulge his homicidal tendencies through you.

Because Barry had died with a bellyful of diamonds, your father had you cut him open to get them out. There would have been too many questions otherwise. The diamonds would be behind the wall of the abdomen but there was no incision where the diamonds had been implanted. It was a physical impossibility.

So your father, who panicked when Barry found out their secret, had you kill him, then cut him open and take the diamonds away.

Back to the matchbook. "I followed Amad for days and I finally tracked him to that warehouse in West Palm Beach. Amad knew who I was and he knew I was getting close. But I was sloppy. While I was following Amad, your father was following me."

"He didn't like you," Milly said. "He told me he didn't trust you and that I should tell you to quit investigating. But I had to know. I had to know the truth."

I looked down at my desk. It made me sad and ashamed to lie to her. She had paid for the truth and she was getting precious little of that. I hoped she would see me ducking my head as simple, uncomplicated regret over what had happened.

It was easier to continue the lie with a question than with a statement. So I asked it: "Do you think he was following me to discredit me?"

"Definitely," Milly replied. "He must have been trying to get something on you, anything, so I'd fire you." I was letting my client make up her own lies for me now. When had I become such a jerk?

She went on helping me lie. "You found out where the warehouse was, right?"

I just nodded.

"You wrote it down on this matchbook. This is your handwriting?"

"When we spoke that first day, you told me to take notes," I offered. Helpful.

"I remember," Milly said.

"I carried that matchbook around for a couple of days. I checked on that warehouse but there was no activity. I couldn't go to the police without a reason. I had to find something incriminating, something linking my suspects to criminal activity. Then I'd convince the police to investigate Barry's death again. That's what I was trying to do when people showed up in black vans, carrying crates. When they went inside, I found a way to get into the building unobserved. They were setting up a meth lab in that warehouse. I got out. There was shouting, but I couldn't see what was happening. I left and shortly after that, there was an explosion. The building burned down and the fire was so intense, the bodies are ash and what's left is crushed."

"My father was in there," Milly said with finality. "He followed you. They caught him."

"I can't be certain," I lied, coloring my voice with concern. "But the police found his car a block away."

Because I had Lonnie's keys and I drove his car and left it there.

"That's why I feel like this is my fault, as much as anyone's."

I'm a jerk. And a liar. And a generally horrible human being.

Milly shook her head. "No," she said. "This is not your fault. I asked you to find out what happened to my husband and you've given me more information than the police ever did. I'm certain now that whoever killed Barry got what they deserved. They're dead now."

She was more right about that than she would ever know.

"My father was not a nice man," she continued. "He was mean and self-centered and he liked to hurt people. He got himself into trouble trying to hurt you. I can't blame you. In my heart, I'm sad I'll never see my father again. He's gone and I'll miss him. You always hope your father will be there for you, you know? But it will be all right. I'll be all right."

I believed she would be.

Milly stood and handed me an envelope. "I hope this will cover any additional expenses with something left over."

I opened the envelope. There were a whole lot of zeroes on that check.

"This is far more than I need," I complained.

"Good," Milly replied. "Buy a pizza." She walked out.

I knew I would be thinking about the things she had said for a very long time. I also knew I'd never cash that check.

EPILOGUE

Erin and I had originally scheduled to meet at the courthouse, conferring with a judge to declare Erin's husband legally dead. We had canceled.

Instead we were at the airport.

Erin had asked me to come with her for moral support and I was happy to oblige. I was. Of course I was.

We were waiting for a passenger to arrive from Maine, of all places, by way of Washington, D.C. Erin looked fantastic, of course. Like she could help it. Though personally it felt like her hair was a little too perfect. Her heels a little too high. Her dress a little too tight. Of course, she also had an ugly black Stain along with her beautiful forest-green ribbons. I was the only person who could see it though, and I wasn't ever going to tell her. I wasn't going to tell her I had one that matched either.

We said barely two words to each other on the ride over, but it was just nerves. Who could blame us? We didn't play any music to fill the quiet. Nothing felt appropriate.

After we parked in the short term lot, we walked toward the arrivals terminal. There was a space of about six inches between us. We were together but also apart. Anyone observing the two of us would never have guessed we'd felt incredibly close to one another a few days ago.

We stopped well short of the outlet where passengers came through from the terminals. We stood there and waited. The flight was a few minutes late and we were caught between baggage claim and a hard place.

After talking to Milly Mallondyke, I had put together a report, much of it fabricated of course, and given a copy to Chief Cuevas. The meeting was perfunctory and done in less than ten minutes.

Most of the details spoke for themselves and were corroborated by the fire department and other reports from the various branches of law enforcement that had investigated the warehouse fire. Lieutenant Kapok had been the one to verify that MacPherson's car was indeed the vehicle found abandoned near the warehouse. The other phony details had no other witness besides me, so the police department really had no choice but to accept what I told them. Cuevas had choked down my story and let me go.

Guess I won't be meeting him next Sunday for golf.

Erin and I watched passengers arriving in batches. Some were excited to have reached their destination and some were tired or bored. I tried to find a calm place within myself, feeling the earth. I listened to the noise of a hundred conversations and the rhythmic mechanical sound of conveyors carrying bags. I chanced a look at Erin. Her expression was a mix of anticipation and anxiety. I wished I could relieve her of the uncertainty and bear the burden of every worry on her behalf. Sadly, I didn't think there was a spell for that.

Finally, a tall guy wearing a pink button-down shirt came into view. He had sparkling blue eyes and a sweep of dark hair. Erin went toward him tentatively, leaving me behind. I was glad she didn't run to meet him.

Over the babble and noise, I heard her ask, "Blake?"

For a pilot in an airport, he looked a little lost, but his face lit up instantly the moment he saw Erin. His teeth were bright, even rows, and his eyes danced with a particular joy that I certainly understood. I wondered if that was what my face had looked like when Erin and I had come together a few days ago at the police station. Right before the phone call. Right before the series of events that had brought us to this time and place.

They shared a brief embrace.

"Hmm. He's a very. Healthy. Looking man."

I didn't have to look to know who spoke. She was responsible somehow for the recent change in events, I knew. But this was about living, breathing people. So I didn't respond in any way. I kept my attention on the reunion taking place nearby.

"I know. What it's like. When you. Want something. And you don't. Get it," she said. Those were my exact words. Coming back at me.

"This isn't about me," I said roughly.

"Why. Art thou here. Then?"

Now I looked at her. Laoch was with her too. She slipped her arm through mine as if we were a couple.

I didn't move a muscle except to turn my head to look back at Erin. She was gesturing while she talked to her human husband, miraculously returned after five and half years. When it suited me, I said, "Friends support each other."

"She is. Not. Thy friend. She is. Thy wife."

"A husband should be a friend as well. But I'm not her husband in this realm. She has a husband here. However, I am her friend no matter where we are. That will never change."

I felt a shrug. "We shall see. If such. Friendship. Can endure. While she has. Another man. With her."

"I told you this isn't about me. It's about family and supporting another person's needs. I know you understand what that means. I may not fully appreciate my relationship with you, but we are a family too, in a way. You and me and Laoch. You care for him as if he were your own child. And he is his own person even though he's a part of me."

I looked past Béil to Laoch. He wasn't wearing his Renaissance shirt but had a modern, kid-appropriate t-shirt instead. Teenage mutant ninja turtle. Michelangelo. He was just . . . normal . . . and he could have belonged to anyone here at the airport. He looked back at me as if he were seeing me for the first time.

I looked back at Erin. "I have to believe that you'd do anything for Laoch, even if it was difficult for you."

I felt a small hand slip into mine. Laoch surprised me by coming around to my side to make contact. I gave him a smile and then I gave his hand a squeeze.

"Today, Erin needs to be here," I said. "She needs to reconnect with Blake and I need to let her."

Erin was coming back my way, bringing Blake with her. They

walked with six inches of empty air between them. A distance of space and years.

They stopped in front of me. Blake was Stained like crazy, but I reached out and shook his hand anyway and said, "Hey, I'm Goethe. Just call me Got."

About the Author

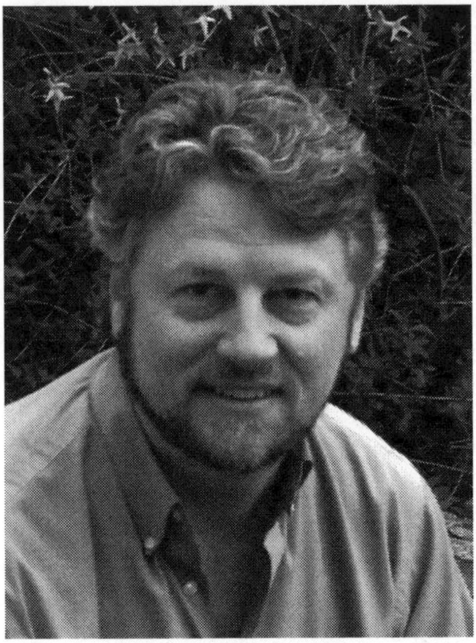

Michael Darling has worked as a butcher, a librarian, and a magician. Not all at the same time. He nests in the exquisitely beautiful Rocky Mountains with his equally breathtaking wife and six guinea pigs, one of whom thinks she's a dog and three of whom claim to be children. Michael's award-winning short fiction is frequently featured in anthologies. Got Luck is his first novel.

Michael graduated from Weber State University with a degree in English Literature and loves to blend the classic with the contemporary in his writing. His early work included short fiction, several plays that were professionally produced, and radio programs that aired in eighty markets around the world. Besides writing, Michael also loves to travel, dabble in languages, and cook tasty gluten-free dinners.

Please visit Michael at www.michaelcdarling.com where you can find more Luck-related content. You'll also find suspiciously easy instructions for stalking Michael on Facebook and Twitter.

If you liked this book, I'd love to hear.
Reviews keep me writing.
Find *Got Luck* online and leave me a review.

Author's Note

The translation of Johann Wolfgang von Goethe's poem "Der Erlkönig" is my own, which means any errors are mine. The poem was originally written in German, but none of the English translations kept the meter of the original, at nine feet per line. My version is less accurate in the text, but it retains the rhythmic structure of the original. Such things make my inner poet happy.

Goethe based the poem on Germanic legends and Danish ballads. The more literal translation of the title is "The Alder King" and that, of course, inspired the character of Got's father. Many scholars translate the title as "The Elf King," but mentioning elves would hinder the world-building and put limits on the creation of the mythical and legendary peoples that reside in the Behindbeyond.

The poem's origin story in Got Luck is fictitious as well but serves to ground and enhance Got's history. I hope the real Goethe doesn't mind my manufacturing events in his life that never happened. Finally, it's worth noting that the poem has been set to music by several composers and Franz Schubert's piece is my favorite.

All the songs referenced in the novel can be found on a playlist and the links are available on my website at www.michaelcdarling.com. You can listen to the songs in order as you read the appropriate chapters. There are a few surprises as well, to coincide with events in the story.

NEVER MISS A FUTURE HOUSE RELEASE

FHP

Sign up for the Future House Publishing email list:
www.futurehousepublishing.com/beta-readers-club

Connect with Future House Publishing

www.facebook.com/FutureHousePublishing

twitter.com/FutureHousePub

YouTube

www.youtube.com/FutureHousePublishing

www.instagram.com/FutureHousePublishing